DARK REIGN OF FOREVER

DARK DESTINIES, BOOK 3

S.K. RYDER

I

KINGDOM OF NIGHT

Two years ago...

Most nights and most places, those who met the Lord of Night never saw him. To those who knew him, the ability to slide past the awareness of anyone near him was Dominique Marchant's most disquieting talent. To Dominique, this skill was still disorienting, even after three months. It was instinctive and often rendered him invisible by accident. All it took was a wish for solitude and it was done.

Only Cassidy was immune. Being bound to her human soul as he was, she was always aware of him, which was as it should be. She was his conscience and his humanity.

At the moment, she was also over fifty miles away. Yet, Dominique still heard her whisper encouragement in their telepathic bond, overshadowing his nerves, which thrummed like an antenna. He had learned to dial it down, but the low-grade hum had suffused him ever since he became the center of the dark web. All the blood drinkers in existence were tethered to him, legions of vampires just beyond his reach, like a swarm of ghosts. They didn't become concrete individuals in his awareness until Cassidy helped him track them down, or he re-sired them in a ritual exchange of blood.

Presently, he sensed one of these ghosts slipping over the locked entry gate at the mouth of the pier on which Dominique stood. He saw it, too, as a single bright white blood-drinker aura standing there just out of cover. The visitor looked around, unsure.

"I am here," Dominique said, letting the salty wind carry his words to the supernatural ears.

The blood-drinker's head swiveled toward him.

Dominique shifted his attitude from solitude to welcome. On the pier's far end, his guest froze, staring, no doubt questioning his own eyes. Or fearing for his immortal life. Dominique couldn't blame him. If someone had barged into his thoughts and talked to him from out of nowhere, he, too, would have run blindly into the night. When the strange blood-drinker had realized that he couldn't outrun the bizarre voice in his head, he started asking questions, and Dominique suggested they meet. That had been two nights ago.

Two nights for a solitary vampire to question his sanity, to wonder if he would find anything or anyone at all at the end of the Lake Worth pier at one in the morning. Now, not only had he found someone, that someone appeared to melt out of the ocean mist.

Dominique turned to gaze over the sea, which heaved with wind-driven swells. A bright patch in the thin cloud cover pointed at a hidden moon, the faint light shimmering on the rippling water.

Emboldened, the other vampire approached, his footfall on the wood planks soft and measured. He didn't speak until his steps had fallen silent for well over a minute.

"Are you the one I heard?" A cultured male voice. British. Dubious.

Dominique peered over his shoulder. "*Oui.* I am that one."

The blood-drinker stood about thirty feet away, out of immediate reach, hands out by his sides, ready to run and disappear in an instant. Dominique listened to him inhale, taking his measure, and waited for his visitor to draw a conclusion from the crisp scent that marked him as a youngling vampire—and the golden glow deep in his dark eyes that marked him as something else entirely.

It took a solid fifteen seconds. Then there was an apologetic little cough. "You...are not what I expected."

"What did you expect?" Dominique turned to face him and did his best to appear as non-threatening as possible in his ominous black motorcycle leathers and heavy boots. Wind ruffled his hair, and he casually gathered most of the jet-black mass in his nape and confined it with the leather string that circled his wrist. The unruly wave that forever fell across his forehead, however, refused to be tamed.

The other vampire was dressed in jeans and a tucked-in navy blue button-down shirt. He was tall, but slender, almost delicate, his own ash-blond hair neatly groomed and only slightly disheveled in the breeze. Except for his pale skin, he could have passed as a gangly young man of any era, but what Dominique could discern about his scent told him that this one's birth to darkness was well over a century in the past.

"Not a Frenchman, I don't think."

Dominique laughed with delight. Instead of terror or attack, this blood-drinker opted for diplomacy and humor. "I like you, Englishman. What is your name?"

"Aubrey Wainwright." His shoulders lost some of their tension.

"I am Dominique Marchant." With a small tilt of his head, he added, "Lord of Night." The title still felt pretentious falling off his tongue to a stranger.

"Indeed."

"I was sired by Kambyses. You may know the name?"

"I have heard legends surrounding that name, yes. They say he is the first vampire."

"He was the root of what we are," Dominique corrected. Even Kambyses hadn't considered himself the first of their kind. "After five-thousand years, he was weary of the darkness." And what darkness there had been in that ancient one. He had teetered on the brink of madness, and all his children along with him. "Three months ago, he chose me as his heir. When he died, the essence of what animates us was transferred to me."

Aubrey stared at Dominique, at the ethereal luminosity in the hyper-dilated pupils, like the reflected light in the eyes of an animal. His own were wide, bottomless wells of darkness. "Interesting. So this gives you the power to intrude into the heads of the unsuspecting?"

"Under the right circumstances." Dominique sobered and separated from the railing. Aubrey did not retreat. "Every blood-drinker's life is bound to mine the way every youngling's life is bound to his or her sire. On some level, I am aware of them all, but they are not aware of me."

"Oh. I'm most definitely aware of you," Aubrey said faintly.

"Do you believe what I told you?"

Small hesitation. Nod.

Dominique waited. Were he a breathing creature, he might have held his breath. It was one thing to have Serge, his closest blood-drinker friend, accept him as the Lord of Night and submit to him, quite another for a complete stranger to do the same. What if he didn't? Would Dominique have it in him to do what was required?

"So. What is it you wish of me?" Aubrey said. His hands slowly tucked into the pockets of his jeans. "Why have you asked me here?"

"To answer your questions, of course. As for what I wish of you...I wish for you to submit to me."

Amusement tucked at Aubrey's mouth. "If you are the lord of us all, have I not done so already?"

"No, not yet. Your life may be linked to mine, but your vampire beast does not know me yet." He let this truth sink in. "The hunger you have to be known and feared, to step out of the shadows when you feed—the thing that drives you to kill—that is Kambyses in your heart. That is his legacy, his madness."

"I have resisted the urge to take lives for decades."

Dominique leaned forward. "But it never leaves you, does it?"

"No," Aubrey whispered. "Has it left you?"

"I hunger for love," Dominique replied just as quietly. "When I feed, I am loved. And I can have so much of this that the need to take it all diminishes to nothing."

The expression on the narrow face hovered somewhere between wonder and incredulity. The twin flames in Dominique's eyes mirrored in Aubrey's obsidian stare. "And...if I submit to you?"

"The dark hunger will leave you." And if he didn't...

"Then I submit." The words were a mere breath in the wind. Slowly, he tilted his head to one side, exposing his jugular in an invitation he may well never have issued before. More than an offer of blood and submission, it was the offer of his mind, his memories, his very life, a surrender of his body and his soul. It was not an offer made lightly, and Dominique took care to accept with all the respect due his new subject. As though welcoming a beloved friend, he embraced him and pierced the artery.

Aubrey's blood was vibrant with the sweetness of spring, full of warm grass and dewy blossoms. When the serum in Dominique's bite found Aubrey's brain, he dropped into a mind resonant with a century and a half of memories. A man of the Victorian age emerged, a gentleman and a trained barrister in his queen's service. Renowned for his diplomatic skill, Aubrey had been sent on missions around the world. It was in Rome where a vampire found him and invited him into the night without fully explaining what that would entail. Aubrey had sought to wield his new powers of persuasion in service to his queen. Instead, he wielded it to appease a hunger that horrified him. After a century of guilt and torment and the resulting ridicule from his sire and other blood-drinkers, he had turned his back on them all. Now he maintained a solitary existence, convinced that he was fit for no company but his own.

You are fit for me, Dominique spoke into his mind, compassion swelling his heart.

Aubrey's arms shook as they came around him, and his hands fisted into the leather jacket.

Long after he had stopped feeding on the blood, Dominique still held him, feeding on Aubrey's roiling uncertainty and hope, his own thoughts in turmoil. How many like Aubrey were out there? How many skulking in the shadows, fighting to live by a moral code opposed to everything they craved?

"I have a gift for you," Dominique murmured when Aubrey at last loosened his grip. Baring his left wrist, he ran the nail of his right thumb deep into his flesh. Blood welled, dark and glistening as he held the wound out to Aubrey. This was where the magic happened. Or at least he hoped it would. He had re-sired only one other, Serge.

Aubrey gripped Dominique's hand and ran his tongue over the injury just before it sealed again. The blood was only a few drops and nowhere near as volatile as Kambyses's had been, but it was enough. It found the serum in Aubrey's veins and ignited, tuning him into the new Lord of Night.

He gasped at the sensation of fire flashing through his flesh, and held on to Dominique's hand, eyes screwed shut, swaying. A long moan slipped past the bloodstained lips, and Dominique knew that Aubrey Wainwright would never again be part of an amorphous gathering of ghosts. The Victorian gentleman blood-drinker was becoming a distinct entity of light in Dominique's awareness.

"I feel it leaving," Aubrey said, awed. "The darkness. It's leaving." When he opened his eyes, small flames of gold flickered in their depths. Moment to moment they grew until they blazed in the night.

Dominique didn't trust his own voice. So he only grinned and planted a kiss on Aubrey's forehead. *Welcome,* mon ami. *Welcome to my kingdom.*

2

THE GIFT

Present day...

The house's landline rang so rarely that Cassidy Chandler associated the sound with nothing good. Mrs. Havashand, she guessed, sitting back in her leather executive chair and stretching stiff shoulders. No doubt Brinkley had left more corpses in her backyard. It was tempting to let the call go to voicemail, but a glance at the caller ID made her grab the extension.

"Good afternoon, ma'am," said the brisk male voice on the other end. "This is the front gate. There's a Jackson Striker here to see you, but we don't have him on our list."

Her thoughts skittering to a startled halt. She stared out the second-floor window, which overlooked an expansive backyard sloping down to the Intracoastal. Hard to decide if it was being called "ma'am" that threw her off or just the fact she even lived in a neighborhood that had a security gate staffed with round-the-clock armed guards. The maintenance crew and maid service had permanent passes. So few others visited during the day, she tended to forget. And at night...well, at night, none of that mattered.

"Ma'am?"

She sucked in a breath. "Yes, I'm here."

"Shall we let him through?"

Cassidy swiveled the chair toward the storm bunker tucked away downstairs at the center of the house. Windowless, made of steel-reinforced, poured concrete, and secured with a door worthy of a bank vault, nothing short of dynamite would dent it.

"Is he alone?"

"Yes, ma'am."

"Okay. Let him through."

"Very well, ma'am."

She returned the handset to its charging station. The clock on the monitor had the time an hour before sunset. If Jackson had reverted to his nefarious ways, he was cutting it damn close. That his asshole uncle wasn't with him, however, ruled out the possibility of dynamite, not to mention random bullets to her head.

Also, this was as good an excuse as any to log off the *V-zette's* Discord server. Four hours of moderating and organizing the hyper-fast postings of a chatty international vampire community was about all she could take for one day anyway.

After changing out of her frumpy yoga pants and sweatshirt into something more suitable for company, she headed for the foyer. Her low heels clacked and echoed in the vast space as she moved down the stairs. Enormous glass walls bracketed the two-story space at both ends, one side overlooking the infinity pool and dock out back, the other surrounding the massive double-door entry which had been hammered in a starburst design. The sun was low enough to pour through the front windows and flood the entire area in a warm glow. In the beams, dust motes danced on the breeze swirling in through the open sliders.

At the foot of the stairs, she paused to absorb the peaceful moment and mentally record it for later when she would share it with the love of her life. This was her favorite room in the house at her favorite time of day and year. Not long now, and

Florida's sticky summer would seize hold again, relegating open doors and fresh air to distant memories.

A polite bing-bong drew her to the door.

Jackson Striker, vampire hunter, stood on the paved stoop, hands in pockets, looking tall and casual in khaki slacks, a polo shirt, and mirrored sunglasses. He pulled them off his nose and folded them. "Hi, Cass."

"Hi," she said, and then considered the strange smile he wore. It wasn't smug, nor anxious. Just normal. There was a new depth to his rugged face and a warmth in the steel-gray eyes that hadn't been there the last time she saw him two years ago. Gone was the young hunter brimming with impatience, replaced by the confident strength of a man of almost twenty-seven with nothing to prove to anyone.

"I'm guessing he lives here?" Jackson prompted.

"What? Oh. Yes." Grateful for the distraction, Cassidy reached down to scratch the little red-and-white cat behind an ear as he stalked through the open door. There was a smear of blood on the side of his furry face, which was probably all that remained of one of Mrs. Havashand's prize finches. "Brinkley came with the house. Just showed up the day we moved in."

With the front door open, a steady breeze swept through the foyer. Swirling in it was Jackson's familiar citrus aftershave and shards of memories she thought to have forgotten long ago.

Cassidy straightened and wrapped her arms around herself. "It's a little early for Dominique to be up."

"Yeah. I know."

"And Sam is out teaching and has dinner plans."

Jackson shook his head. "I can talk to my sister any time. The person I was really hoping to talk to before sundown, though, is you." She couldn't keep the shock from her face, and he laughed, raising both hands, one of which held a small black case. "No, don't worry. I won't try to talk you into leaving him again." He looked her over, taking in the gold, kitten-heeled sandals, white palazzo pants, peacock blue patterned tunic, and the thick mass of her chestnut hair falling around her shoulders. Noticing her suspicious glare, he sobered. "You're looking good, Cassidy."

Her cheeks warmed in a way she didn't appreciate. "Flattery will get you nowhere. But since you're here, fine. I'll listen."

Jackson followed her through the living room. Last night's blankets and empty popcorn bowl still decorated the sofa. The adjoining kitchen was a lake of jade granite counters, maple wood cabinets, and stainless steel appliances.

"Cozy place you've got here," he said.

She snorted and opened the fridge. "Only you could describe this multi-million-dollar palace as 'cozy.'" His own home, the Striker family compound, was three times the size—and price. "I swear I still lose stuff in just this kitchen on a weekly basis. It's way too much house for me." But bomb-grade storm shelters and twenty-four-seven armed security generally came with substantial real estate attached. "What would you like? Beer, wine, water, or juice?"

"Juice."

Cassidy set out two glasses, careful how hard she placed them on the unforgiving granite surface.

"You know you're supposed to have staff for a kitchen like this," Jackson pointed out as she poured the apple juice.

"Kind of a waste for just one person. I don't need much." What meals she did need, Dominique enjoyed preparing for her. Samantha, who lived out in the pool house, kept her own, strictly vegan kitchen.

He settled himself on a cast iron barstool and placed the little black case on the counter beside him. His hand lay on it for a moment, as though reluctant to let it go. Curiosity made Cassidy's eyes cling to it. "You're in here all alone? All day?"

She shrugged. "I get caught up on stuff." Like sleep. "My nights can be busy."

"Yes, I would imagine they are."

Cassidy eyed him over the rim of her glass and waited.

He cleared his throat. "So. I have some news. Two bits of news, actually. Well, three if you count the news I have for Dominique." He patted the case.

She waited some more.

"I'm getting married."

Three pieces of news, and that's what he was leading with? Unsure she wanted to know the rest, Cassidy swallowed the last of her juice along with an impulse to express condolences for the bride-to-be. His expression hovered just a notch below pained.

"So your uncle finally broke down your resistance with his parade of 'suitable brides' to choose from?" None of which had captured Jackson's interest in the past, as far as she knew.

"No." Wry grin. "Actually, my mom set me up with this one. Ollie's the daughter of a friend of hers."

"Ollie?"

"Olivia. Henning-Toliver."

"Oh. One of *the* Henning-Tolivers?" This was a name with weight in local banking and financial circles. Socially then—unlike middle-class Midwest Cassidy—this Ollie was a good match for the heir to the Striker fortune.

"The youngest daughter, yes."

"Okay. And you're marrying this one because...?"

Jackson sat back. "Turns out we have a lot in common. She's got an MBA and a future at her father's firm, and neither one of us wanted to be forced into a marriage." He laughed a little. "After we got done bitching about the manipulation, we actually had a lot of fun on our first date. She's got spirit." He sobered and dropped his gaze into his glass. "And she's pregnant."

Cassidy watched him toss back the juice as though wishing it was something stronger and wondered if she had heard correctly. More than that, she wondered what that peculiar niggle was doing at the bottom of her heart. Children had never been a priority for her, nor were they even possible for her and Dominique. Full stop. The end.

"I see." She leaned on her forearms, studying him. "You must really have it bad for her if you forgot how to use condoms."

He still didn't look at her, but he nodded, and his face pulled into a *don't-I-know-it* grimace. "She's okay, considering—" He caught himself before adding the "she isn't you" Cassidy heard anyway.

"We may have vodka around here somewhere," she murmured and turned away to cover her own discomfort.

"No. Thank you, but no. I need a clear head when I talk to Dominique. Juice is fine."

"Okay." She refilled his glass. Her own head was a muddle. He was moving on with his life despite still loving her. While she felt a grudging respect and a hard-earned but cool friendship for her former fiancé now, she had loved him once—back before she knew he would walk over bodies in the name of revenge.

An awkward silence settled beside the quiet hum of the refrigerator. Outside, the daylight had dimmed. Night would fall like a dropped shroud within minutes. She wanted to count the seconds. Instead, she said, "Don't you usually talk to Dominique on video?"

Again, he placed his hand on the case. "This is something he and I need to discuss in person."

"What is it?"

The discomfort evaporated in a broad smile. "A gift."

She arched a brow, relaxing as well. "Now what sort of gift would a vampire hunter give the lord of the vampires?"

"Enforcer," he corrected. *Daytime* enforcer, to be exact. He and his uncle Garrett both were enforcers. Not everyone agreed with the Lord of Night's new directives, especially the younger ones and those in far-flung places who imagined themselves immune from his influence. With Dominique's blessing, the Striker Foundation, once dedicated to exterminating all vampires, now used its considerable resources to locate and bring under control—or destroy—these rebels. The arrangement freed him to concentrate on bigger goals and gave the hunters an outlet for their well-honed skills.

"Which brings me to what I wanted to talk to you about," he continued.

"Oh?"

"I need to figure out how to tell Ollie what I'm really doing when I go on all those 'business trips.'"

Like you were never going to tell me? She bit back the words and instead said, "I wouldn't think that'd be so hard. Just introduce her to an actual vampire. We've got two living right here." She waved at the cast iron gate at the back of the kitchen that fronted the vestibule to the storm shelter, which doubled as a wine cellar.

Which doubled as a vampire lair.

"People rarely react well to that sort of news."

"They could compel her to accept the truth without fuss."

"No. Absolutely not. No compulsion." He made a slashing motion with the edge of his hand before running it through his short-cropped, dark blond hair. "I want to be honest with her, but I don't want her exposed if she doesn't want to be."

"Ah." Cassidy chewed on her bottom lip. "So what exactly is it you're asking?"

"Well. I was hoping you might talk to her with me?"

Her jaw dropped.

"You know, a neutral third party."

"Oh, I'm hardly neutral."

"You know what I mean."

"You want someone to help you sound less like you've lost your mind. Right."

He gave a sheepish shrug. "Will you consider it at least?"

"Does Garrett know you're planning to tell her?"

"He does, and I'm not asking him for permission."

"Wow. I guess you really do like her." Traditionally, no one not born and raised in the Striker household was ever told about the family's clandestine operations.

"She will be my future. The mother of my kids. I owe her the truth."

"Who are you, and what have you done with the bastard who was hell-bent on keeping me oblivious?"

"Cass—"

Cassidy held up a hand. "It's okay, Jackson. If not for you being such an ass, I would have never met Dominique. And he is *my* life now," she added with a pointed look and watched his eyes dart to the sapphire and diamond ring on her finger. It was a gift from Dominique and the only piece of jewelry she wore, as close to a wedding ring as she ever wanted to get. "I really am happy for you, Jack. I mean it. This Ollie sounds like a girl I'd like to meet and—yes—talk to."

"Thank you, Cassidy." He splayed a hand over his sternum. "Thank you."

"Don't thank me yet. I have all kinds of dirt on you I might want to share."

The look of mock-innocence made her laugh. "So, when do you want to do this?"

Jackson had a plan. He always did. They discussed the details at length and had finalized their plot to shepherd one Olivia Henning-Toliver into their supernatural reality when a decidedly supernatural sensation stole over Cassidy. Every night it started like this, with a sense of an expanding awareness, like doors opening in her mind. Like quiet energy surging from a deep well. She closed her eyes and welcomed it with a sigh.

"Sunset?" Jackson wondered.

"Sunset," she confirmed.

Right on cue, a small, furious growl sounded. Brinkley crept into position behind a cabinet corner, his green eyes narrowed on the gate to the wine cellar/storm shelter/vampire lair. The cat considered the vampires invading predators, and he wasn't having it, no matter how hard Dominique tried to persuade him otherwise.

Cassidy picked up Brinkley by the rising scruff and turned to the kitchen door. "None of that tonight."

By the time she deposited the unhappy cat in the side yard, Dominique had become fully conscious. With their bond renewed only the night before, their minds functioned like two adjoining puzzle pieces clicking into place. He contemplated the last hour of her memories. The mysterious gift Jackson brought intrigued him. But what really captured his interest was the news of Jackson's impending fatherhood.

They had never discussed it. There was no point. Offspring between a vampire and a mortal was impossible. While Cassidy accepted this with little sentiment in either direction, Dominique ranked his inability to have a family high on the list of immortality's shortcomings. He never said so. He never even thought about it, not consciously anyway, but Cassidy sensed it just the same.

The vault door in the vestibule unsealed. A vampire appeared and stood with his arms draped over the decorative gate, his unshaven face split by a lecherous grin that made Jackson rise from his chair in alarm.

"Cassidy." Serge's baritone voice purred with appreciation. "You ordered takeout." Unlike his lord and master, who still digested the events of Cassidy's day, Serge didn't know what the human was doing there.

"Be nice," she said. "He comes bearing gifts."

"Oh, yes, he does." Serge unlatched the gate and sauntered across the kitchen, barefoot and rumpled, his curly caramel hair sticking out in every direction, the vampire equivalent of a man in search of coffee.

Jackson glared at him. "Sleeping with the boss now? You've come up in the world."

"Sleeping? No. Not I." Serge puffed out his barrel chest with pride. "I stand guard over my lord."

His lordship materialized beside Serge and delivered a brotherly slap to the back of his head. "More like *lie* guard flat on your back," he said in his lyrical French accent.

Serge growled, much as the cat had earlier. "But I am always with you."

"I know," Dominique concurred with a dramatic sigh. "There is no getting rid of you."

"And you are glad for it, blood-child. Admit it."

Cassidy smiled at their antics. Tall, lean and grace incarnate, Dominique was the polar opposite of both the stocky Serge and muscle-bound Jackson. Even dressed in his usual exercise pants and T-shirt, both black, few would mistake him for the ordinary man of twenty-seven he had been when he was turned into a blood-drinker. Carved cheekbones and a knife-blade nose dominated his profile, and his expressive mouth could instill terror as easily as convey gentle humor—not to mention bestow mind-blowing kisses.

But it was the eyes that were the most striking thing about him. Their quiet depths missed nothing and could flash from warm and beguiling to full black and disturbing in the space of a heartbeat. Gold flecks danced in the hazel irises as he looked at her.

"*Bonjour, mon amour*," he murmured and held out his hand.

"*Bonjour*," she said, moving into his embrace.

The world around them fell away, and they stood together in her memories of the sunlight streaming through the foyer. He rubbed the back of her neck with his thumb while she nuzzled into his thick hair, inhaling his heady clean scent that reminded her of an early spring day.

"Indeed. He brings gifts," Serge said, pulling them back to the moment.

Uh oh, she thought.

His tone had lost its swagger and turned dreamy. It meant he saw "shadows" in the aura of whoever he was looking at, or impressions of the future. When Serge had his visions, disjointed and insubstantial as they were, changes were coming—usually not for the better.

Though Dominique appeared unconcerned, Cassidy felt the tension skitter through him. Neither of them dared to interrupt Serge as he studied Jackson with an intense interest that no longer had anything to do with his warm blood. The human man returned the stare, his hands wrapped over the back of the bar stool as though preparing to pick it up and use it as a weapon.

Serge turned to look at Dominique with a wide, gap-toothed grin of wonder. Then he chuckled with obvious glee.

"*Oui?*" Dominique prompted. "Did he bring a good gift?"

Serge laughed.

Jackson offered a tentative smile. "I suspect you'll like it."

Just like that, Serge stopped laughing.

In a flash, he was by Jackson's side, his eyes bugging out of their sockets. "Beware the fire," he whispered in a hiss that made Cassidy's skin crawl.

Jackson took a hasty step back.

"Beware the fire," Serge repeated, now looking at Dominique. Then he laughed uproariously and disappeared.

Dominique closed his eyes and struggled for patience.

"What...was that?" Jackson said.

Cassidy rubbed the chill out of her arms. "That was Serge. You remember him, don't you? The vampire you tried so hard to kill?"

Discomfort tightened his mouth as he looked away.

Dominique placed his hands on the edge of the granite countertop as he faced Jackson. "So, did you bring me fire, Jackson?" His gaze darkened as he let the vampire rise and his senses expand.

Looking through his eyes, Cassidy saw Jackson had changed more than she realized. His aura, once muddy red with anger, had brightened into the powerful crimson of a man whose mind and purpose were clear.

Jackson took a deep breath and pressed a fingertip onto the little black case. "In a way."

Dominique tilted his head, brows drawing together. "This is from the lab?"

"Yes, it is."

The lab was the Striker Foundation's clandestine research facility, staffed with bright scientific minds compelled to maintain absolute secrecy. The lab existed for one reason, and one reason only, and it was that reason that caused Dominique and Cassidy to become stone-still with anticipation.

"They did it, Dominique. They found a way. You can have the sun again."

3

Beware the Fire

Dominique's mind went as still as his body. He could only stare at Jackson, incapable of speech or reaction. Cassidy leaned against him, seeking support, providing comfort. Her mind, too, was silent.

The sun.

For all his determination to see daylight again, he realized now he had never truly believed it was possible, or at least not so soon. Certainly not now that he was the literal center of the vampire world. The mere possibility of such a thing rendered him near senseless.

"I think I was expecting a little more excitement," Jackson said, uncertain.

Cassidy wiped at her face. "We're speechless," she croaked.

Dominique found his voice, low and soft and in words that felt safely removed from his exposed nerves. "Have you eaten?"

Jackson's turn to look startled. He shook his head.

"Then sit," Cassidy said. "We'll make something."

"You—" He looked between them. "Okay."

Dominique opened drawers and retrieved two pots and utensils before checking the fridge for the meat he had set to marinate last night. Cassidy poured more juice for Jackson and herself, collected her hair in an efficient pile on top of her head, and headed to the pantry to collect the ingredients Dominique had in mind. Meanwhile, his thoughts circled Jackson's revelation at a wary distance. There was nothing to be done with it right at this moment. The night had only just begun. He needed to stay busy, and staying busy for Dominique meant either getting on his bike and hunting for fresh veins to seduce, seducing Cassidy until she fell into a sated sleep, or cooking a meal he would never eat.

Maybe never eat, he amended, and paused, stunned all over again.

He didn't trust himself to speak until the flank steaks were seared on one side and flipped to the other on the stove-top grill. He didn't look at Jackson. "Tell me about it."

Jackson shifted in his seat. "Well, it's not a cure, but it could be in the future. For now, this compound can only suppress the condition when it's at its weakest, during the day."

Dominique turned to the pot with the stewing vegetables. So, not a permanent cure, but if it would allow him to experience daylight again? Even for an hour? He would take it.

With a comforting touch on Dominique's shoulder, Cassidy turned to face Jackson. "The 'condition' is genetic. Not an infection."

"Right. And this targets the genome."

"Gene editing?" she said dubiously.

"Gene editing," he confirmed. "CRISPR. I can't explain the exact science, but..."

"It's increasingly used to cure genetic...conditions," she finished, sounding as astonished as Dominique felt. In a regular research setting, there were likely many standards and guidelines that would try to keep the science from getting ahead of the ethics. Nothing about the Striker labs was regular.

Jackson placed a hand back on the case beside him. "Correct. This targets the vampire mutations we've been able to identify and neutralizes them. Most of them, anyway. There are others we haven't been able to isolate that reverse the process once they become active again at night. So, for now, this is a suppressant more than a cure."

"For now," Dominique murmured as he seasoned the meat and fought the excitement simmering in his blood. So far, this was all just talk. "How do you know this works?"

"I've seen it work."

Dominique dropped the fork and turned around. "You what?" both he and Cassidy said in unison.

"They tested this. I was there when they did."

"On *who*?" Cassidy demanded.

"Not a *who*. A what."

Dominique narrowed his eyes. A *what*? How badly had he misjudged this man now?

Jackson held up a hand. "Rats. They tested it on rats."

"Rats?" he repeated.

"*Vampire* rats?" Cassidy asked, incredulous.

Jackson nodded. "Yes."

"They turned *rats* into vampires?" Dominique could barely comprehend.

"They had the serum and blood you donated. There's nothing magical about the mechanics."

He was speechless.

Rats. Forged into immortal beings with his serum and his blood, his DNA. Linked to the dark web. Linked to him.

Your younglings, Cassidy said, her silent voice outraged, her fingers curling into fists.

Dominique closed his eyes. *No, rats. They are only rats. I have no sense of them.*

"They're dead now," Jackson said, hesitating, clearly unsure of just how much trouble he was in.

Cassidy clamped her mouth shut against an outburst, but her chin jutted forward and her eyes blazed. Dominique had to smile despite himself. His love, his queen, his lioness charging into battle on his behalf. There were no words for what he felt for her.

Sensing the warm emotion, she turned to him, surprised. Her shoulders relaxed. A small nod and she tucked an escaped strand of hair behind one ear. The rats didn't matter. Not in this context.

"Did your suppressant kill them?" Dominique asked.

"No. With the suppressant, they were fine during the day. Normal in every way. But once the sun was down, they became vampires again. We tried to see if the suppressant would kick in again the next morning. It didn't." The rest was easy to guess. The scientists left the animals exposed to daylight, and the rodent vampires did what vampires did in daylight.

"So, one dose will buy me one day."

"Yes."

"How is it done?"

"It's an injection. But it has to be administered directly to the heart at or after sunrise. Too early, and the suppressant gets overpowered and purged before it can take effect."

Which meant someone else would have to administer the shot. Someone human. He glanced at Cassidy who hunched her shoulders almost imperceptibly.

You don't know nearly enough to take a risk like that.

His mouth twitched. *I will by the time the night is done.*

Cassidy cocked a brow at him, glanced at Jackson, and went to retrieve a bottle of wine for herself. *I'm going to need this.*

As Cassidy and Jackson enjoyed the meal he prepared, Dominique sipped Perrier water, relishing the effervescence in his mouth, and let the liquid take the edge off his other appetites. He asked more questions. Jackson answered what he could. Nothing about his manner betrayed deception, but if there was one thing at which Jackson Striker excelled, it was deception.

Under the influence of the wine, Cassidy grew animated. Dominique faded into the background of the conversation. He watched her heart-shaped face flush until her freckles glowed. Her ocean blue eyes darkened, drowning him. Over old memories and new perspectives, she and Jackson became reacquainted. They shared much, these two, not all of it ugly. She had once cared for Jackson, and judging by his warm laughter and dilating pupils, he still cared for her.

As for Dominique and Jackson, they trusted each other, though only to a point. Jackson and his uncle were capable, ruthless hunters, and while it suited them to work on his behalf, Dominique was under no illusion that they wouldn't come after him again the moment he gave them the slightest cause—or became vulnerable.

Vulnerable as he would be if he allowed himself to be injected with a mysterious substance during the day.

Yet, how could he refuse such a gift?

Beware the fire. Alarming as that warning was, Serge's prognostications were never literal. Nor did he convulse in a fit of laughter if he perceived a genuine threat. Whatever this fire, it wasn't sun fire.

"Well, it's getting late," Jackson said when the conversation lulled after almost three hours. "I should be going."

Cassidy emptied the remnants of her wineglass.

Dominique said nothing.

"So, what do you think? Want to give this a try?"

Dominique leaned on his elbows and toyed with the empty water glass. "I have one more question."

"Sure. Fire away."

"Why are you giving me such a gift?"

"Why? Seriously? Isn't this what you've wanted for as long as I've known you?"

"It is. And I always hoped that you would be true to your word and genuinely attempt to find a cure for me, for all of us, but—"

"But you never expected I'd deliver? Nice."

"You have a way of surprising me, Jackson Striker."

The human man glanced at the empty plates and bowls, all that remained of the feast a vampire had prepared. "I could say the same for you."

Dominique smiled and sat back in his chair. "Then allow me another surprise. I will not accept your gift without one more concession from you."

The hunter's wariness was instantaneous. "Oh?"

"I need to know your mind. Your true mind."

Every muscle in Jackson's face hardened. Vampires had fed from him, but none had ever asked permission. It would be a simple thing for Dominique to do the same, leave no trace, and make Jackson forget it ever happened. But the hunter was skilled at recognizing and reversing compulsions placed on him. He would remember eventually, and whatever respect Dominique had earned with him would vanish.

Cassidy propped her face in one hand. "You didn't expect Dominique to trust you with his life on your word alone, did you?"

"Oh, I don't know," Jackson said, sitting back, tension bunching his shoulders. "I guess I thought we were past the trust issues."

"Too many depend on my continued survival, which makes trust a luxury I cannot afford." Dominique lowered his voice. "But what you offer is irresistible. That I ask you to open your mind to me instead of simply tearing it open along with your vein should say much about my regard for you."

"I see. And...if I don't agree?"

"Then you may take your gift...and go." He had to scrape the last two words out of his throat. More than his dream of seeing the sun again was at stake here. If Jackson refused this request, the implied deception would forever alter their relationship—and not for the better.

Jackson considered while he rubbed at the stubs that remained of the ring and pinkie fingers of his right hand. "You're willing to turn your back on a chance to see the sun again...because I refuse to give you something you could simply take?"

"I am."

"You're right. I'm surprised."

Dominique waited, flattened by the power of his sudden longing for Jackson's blood, his mind...his trust.

Jackson pushed back his chair and stood. "Fine."

"Fine?" Cassidy repeated, straightening.

"Yes. Fine. If that's what it'll take for you to trust me with this, then you can—" He gestured resignation with one hand. "You can—God help me—*feed* from me." He scrubbed the same hand over his face. "Fuck, I can't believe I'm saying this."

A nameless thrill raced along Dominique's nerves.

Hell may have just frozen over, Cassidy thought, but kept her expression remarkably neutral.

Nonsense. I am impossible to resist, non? Dominique countered, grateful for the humor to break the tension. She squeezed her lips together, but he heard the derisive snort in his mind.

"You realize that once my serum is in your blood, there is nothing you can hide from me."

"Plus, I'm opening myself up to major compulsion. Yes, I'm very aware. Remind me again, why don't you, and I'll change my mind."

Dominique got up and moved around the dining room table, one hand caressing the brocade backs of the chairs he passed. The thump of Jackson's heart began to drown out the Euro-jazz streaming over the house sound system. "Blood offered without compulsion or deception and with full knowledge of the consequences...that is precious to me beyond words. I shall not abuse such a gift."

The human's bright eyes blazed. "I'm letting you see what you need to decide. That's all this is. Get what you need and get out."

Dominique stopped in front of him and produced his most disarming smile. That wasn't how he fed.

"I know why seeing the sun again means so much to me, but tell me this..." In a blur of speed, he had his mouth against the slightly taller man's ear and whispered, "Why is this so important to you?"

"What the fuck?" Jackson yelped but caught himself, jerking his head aside only a little. The artery in his neck pulsed with shimmering life energy, but the thin, silver chain stuck to his clammy skin drew more of Dominique's attention. If he wanted to avoid having his mouth burned by this, he'd have to take care, which was probably why the hunter wore it. "Maybe turning you back into a human is less trouble than having to kill you."

"Aww *chèr*," Dominique said with a sigh. "I always knew you cared."

"Don't get all weir—" The last word ended in a gasp as Dominique's teeth pierced the skin.

Hot, intoxicating blood filled his mouth, thick, salty, and powerfully male. One swallow, two, and then the blood no longer mattered. Then he had the mind.

Though Jackson wasn't aware of him in his mind, his thoughts bristled with a well-practiced obscuring anger. Dominique brushed against it like a summer wind over a frozen lake. Without something concrete to rail against, the anger quickly crumbled.

No, Jackson was no blood-drinker advocate. Far from it. He either pitied or despised them, and could kill them with the same ease others crushed bugs. There was only one vampire he credited with any honor at all, even if that individual was a rival for the affections of a woman he knew would never have him again. So it was for his lingering love for Cassidy and for his growing respect for Dominique that Jackson Striker had spared no expense in finding the cure Dominique sought so desperately.

It was all there. The researchers, the experiments, the fascination and the hope. Even the rats. Their tiny fangs and supernatural reflexes appalled Dominique, and he was stunned when they succumbed to the day and then were dosed with tiny needles. Within moments, they jerked back to consciousness.

At the awe-filled memory of seeing them blink peacefully in the light of day, Dominique stopped drinking. He licked the punctures closed slowly, but did not release Jackson, who remained stiff in his arms.

The rats reverted to their true natures as night returned. In their steel security cages, they were ruthless with their mortal brethren and with each other. In his memories, Jackson flinched to see a vampire animal dispatch its mortal companion with bloody brutality.

Instantly, his memories flashed to another place only five years in the past. Deep underground, in a long-abandoned sub-way station, Jackson's mirror image, his twin, Justin, stood cornered and bug-eyed by a male vampire. To Dominique, the blood-drinker appeared uncoordinated and panicked. To the humans, that didn't matter.

"Why isn't it asleep? What's wrong with it?" Justin shrieked. They were to be his last coherent words before he was shoved against the filthy tile wall, his throat torn open.

The hunters had tracked the vampire there. With the sun up for almost an hour now, he should have been an easy target to dispatch. He was anything but. Justin screamed and clawed at the creature while Jackson threw himself onto its back, roaring with bravado, and drove a small dagger into the vampire's collar. In the next instant, a geyser of blood hit his face. Then he was airborne, followed by a hard tumble over the ground.

When he righted himself, ready to spring up again, he saw the vampire come for him, fangs bared and covered in blood, morphing into a snarling, skeletal incarnation of terror. Jackson raised his hand, blocking the inevitable, when a sword blade flashed from the side, taking off the vampire's arm. Not until much later would Jackson realize that two of his fingers had also come off.

The sword slashed again, and this time hacked off the head. The body pitched forward. One of the clawed hands slammed into Jackson's leg and scraped downward, cutting a deep gash into his inside thigh. Uncle Garrett kicked the head and the arm into a sewer drain. Jackson's fingers went with them, though he didn't know, nor care, petrified with shock. He swayed on his feet, ears ringing. The room spun.

Garrett, looking every inch the blood-spattered warrior, surveyed the scene, his face hard with rage. Only when Jackson staggered and crumpled to the ground did Garrett turn to see the blood pooling around his nephew. He fashioned a crude tourniquet high on the leg with a strip of rope and the dagger. "We need to get you to a hospital," he said, pulling Jackson back to his feet and preparing to half-carry him. "Hold it together."

"Justin. We can't...we need to—" He strained toward the motionless body, but froze when he saw the ragged stump of his brother's neck, the head gone.

"It's too late for him, kid, and I'll be damned if I lose you, too."

While Jackson recovered physically, his twenty-one-year-old self felt ripped in half and poured out. He tried to live the life he was supposed to live and, when asked, shared that his twin had died in a hunting accident. No one ever asked about the prey they hunted, the mystery of why it had been conscious at that time of day was never solved, and Jackson wanted nothing more to do with his family's legacy.

He was done.

But he realized how not done he was when he found the girl trying to fight off the unwanted attentions of two drunken coeds. Never had he known the kind of rage that fueled his punches on them. That girl had been Cassidy, and in the months that followed, she had taught him to feel again. By the time he brought her home as his bride-to-be, he was ready to hunt again. He was ready to avenge his brother.

Then Dominique had entered his life and upended everything Jackson knew about vampires and tolerance.

"Goddamn you," Jackson choked out and tried to break free. "Why am I remembering this? Get the fuck out of my head!"

Another pair of arms came around him. Cassidy's warm female scent merged with Jackson's bitter anger. Through their link, she had experienced every one of these memories, just as Dominique had. Her sigh was one of care and sorrow. "Oh, Jackson."

He trembled between them, fighting he knew not what. His right hand, the one with the two truncated fingers, found one of Cassidy's on his chest and pressed tight.

A strange harmony vibrated through Dominique, as though somewhere deep in his heart a secret string of kinship had been plucked. He understood the agony of loss, just as this man did. And he knew the power of one woman's love to dull that torment. It felt natural to take the human's face in his hands and kiss him in a gesture of affection and understanding. At first Jackson made only a slight effort to break the intimacy, but he struggled harder when Dominique pricked his own tongue on the tip of a razor-sharp canine and pressed it into Jackson's mouth.

"Son of a—" Jackson's head snapped back, eyes widening as the drop of vampire blood heightened his senses to near supernatural levels. He wiped at his mouth.

"Relax," Dominique whispered.

It wasn't a compulsion. Jackson could have stormed away and never looked back. But he didn't. Instead, he closed his eyes, collapsed into Dominique's arms, and muttered a grudging "Fuck you."

4

SWEET DREAMS

They stayed like this, the three of them, in a quiet embrace of bodies and spirits. Breath by breath, Jackson's anger loosened its iron grip on him. As it faded, new feelings of relief surfaced, along with gratitude. But it was the undercurrent of surrender that captivated Dominique the most. Cassidy sensed it draw him in like a moth to a flame. Raw emotion was right up there with freely offered blood on the list of things guaranteed to draw a vampire's undivided attention.

Jackson's hands fisted in the material of Dominique's shirt. Never had he been this vulnerable, this trusting. Dominique's eyes darkened as his interest sharpened, and he sounded distracted when he said, "I am sorry, *mon ami.*"

Slowly, Jackson disengaged and stepped back. He glanced between them, spots of awkward color blooming on his cheeks, and raised a hand to touch the twin St. Christopher medallions around his neck. She had always known that one of them had been his twin brother's, but only now did Cassidy realize that Jackson had pulled it from the gore of his brother's body. It had still been smeared with blood when he added it to his own. "It's not your fault. I'm sorry for ever blaming you for Justin's death." When he saw that only the slimmest band of hazel surrounded the vampire's pupils, he dropped his hand and retreated two more steps. "I—I should go."

"No. Stay," Dominique whispered.

Cassidy arched an inquisitive brow.

His expression softened with a pensive smile. "I need you at sunrise."

Jackson stared at him. "What do you mean?"

"You brought the suppressant, did you not?"

He gave a wary nod.

"Then I will need you to administer it."

"So, you will do it then? You trust me not to kill you at the last moment?"

"You trusted me with your life tonight," Dominique said, his tone solemn. "Now I will trust you with mine."

"I see." He looked around, rubbed the back of his head, unsure. "Well, I guess I'll—"

"Get some sleep," Dominique finished. The compulsion was only a suggestive touch against Jackson's mind, but it slid in between his tattered defenses and found its mark. He shook his head but lost his coordination just before his eyes closed. Dominique swooped in to catch him as he slumped.

"Sweet dreams," Cassidy murmured to the limp body in the vampire's arms. Then she met Dominique's eyes. "Are you sure about this?" She knew the answer, of course, but they had found that saying things—important things—out loud, lent them gravity.

"I have never been more sure about anything," he confirmed, and hoisted Jackson over one shoulder as though he didn't weigh north of two hundred pounds.

"It's not a cure. It's just a tease for something you can't have."

His sensual mouth curved, pressing a mischievous dimple into his left cheek. "What I intend to have, *mon amour*, is you. I want to see you make love to me with your eyes sparkling in the sun."

The visual, together with the husky purr thickening his accent, made her belly quiver in delicious ways. "Oh, you think you can have that, do you?"

He leaned in to press a kiss to the sensitive spot beneath the corner of her jaw, which made other parts of her quiver as well. "I know I can."

Her mouth went dry with heat. "I don't know, lover. You may need to practice."

Avec plaisir, he agreed. *Meet me upstairs.* He blurred away with their passed out guest.

Her senses already reeling, Cassidy kicked the dainty sandals off her feet before jogging after him.

A set of double-doors opened into Dominique's private sanctuary at the top of the stairs. Unlike the rest of the house, this bedroom was ponderous and dark. Gone were the airy pastels and desert-southwest accents she favored. Rich woods and deep-blue fabrics predominated here. Curving over the entire room was a vaulted ceiling, which, at first glance, appeared to be open to the sky at dusk or dawn, but was, in fact, a delicate mural, exquisitely illuminated by recessed lighting. Beneath this vista, they had spent countless nights in the ornate, king-size bed, making love, laughing, plotting, and dreaming.

There was no mistaking which of these was on the agenda now. Having deposited their houseguest in a spare bedroom, Dominique had already pulled back the brocade spread, shed his clothes, and crawled in amidst the pillows. His sinuous body gleamed against the indigo sheets. The dark pools of his eyes were riveted on her.

Cassidy forced herself to slow down. She removed each item of clothing with tantalizing movements until she heard her vampire lover growl with impatience. But he didn't move, not until she came to him, and even then, he let her take the lead. Obediently, he lay back as she directed, allowing her hands to do as they wished. When she finally joined her body to his, he groaned with unreserved enthusiasm.

More than their conscious minds merged now. Physical sensations echoed between them, blurring their edges further. It still threatened to overwhelm them, this feeling of simultaneously taking and being taken. Which is why, at this point in their lovemaking, if they didn't want it to be over in seconds, they always paused to refocus on only one of them, usually Cassidy.

Sitting up, Dominique undid the tie on top of her head and ran his fingers through her hair as the coil dropped halfway down her bare back. Then he kissed her, slow and deep, filling her with the cool, earthy taste of him. She moved at a leisurely pace, riding him, riding the edge, drawing out the pleasure until she could hold it no more. When she threw back her head with a hoarse cry, his teeth nipped her jaw.

Her body still shuddered when he rolled her onto her back with a possessive growl and let his own need take over. As he did, a familiar spiral of crystalized light pulsed into existence around them. It moved in tandem with him, twisting up and out with increasing urgency, disappearing into the sky mural. This was how Cassidy saw the beast slipping out of Dominique's control. This was his true vampire soul, the insatiable hunger for blood and life.

It was this that got the mortal lovers of vampires killed.

Beneath her hands, Dominique's shoulders tightened into something leaner and harder than mere muscle. Beneath her ear, his teeth grazed her skin. She let her spirit unfurl around him and spread out into the spiral, giving herself to a fresh wave of cresting ecstasy.

"*J't'aime*, Dominique," she whispered, and backed up the words with thoughts and feelings. *I love you. All of you. Always.*

For a singular moment, at the height of his climax, his alter ego's alien presence rippled through her like a touch from the grave. It withdrew as suddenly as it appeared, sated by her love. Also, she was too much a part of him to register as a separate entity.

They sprawled in a spent heap in the middle of the bed. She stroked the back of his head where it lay against her shoulder. The mingled aromas of sex, winter ice, and spring growth saturated the air. When her breathing calmed, he propped himself up and playfully bumped his nose against hers before finding her mouth for a tender kiss.

In the next room, Jackson moaned.

Peering over Dominique's virtual shoulder, Cassidy saw Jackson was dreaming. Or rather, he was taking the experiences flowing out of their unguarded minds and making them his own in vivid, breathtaking color. "Good God."

"*Intéressant.*"

Cassidy screwed her eyes shut as though that could block anything out.

Dominique throttled down his connection with Jackson's psyche. "It seems we have set him free, even if only in his dreams."

"That is so way more than I wanted to know."

He rolled his forehead against hers with a wistful sigh. *I know.*

The small frisson of regret in his mind made her catch her breath. *No. You can't be serious.*

He pulled her into his arms in mute apology for thinking about what he had, however briefly.

You...you would have been okay if...if we had...and...and...wow. She couldn't even finish the thought.

I don't know, he admitted. But the fact remained: he yearned for a human child—with her, or, failing that, *from* her. If he couldn't be the biological father, then the oblivious man in the next room was, after this evening at least, the only one worthy of that honor. *Nothing but a fanciful dream.*

Cassidy released the breath she had been holding. *Oh, Dominique. You know if I could give you such a gift, I would, but not like this.*

I know. He kissed the top of her head. *Forgive me. That would have been one miracle too many tonight.*

She wound her arms around her troubled vampire, holding him tight. There was nothing to forgive. For as long as she had known him, he had grieved for his human life. But not until tonight did she grasp the full lengths to which he was willing to go to reclaim any part of it.

She only wished she could veto the sunlight experiment as easily as the baby plan.

5

A Shot at Dawn

C assidy and Dominique sat at the kitchen counter and contemplated the black case when tentative footsteps approached from the foyer. They looked up to see Jackson, who had shoved his hands into his pockets and looked anything but at ease.

"Good dreams?" Dominique wondered with a knowing smile, which only compounded their guest's obvious discomfort.

"Coffee is over there," Cassidy said quickly, pointing at the coffeemaker, which sighed and burbled in the far corner. Jackson beelined for it.

God help us. He remembers his dreams, she lamented, wishing she didn't remember them, too.

And he suspects we are aware of them, Dominique added with wry amusement.

Well, I'm glad one of us is having fun. Toying with Jackson's uptight equilibrium had long been a favorite sport for the vampire.

"Ah!" Serge exclaimed as he trundled into the kitchen and spotted Jackson. "He survived the fire."

Half the coffee Jackson was pouring splattered on the counter. He jammed the carafe back on the hotplate and pinched his mouth against a string of obscenities. Ripping a wad of paper towels off the dispenser, he mopped up the mess.

"Our night was...very enjoyable," Dominique said suggestively before taking pity on Jackson and changing the subject. "But I intend to enjoy my day even more."

"Ah, yes. That." Serge sucked in his lips and touched his fingertips together.

"What does that mean?" Cassidy asked. "Is it safe? What do you see?"

Serge tilted his head to one side, then the other, his full face narrowing as he considered Dominique. He shrugged. "Turmoil, but nothing of consequence."

It will not work, Dominique thought, shoulders slumping.

Cassidy gripped his forearm as she implored Serge. "It won't kill him, though. Right?"

"Bah! Nothing will kill him," Serge sniffed with a dismissive flick of a wrist.

"So, you...um..." Cassidy glanced at Jackson, now clutching a steaming cup of determination and maintaining his distance. Whether or not he realized it, he really had touched fire last night when he offered his vein to Dominique. The searing dreams that resulted were just the smoke. "You weren't talking about the sun last night with, um, 'beware the fire?'"

Serge gave her an exasperated look. "We must *always* beware the sun, sweet one."

I give up, she thought and dropped her head on Dominique's shoulder.

He leaned in, his hair damp against her face. *I did years ago.*

Serge eyed Jackson, but no more vagaries were forthcoming. Instead, he turned to Dominique, pressed a hand to his sternum, and bowed at the waist. "My lord, I will find my sanctuary in the earth. I bid you a pleasant day. May it be all you hoped."

With that, the barefoot vampire vanished. He would have no part of their experiment. Or risk being vulnerable.

This sent a chill creeping across Cassidy's shoulders. *He doesn't trust Jackson. Should we?*

We have more reason to trust him than Serge does, Dominique countered. *Also, if there were true danger, Serge would never let me do this. Which means…this probably will not work. You will need to seal the door to the sanctuary from the outside.*

Cassidy thought she'd consider herself lucky if that's all she would need to do in the next few minutes.

Jackson cleared his throat. "So, I guess we should get started?"

"We should." Dominique scooped up the case and headed for the wine cellar–lair. Cassidy followed.

"What? In there?"

"Just in case." She inclined her head in a gesture meaning *come on*. With his mug cradled in both hands, Jackson did.

Dominique sealed the door behind them. The silence inside the poured-concrete room enveloped them like shrink wrap.

"I know the exit code," Cassidy said when Jackson acquired the pallor of someone being shut in a tomb.

He put his cup down on a small table that, together with two chairs, occupied one side of the shelter. A rack of wine bottles took up the entire far wall, filling the air with the smells of corks and dusty labels. Two cots padded with blankets lined another wall. On one of these Dominique sat now, eyes drooping. Cassidy could hear the sun's inferno roaring in his ears and felt its weight crush all coherent thought out of his head.

Jackson picked up the little black case from the cot beside Dominique and unzipped it. Inside, encased in foam, was a large vial of clear liquid and a pair of syringes. He pulled out the vial and a syringe, uncapped the sharp and substantial-looking needle with his teeth, plunged it into the vial and drew out the contents. Against the weak light, Cassidy could just make out a pink hue to the suppressant.

"How are you feeling?" Jackson asked, watching the filling hypodermic. "How much time do we have?"

"One or two minutes," Dominique replied, drooping eyes locked on the liquid.

"I suppose now's not a good time to talk about last night, then, is it?"

Dominique cut him a sly look. "We can talk all you want after sunrise. I will make you breakfast."

"I'll hold you to that." Jackson flicked the syringe with a fingernail and squirted out an air bubble.

Dominique lay down and pulled up his shirt, baring his torso.

Jackson hesitated.

"What?" Cassidy said.

"I don't exactly stick needles in people's hearts on a regular basis, or, actually...ever."

"Well, don't look at me."

Have him get on with it, Dominique snarled.

Cassidy placed a hand on his chest and located the slow heartbeat. Like the last grains of sand in an hourglass, his consciousness drained out of her as it did every morning, leaving her bereft. "Now, Jackson."

"Okay. Okay then." Jaw clenched, he leaned over the prone body. While Cassidy braced for the pain about to shimmer across the link, Jackson winced as he pushed the needle in all the way.

Cassidy felt nothing.

The plunger came down. The syringe emptied.

Still nothing.

He pulled the needle out. A small red bead formed where it had been.

Beneath her hand, the vampire's heart still beat, slow and steady and undeterred.

"Are you sure you hit the heart?"

He stepped back. "Pretty sure."

"*Pretty* sure? What do you mean—"

Dominique drew a breath. Exhaled. Inhaled again.

"Yeah. That's how it starts," said Jackson, putting the cap back on the used needle. "I hit it alright."

"Dominique?" Cassidy said. She had no sense of him in her mind. The daytime emptiness persisted, but he was breathing, something he never did without a conscious thought at night.

"Dominique, *mon amour*. Wake up," she whispered. "*Réveillez-vous*." After almost three years of sharing a Frenchman's mind, her command of the language even during the day approached fluent.

She wanted to weep with joy when she saw his eyes open. "*Bonjour*," she said.

He stared at her. Hard. His eyes held no trace of vampire, but there was no warmth in them either. In fact—

"Dominique?"

"*Oui. C'est moi.*" He sat up. His eyes darted through the shadowy little room, flicked between Cassidy and Jackson, and finally settled on the empty syringe in Jackson's hand. "*Mais qui êtes-vous? Et où suis-je?*"

All the air left Cassidy as though someone had kicked her in the gut. "No. Oh, no."

"What?" Jackson said. "What's he saying?"

"He—" *Oh my God, no.* "He wants to know where he is." She could barely form the words. "He doesn't know. He doesn't know who we are."

6

THE STRANGER

"Holy shit," Jackson muttered. "Holy fucking shit."

Cassidy turned aside, bracing herself against the wine rack, one hand pressed to her mouth. Her whole body slumped.

"Can you feel him?" Jackson asked. The panic edging his voice only fueled her own. She shook her head. "Even a little?"

"Nothing." The word strangled in her windpipe. Nothing. The Dominique she knew and loved was gone, dead, body-snatched. The man struggling to stand on uncooperative legs might as well be an alien.

"What is this shit?" he blustered, the French accent more sibilant than ever. "What have you done to me? What do you want?"

"Easy," Jackson said and raised both hands, one still holding the ominous needle. When Dominique's eyes widened at the sight, he dropped the thing on the table together with the open case, backup syringe, and empty vial, all of which remained in full view.

"What have you done?" Dominique demanded again.

Yes. What have we done? Cassidy's eyes filled with tears.

"You were sick," Jackson tried. "Asleep. But you're getting better now."

"Asleep?" He waved a hand around at the cramped space. "Is this how you keep your guests? In"—his eyes caught on the heavy-duty door with the keypad glowing on the wall beside it—"a prison?"

"No, not a prison," Cassidy said. She wiped at her eyes before stiffening her back and facing the alien. She had to get through this day somehow, one interminable minute at a time. "This is protection. For you."

"Protection?" Dominique snorted. "Do not tell me fantasies."

She pushed past Jackson on her way to the door and punched in the code.

"You sure about this?" Jackson wondered.

"Oh, yeah. I'm sure." Never mind the vampire who forgot he was one. If she had to spend the whole day locked up in here with these two, she'd be the one making an attempt on Jackson's life.

He lowered his gaze. "I'm sorry."

"Too bad rats can't talk," she snapped under her breath. The handle clanged in her hand. The door swung open. Turning back to Dominique, she said, "C'mon then. I'm told it's safe for you now."

Dominique hesitated. When he finally walked forward, it was with great care, but each step grew more certain. In the kitchen he stopped again, looking around. Unlike his vampire face, his human face hid none of the confusion, nor the simmering panic. She clasped her hands tightly to stop herself from comforting him with an embrace that would surely be rejected.

"How do you feel?" Jackson asked. He sounded a little calmer, like he had a plan.

Dominique looked down, spread his hands out before him, and inspected his bare arms. At night, his skin could pass for a natural pale. Now it looked paper white. "How long have I been...asleep?"

When Jackson opened his mouth, Cassidy gave a slight shake of her head. He opted for a vague "A while."

"I look like a corpse. For how many months have you kept me confined?"

"You're not confined," Cassidy said.

"Oh? I can leave then?"

The question took her aback. *Leave?* Dear God, where would he want to go?

Dominique turned and walked toward the living room. She dared not move, not even breathe, as he rounded the corner and stepped directly into the bright sunlight streaming through a wall of glass. He raised his hand to shield his eyes, but didn't flinch. His skin remained a pristine white.

Weak with relief, Cassidy hurried after him, Jackson on her heels.

The sliding doors opened. Dominique walked out and studied the infinity pool and the meticulously tended backyard. Serge's sailing catamaran lay tethered at the end of the dock, awaiting her pirate captain at nightfall. By the pool's far side, close to the guesthouse where she lived, Samantha was engrossed in her morning yoga practice, while nearby, Brinkley stood on his haunches to inspect the contents of a terra-cotta planter.

"*Ce n'est pas Saint Barthélemy.*"

"You're right. It's not," Cassidy agreed, coming up behind him. "This is South Florida."

He stabbed the fingers of both hands into his hair and clutched his head. "*Comment est-ce que je suis arrivé ici? Pourquoi est-ce qu je suis ici?*"

"Please, Dominique, listen to me," she tried. "I know this is disorienting, but how you got here is a really long story that'll take time to tell. And you really are safe here."

The outburst caused Samantha to glance over her shoulder and promptly stumble out of her balance pose. Mouth gaping in astonishment, she came toward them. Beside Cassidy and out of Dominique's view, Jackson tried to wave her off. She ignored him. "Dominique?"

"*Oui?*"

"What are you doing? Why are you...what...how?" she spluttered as she gestured at the sunlit landscape.

"Do you know me, *madame*?"

Samantha reared back. "Do I what?"

"He doesn't remember," Jackson said. "Anything," he added with great emphasis.

His half-sister looked dazed. "I see." She shook her head. "Yes. Yes, I know you."

Cassidy put a tentative hand on Dominique's shoulder. "What is the last thing you remember?"

He shot her a guarded glance. Then he walked away again, rounding the pool, putting distance between them. Wind ruffled his wild hair. The morning sun bathed him in warm brilliance. He was living his most impossible dream—a dream he no longer remembered. Cassidy's eyes stung with fresh tears.

"Jack, is this the 'gift' Serge said you brought for him?" Samantha whispered.

"It is," he confirmed.

"My God, baby brother. What have you done?"

"What we all do, Sam. What he wants us to do. And now I'm going to do what I need to do."

Cassidy grabbed his arm before he could take more than a single step. "I think you've done quite enough." She swiped at her cheeks and set her jaw, then went after Dominique.

The day-walking vampire had come to a halt at the far side of the pool, and stood with arms crossed, staring into the sunrise. Cassidy didn't touch him again. She wouldn't be able to handle him turning away from her one more time. "Please. Tell me what you remember. We really are trying to help."

The sneer on his lips was scathing. "You must think I'm an imbecile. If I were sick, I would be in hospital, not locked up in a house in a foreign country."

"You're right. You're not sick." And he definitely didn't need any damn "cure." "I'm guessing the last thing you remember is leaving your house, your parents' house, on Saint Barthélemy. You were very sick then. Am I right?"

The sneer faltered. "*Oui.*"

"You haven't been...yourself since then." Her eyes brimmed with more moisture, but she blinked it away. The only "self" she had ever known of Dominique was buried together with four years' worth of memories in a brain that could apparently only function at night. *Temporarily buried,* she reminded herself. But she felt her knees quake at the possibility that he would wake up tonight like Jackson's lab rats, and remember nothing of who and what he was. Who *she* was.

Or how to control his deadly instincts.

"You have kept me drugged ever since then?"

"No, of course not," she said too quickly.

Dominique's gaze shifted to Jackson, who had trailed after Cassidy together with Samantha. "So that was not a spent shot I saw you holding?"

"It was, but—"

"Something went wrong?"

Jackson swallowed visibly. "Wrong" wasn't even a word for this.

Cassidy managed a wobbly smile. "This is not as bad as it seems," she said, trying to convince herself as much as Dominique. Her heartache in every word, she introduced herself to the love of her life like he was a complete stranger. "And this is Jackson and his sister, Samantha," she added to fill the silence that followed. "We are your...friends."

Jackson cringed.

Samantha gave her a look of raw pity.

"Right," Dominique said with a soft snort and looked down. Brinkley stood by his bare foot and must have bumped his leg. The cat blinked up at him, his tail waving in a friendly hello. There was no trace of the ferocious feline from the night before.

Nor was there a hint of the vampire who leaned down to pet it. Brinkley rose on his hind legs to push into the head rub. "I think the only friend I have here is this one."

When he straightened, his face shuttered at the sight of the three people staring at him. Cassidy no longer fought to contain her emotions. Her tears flowed unchecked, dripping off her chin. After months of trying to cajole Brinkley into tolerating him without success, this alien in Dominique's body was welcomed without so much as a hint of feline challenge.

"Oh, you are *magnifique, madame*," Dominique scoffed. "You can weep at will? Are you an actress by profession?"

Cassidy sucked in her breath at the vicious verbal sting.

Beside her, Jackson moved.

Samantha yelped. "Jack, no!"

Too late. Jackson's balled fist landed on Dominique's jaw with unrestrained power, sending him reeling into a hedge.

Cassidy flinched.

Jackson clutched his hand. "Mother *fucker*, his bones are hard." Dominique staggered upright. He touched his face, dabbing at a split lip, and voiced several fervent French obscenities.

"Oh, shut up," Jackson snapped. "You've had that coming. For years."

7

THREE FOR BREAKFAST

The punch reined Dominique in a little, or at least curbed the acid flowing off his tongue. It also surprised him enough he didn't stop to consider how badly he was hurt—and how the injury healed in a matter of minutes. At night, the cut would have disappeared in seconds.

He remained quiet as they shepherded him back into the house, but Cassidy saw the way his body moved around Jackson now, constantly on guard. His Aikido training had him on full alert. Jackson wouldn't be able to get away with another stunt like that.

Cassidy busied herself preparing a basic breakfast of scrambled eggs, bacon, and toast. She moved through the motions, opening drawers and cabinets, looking for everything in all the wrong places. Her head felt like a quicksand pit, full of random thoughts, refusing to focus.

"You are clueless, woman," Dominique muttered as he watched her snatch the blackening bacon from a too-hot pan. He sat at the kitchen counter under Jackson's watchful eye.

Cassidy shot him an ugly look. She didn't need him telling her that her culinary skills—never top-of-the-line to begin with—were disintegrating into the realm of abomination. "Everything I know about cooking I learned from you."

This earned her a scornful snort.

Turning to Jackson, who was nursing another mug of coffee, she said, "You're staying for breakfast?"

"I'm staying the day," he said, answering the question she really asked. On a mutter, he added, "Least I can do."

"Thank you."

With an impatient gesture, Dominique pinned his hair behind his ears. "You are my guard, then? Here to prevent my escape?"

"This is your home, buddy. Trust me, you don't want to escape it."

"My home is on Saint Barthélemy. Does my family know I am here? I will need to contact them."

Jackson glanced at Cassidy. Did she want to handle this one? She did.

"Your family believes you're dead," she said, wiping her hands on a towel. "For their safety, it's better if they keep believing that." Not to mention safer for him to believe they were all alive and well in their peaceful island paradise.

Dominique became still, and for a horrifying moment she feared he remembered what he had done the night he was turned—and since. Who he had killed—and how. Then a corner of his mouth tilted up. "Is everything coming out of your mouth complete bullshit?"

Oh, the things I could tell you that would spin your head, my love. But none of them found their way to her tongue. This day would pass. Somehow.

She tossed the towel down and went for plates. The abomination was ready to be served. "Are you hungry?"

"Starving," Dominique said. "But not for this shit you have made."

"Oh? Pray tell, what shit are you hungry for then?"

Jackson shifted a little, his coffee back on the counter.

Dominique looked between them, uncertain for the first time since waking.

"Well, I'm starving," Jackson said. "So, how about we eat? Then we can talk." He didn't wait for a response before joining Cassidy, collecting utensils and condiments, and placing them on the breakfast table nestled in a bay window. He poured himself more coffee and filled two additional mugs. Also, three glasses of OJ. As Samantha had retreated to the guesthouse, the third setting was for the vampire who hadn't eaten solid food in years.

"Did your little fury friends eat?" Cassidy asked casually.

"They did," Jackson confirmed.

Dominique seemed to decide he was hungry. And not just a little. "This is atrocious. Are you familiar with salt, *madame*?" he demanded after the first forkful of rubberized eggs. But that didn't stop him from taking a bite of the toast he had buttered and slathered with jam. Seconds later, his face rumpled with disgust as he tossed the bread on top of the atrocious eggs. "This tastes like nothing."

Cassidy swallowed a mouthful of eggs and then stopped to watch, mesmerized. Seeing Dominique eat her cooking was something she never thought she'd see. Now she wished she had put more thought into her efforts.

Jackson shook his head in wonder. Then he pulled out his phone and pointed it at Dominique.

Dominique paused. "What are you doing?"

"Evidence," Jackson said, capturing the wary vampire glower over the plate of human food.

Cassidy sobered. "You don't think he'll remember this?"

"No, I'm sending this to Garrett."

"And who is this Garrett? Another supposed friend of mine?"

Cassidy opened her mouth and shut it again. Then she said, "He works for you."

Dominique made a disgusted noise of sheer disbelief and shoved at his hair again. His chair scraped on the tile as he pushed it back, got up, and carried his plate into the kitchen to toss it, half-eaten contents and all, into the sink. Next, he tackled the fridge, pulling out more eggs along with herbs and mushrooms and a package of smoked salmon.

"I'll wait for what he's making," Jackson said, pushing his own plate away. "Sorry, Cass."

"No need." She put her fork down and made use of her napkin. "It truly is awful."

Jackson leaned on his folded arms. "I also owe you an apology for last night. For whatever you and Dominique may have...well...seen, I guess."

"Also no need," she said, keeping her eyes on Dominique and her voice low.

"I wasn't...I don't know where all that came from. I'm sorry if anything...upset you."

You were accidentally compelled by a powerful vampire in the throes of passion with an open circuit to your brain, she thought, but saw no point in discussing it further, given present circumstances. Turning away from the kitchen to face him directly, she said, "You didn't upset me, Jackson. Not until you gave him that damn shot."

His square jaw tensed. "I didn't know."

"And you don't know if he'll remember who he is tonight, do you?"

Jackson's gaze slid away. His voice sounded strained enough to fracture. "No. I don't."

Cassidy inhaled as deeply as her tight chest would allow and forced herself to recall Serge's relaxed attitude about this insane experiment. If the Dominique they knew was gone for good, he would have seen it and sounded an alarm, wouldn't he? She clung to that hope like she did her coffee cup.

Jackson's phone buzzed with a text message. He scowled as his thumbs tapped a response. Before he could send it, the device rang. He cursed and turned away, shoulders hunched, to accept the call. She marveled at the awkward excuse he spun for missing his Sunday morning run with Olivia today. The Jackson she knew was a far smoother liar than that.

After the call ended, he dropped the phone on the table and buried his face in both hands. "God, I really want to do right by her, but fuck. After last night? I don't even know where to start." He dropped his hands to look at the ceiling, fresh color in his unshaven cheeks. "Maybe we should wait a bit before you talk to her. About anything."

"Well, I certainly wouldn't be mentioning anything that...um...didn't really happen."

Jackson gave her such a frazzled look she almost felt sorry for him. Then he glanced into the kitchen behind her and all the exhaustion vanished. In the blink of an eye, the hunter was back. "Where the fuck is he?"

She spun in her chair. Breakfast lay abandoned in mid-prep on the countertop. The door to the side yard swayed in the breeze.

The cook was nowhere to be seen.

8

SIDE EFFECTS

Dominique woke at dusk to his stomach punching into the back of his throat. His whole body convulsed, determined to turn inside out, as he hunched on hands and knees. Powerless, he could only let it happen, could only watch a thick stream of pulp hurtle out of his gullet and explode on the paving stones.

"Yeah. I thought that might happen," said a man he vaguely recognized. He reached for the man's—Jackson's—mind, but it was like feeling the shape of a thing through a thick layer of cotton. Only fear and tension greeted him. More of the same came from a woman—Cassidy—muted and distant. So much fear.

"Dominique?" she asked, her voice tentative. "Please tell me you know who I am."

He rolled to sit on his hip and looked up at her. She was borderline frantic. His hand shook as he wiped the back of it across his mouth. "Cassie, *mon amour.*"

She was in his arms before the words had fully left his lips. "Oh, thank God. You're back."

"What...what happened?" Only a storm of conflicting impressions met him in her mind. "How did I get out here?"

"Really?" Jackson said. He stood over them with hands on hips. "You don't remember the total fucking asshole you've been all day?" Samantha stood by her brother's side, arms crossed, fingers of one hand pressed to her mouth.

"The suppressant," Dominique murmured. Watching that syringe fill was the last thing he remembered with any clarity.

Over the next few minutes, they filled him in on the harrowing events of the day he spent in the sun. Their words sketched the outlines, while Cassidy's memories filled in the details. He had verbally abused them, insulted them, tricked them. He even attempted an escape.

"Of course, you forgot how fast you really are, so I tracked you down quick enough." Tracked him down and tackled him in Mrs. Havashand's backyard. Jackson had survived the altercation that ensued only because Dominique also forgot how strong he was. That and the drop of blood he had forced on Jackson the night before, had given the human the edge.

Mrs. Havashand had called the police. Jackson smooth-talked the officers out of making reports. Dominique held his tongue because Cassidy implored him that it was in his best interest to stay with them and hear them out. They told him tales of being ill, of running from criminal organizations, of fighting to keep his family safe by remaining in hiding.

Anything but the fantastical truth.

Through it all, Dominique of the day sneered at them, tried their every nerve, and emotionally tortured Cassidy to the breaking point. Spending the day with him was supposed to be a joy. Instead, she was forced to spend it with a bitter, suspicious stranger. She had no sense of him, no connection, no rapport at all. He was a walking, talking blank spot in her house and mind. The most brutal abandonment of all.

"You were a first-rate, unmitigated son of a bitch," Jackson finished with feeling. They had moved to the kitchen by now. Samantha and Serge—who had stopped by long enough to confirm Dominique's continued existence—had retreated to the pool house. "I can't believe I'm saying this, but I'm actually *thrilled* to have the blood-sucking demon lord version of you back."

Dominique was appalled. "I recall none of this. I walked in the sun and...remember nothing."

"You were busy plotting escape."

He shook his head. "I must have been terrified." He emptied the bottle of Perrier Cassidy had put on the kitchen counter in front of him. "That must be why I remembered nothing. Next time I will be better prepared."

"Next time?" Cassidy asked, incredulous.

"*Bien sûr.* This is only the beginning. There has to be a way for this to work. We simply have to try until we find it."

"No way," Jackson said. "I'm not spending another twenty-four hours like I just did."

"Then don't. Get me the shot and go. *Non,* get me several."

"You're out of your fucking mind if you think I'm going to let you do this to yourself again."

"Ah, Jackson, *chèr,*" Dominique crooned. "You do care."

"Oh, for fuck's sake." Jackson raised his hands. "I'm done. We're done. I need to leave. I owe Ollie a dinner out tonight."

He hadn't taken two steps toward the door when Dominique moved in a blur and planted himself right in front of Jackson, who bounced off him. He was done asking nicely. "By when can you get me more?"

"Goddamn you, Nick. I liked you less today than I even do right now. And I'm willing to bet the same is true for Cassidy." He gave her a quick glance. "I think neither one of us wants to see that side of you again. Ever."

Dominique's building frustration erupted in a growl. He could still smell daylight on his own skin. He'd be damned if he didn't fight to see it and remember it, too.

"Nice," Jackson sneered.

"It's okay," Cassidy said, joining them. "We can try it again, but we have to make a plan. Today was chaotic."

"By when?" Dominique pushed.

Jackson glowered. "I'll get with the lab tomorrow and see what they can do. A few days, I'm guessing. I'll be in touch."

"*Merci*," Dominique said, a smile bursting onto his face.

The door hadn't quite shut behind Jackson yet when Dominique turned to Cassidy and folded her into his arms. She softened against him. Her exhausted relief seeped into his body like a calm tide. *Can you ever forgive me for what I did to you today?*

It wasn't you. It was a version of you that didn't know he... She swallowed the thought.

Didn't know he had died, Dominique finished. *I know. I will figure this out. We will figure this out.* He revisited her memory of him walking in the morning sun, experienced her wonder and awe, and he knew she would move mountains to help him make real at least this one dream.

Following his thoughts, she said, "You can always sire some worthy soul if you're feeling so parental."

He held her closer, hands caressing her back. "There is only one worthy soul I wish to sire, Cassie *amour*. And when you are ready, I promise you there will be nothing parental about it."

9

THE COMPLICATED LIFE

For the rest of the night, Dominique struggled to regain his full strength. He didn't realize how much of a toll his daytime adventures had taken until he caught a jogger trotting through the exclusive neighborhood. Only after feeding to within an inch of the man's life, did the fog clear out of Dominique's brain. The suppressant's lingering effects were unnerving, stealing memories and control, almost like being turned again, only on a much smaller scale.

Still, he couldn't wait to try again, and thought of little else for the rest of the week. Jackson promised him another dose by Saturday morning, and by Friday night, Dominique had a firm plan. He laid it out for Serge before they left the vault.

Serge sat on his cot with his face in one hand and sighed. "Don't you have better things to do than chase this ghost, my lord?"

"Think of the advantage, Serge. A blood-drinker who doesn't have to hide from the sun? I could travel anywhere, anytime. How simple that would make it to control this kingdom."

His friend tucked in his chin and gave him a look that said he knew an excuse when he heard it. But there was none of the frantic panic Serge fell into when he saw misfortune in their immediate future. That was good enough for Dominique.

He got up and unsealed the vault's door. "Besides. This may lead to a cure for all of us."

Serge snorted.

Dominique kept himself busy by teaching his regular Friday night Aikido class. His dojo shared space with Samantha's yoga studio and served as the official address for the Lord of Night. Also, teaching was a way of keeping his own skills sharp—not to mention his self-control around his mortal students—and to be a visible, active member of the local community.

Afterward, he hunted, drinking his fill several times over in numerous local bars and event venues, gaining more strength. Though he spent a fair amount of these energies in his bed with Cassidy not much later.

His grand plan for his second attempt at day-walking began an hour before dawn when he got busy in the kitchen. The gourmet breakfast experience he prepared was one he intended to enjoy together with Cassidy and Jackson after sunrise. As he prepped ingredients and utensils, he had Cassidy record him talking to himself in French. He was whisking eggs, cream, cinnamon, and vanilla for the toast when the phone in his pocket doodled with a video call.

He retrieved it one-handed and touched the video button to answer.

"I hope I'm not disturbing you, my lord," said Aubrey Wainwright. He looked his usual put-together self. Smart jacket, close shave, impeccable hair. Every inch the Victorian gentleman. Far too much the gentleman to notice or—God forbid—comment on Dominique's own appearance. In the tiny video image of himself, Dominique spotted a dusting of powdered sugar in his hair.

Cassidy stopped the recording on her phone and went to load the coffeemaker. He gestured with the dripping whisk. "I'm making breakfast."

"Of course," Aubrey said, as though that were the most natural thing for a vampire to be doing this time of day. "I shan't keep you long."

"Very well. What is so urgent?"

"I'm in San Francisco, and I have made the acquaintance of a highly intriguing lady of our kind."

"I am pleased to hear it, Aubrey," Dominique said with a grin. Aubrey needed to loosen up. A lover could be just the thing.

"Er—" Aubrey stammered, then cleared his voice. "Actually, she is of interest to both of us."

"How so?"

"She refused the re-siring."

Serge silently appeared in the kitchen and peered into various containers arrayed on the counter. "And you are letting her refuse because...?"

"Because she has requested time to consider. Apparently, forcing the issue right now might present problems for her with the leader of her group, or 'colony' as they call themselves. She has given me to understand that he is...challenging."

"I see." Aubrey's mission of locating and re-siring blood-drinkers on Dominique's behalf was straightforward. He told them of the change in leadership—often having to explain the old leadership as well—and offered an alternative to living with a constant need for terror. Simple. But approaching a group of more than two or three could be dangerous, and not something Aubrey was willing—or expected—to do.

Serge had sidled around him and studied the griddle warming on the gas flame. When he made to poke a finger at the melting butter pad, Dominique swatted his hand with the whisk. "So you are requesting the hunters?" he asked. He hoped not. Jackson was his only source of suppressant.

"Actually, my lord, if I may—" Aubrey stopped, appearing to think better of what he was about to say. "The colony numbers over two-hundred members, some of them quite old. With all due respect to your mortal aides, that is considerably more than I think they could safely handle. Even during the day."

"*Merde!*" Dominique put the whisk down and rubbed his forehead with two fingers, chasing a spontaneous ache. This wasn't what he wanted to have to deal with right now. When he sent the Strikers to aide Aubrey or one of his other emissaries, they located the comatose blood-drinkers during the day and secured them so that when they woke the next night, they had a very clear understanding of the new regime's true reach and power. Only rarely did a blood-drinker decline to be re-sired at that point, which was when Jackson and Garrett "cleaned up." Two hundred vampires was a large group by any standard—one that required a territory rich in prey.

Serge leaned against the counter on the kitchen's other side, his attention now solely on Dominique.

"Are they in San Francisco?"

"No, my lord. They do business here, which is how I came to meet Miss Natalia, but—"

"Business?"

"Yes, indeed. Their leader has fashioned himself the head of an international conglomerate based in Vancouver, Canada. As I understand it, he uses the fortunes he earns from this enterprise to provide the sort of lifestyle for his followers that they find difficult to resist."

"No doubt."

"I should mention that I was extended an invitation by the charming Miss Natalia to visit there, and I contemplate doing so. Although, perhaps, not in my official capacity as your emissary," he hedged.

"A social call. Of course. That is a brilliant idea. Get to know your new lady friend in her home territory and see what goes on there. Then we shall decide how to proceed."

"Thank you, my lord."

A strange flicker in Aubrey's eyes stopped Dominique from disconnecting. "What else is on your mind, *chèr*?"

"Forgive me, but—" He paused and grew a little more regal. "I thought perhaps you might like to join me."

Dominique didn't respond right away, though his teeth were now on edge. Traveling long distances was complicated for someone who couldn't function in daylight. More than that, he would have to delay his day-walking project. Then again, if he could make the latter work today, the former would be no problem. "My schedule is spoken for right now," he said.

"Making breakfast, yes. I see."

Serge chortled under his breath. Dominique shot him a stern look. "It is a related project, one with great promise for us all. I will let you know if my availability changes. In the meantime, go see this colony. Tell them nothing more of me than what you have already shared with Natalia. See what you can find out and report back."

"Very well, my lord. Expect to hear from me in three night's time at the soonest." The connection dropped.

Dominique considered his phone for a long moment before pocketing it and going back to whisking the dip. The more his control over his kingdom solidified, the more complicated his life became.

"That's a lot of vampires for him to handle," Cassidy said, echoing his thoughts. She was setting the table in the nook. Beyond the windows, the sky grew light.

"Too many," Serge agreed, all serious now.

"There is nothing to handle. Just a visit." He dipped the thick slices of challah bread in the sweetly fragrant emulsion.

"A visit you would do well to join him in, blood-child."

"I would only get in his way. I think he may like this Natalia more than he claims."

"Too many," Serge said again. "I have a feeling."

"A feeling? Or a vision?" Dominique wondered as he plopped the dripping bread onto the griddle. He glanced at his best friend. Discomfort, yes, but not disaster coming their way. "Why are you still here? The sun isn't far."

Serge fidgeted in place for a few more seconds before grunting an "as you wish, my lord," and vanishing out the kitchen door.

Cassidy stopped placing flatware and turned to him. "What if Aubrey gets himself into trouble with them? Or their 'challenging' leader?"

Yes, what about that creature? Whatever else Aubrey knew about him, he hadn't thought it important enough to mention. Dominique shook his head. "Aubrey is an accomplished negotiator. If he has to, he can make his case to two-hundred as well as to one."

As Cassidy returned to finishing the table, he felt a new well of worry bubble in her heart. "I hope you're right."

IO

Insufficient Proof

By the time Jackson arrived, breakfast was ready and night hung on the verge of vanishing.

"Something smells good in here," he said as he entered the foyer, holding a somewhat larger black case than he had a week ago.

"He made breakfast for us," Cassidy said, closing the door behind him. "*All* of us."

"You're joking."

"Not one bit." She extended her hand for the case.

He handed it over. "Like that worked out so well for him last time."

"How much is in here?"

"Two opportunities to throw up."

Dominique had expected one. He'd be beside himself with two. In fact, she could already feel his exhilaration in the kitchen. "He's thrilled."

"He's crazy."

"That, too." Though obsessive was more like it. Where the suppressant was concerned, his common sense had evaporated faster than vampire blood in sunlight.

"Just so we're clear, Cass," Jackson said, touching her arm with his fingertips. "I'm prepared to stay today if this goes sideways again, but—" Apologetic shrug, "I can't keep doing this. I have other places I need to be."

"I know, Jack. Let's hope this works today."

With the coming sun, Dominique the vampire faded. He sagged onto his cot and grasped Cassidy's hand. "Make me remember."

She swallowed the sudden knot in her throat and fought to hold on to her awareness of him, even as it dropped out of sight, into an abyss.

Minutes later, Dominique—the human—staggered to his uncooperative legs. "*Merde!* What have you two idiots done to me now?"

"Fuck," Jackson muttered. "Mr. Sunshine is back."

The offer of breakfast checked Dominique's building panic. As did Samantha, who joined them this morning to bear witness so that Serge could see this in her memories tonight. Her upbeat demeanor seemed to lull Dominique, or perhaps it just confused him. Of all of them, the peace-loving, ever-optimistic Samantha was the least likely to take anyone hostage.

"How do you like it?" Cassidy asked after Dominique had taken a bite of the fluffy, vanilla-sugar encrusted toast.

His brows drew together as though he was trying to decide which criticism to throw at her. "You have improved." Cassidy felt her face warm. "Some," he added and reached for the blackberry syrup. "It still tastes like nothing."

Cassidy laughed for the first time since this madness had begun. "Well, you can't blame me for that. It's your cooking."

"*Moi?*"

"And it's divine," Samantha pronounced, closing her eyes in bliss.

Jackson nodded as he cut a sizable chunk of toast on his plate. "Gotta hand it to you. You really know your way around a kitchen." The hunk of toast disappeared in his mouth.

Uncomprehending anxiety glimmered in Dominique's wide eyes. He remembered none of this.

"Hold on. I have proof." Cassidy got up to retrieve her phone from the kitchen counter, queued up the video and touched *play*. Dominique of an hour ago moved on the small screen with confident enthusiasm. Dominique of now sat with his face going slack with shock. He reached for the phone, and Cassidy let him lift it out of her hand.

"*Comment*," he whispered. "*Comment est—*"

"Remember, Dominique." She put her hand on his arm. He ignored her. "Please remember."

Recorded Dominique's phone doodled with an incoming video call.

"I hope I'm not disturbing you, my lord," said Aubrey's tiny voice just before the playback ended.

Cassidy chewed her lower lip. Why hadn't she stopped the recording before that confusing bit of conversation? Or, better yet, why hadn't she kept recording? It seemed so insignificant at the time, but it wasn't insignificant to Dominique now. The bewildered look he cast around the table would have made Cassidy burst out laughing if she didn't know how much fear and pain hid behind it. None of this would make any sense to him, and trying to explain it honestly would sound insane. They couldn't tell him. He *had* to remember. Somehow.

He keyed the phone to replay the last thirty seconds. Then the last ten twice more.

"I hope I'm not disturbing you, my lord."

Dominique put the phone down. "What...what is this?"

"It's you, Dominique," Cassidy said gently. "It's the you we have known for three years now."

"*Ç'est des conneries!* That is bullshit."

The outburst made both Cassidy and Samantha jump in their seats. Jackson only sighed.

"I know how technology can lie," Dominique fumed. "This is not me. This *cannot* be me."

Jackson matched his strident tone. "For fuck's sake, Nick. Why would we waste that kind of time and effort? For *what*?"

A calculating, narrow-eyed quiet settled over him. "You tell me? Why do you want me to doubt my mind?"

"They're trying to help you remember who you are," Samantha said. "Please listen to them."

Dominique pinned Jackson with his eyes. "You cannot just tell me? You have to play some bizarre game? Create some past in which strangers call me 'lord?' What makes you think I would ever believe such a thing?"

"Actually, right now, that's the most believable thing about you," Jackson countered.

Cassidy jumped into the fray. "You inherited a kingdom from someone—" *who turned you into a vampire.*

"Yes? Go on. This is fascinating," he snapped, his accent thick enough to cut with a butter knife, his gestures small but abrupt.

"You don't...you don't remember him now, but he was, well, crazy."

"And obsessed with you," Jackson added and stuffed another piece of toast in his mouth, as though trying to keep a torrent of other words from pouring out.

Dominique pursed his lips. "Some of my lovers can be a little obsessive. This is true."

Cassidy stared at him. She knew his every memory as if it were her own. While there had been no shortage of lovers in his mortal life, not one of those relationships had been anything but casual, and none ended in anything darker than bittersweet memories. None but one, the last one, the woman he had cared for—before he killed her. Like he killed his father and sister. All of them among his first victims after being turned.

All of them still alive and well in his mind now.

She looked away, suddenly aware of what they were really up against. He was fighting them too hard. On some level, he must know what he would find if he remembered the truth.

And he didn't want to.

"Is this what is happening here?" Dominique ventured, placing his elbows on the table and folding his hands. He peered at Jackson, whom he had apparently determined as the mastermind behind this nefarious plot. "You have some twisted obsession with me, have lured me from my home, and kept me—"

"You need to stop right there." There was no mistaking the menace in the hunter's face or in the warning finger he raised.

Dominique waved at the phone on the table. "—in a drug-induced haze?"

Another chirp sounded, this one from Jackson's pocket.

"What manner of sick pleasure do you take from me...when I am not even in my right mind?" Far from outraged, the words twisted in a sultry dance. "Tell me, Jackson. Do I make you moan?"

Samantha put her utensils down and covered a delicate cough with her cloth napkin. Cassidy's face tingled with heat as she recalled the moaning Jackson had indeed done in his sleep—and why. He still remembered, too, if his rising color was anything to go by.

"The only thing sick here is your head," Jackson snapped. His pocket chirped again, and he yanked out his phone, glanced at the screen. "Fuck. The Grid has a hit in Europe. Three dead."

Cassidy's heart dropped. "Oh God."

The Grid was the Striker Foundation's global, high-tech alarm system for potential vampire activity. Inevitably, this involved the victims of violent deaths.

Jackson glared at Dominique. "This is where Garrett and I usually warm up the jet, but instead I'm stuck here, watching you scatter your marbles." Another chime. "And now Garrett is looking for me. Great."

Dominique brushed his folded knuckles against his lower lip. He studied Cassidy's and Samantha's solemn demeanor, studied Jackson come unglued, and smirked. "So you are obsessed, *non*?"

Furious color climbed up Jackson's bulging neck. "You son of a bitch. You and your *obsessive* delusions are what got us here. This experiment doesn't work. It didn't work the first time. It's not working now."

"Jackson," Cassidy warned.

He got up to lean over the table toward Dominique whose smug demeanor faded. "There is no going back. Not for you, not for any of us. Deal with it. Deal with what you are and do the fucking job you signed up for."

"Jack!"

His nostrils flared with agitation as he looked at her with eyes as cold as any predator's.

"Don't," she said, shaking her head a little, praying that Jackson would pick up on her meaning.

Samantha did. "He's not ready," she said under her breath. "He has to remember on his own."

"In the meantime, we babysit him? Nice."

Cassidy threw up both hands. "Oh my God, Jackson, go. Meet your plane and go to Europe. Do what you have to, but don't do it here."

"You're not serious."

"I am. Very." She touched Dominique's forearm where it lay on the table. The familiar tendons twitched beneath her fingers. "We'll be okay on our own. We always have been."

"He's not in his right mind. What if he pulls another stunt like last time?"

"He won't." Not without Jackson around to provoke him.

"I can't let you—"

Samantha pushed her chair back and stood. "She'll be fine. C'mon, Jack. I have a class to get ready for and Garrett is waiting for you."

Jackson met Dominique's glower with his own for several more seconds. Finally, he shook his head, disgusted. "I don't know why I give a shit. I really don't."

Dominique inclined his head, making a wave of ebony hair—still dusted with powdered sugar—fall across his forehead, and blew him a kiss.

"Fuck off. Cass, you're on your own." He turned to go, turned back. "If you know what's good for both of you, lose that other shot before sundown." The front door slammed behind him moments later.

His half-sister broke the awkward silence by thanking Dominique and Cassidy for breakfast. "I'll be home this afternoon if you need anything."

"Thanks, Sam."

After Samantha retreated out the kitchen door, Cassidy slumped back in her chair. Dominique regarded her curiously. "We are always okay, *chère*?"

"Always," she said without hesitation and met his warm human gaze. A stranger stared back. "We've been through far worse than a little amnesia."

He flashed her a seductive smile. His voice purred in a way that would have sent shivers down her spine if not for the words. "So you are—what is it—the 'good cop?'"

"No. I'm—" *your lover, your partner, your friend, your reason for being, your tether to humanity, to life, the other half of your soul.* She swallowed it all down into her sore heart—"here for you."

"Truly? Then please help me return to my home."

Cassidy rubbed her right temple against the pressure building there and opened her mouth to explain, to argue, but couldn't. She couldn't give him facts that didn't fit with what he believed, no matter how benign. He wouldn't trust them, maybe not even hear them. Just like he wasn't seeing the clues all around him—the speed with which his injuries healed, the unnatural paleness of his skin, the hard edges to his inhumanly beautiful face, even the fact that he hadn't used a toilet that entire first day. He questioned none of this because he already knew the answers.

And he didn't want to.

Cassidy reached out and wrapped her fingers around his unresponsive hand. "All right, Dominique. If you want to go home...I'll take you home."

II

Coming Home

T he only thing Cassidy dared not do today was let Dominique out of her sight. The amount of damage and grief he could cause with a single international phone call was incalculable.

Which is why she escorted him to his closet and watched him take in the mostly empty miles of Cherrywood shelving and stacks of drawers. A handful of T-shirts and gym pants, plus some dress shirts and jeans, and a grand total of three pairs of shoes were the entirety of his wardrobe. That and the black leathers and silver-buckled boots waiting in a far corner. He studied this last but made no comment before turning away, ignoring the outfit and the blood-soaked history it represented.

"They all fit. They're all yours," Cassidy said, giving no hint about what he might select.

He pulled off the T-shirt and dropped his gym pant bottoms, affording her a glimpse of the bare assets with which she was so familiar, but which were oddly new in the light of day. He arched a sweeping brow at her. "Underwear?"

"Hmm? Oh. Right. That drawer." She pointed. A minute later, he was packaged in briefs, a pair of jeans and fresh shirt, and stuffed his bare feet into the sneakers. She tossed the leather jacket at him and gestured for him to follow her.

Though she didn't spend much time there most nights, Cassidy maintained her own suite in the house, a place that was distinctly her own, and her walk-in closet was far better stocked than his. While she eyed the tidy collection of colors and styles, she shed her tunic and shorts without thinking.

A soft groan sounded behind her. Dominique stood with one shoulder leaning against the frame of the closet door, arms crossed, a slow smile curving his sensual mouth.

Oh, right. This version of him would be a stranger to her body. The thought made her skin tingle.

Raising her arms to gather her hair in a messy bun, Cassidy gave her amnesiac lover a coy look and her most evocative French to inquire if he saw anything he liked.

"Oh, *oui, madame. Beaucoup*," he agreed with unfettered appreciation, but didn't move from his spot, content to ponder her underthings and the treasures they barely concealed.

Cassidy took her time selecting a pair of jeans and a flirty off-the-shoulder top, giving him plenty of opportunity to admire the view. It was a challenge hiding the grin that threatened to burst across her face. Everything else about him and their relationship was so radically different that the possibility he might show any sexual interest in her hadn't even crossed her mind. Yet, there it was. She could feel the primal heat of his gaze raking over her body.

"Where are we going?" he asked as she considered an all-out seduction.

She sighed, slipped into a random pair of shoes that were sturdy enough for what she had in mind, and grabbed her purse along with a light jacket. "You'll see. C'mon."

In the garage, she ignored her own new Mercedes coupe and walked up to Dominique's BMW motorcycle. The thing looked like it was flying, just sitting there. Tricked out by a previous owner with more ego than sense, the low-slung, pitch-black bike could move at two-hundred-plus miles per hour. Amazingly, it wasn't the bike that had killed the guy—a player in South Florida's drug trade—but the vampire who claimed it. Dominique had used it to carry him far and fast when hunting meant making bodies. While he had killed no one in years, he still preferred the bike as a convenient mode of transportation.

"Want to ride?"

Dominique scoffed. "You are joking. I have never been on one of these things."

"Fine. I'll drive," she said with forced confidence. Dominique had taught her how to ride, and she had a license issued by the state of Florida. But this machine was a whole lot less menacing at night, when Dominique was there to keep control of it with his supernatural reflexes. Now, during the day, driving it with her mere mortal skills felt like asking for trouble, but if there was a chance of reaching him, she'd risk it.

Of course, having him climb up behind her and feeling his hands steal around her waist was also worth a few risks. The embrace felt more sensual than practical, as if he had been looking for an excuse to touch her. It was all she could do to collect her scattering wits and ease the bike on its way.

The five-mile trip took fifteen minutes. After the first five, Cassidy relaxed enough to enjoy what was a glorious morning. A late-season cool front had brought what was sure to be the last dry air for months, leaving the sun to blaze diamond-bright in a sapphire sky.

All that, and Dominique was with her. If not for his amnesia, she would be the happiest girl on the planet.

"This does not look like an airport," he observed after she had parked and they pulled off their helmets. When he squinted against the light, she handed him the wraparound sunglasses she wore and retrieved a more stylish secondary pair from her purse.

"Nope. It's the Beach Tiki." She pushed the glasses onto her nose. "It's one of your favorite places to catch a bite," she added, and grinned at her personal joke. The blood supply here was always varied and plentiful and often steeped in the relaxed hormones of vacationers who spent their days playing in the surf and their nights partying.

"Another breakfast?"

"If you want." She paused a beat. He didn't react. "Though I was thinking we might go for a walk."

"To an airport?"

Her smile grew rueful. "In a way."

On the beach, miles of sand stretched north and south, and to the east, blue-black waters foamed under a stiff wind. Only a handful of people dotted the sand, and the distance disappeared into the thick mists kicked up by the rolling waves.

Cassidy hunched her shoulders against the salty gusts, which were stronger than she had expected. Dominique didn't appear to notice. As she knew he would, he became absorbed in the view of the churning water, his hands tucked into the pockets of his half-zipped jacket. With the wind in his raven hair and the sun on his chiseled features, plus the mirrored, futuristic sunglasses, he looked like something straight out of a glossy fashion magazine—even a movie star. Admiring eyes turned their way from the Beach Tiki's back deck.

"This is nothing like Saint-Barthélemy."

"I know," she agreed, strolling away from the gawkers. "Tell me about it."

Not that he could tell her anything she didn't already know, but that wasn't the point. He talked. Slowly at first, then more freely as he got lost in memories of the life she knew he mourned. The warmth of his island home, the peace, the love of family and friends. He spoke as though it were all still real, as though long-dead loved ones still lived. With every word, her sorrow grew, but she smiled and was glad for the oversize sunglasses hiding her eyes.

After a while, he asked about her past, and she told him about her life in Colorado, all the grief she had left behind there, and how some of it had followed her here in the guise of her father. Her father, who now lived in Fort Lauderdale, where he managed a string of car dealerships belonging to his latest wife, the widow of a friend—the friend Dominique had accidentally scared to death with his beast. That last bit, she didn't mention.

"But you live very well now," Dominique said when she fell silent. "Did you win the lottery?"

"You could say that. I fell in love."

"Ah, of course." He nodded. "Jackson."

"What?"

"The man with his own plane. It makes sense. The house is his, *non*?" He gave her a long look. "As are you?"

She stopped, feeling hit over the head. "No. I'm not *his*. Where would you get that idea?"

Dominique shrugged. "You wear no jewelry except for one exquisite ring. It must mean much to you."

She lifted her hand. The sapphire was set in platinum and surrounded by two glittering waves of diamonds. It looked like a drop of ocean on her finger. She felt awe every time she looked at it. Not because it was worth a fortune, but because of what it represented.

"It's only a ring," she said and watched Dominique raise her hand by the fingertips to admire the jewel more closely. "But the person who gave it to me...he is my world."

"*C'est magnifique.*" Dominique pulled down his sunglasses far enough to peer over the top. "Two souls. One body."

"Yes," Cassidy whispered, and closed her hand around his. She felt faint with hope when he returned the squeeze. She waited, praying he would take her into his arms and kiss her senseless.

He released her hand. "He is a very fortunate man."

Breath escaped her in a pained rush. He wouldn't acknowledge their connection. Their relationship was part of a life he didn't want to face right now, so he didn't.

Cassidy's heart ached all the way back to the Beach Tiki, an invisible cloud now obscuring the day's brilliance. The truth longed to be told, but she remained silent. She couldn't face the possibility of him refuting her outright with another fantasy he would spin to protect his own sanity.

As if sensing her despair, he regaled her with humorous anecdotes from his life and travels. She knew them all, but they still made her laugh for the sheer joy of listening to him share them as though for the first time. As they strode across the Beach Tiki's dune walk, they both smiled, and the people they encountered smiled back.

"Two for lunch?" the hostess asked when they were about to pass the entrance. Lunch already? The clock hanging among the decorative driftwood on the wall read eleven-forty-five. They had walked and talked for longer than she thought.

Dominique studied the chalkboard menu. "*Oui. S'il vous plaît.*"

"You're hungry?"

A lopsided smile and one-shoulder shrug. "Always."

They were shown to a prime location table at the rail on the back deck. Delicious aromas wafted in the sea air, and Cassidy realized that not only was she hungry as well as thirsty, she was also in dire need of a restroom. She paused before deciding to take her leave with as little fuss as possible. They had forged a new connection this morning, a level of trust, however tentative. Dragging him to the ladies' room so she could keep tabs on him wasn't workable and shouldn't be necessary. Besides, he was engrossed in the menu.

When she got back, she found him staring out at the waves, and she chastised herself for doubting him.

They continued to talk over their food—a steaming bowl of mushroom soup for her and a gourmet jalapeño cheeseburger for him that somehow managed to "not taste like anything." He wolfed it down anyway.

"You should try riding it home," Cassidy told him when they returned to the bike, now covered in a dull sheen of salt spray.

"You cannot be serious, *chère,*" he said, but his smile encouraged her not to let it rest there.

She pressed the helmet into his midsection. "I'll show you. It's easy."

To her relief, he grabbed the helmet without argument. Though a small, cynical part of her wondered if he considered the bike a potential escape vehicle, she was encouraged by his curiosity as she showed him how to work the controls—and by his amazement at how natural riding felt. Once on the road, he opened the throttle for a brief burst of speed that had Cassidy yelp and clamp her arms around him.

"*Mon Dieu!*" she heard him exclaim. The machine hummed beneath them, motoring along at a traffic-clogging twenty-five miles an hour all the way home.

And it was home they went. He found his way there without directions or hesitation.

"Not looking for the airport anymore?" she asked when she had pulled off her helmet and sunglasses and shook her hair out of the untidy bun.

His expression turned mysterious and a little sheepish. "You say this is my home? Perhaps I should...explore it some more." He pushed his sunglasses to the top of his head, revealing a playful twinkle in his eyes.

"Oh, *oui*. You should," she agreed. Then, before she could stop herself, she had her mouth on his and swooned into his arms when they came around her. Unlike almost every other intimate moment they had ever enjoyed, this time they were not in each other's heads, did not share every emotion, or feel every sensation. They were two souls in two bodies, connecting on a new—but no less profound—level that affected them both.

For long moments after the kiss ended, they stood, embracing. Breathless.

He sounded a little hoarse. "Cassie, *chère*. What are we to each other? Truly?"

"Everything," she whispered. "Everything."

He pulled back to study her face. She could tell by the wary pinch at the corner of his eyes that her serious tone took him aback. Enchanted by her, he might be, maybe even suspect a history between them, but he was also a man without a memory who feared being manipulated.

She forced a more relaxed demeanor and took hold of his hand. "Come. I'll show you."

Just outside the garage, a path ran between the house and a box hedge that shivered in the breeze. Once past the guesthouse, round stepping stones curved across the plush lawn to an alcove shielded by tall, jungle-dense landscaping. There, a burbling Jacuzzi tub with a small waterfall took up most of the space. Beside it sat a double-wide wicker lounge, well-padded and full of pillows.

"We have spent quite a bit of time here," Cassidy said, removing her jacket and dropping it on another chair.

Brinkley unrolled from a discarded towel among the pillows and produced a huge, toothy yawn. Dominique gave him a quick scratch under the chin. The cat closed his eyes in bliss.

"Have we?" He glanced back at her and paused, forgetting about the cat. Given the cool wind at the beach, the off-the-shoulder top hadn't put in an appearance over lunch, but Dominique's gaze was all over it now.

"Oh, yes, we have," she assured. Her shoes came off next.

"Doing what?" He had a good idea, his tone said.

"Mostly we watch the stars." She stepped close to him and unzipped his jacket to slide her hands up his solid chest and over his shoulders. "Afterward."

He let the jacket slip off his arms and drop to the ground. His gaze became hooded. "Oh, *oui*? After what?"

Her answer was a soft, teasing kiss.

"Is this where you seduce your helpless prisoner into docile compliance, *madame*?" he murmured.

"No. This is where I tell the not-so-helpless love of my life to kiss me like he means it."

For two long beats, he stared at her, letting those words sink in. Then he claimed her mouth in a kiss that left no doubt that he meant it. That primal craving she had glimpsed earlier surfaced with a vengeance. Grasping her face in both hands, he kissed her hard and deep. Heat blossomed in her belly, stoking a passion at once familiar and strange. This was no supernatural hunger reverberating between them. This was her own female reaction to him as a man.

When he trailed wet kisses down her neck, she arched back and nearly wept at the sight of that deep-blue sky. They *would* make love in the sun, and he *would* remember it, so help her God.

After she freed him from the confines of his jeans and briefs, she grinned up at him. He looked uncertain again. "Do you have something for—?" He gestured at his erection.

"No. No condoms for us," she said, sobering a little. "We don't need them. For anything."

"*Non?*" Still doubtful.

"No." She kissed him until he was convinced. More clothes came off.

Dominique allowed her to pull him into the creaking lounge and let his fingers explore her body. When she straddled him, he moaned in lusty French that made her giggle. Oh, *oui*, she knew exactly how *fantastique* she felt to him, how much he wanted her—*needed* her—to feed this fire in his blood.

Cassidy held back nothing.

With sunlight glistening on their straining bodies, they surrendered to each other as they had a hundred times before by the light of the moon. And as he had a hundred times before, Dominique rolled her beneath himself with impeccable timing and an easy strength that was anything but human. His smile was dazzling and full of wonder.

"*Salut, mon amour,*" she murmured.

His answering kiss was thorough, but merely the opening salvo of him getting down to business. Oh, dear God. He didn't need to read her mind to play her body like a fine instrument. He was—and always had been—a virtuoso.

When he brought himself home, there was no sign of the spiral, no trace of the beast. It was only the two of them this time, and the sight of his beautiful face, wanton with ecstasy and bathed in sunlight, made her eyes fill with tears of joy.

But she stopped breathing when she saw that same face become sharper, almost skull-like.

His eyes snapped open, full black and bereft of all humanity.

The vampire was awake—staring into the sun.

"Dominique," she whispered.

He began to shake. His fine skin darkened to a furious red.

"Dominique!"

He looked down at her, uncomprehending. Then his arms buckled, and he collapsed on top of her.

Cassidy pushed at him, shook him, yelled for him. "Oh my God, Dominique, wake up!"

Nothing.

With a mighty heave, she rolled him onto his back. Blisters erupted all over his face, along his neck, and across his chest, their edges quickly turning black.

Hysteria clanged against her ribs. The suppressant was gone. He was a comatose, naked vampire sprawled in a poolside lounge on a sunny afternoon. Soon to be ash.

Cassidy's head spun as she pulled closed his shirt, then snatched at the forgotten towel crammed in between the pillows and spread it over his face and neck. She piled pillows over his groin—where the most painful sunburn in history was taking shape—and did her best to cast as much shade over his legs and feet as possible. This slowed the sun's ferocious progress, but didn't stop it. More and more of his still-exposed skin darkened, and wisps of noxious smoke drifted off him everywhere. She had to get him under cover, and fast.

But where? How? Serge lay buried somewhere in the foliage surrounding the alcove, but there was no way she'd be able to dig a grave in time with her bare hands. Drag him into the house? No. That would take too long and cause him too much damage.

But compared to what? Spending the rest of the day out here? Either way, he would die.

A wordless, frustrated scream tore out of her. *Get your shit together, Chandler. Think, damn you!* Thoughts bolted around her head like frightened rabbits. *Oh God oh God oh God...*

"What's going on out here?"

Cassidy jerked around to see Samantha rush into the alcove and come to an abrupt halt, her hand flying to her mouth. "What...is that—?"

"Sam! Help me. We need to get him out of the sun."

Samantha spun on a bare heel and disappeared. "Back in a sec."

"No! Where are you going? Help me!" More tears burst from her eyes.

"I am!" Samantha called. Ten seconds later, she was back, carrying a stack of towels, likely everything she could grab out of the cabinet by the pool shower. "Here. Start wrapping. Then we can worry about moving him."

They made a towel mummy of Dominique. Multiple layers of terrycloth swaddled him, corners strategically tied together. The smoke oozing out between the folds lessened but didn't stop, and it smelled alarmingly like roasting meat. When they were sure the wrapping would stay more or less in place, Cassidy grabbed him beneath his arms while Samantha tackled the feet.

"Shit, he's heavy," she huffed. It was the first time Cassidy had heard her friend swear.

Stumbling and tripping, they carried and dragged his limp body to the back door of the guesthouse, which was the closest entrance to an interior space. There, they maneuvered him into a tiny blue-and-white-tiled bathroom with only one small window high up the wall. "I'll get the shutters," Samantha said, rushing back out. Moments later, the accordion storm shutters attached to the outside of the window rattled into place, plunging the room into a crypt-like gloom.

Cassidy turned on the vanity light. Smoke had stopped puffing out of the mummy the moment they had moved him inside, so she decided to risk unwrapping him a little. Though she braced herself, she wasn't prepared for what she found. The oozing blisters...those were the "mild" injuries. His hands and feet weren't blistered anymore—they were charred. And his face—*Oh my God!*—his face looked like it had been planted in a bed of red-hot coals. His fangs were out, thinned lips pulled back in an agonized grimace, his nose and one ear blackened. One of his eyes was swollen shut. The other was shrunken and cloudy.

Cassidy didn't breathe. She stared at what should be a corpse. Tiny changes seemed to be happening, supernatural cells struggling to repair themselves, but she couldn't be sure. The only thing that *was* sure was that there were no flakes of glittering ash coming off him—he wasn't disintegrating. He would—God help him—wake up tonight.

"I'm so, so sorry, my love," she whispered, and carefully kissed the relatively undamaged top of his head. Covering him back up, she prayed that the bit of light creeping around the shutters for the rest of the day wouldn't be too much for him.

Samantha appeared in the doorway. She had shuttered the other windows as well and now wiped at the sweat on her brow. Strands of her long, golden hair clung to her flushed face. "What happened out there?"

"The death of a dream, Sam." Cassidy stood and leaned on the vanity. The oversize, off-the-shoulder blouse she had hurriedly pulled back on only just covered her crotch. She tugged at it a little, gave up. "He woke up when, well"—she indicated her state of undress—"he woke up. The suppressant stopped working. He was totally himself." She glanced at the motionless heap of towels on the floor. "He still is."

Samantha's eyes glistened. "So he can never be awake during the day and know how special that is for him, can he?"

Cassidy stepped out of the bathroom and closed the door behind her. She opened her mouth to speak, but there were no words. All she could do was fall into her friend's arms and sob.

12

CONSEQUENCES

J'ai vu le soleil!

That was the only thought that kept Dominique from losing his mind the following evening, when he awoke looking and feeling like a patient in a burn-care ICU.

I have seen the sun!

True, it was only a moment, a singular, sublime moment of feeling the sun's warmth on his face—before it turned into a kiss from a blast furnace—but that moment would be seared into his mind for years, decades, centuries. And the woman who took him there—the one he thought he couldn't possibly love any more—her he would worship for the rest of time.

He had seen the sun. But the price was beyond steep.

For starters, there was the excruciating pain. Even without the suppressant in his blood, his injuries would have challenged his capacity to heal. But under its lingering influence, they overwhelmed him, leaving him blind in one eye, his legs uncooperative, and his hands and feet mostly useless. Worst of all, every time he moved or spoke, delicate new skin cracked open. The wounds bled, tried to mend, only to open again, bleeding more.

Serge and Samantha fed him all the blood they could spare, which was just enough to get him mobile again. He didn't regain use of his eye until Serge organized more feeds for him by summoning the security detail from the front gate. After that, it took two solid nights of hunting until his skin stopped feeling like parchment paper and his extremities were fully restored. Three more after that before he recovered most of his strength.

Guilt, too, was another price of this madness. Serge was racked by it as he watched over Dominique throughout his recovery. The old pirate was convinced he had misinterpreted his visions when Jackson first brought the suppressant. "It was fire I saw, but bodies in rut, too," he insisted, wide-eyed, whenever Dominique moved gingerly, which was often.

"And you were right," Dominique assured him every time. He didn't have the heart to tell his friend that more dire warnings would have made no difference; he had wanted this too much to heed them.

Cassidy agonized as well. "I should have known what would happen. Your alter ego always wakes up when we make love. I was an idiot to take a risk like that."

"No, you did right," he told her. "I had to remember, or none of this would have mattered."

And he remembered. A few glorious seconds of sunlight. That was all he would ever take from this mad experiment. He had neither the luxury nor the stomach to try again. The possibility that he might lose his immortal life—along with the lives of every other blood-drinker in existence—had never even crossed his mind. He was horrified at how close he had come to exactly that, thanks to his obsession with daylight.

But all of this paled compared to another possibility he hadn't considered, one that didn't materialize until a week later. When he awoke that night, anxiety plowed into him hard enough to make him gasp. It took him a moment to recognize the source. His telepathic link with Cassidy was currently ebbing, making the exchange of distinct thoughts impossible without physical touch. Emotions, however, still came through. The stronger the feeling, the louder the echo. This one reverberated in his bones.

He reached out, trying to soothe her.

Then he caught a hazy impression through her eyes and felt his world tilt off its axis. Non. Non...

He sat up, grabbed his tablet and called up the security camera in the patio at the other side of the house. It couldn't be, it just couldn't, and yet...it was. Right there, sitting across from Cassidy...

"*Maman...*"

Tall and stately in taupe linen slacks, cream silk shirt, and a stylish maroon cardigan, Francesca Marchant was everything Dominique remembered of his mother. She had cut her hair, though. Instead of carefully upswept brunette locks, she now sported a short precision cut and a wave of silver that flowed from her distinctive widow's peak. She looked older, her face more drawn, but also fiercer than he had ever seen her: a woman on a mission.

The man sitting beside her, with the cat curled in his lap, was another shock. Dominique hadn't seen his cousin, Étienne Pélissier, in more than a decade. Yet, there he was, not the sophisticated patron of Parisian cafés Dominique remembered, but dressed in shorts and an untucked white button-down shirt, the nut-brown embodiment of a beach bum.

Francesca and Étienne. In his house. Dominique trembled.

Out on the patio, the halting conversation stopped. Francesca's expression softened into concern as she spoke to Cassidy, who had put down her glass and gripped the armrests of her chair. She nodded in response to Francesca, but he could tell she was grimacing. The onslaught of his rising panic and despair threatened to overpower her, even across their weakened link. Closing his eyes, he tried to quiet his reaction. Finally, he sensed her getting up and moving toward him.

By the time she got to the kitchen, Dominique had the vault door unlocked and swinging open. She rushed into his arms. The moment they touched, her memories came into focus...

It was like a bomb going off in his skull, the culmination of his every fear.

Four years ago, in the horrific aftermath of becoming a blood-drinker, he had done the unspeakable, killing not only his father but also his younger sister. He had left his mother and surviving sister to pick up the pieces of their lives by staging his own death. Then, a week ago, Francesca had received a call from Dominique, saying he needed her help. He gave her the address of this house, which she could barely write down before he hung up, leaving her badly shaken. Étienne later prompted her to call back the strange American number. The woman who answered said the man who borrowed her phone earlier seemed perfectly fine. The description she gave matched Dominique's. Which was when Francesca recruited Étienne to help her find her son.

And now, here they were.

"*Mon Dieu.*"

"The five minutes I left you alone at the restaurant," Cassidy whispered. "That's the only thing I can think of. You got your hands on a phone."

Merde. Given the near-cataclysmic way that day ended, the idea of him reaching out to anyone had never been considered.

"I couldn't send them away. Samantha and I were ambushed. They saw we knew something when they mentioned your name," she hurried on. "I'm so sorry, Dominique, but I had to tell them something. I had to do...something."

What she had done was invite them in, serve refreshments, and tell them as little as possible. For two hours, she played the considerate hostess, watched every word that left her mouth, and counted every second to sundown. When her guests insisted on knowing why she couldn't produce Dominique on the spot, she told them he was out, teaching a class, and would be back soon.

"Teaching?" Étienne wondered, his thick brows rising.

"Aikido," Samantha jumped in. Her cheeks flushed as she met Étienne's eyes. "He's really very good."

"The martial arts have long been a passion of his," Francesca agreed, relaxing a bit into her chair and looking around at the lavish home and expansive gardens. "He seems to live comfortably here, coming and going as he wants, while we thought he was dead." She shook her head a little, as though still unsure she believed he wasn't. "*Mon Dieu*, why did he not contact us sooner? And why does he say he needs help?"

"He...he felt you'd be...safer that way," Cassidy stammered. "From the cartel." Francesca blanched. Officially, the killers of her husband and daughter were the men Dominique had fought off when he found them raping his little sister, Anastasie. Not only had he caused them serious injuries with his martial arts abilities, he had killed one of them. As they were high-ranking affiliates of a notorious Colombian drug cartel, Dominique's supposed kidnapping—and the murder of his father and Anastasie—were all attributed to them. There had been no proof, though, so no charges were filed. They left St. Barth free men. "He had to make everyone believe he was dead, so there would be no point for them to come after you," Cassidy added quietly. "As for why now...he'll have to be the one to explain that."

More questions followed, most of which Cassidy deflected with variations of this last statement. There wasn't much about Dominique's current circumstances she could explain without straying into the supernatural. But when Francesca shifted her focus and wanted to know who Cassidy was in her son's life, she had to stop and think. Then, to everyone's astonishment—including her own for the monumental understatement that it was—she said, "I'm...his wife."

Dominique let all these memories wash over him. Cupping her head in one hand, he pressed it to his shoulder. "*Oh, mon amour*," he murmured. "I am so very sorry."

Serge roused from his cot and rubbed his eyes. "My lord? What happened?"

Catastrophe, he thought, and released Cassidy. This was an explosion that couldn't be stopped, but maybe it could be contained. He turned to Serge, who had his head cocked as if listening to something only he heard. Samantha's mind, no doubt. "Go to them and compel them not to notice anything out of the ordinary. And...convince them that I called them with an invitation, not a request for help."

The corners of Serge's eyes pinched. His mouth went white. Something in Samantha's thoughts did not agree with him.

"Serge?"

His gaze focused on Dominique. "Yes, my lord?"

"Did you hear what I asked?"

"Yes. But why me?"

"Because I will not compel my family. I have done enough damage to them. Now go. And be gentle."

"As you wish." Serge took his time ambling out of the vault and across the house, reluctance in his every barefoot step.

Dominique sped upstairs and traded his usual T-shirt and gym pants for jeans and a dark gray dress shirt. He rolled the sleeves up his forearms, tied his hair back, stuck his feet into the only pair of leather loafers he owned, and returned to Cassidy and Serge, where they waited at the bottom of the stairs.

"It is done, my lord," Serge said and disappeared out the back of the house in a blur of motion.

Cassidy shook her head and sighed. "Étienne."

"Étienne," Dominique agreed. Serge sensed a rival for Samantha's affections, and, based on what Dominique had seen in Cassidy's memories, with good reason. Any other time, Dominique would have been amused. Now he could barely believe that Étienne was even here. As Francesca explained it to Cassidy, her nephew had volunteered to stay with her on St. Barth and help with the restaurant after she lost her husband, a daughter, and only son within days of each other. Island life seemed to agree with Étienne, for he hadn't left since.

Cassidy took his hand in mute encouragement. Through her touch, he saw himself as she did: a hard, pale, mesmeric beauty. Not a look he wanted to expose his mother to. It took him only an instant to deploy a bit of silent compulsion and make himself appear as his suntanned mortal self to all who saw him.

Cassidy raised a doubtful brow but said nothing. She had never been susceptible to his persuasive talents, but she sensed when he used them.

"A small aide to ease their minds," he said and tucked her hand into the crook of his elbow.

She squeezed his arm and nodded. "Okay."

Steeling himself for the moment, he rounded the last corner and became visible to his mother. Dominique thought he knew what to expect. He didn't.

The sliding doors to the side patio stood open, admitting evening air soaked in rain and ozone and a delicate, familiar perfume. Catching the scent of lavender and orange, he was instantly transported back to another life, one filled with the warmth of sunshine and family.

His steps faltered, preparing to turn back, but too late. His mother's gaze found him and pinned him in place.

The practical, reserved, always-in-control woman he had known all his life disintegrated before his eyes. She stood up, mouth falling open, her eyes brimming with moisture. Her hands made to reach for him, then clapped to her mouth, stifling a sob.

Beside her, Étienne stood and touched her elbow in support, though he, too, only had eyes for Dominique. "Cousin," he greeted with a tentative smile. "You look well for a dead man."

Samantha didn't get up. She gaped at Dominique, or rather at the vigorous mortality he conjured for them. Even the cat looked confused. Instead of launching his usual attack, Brinkley cowered under the table, growling, every hair on his body standing on end. No one else noticed.

"*Madame?* Your son," Cassidy said with a warm, if nervous smile in her voice.

"*Maman?*"

With a cry, Francesca rushed forward. In her haste, she knocked the table, jostling an array of half-empty glasses, then stumbled over the sliding door track. Dominique moved a touch too fast to catch and steady her.

"*Mon fils*," she whispered, her hands clutching his arms. "*Mon petit*."

"*Oui. C'est moi.* Welcome to my home." It was an automatic response, the only thing his stunned mind could come up with.

She caressed his face with both hands, kissed both his cheeks three times each, then clutched him in a shaking, sobbing embrace no French person would allow themselves—unless the recipient had risen from the dead.

Dominique held her, breathed her familiar scent, and wondered how different her reaction might have been if she saw him as he truly was. Tears tracked down his cheeks and dripped into her hair. She felt fragile as a bird in his arms as she continued to shower him with kisses and endearments, along with her relief, her love, and her gratitude. She was reborn, she said. God had heard her prayers and answered them.

It was too much.

I'm not worthy of this, he thought, but found it impossible to let go of her. *It is all a lie. I am the one who destroyed her life.*

And now you're making up for it by giving her a priceless gift, Cassidy replied. She stood behind him and to the side, her hand on the small of his back to strengthen the remnants of their connection.

Dominique closed his eyes and pulled as much strength and humanity as he could from Cassidy. "*Maman*," he murmured. "How I have missed you."

It took several minutes before she calmed enough to gather her shredded composure and let him go. Étienne greeted him with the traditional kisses, but also bestowed a quick, shoulder-slapping hug. "You dolt. We were all crazy with grief."

At first, the words stuck in Dominique's craw, but they came easier as he went along. Bit by bit, he fleshed out the scant details

Cassidy had already shared with half-truths and allusions, but not an ounce of compulsion. Bit by bit, their doubts turned to amazement and then relief. He imagined that even Jackson, the master of spin, would have been impressed.

But where to from here? Thanks to Serge, they believed that, rather than asking for rescue with his surprise phone call, Dominique had invited them for a visit. He could not send them away without compelling them to forget they had ever been here. Two weeks ago, he would have done just that—or asked Serge to—but that was before he was seized by the possibility of reclaiming a small part of his lost life. The suppressant hadn't delivered him the sun, but it had brought him something even more profound: his family.

Not only did he not send them away, he uncorked several bottles of wine and cooked them all dinner.

Étienne joined him in the kitchen and delighted in showing off his culinary skills. Or rather, showing them off to Samantha, who sat at the counter, spellbound by his every word and gesture. Dominique's cousin was an endless fount of breathtaking flirtations for the blushing woman. And the teasing rejoinders he tossed at Dominique harkened back to the long summers the two had spent running wild around Étienne's family estate outside Bordeaux.

Francesca's confident, throaty laugh rang out often as she joined in with stories of her own about the family's history, and shared happy recent events. Most notable of these was the news of Dominique's older sister, *Geneviève*, who had been newlywed when he last saw her. "*Frère préféré*," she used to call him, her "favorite brother," despite her having only one brother. Close in age, they had grown up together, partners in childhood games and adolescent dramas, always each others' confidante, protector, and biggest fan. It staggered him to think that she was now a mother herself to a baby girl of eighteen months. The doting grandmother had a phone full of pictures to show off, and Dominique dutifully admired his new niece, but not without a pang of regret. Thrilled as he was that *Geneviève* was moving on with her life, this child was a poignant reminder of how much he had truly lost.

Beside Francesca, Cassidy sat with a wineglass in hand and glowed with high spirits. Sensing his turn of mood, she stirred the conversation into new avenues.

Silently, he sent her his love and his thanks.

Their hands touched as he passed her on his way back to the stove. She looked up at him, eyes bright. *I love you, husband of my soul, and I adore your family.*

As the evening progressed, the years of darkness lost a little of their weight, and his regrets some of their sting. Reality as Dominique knew it faded into the background, supplanted by a dream of his former life. For this moment, at least. But then, with the past done and gone, and the future eternal and obscure, wasn't the present moment all that really mattered?

He thought so—and he vowed to stretch it for as long as it would go.

Which was why, long after midnight, he offered his mother and cousin the two best guest rooms in the house and invited them to stay for as long as they wanted.

13

Drop-Ins

For Samantha, this entire day ranked near the top of her personal excitement scale, which was saying a lot for the half-sister of a vampire hunter living with vampires. Best of all, none of her current preoccupations had anything to do with the supernatural.

Well, so far anyway.

At the moment, her entire late afternoon yoga class groaned and huffed through the poses. They would all remember this session, if perhaps for slightly different reasons. The eight ladies were all devoted regulars, Samantha's most advanced students. Both of the two males were drop-ins and claimed never to have done a day of yoga in their lives. Which did not, of course, stop them from trying to show off—to the women and to each other. The women didn't mind, instructor included. Both men were the picture of vigor and health, even if somewhat less flexible than they might have imagined.

"Exhaling, come down," Samantha directed. "Aaand child's pose."

"Thank you," one of her long-time students said as she folded into a happy heap on her mat.

"Just trying to keep your mind on the work, Evelyn."

This earned her several snorts and made her face tingle. Had she really just said that? Every one there would know what was distracting them—including the distractions.

"*Mon Dieu*," one of the latter gasped. "You are a cruel mistress."

"Just breathe," she told Étienne, grateful she couldn't see his eyes right now. Oh, those eyes! Every time she looked into them, it was like falling into a soft, warm pillow made of sky. That, plus the French accent and that dazzling smile, all packaged into the sun-bronzed physique of an Adonis who seemed to have fallen under her unwitting spell, and Samantha's wits were all but scattered.

They had spent much of the day together, with her acting as his tour guide to the local attractions, while Cassidy doted on Francesca and made excuses for her son's absence during the day. Étienne was an easy-going version of Dominique, charming and quick-witted, ruggedly beautiful and—most importantly—human. He was also the perfect gentleman, flirting without shame, but crossing no lines, even when Samantha fervently wished he would. In all of her thirty-one years, no man had ever gotten to her this hard, this fast.

"God, this is intense."

"Yes, it is," she agreed before realizing that the speaker, the other new male student, wasn't talking about her raging attraction to Étienne. One by one, the students sat up on their heels. Several of the ladies who knew her well, slanted sly looks in her direction, reading her like an over-sharing social media feed. Her cheeks flamed. "This is an advanced class," she amended. "You should only take the poses as far as you're comfortable."

This guy, this Ryan Gardner, shouldn't be here any more than Étienne. But, eager to involve Étienne in her life, she had invited him to join in. So when Ryan showed up ten minutes before class, nervous but game, she could hardly advise him not to take part based on his lack of yoga experience.

"It's all mind-over-body, right? I can do that all day long." He glanced at Étienne who looked casual as a cat stretching out its limbs. The two men couldn't be more different. One golden brown, limber and European, the other pale, brawny and Canadian, complete with a full, neatly trimmed, dark beard that gave him a rugged outdoors-man appeal. To the delight of the rest of the class, the two had been in an undeclared competition since pose one.

To the relief of the instructor, they both made it to the end of class without sustaining serious injury.

"I don't think I'll be able to feel my legs or arms tomorrow, but best class ever," Evelyn said on her way out the door. Several others echoed this sentiment as they dispersed amidst chatter and giggles.

Ryan took his time finding his shoes and then loitered around her desk as she updated attendance records and answered two email inquiries. "Do you have any questions?" Samantha prompted, hoping what questions there might be would be brief. She had plans for an intimate dinner with Étienne in the pool house.

"I do, yes." He glanced over his shoulder at Étienne, who lounged by the door, waiting for Samantha. "Well, don't get me wrong, I really enjoyed the class, but...I...well, I—"

Samantha's mind finally roused from the fog of distraction. "You were hoping for a...different instructor?"

His gaze flicked toward the window, which had gone full dark with night over the past half hour. "Maybe a different class? This is the address of the Lotus Blossom Center of Martial Arts, isn't it?"

She sat back and touched two fingers to her lips in thought. Usually people who came looking for the dojo and its sensei didn't surface until well after dark, which was why all her classes were held—or at least started—while the sun was still up. "Yes, and I teach yoga here. We have Aikido classes on Monday, Wednesday, and Friday nights." Except last night when Dominique had asked his senior student to run the class while he was handling his family emergency.

Ryan nodded. His beard closed in around his flattening mouth. "I see. So...not tonight."

"You hardly survived yoga class," Étienne scoffed. "You would not last five minutes in Dominique's class."

Ryan turned. "Dominique? Dominique Marchant?"

"*Oui*. My cousin."

Samantha tensed. Whoever this Ryan was, he knew more about Dominique than Étienne could even imagine.

"Where is he? We have to talk to him."

Étienne frowned at the sudden burst of intensity from the quiet Canadian.

"We?" Samantha asked.

Ryan turned back to her and made a visible effort to stay calm, though his fingers wrapped around his thumbs until they cracked, all the relaxation from class draining away. "My girlfriend and I. It's important that we reach him soon."

"Do you know him?" Étienne asked, sounding baffled, but Ryan ignored him.

"Well, he'll be here tomorrow night. You can also email. Through the same site I suspect you found this address on," she added with a raised brow. This was all she wanted to say out loud about the *V-zette* in front of Étienne.

"This is something she needs to discuss with him in person," Ryan replied. "And quickly. He'll want to hear about this."

"Très mystérieux," Étienne murmured.

No, not mysterious at all, Samantha thought. Somewhere out there was a vampire desperate to speak with Dominique. In recent months, this had happened several times; though usually the vampires didn't send their human helpers to take a yoga class first. Ryan wasn't typical. He wasn't just conducting daytime business for his nocturnal mistress. He seemed to care about said business. Vampire business.

Samantha sighed and pulled her phone from her bag. "Just you and your...girlfriend?"

He nodded. "Is there any way she can see him tonight?"

Samantha tapped and sent her message to Cassidy and Dominique. An affirmative pinged back within thirty seconds from his highness himself. "All right. You can follow me."

"Thank you," Ryan said, gushing gratitude.

"What was all this?" Étienne wondered after the door had swung shut behind Ryan.

"Just my world living with your very popular cousin, sweetie." She grabbed her bag, toed into her sandals and turned off the lights. "C'mon."

Outside, she glimpsed the vampire behind the wheel of the Nissan SUV Ryan slipped into. Female, blond, petite. Trouble. The SUV followed Samantha's Prius at a polite distance out of the lot and down the road. Samantha chewed her bottom lip.

"So these are friends of Dominique's?" Étienne said, drawing her out of her musings. Unbelievably, she had almost forgotten about the French hunk in the passenger seat.

"We'll see, I guess."

A mile of silence slid by. "He has changed," Étienne said, thoughtful. "He never was this serious."

"He has a few responsibilities. With his business," she added when Étienne gave her a questioning look. Last night, Dominique had hinted that he was involved in something far-reaching that kept him quite occupied, but shrugged off all inquiries about the details as trivial, uninteresting things. His mother had been too happy to have him back to pry. Samantha prayed Étienne wouldn't start digging now.

"As a boy, when he came to spend summers in France, he was two years younger than me, but he was my hero."

"Oh?" she said and made note of the fact that this would make Étienne about her age.

"He could charm anything from anyone. All he had to do was smile and people—women, men, any age," he clarified with an emphatic gesture of one hand. "They just fell over for him."

"Fell all over themselves for him, you mean?" She could see it. She had done a fair bit of falling herself when that dimpled, mischievous smile appeared.

"*Oui, ça.* They did. It was his secret weapon. As long as I was with him, we could get away with anything. It was...*magique.* He was *magique.*"

He is still magical, Samantha thought. *More than ever.*

"Everything was so easy for him. Nothing was ever serious. And now—" Another shake of his head. "He still has the same charm—and he still attracts everything and everyone near him—but...there is an intensity I don't recognize."

"It's been a few years since you saw him. People change."

"Hmm. *Oui. Je suppose.* Now he has a business that has people looking for him in the night. Do you know anything about this?"

Her hands tightened around the steering wheel. She hated lying. So she hedged with "it's complicated" and changed the subject. "Étienne, do you mind if I asked you a personal question?"

"You, *ma belle amie*, may ask me anything you wish." His smile didn't have dimples, but the white teeth flashing in his sun-tanned face were enough to put butterflies in her stomach.

She almost reconsidered her question. The direct approach wasn't her style. But, damn it, she was falling for him, and before she fell any harder, there was something she had to know. "Do you...do you like—well, I mean..." She rolled the car to a stop at the last red light before home and checked to make sure the vampire still followed. There didn't seem to be any conversation going on in the car behind them. Both faces were grim. Their business with Dominique might not ever affect Samantha. Or it might turn the world of night upside down, and her own world right along with it.

Better get this settled before the apocalypse then. With a deep, fortifying breath, she turned to her passenger. "Are you gay?"

Étienne guffawed. "Why would you think that?"

"Because you're the most beautiful man I've ever met. Even more than Dominique," she added, thinking of the vampire lord's true appearance, which Étienne had not seen, and which, though breathtaking and hypnotic, could also be hard and terrifying. The only thing hard about Étienne were those muscles she itched to touch.

"Oh. *Merci, mais—*"

"And because I think we have a connection, and I might be falling for you, but you've been nothing but a gentleman." There. She said it. It was all out there now.

Étienne closed his mouth and swallowed. He wasn't smiling anymore. He might even be blushing, though she couldn't be sure in the low light. He definitely sounded husky. "And...you did not want me to be a gentleman?"

"Depends. Would you like to kiss me?"

"Oh, *oui*, yes. Very much."

"Well, then...?"

"In France, a gentleman waits for the woman to..."

Samantha leaned toward him. "We're not in France."

A corner of his mouth quirked up as he leaned to meet her. "And I am not gay," he whispered and backed up his words with the kiss she had fantasized about since first laying eyes on those lips. It was everything she imagined and more. Very gentlemanly, but with a passionate edge and a swoon-worthy attention to detail.

The polite honking behind them turned into a blaring blast before they separated. Samantha waved an apology at the vampire and made her turn. "Let's continue this conversation at home."

Étienne had his elbow propped against his door and looked ruggedly casual as he stroked his lips with one finger and studied her. His smile was full of sensual promises. Their "conversation," it said, would not be held in words.

14

Urgent Business

D ominique waited with Cassidy and Serge in the entrance hall, keeping a tight lid on his temper. Every few months, a blood-drinker found his or her way to his dojo's door. They had heard rumors of him, they would say, found the address listed on the *V-zette*. They wanted to know if it was true that there was a lord of their kind. They wanted to know what it meant. He answered their questions, re-sired them, sent them on their way. It was part of the job, but he also enjoyed flipping their world upside down, turning them away from fear and darkness and into love and light.

But why did one have to show up tonight?

"It'll only be a little while," Cassidy said earlier when Samantha's text hit both their phones. Dominique had been preparing to go out to hunt. He needed the sustenance for his plans tonight. He wanted to renew his bond with Cassidy and spend more time with his family in the happy illusion of being human again.

Instead, there were hunger pangs in his belly, Cassidy was only a remote whisper in his mind, and his mother was occupied in her room, catching up with the rest of the family via video—as Serge had "suggested" she do.

Dominique waited.

Finally, the garage door rumbled open and Samantha's hybrid whispered in. Another car rolled up the driveway. He settled into one of the plush, high-backed chairs in the far corner of the foyer. Serge took up position behind him.

While Dominique wore jeans and a dress shirt with his loafers, Serge was his usual disheveled self in board shorts and a Hawaiian shirt. In honor of this "official" occasion, he had donned flip-flops. Dominique didn't insist on formality. The casual dress was a convenient way of soothing the jangled nerves of blood-drinker visitors—or lulling potential enemies into underestimating the true extent of his power.

Samantha hurried in from the garage through the kitchen, her new shadow, Étienne, trailing behind her. Both were flushed, their eyes shiny, and their heart rates elevated in ways that did not speak to looming danger.

He allowed himself a tiny smile.

"Sorry, Dominique," Samantha said. "I didn't mean to ambush you."

"But you were ambushed, *non*?"

She nodded. "Her—" her eyes flickered to Étienne "—boyfriend made it sound pretty grim."

"*Très mystérieux*," Étienne supplied.

Dominique's mood darkened further. His cousin was getting far too exposed to things he would be better off not knowing. "Thank you. You may go."

Étienne cocked a brow at the official tone. "'I may go?'"

Serge zipped around the chair, eyes flashing black, mouth open, compulsion ready to fly.

Samantha clamped her hand to Serge's shoulder. "No. I've got this."

The softest of growls escaped Serge, but he relented.

Étienne blinked, uncertain. Samantha took his hand. "Shall we leave them to boring business and continue our...conversation?"

He smiled down at her, trapped in her wide, beguiling eyes. "Yes. Let's." Bidding them all a good night, he let Samantha lead him away.

Serge watched them go, still growling, and Dominique feared that if Étienne were not related to him, the man would be short serious amounts of blood at this point. He sent the mental equivalent of snapping fingers at Serge to gain his attention.

Shooting his lord an unhappy glance, Serge returned to his post behind Dominique's seat.

When tentative steps approached the door, Dominique nodded to Cassidy, who turned to open it before anyone could ring the bell. "Welcome," she said warmly.

The vampire who entered was a petite work of art, determined to disappear into the background. There was next to no color about her. Only a hint in her ice-blue eyes and soft pink lips, but none in her white-blond, up-swept hair or translucent skin. Even her choice of dress—a pantsuit ensemble of white and peach beneath a cream duster—seemed to work toward making her disappear. Despite this, she carried herself with the regal posture of royalty and an impassive expression that bordered on haughty.

Her heart told a different story. He listened to it race as she approached, the click of her stilettos tentative. Dominique smelled the hint of fear in her still-wintery scent. Young. Perhaps a decade as a blood-drinker, no more, and perhaps all of twenty when she had been made.

A human male carrying a leather shoulder bag entered with her. He was the polar opposite of her. Tall, muscular, with a dark beard, and dressed in black workout shorts and a sports hoodie. After murmuring a greeting to Cassidy, he stood by the door, hands clasped before him. He, too, oozed a fine mist of fear.

The vampiress stopped before Dominique, but her enormous eyes were for Serge alone. Her chin pointed up another notch. "I am Natalia Bogomolov." Even her hard Russian accent sounded delicate in her crystal voice. "I have come to find the friend of a friend: Dominique Marchant."

"You have found him," Serge said with little enthusiasm, his mind clearly still with his personal problems.

Her chin lowered a bit, her hands flattening against her hips, uncertain.

"Our common friend is Aubrey Wainwright?" Dominique asked. He recognized her name as that of the woman who had so charmed the Englishman. He frowned. That had been five eventful nights ago, and no word from Aubrey since.

Natalia's gaze flicked to Dominique, as though annoyed he had spoken. "Yes, it is," she confirmed, looking back to Serge.

A mental nudge made him glance in Cassidy's direction. "She can't see you," she mouthed, and he realized he was still holding himself shrouded in the illusion of humanity he had adopted for his family's sake. The only vampire Natalia saw in the room was Serge.

Amused, Dominique tented his fingers before him. "Did he send you here?"

Fire flashed in those pale eyes at the human meddling in her business, but seeing no objection from Serge, she turned to Dominique. "No, he did not. But he told me this vampire had great power and would rule us all." She glanced at Serge, as though unsure about applying this statement to him. "He spoke highly of him and called him a friend."

"And so he does," Dominique said and let the soft, sun-bronzed human guise melt away into his stark, pale, blood-drinker reality.

Natalia gasped and dropped to her knees, folding over so far her head touched the floor. Her cream duster flared out around her, all but vanishing against the cream tile.

Dominique was too startled to react. Serge made a tiny, troubled sound deep in his throat.

Cassidy's mouth dropped open. The man beside her shifted nervously.

Blood-drinkers always accorded Dominique the respect he was due once they realized the true extent of his supernatural gifts, but not one had ever prostrated themselves to this degree. Of course, he had never frightened one as thoroughly as he had just frightened this hapless soul who didn't know him at all.

"Be at ease, Natalia," Dominique said. "This is not required."

She sat up, uncertainty hunching her shoulders. "I am so very sorry, my lord. I meant no offense. I didn't—"

"No offense taken. Please. Get up and tell me why you are here. As a friend, *non*?"

Natalia gracefully rose back to her feet, but her head no longer rode quite so high. "I'm afraid I come to bring sad news, my lord. Our friend, Aubrey. He...he is dead."

15

PRETENDER

D ominique didn't react. He could not have heard what he just heard. This could not be true. Not of Aubrey.

When the stunned silence lingered, Natalia's companion hurried to her side and held open the bag he carried. She reached inside and retrieved a finely made red metal urn. "You are the only relationship he mentioned in our brief time together. I thought perhaps you would like to receive his remains." She placed the urn on the table beside Dominique. The man and the bag retreated into the background, his eyes downcast.

Dominique touched the cool metal with his fingertips. He had no reason not to believe her. Aubrey had not reported back as he said he would. Then again, if there was one thing blood-drinkers were good at, it was playing cruel games. The blood-drinkers of old anyway, the ones who still fed on terror and pain. The ones not yet re-sired to him.

Like this one.

It was paramount that he not react without solid proof. "How?"

Natalia's voice practically disappeared. "He was executed."

Dominique got out of his chair. She took a step back.

"Considering he was over a century old and one of the most well-adjusted and honorable blood-drinkers I have ever had the pleasure of meeting, that, *madame*, is sadly self-evident."

Somehow, he kept his voice level despite the anger blazing up his chest.

Natalia shrank into herself a little more, and her eyes darkened with fear. "I should not have invited him to visit with us. I should have warned him about Adilla. I tried to stop them, but I'm young and new there, and—"

Dominique raised a hand to stop the flow of words. Her mouth snapped shut. Tremors raced through her small body. "What happened?"

She wrung her hands before her. "He spoke to me about you. He said you were our true lord and that he had found peace in your blood. I doubted such news would be welcomed by Adilla and Esteban, but I didn't think...I didn't—" She tried to swallow a sob, failed, lowered her head. "Forgive me. He was, as you said, an honorable man."

Dominique stared at her. His leashed anger emerged as a growl. "What. Happened."

When she looked up, her eyes had gone almost full black, a vampire skirting the edge of mindless panic. Very deliberately, she tilted her head aside, exposing her neck. She would not—or could not—speak the words. She would show him.

He struck with lightning speed, grabbing her and driving his teeth far deeper than necessary. Turmoil and secrets spiced her blood, and one of the first things that surfaced was about the human man, Ryan. He was in her mind with her, aware of her and everything she experienced and thought. They had a bond like Dominique had with Cassidy, rare and—in a world where humans were considered servants and food—dangerous.

Dominique saw the other blood-drinkers as she had, beautiful city sophisticates, gathering at a spacious private home overlooking a bay. They all orbited around their host, the regal figure of Adilla Khan. The ancient vampire wore jeweled rings on almost every finger, and an emerald glinted in one earlobe, but in every other way he was the embodiment of a successful Western business tycoon: impeccably trimmed sable hair, a bespoke suit, and a dazzling smile. He turned that smile on Aubrey as he greeted him with a handshake and offered a crystal tumbler of warm blood. He still smiled several minutes of small talk later, when he said, "You say you spend much time in the south. Are you familiar with...Dominique Marchant?"

Aubrey must have known that his subtle hesitation gave his recognition of the name away. "I am."

"My sources tell me he calls himself our...new lord?"

"You're sources are well-informed," Aubrey allowed and took a sip of the blood, his first. "Oh, this is excellent."

"It is, isn't it? My own special vintage." Adilla sniffed his own drink appreciatively. "I'm curious. What are your thoughts regarding this...new lord?"

Aubrey hesitated before shaking his head with an affable chuckle. "Ah, politics. Please, I beg you, let's not spoil an enjoyable evening with such talk."

"Oh, but why not? It's what you do, isn't it, Aubrey Wainwright? Convince the more feeble-minded among us of this sheer fantasy? Don't you want to at least attempt it with me?" At Aubrey's shocked expression, the glint in Adilla's deep green eyes turned predatory, belying his easy-going smile. "Your reputation precedes you as much as your master's."

"I see." Aubrey coughed delicately. "Well, then allow me to assure you that my sole purpose here tonight is to accompany a charming new friend." He turned to Natalia with a reassuring smile, which she returned automatically, hiding her growing unease.

Adilla would not be dissuaded. "Then I'm curious about something else, Mr. Wainwright." He took a deep drink from his glass, leaving his lips glistening red until the tip of his tongue licked off the excess blood. "What thoughts do you have regarding us?" A slight gesture encompassed the room and everyone in it.

"I have only just met you, sir. But Natalia tells me good things."

"Has she really?" Adilla's gaze settled on her like a suffocating weight. "What a pleasant surprise."

Aubrey did his best to defuse the escalating situation with compliments and good humor. Adilla continued to counter with snide insinuations and increasingly less veiled insults. In Natalia's memories, Dominique could see how his friend's discomfort mounted, how he struggled to maintain his steadfast composure, until he had at last been maneuvered into a corner from which the only escape would have been to flee. It was what Adilla wanted; that much was obvious in his darkening eyes and the elongating tips of his fangs. The ancient one was hunting—and Aubrey was the prey.

The prey stood its ground. "Yes, Dominique Marchant is my lord, which is how I know he wishes no one here any harm, least of all you. He is young, as you say, but wise. He would respect your wisdom and welcome you by his side."

The hubbub of the party faded as though a ripple of disturbance shuddered through the house. What remained of Adilla's pretended geniality evaporated, his expression turning hard and cold, almost reptilian. "As...his subject?"

Aubrey didn't hesitate. "We are all his subjects, sir."

"Not all, you pompous little fool. I bow to no one."

"He is heir to Kambyses, the—"

"How *dare* you use that name to me?"

Everyone else had gone as still as rabbits sensing a circling hawk. Aubrey forged on. "I merely state fact. Kambyses is his sire. I have seen this in his—"

Adilla leaned into his face and roared, "There is only one true heir to the great Kambyses, and that is I. He chose me, a true prince of my realm, sired me with his blood, mentored me, and bequeathed me his kingdom when and if he so decrees."

Aubrey fell as silent as the others, as still as Natalia by his side, who was now terrified for both their lives.

Then Adilla took a single step back, his voice almost calm when he spoke again. "You have been sadly misled. The...*fact* is that neither you nor your so-called lord are worthy of uttering the name of Kambyses. You are not even worthy to *think* mine. Your lord is a pretender, a fake. I, however, have worked diligently for countless centuries to prepare for the night that I will rule. I have built a community here unlike any other of our kind. They are thriving together, because of me, as all of us will thrive under my guidance. That, Mr. Wainwright, is inevitable."

Natalia heard the threat in the calm words, as did everyone else. No one moved, their attention riveted. Even the soft background music had stopped.

Adilla placed his drink on a tray brought by one of the enslaved humans and straightened the cuffs of his jacket as he continued. "You understand, I'm sure, that such a great society does not run itself. There are rules and procedures by which we have all agreed to abide."

"No," Natalia whispered into the silence. "No, you—"

Ignoring her, Adilla nodded at Esteban, his chief of security. An instant later, four of Esteban's delegates rushed in. Aubrey gave himself over to his beast in a fight for his life, drawing more than a little blood, surprising his attackers with a ferocity even Dominique had not imagined possible of his gentle friend. But he couldn't prevail. Soon he was subdued and bound hand and foot in silver by a fifth man, who carried shackles in gloved hands. A thick silver collar was snapped around Aubrey's neck, raising boiling blisters on his skin within moments.

Despite the pain he must have endured, he stood straight and defiant in his torn, bloodied clothes and disheveled hair, his eyes still black as tar. "You are making a very big mistake," he wheezed with unflinching dignity.

"But...you broke the rules," Adilla chided.

"He doesn't *know* the rules," Natalia protested.

"And whose fault is that, hmm?"

Natalia shrank back, horrified. She had shared with Aubrey everything she thought might matter before this meeting, but she had not expected the lengths to which Adilla would go to bend the rules to his whims.

"I apologize if I gave offense," Aubrey said, finishing on a gasp as the silver collar burned against his bobbing Adam's apple.

Adilla shook his head. "I'm afraid that won't suffice. You broke the cardinal rule by acknowledging an allegiance to another. After Kambyses, I am the lord of our kind. The *only* lord." All around, heads bowed in grim acknowledgement.

"He meant no challenge," Natalia tried again.

Aubrey said nothing, serving the challenge now by refusing to refute his own words. Or maybe he understood that to one such as Adilla, nothing he could say would have made any difference now.

Adilla's smile broadened with satisfaction. "Mr. Aubrey Wainwright, according to established procedure, your challenge has been heard and witnessed and will be answered accordingly."

This time, Esteban nodded to the men holding Aubrey. In a blur, they hustled him away.

Disbelieving horror rooted Natalia to the spot. "No. No, you can't do this. There is a rule about guests. This is a violation!"

Adilla turned away, reaching for a fresh glass of blood. As the music started again, Esteban appeared by her side. "Careful, pet," he said under his breath. "Or we might think you'd like to meet the dawn together with this heretic."

Dominique's legs buckled beneath him the way Natalia's had buckled. He had stopped feeding, but he still held her, still swam in her memories.

She had said no more, done no more. She had no choice. Someone else depended on her survival far more than Aubrey did. Though near dawn she had gone downtown, hoping against hope to gain access unobserved to the high rise that was Adilla's business headquarters. Esteban's men patrolled the street, and she was too young to outlast them against the coming dawn. They were gone the next evening, when she returned and rushed to the top floor unimpeded. There she found the room she had only heard about, a small space with shackles on one wall opposite a floor-to-ceiling window. A window that faced east, faced the sunrise over the North Shore Mountains.

A sunrise Aubrey had seen.

His fine clothes lay piled beneath the empty shackles, filled with glittering ash.

Natalia had fallen to her knees, weeping. She wept again now, in Dominique's arms.

His wretched sob broke the silence. Aubrey was dead, and he, Dominique, could have saved him—if he had been there, if he had joined Aubrey, as his friend had asked. If he hadn't been so selfishly caught up in the promise of seeing the sun again...Aubrey would have lived.

Anguish threatened to rip Dominique apart right down to the bone. But something held him together. Fear. Not his, but Natalia's. Fear for her mortal lover.

The vampiress had been hiding the secret of their bond for weeks, passing him off as her favored slave to the others. Aubrey had told her about the bond between Dominique and Cassidy, which was her primary reason for volunteering to deliver Aubrey's ashes to Dominique. More than running an errand, she was fleeing the colony, which would sooner kill her beloved than acknowledge him. She trusted Aubrey's words with blind desperation, placing her and her lover's lives into the hands of Dominique, an unknown entity...for love.

Releasing her, Dominique crouched on the floor beside her. His eyes stung when he met Cassidy's look of sorrow. Slowly, the knowledge of her unfaltering support and the weight of his responsibility forced the grief to settle and his thoughts to focus. He had eternity to chastise himself for this many other mistakes. Now was not the time to dwell. He allowed Natalia to recover her composure before saying, "Aubrey shared with you how to find this peace."

She wiped at her eyes with one small hand. "Yes. The re-siring. He offered this, but...I was unsure. I thought Adilla might not be pleased. Now I know he would have killed me. And without me, Ryan..." She looked up at him, her words echoing what he could feel in her mind. "I will never return to them. I can't. It's peace I want, and for this, I submit to you, my lord, in whatever way you wish."

Not that she really had a choice. Dominique always asked, and they always accepted, but the truth was that he would not tolerate blood-drinkers who continued to feed on terror.

Natalia felt so raw and alone sitting there before him, her hair undone, her face almost childishly young. Despite her bravado, she was fragile, her resolve thanks to Ryan alone. If not for him, she would be nothing but an obedient shadow in Adilla's court of horrors.

Dominique pressed a thumbnail into his palm and waited for the blood to pool before offering it to her. "You are safe with me."

Her touch was gentle as a butterfly's feet when she took his wrist, though once his blood ignited in her veins, her fingers convulsed like claws. Then she gasped and let go, falling back to the tile floor.

"Natalia!" Ryan rushed forward, dropped to his knees, and scooped her into his arms. There was fire in his eyes when he glared at Dominique. "What did you do to her?"

Dominique licked the rest of the blood off his hand and got up. Already he could sense her more clearly in the web. "She is fine."

"She better be."

The outburst made him smile. Ryan was as devoted to Natalia as Cassidy was to Dominique, and clearly just as willing to defend her against forces far beyond his abilities.

Natalia stirred with a small moan. When her eyes opened, they were fully dilated, and in their depths glowed the familiar golden light.

"Natalia? Sweet pea? Are you all right?"

"Yes. Oh, yes, my love." She touched his face, her heart in her eyes as she looked at him. "It's as Aubrey said; the fear is gone."

The mention of Aubrey's name made Dominique glance at the urn, then at Serge, who stared at Natalia with a thoughtful frown wrinkling his brow.

Dominique cocked his head in question.

The corners of Serge's mouth turned down, but then he said, "This Adilla could be a great ally...if you can sway him."

Dominique squashed the impulse to argue. Killing that arrogant menace was more in line with what he had in mind. Too bad that wasn't the peaceful, loving way he preached.

"He is old," Serge offered when Dominique remained silent. "Many would perish if you ended him."

True. Since Kambyses had not fully sired any younglings for a thousand years—only infecting them with his serum, but withholding his blood—Adilla was at least that old. Any blood-drinker that age had the potential to have sired many others who, along with their descendants, would depend on his survival. It was the dark web that bound them. Break one strand, and all the strands that branched from it unraveled. As the center of this web, if Dominique was destroyed, they all would be.

"What do you know about him?" Dominique asked.

"I may have heard of him." Serge looked away. "Once or twice."

As he often did around his friend, Dominique felt like he was missing something, a sensation that never boded well.

"Adilla is no one's ally but his own," Natalia said. She was back on her feet now. Ryan hovered close, one of his arms around her, providing support she surely did not need.

"Once he tastes your blood, he will see reason," Serge countered.

"Is that what your visions tell you?" Dominique asked.

Shrug. "They all see reason, don't they?"

"That whole setup with the colony gave me the creeps," Ryan broke in. "Adilla gives them anything and everything you can think of. Money, homes, security, entertainment, and all the blood they can guzzle. In return, he demands their blind devotion, and let me tell you, he's getting that in spades. Those vampires are more than willing to bow down and agree to everything he says. Their loyalty is bought and paid for many times over."

"And I would gladly have been one of them," Natalia said. "Until the night I found Ryan." She looked up and they exchanged a brief smile. "He could hear my thoughts, and I was no longer alone. I saw things differently then."

Cassidy joined Dominique and slid her hand into his. He lifted it to press a kiss to her knuckles. "I know the feeling."

"I'm so glad we're free of that mess," Ryan said.

"And I am so sorry that it took Aubrey's death to make me see how badly we needed to get away," Natalia added.

"My lord, you must persuade him to join you," Serge blustered.

Dominique tried to picture standing across from Adilla—the first millennial blood-drinker he had encountered since claiming his kingdom—and felt his confidence flagging. "Fake," Adilla had called him. "Pretender."

The words echoed in his bones. Not because they gave offense, but because they were true. He pretended to be something he could never be again for his mother.

Fake human.

He was supposed to be master of the world of night, but few of his subjects knew he existed, much less that he forbade them to kill or make others against their will. Yet he went through the motions of ruling—while distracted with every shiny possibility of turning back time, of being human again.

Pretend leader.

Cassidy squeezed his hand, disrupting the black spiral of his thoughts. Her silent voice was faint in her touch. *Those who know you know better. What you do for yourself, you do for them all.*

Aubrey died for me. I was too obsessed with seeing the sun again to stand by him, and he died. Because of me.

Maybe, she allowed after a moment's thought. *Or maybe, because you wouldn't have known what to expect, they might have killed you both. Aubrey died because he believed in what you are trying to do. Now you know what you're up against, and if you don't use that knowledge, if you doubt yourself, he will have died for nothing.*

He turned his head to meet her eyes, deep blue pools of stubborn strength. His lioness in battle mode.

The others waited, brows folded with worry.

"It appears I will need to meet this Adilla for myself," Dominique said.

"He will destroy you," Natalia burst out, then caught herself and lowered her eyes. "My lord."

Jackson and Garrett should come, too, Cassidy said, and Dominique agreed.

Serge's hands fidgeted in front of him. "You must make him an ally. Destroying one so old...no good will come of that." He shook his head. "No good at all."

16

STRANGE NEW WORLDS

Cassidy watched sullenly as Dominique pulled the plunger, and the soft pink suppressant filled the syringe. When he was done preparing the shot, he held it out to her. She didn't react for several seconds, then reluctantly took the instrument of demonic possession into her hand. At thirty-thousand feet, her options were limited.

"I don't like this."

He took off his jacket and shirt and lay back on the double bed in their jet's private compartment. Though they had taken off well before dawn, they wouldn't make it across the entire continent before the sun caught up with them. "Neither do I, but it is necessary. So you will do it, *non*?"

"You don't know that. Maybe I'll stuff you in the lavatory. Maybe I'd rather spend the day guarding the door on this plane than dealing with...with *him*."

"Give him whatever he wants," Dominique said, closing his eyes. His face tensed as he fought the mounting urge to take shelter. "Make him remember."

Cassidy glanced out the window. Red light strobed from the tip of the wing in the predawn gray, above a solid blanket of clouds. The flashes only underscored the warning bells going off in the back of her head.

Taking his hand in hers, she reached for what remained of their telepathic connection. Not only had events derailed their plans to renew the link tonight, now Dominique was convinced she'd be safer without it. Taking the suppressant made him vulnerable the next night. A deep link with him, he said, would compromise her if anyone got their teeth into him. In fact, he wanted her to stay safe at home, but given his decision to travel fast and without regard for the sun, her presence was essential.

Someone had to push that damn plunger.

She would have preferred to send in the Strikers as an advance team, but thanks to a vampire named Abdul, the hunters weren't leaving Germany any time soon. Even bound in silver shackles, the jihadi vampire had surprised Garrett with a violent head-butt that landed the man in a hospital. Garrett spent eight hours in surgery, getting his insides put back together. Jackson spent eight seconds turning Abdul into ash. Now, not even a thousand-year-old target was tempting enough to budge him from his uncle's bedside.

The Strikers were going nowhere.

None of this stopped the Lord of Night. Not with a magic daylight shot in his pocket.

Cassidy looked at the syringe in her hand, at the large-bore needle, remembered how he had ended up the last time, and felt ill. His fingers twitched against hers. "*Embrasse-moi,*" he whispered.

She tucked her hair behind one ear and leaned forward to deliver the requested kiss. It lingered as the sun gained on the plane. Over their faltering connection, past the drone of the engines, she thought she could hear its crackling roar the way he did, could feel the fear skittering along his nerves.

The kiss was a distraction, and an effective one at that. When he had gone corpse-still, eyes closed, lips parted, Cassidy sat up beside him. "Damn you for making me do this, Dominique."

But do it she did, if only because she could never drag him into the lavatory on her own. She aimed the needle toward the heart the way she had seen Jackson do it and shuddered when she felt the powerful beat against her hand.

The plunger descended. The suppressant disappeared. The syringe disappeared into its case.

She waited.

The sun bathed the cloud blanket below in rosy pink, but there was no sign of its scorching touch on Dominique's bare skin. A minute later, he inhaled and opened his eyes like a man waking up from a nap.

"Good morning," she said.

He sat up. "Where am I?"

"On a plane."

His hands moved over the bed to either side of him. His eyes found the large, round windows. "We are going to—"

"Vancouver, Canada."

"Canada," Dominique muttered. He scooted to the edge of the plush mattress, shoulders pulled up to his ears, and put his bare feet on the carpet. A shock of hair fell across his brooding scowl. "This is intolerable. What are you doing with me, *madame*?"

Cassidy leaned back on one hand and couldn't help being charmed by his befuddlement. "What's the last thing you remember?"

His sweeping brows gathered, then smoothed as he looked at her. "I remember you." His voice dropped a notch, approaching husky. "We made love, *non*?"

"Oh, *oui*. We did. What else do you remember?"

The warmth blossoming in his eyes dimmed. "At the end..."

"Yes?"

He stared at the floor. "Nothing."

He was lying. She knew he was, even to himself, but she let it go. Whatever he remembered of that moment when his vampire self re-emerged, his human self still wanted no part of it.

She fished his phone out of his discarded jacket. "Here. You should watch this."

On the small screen, Dominique of an hour ago spoke for several minutes in concise, no-nonsense French. His eyes flashed confidence and resolve as he explained they were going to Vancouver on business, and they were expecting trouble. Under no circumstance was he to leave Cassidy's side. She was the only one he could trust.

Vampire Dominique leaned in. "One more thing you must understand: Cassidy is my beating heart and living soul. I entrust you with her safety. If anything happens to her—anything at all—I will never allow you to wake again."

Human Dominique cursed under his breath. "How is this possible? How are you doing this?"

"If you let yourself remember—"

He held up a hand to stop her. "*Non*, do not misunderstand me. You are *très charmante*, and I have enjoyed our *rencontres*, but"—he leaned closer—"*Je veux rentrer chez moi.*"

She touched his cheek. "I know you want to go home, my love." *Give him whatever he wants*, Dominique had said. *Make him remember.* "Would you...would you like to call your mother? Again?"

The look he gave her was one of pure incredulity. "You would allow this?"

She gestured at the phone attached to the wall beside the bed. "You'll want to call her mobile. Seems you invited her to come stay with us," she added deadpan.

He looked suspicious until Francesca answered her phone. "*Maman?* Is it you? Where are you? Oh, yes, of course. No, nothing is—I don't know—I am...fine. I'm on a plane. Vancouver?" He glanced at Cassidy, who nodded. "On business. Yes. Yes. Right. Very important." He dropped his forehead into one hand and slid long fingers through his hair. "Yes, we left in a great hurry. I will be back soon. Yes, you stay as long as you like. Enjoy the house. I know. I love you, too."

Slowly, he replaced the handset on the hook and sat back down beside her. Cassidy let out the breath she didn't realize she'd been holding. "Tell me, Cassidy. Just what sort of...business does my mother think I do?"

"Security," she said and leaned companionably against him. He met her wide, innocent eyes out of the corners of his narrow, suspicious ones. "And you're a stupendous success."

She could tell he wanted to know more. Or not. He looked away, shoulders rounding. Then he spotted the protective bags carefully clipped to a utility hook. Their long, thin shape betrayed their contents: swords. He stared at them, and Cassidy held her breath again.

Without a word, he got up, retrieved the longer of the bags and carefully extracted the *katana* inside. The magnificent sixteenth century weapon was sheathed in a black scabbard festooned with writhing dragons. He studied the hilt, the small gold dragon embedded there glinting in the warm morning light pouring into the cabin. His thumb rubbed the brass hand guard, which featured another dragon. A tiny notch marred the edge, she knew, a remnant of a long-ago battle that would confirm the sword as his. Together with its mate, it had entered his life just before he was transformed and would still be fresh in his human memories. "Why are these here?"

Oh, of all the questions... She licked her lips, considering the minefield ahead. "Well, they're yours," she began. His brow furrowed with impatience. "And...you, well, you use them to—"

"These are *antiquités*. They do not get *used*."

Cassidy exhaled, the "to decapitate hostile vampires" left blessedly unspoken. "For your work," she finished instead.

"In...security."

"*Oui*," she confirmed brightly. The frown deepened, and she sobered. "You have...told me that the dragons guide you...sometimes."

He looked at the scabbard in his hands again, brow smoothing. "These were a gift from my friend Jérôme when I earned my first degree black belt. The dragons were supposed to remind me that strength is nothing without the wisdom to use it."

"A fitting gift," she said, dangling verbal bait. "Considering how much greater your strength has become." She waited. Would he bite?

Dominique slipped the scabbard into its bag and hung it back up with its mate. "*Très bien.*" When he turned back to her, it was like the swords had ceased to exist. He stuck his fingers in his pockets and smiled. "Is there any food?"

There was. Because of their often unpredictable schedule, the jet and its rotating crew were always on standby, and the galley was always stocked with the basics. The microwaved breakfast casserole served by the bleary-eyed steward wasn't lavish, but it was tasty, as were the fresh OJ and the mostly fresh pastries. The best part was the large thermos of hot chocolate. Dominique had hurriedly made it before they left. Now, Cassidy smiled as she watched his reluctant pleasure at finding the drink spiced "almost" the way he preferred.

Later, while he stared out the window, she tried to nap, but failed miserably. Even here, she was too anxious about leaving him on his own, too worried about what he might scheme about, or, worse, the suppressant spontaneously wearing off. Giving up on getting rest, she got up to raid the remaining pastries.

When he saw her return with the entire bin, he shook his head. "*Madame,* your appetite is...impressive."

Stress will do that to you, she thought, but smiled as she selected a chocolate-stuffed croissant. "It's nothing compared to yours, *monsieur.*" Pushing the pastry container in his direction, she added, "Have some." He looked unsure. She gave him a seductive smile and purred, "I know you want to."

He did. Though still not a fan of the "strange" taste, he declared it passable. For the remaining two hours of the flight, they nibbled and talked, mostly about carefully inconsequential things. It wasn't for a lack of trying on Cassidy's part. She gave him countless hints and loose ends, silently begging him to follow up.

He didn't. The truth and his human mind continued to repel each other like water and oil. By the time they touched down, the pastry bin was empty and Cassidy was exhausted.

On the ride to the hotel, she took stock of Vancouver. As cities went, this one had a lot going for it. It was a busy glass-and-steel metropolis, with green spaces exploding out of every crack and crevice. Late spring rode in the cool, fresh air streaming through the open window. There was even a tang of cedar mixed with ocean brine. Despite her fatigue, she smiled into the watery sunlight, new energy coursing through her body.

Beside her, Dominique hunched deeper into his jacket.

"Are you okay?"

"I am cold," he grumbled.

"But the sun is out. You should be thrilled."

She waited for an argument or a scoff. Instead, he gave her a strange look and turned back to his window.

The room they had waiting for them at the Pan Pacific was enormous. Cassidy tried not to look as awkward as she still felt in situations like this. In her previous life, she would have booked into the cheapest motel on the outskirts of town. Now she had two bellmen wheel her luggage into an apartment-sized space featuring a separate bedroom, cozy sofa group, and elegant dining area, even a small kitchenette. The style was clean, modern, and neutral so as not to detract from the shimmering harbor and misty mountain views beyond the floor-to-ceiling windows.

Dominique seemed a little more at ease, looking around casually with his hands in his pockets. From a more affluent background, he was used to traveling in some style, but this was extravagant even by his former standards. After the bellmen concluded a tour of the amenities, filled the ice bucket, collected their tips, and departed, Dominique gestured at the expansive space and tidy furnishings. "I booked this?"

"You sure did." In fact, it was the last thing he had done before prepping the suppressant. He even used a fake name. They were entering the territory of a hostile blood-drinker. The fewer people who knew where they were, the better. Even during the day.

"And I can afford this?"

She walked up to him. "This and the plane that brought us here. You could afford to buy the whole hotel without missing the change."

"Security," he murmured. "Hmm." He curled an arm around her waist, drawing her close. "But I...he would give it all up for you, would he not?"

Cassidy sobered, her hands on his chest. "The money is a tool. Nothing more."

"I remember some things. Nothing clear. Just...shadows. Like nightmares in the morning. Does that make sense?"

"Yes."

His eyes filled with uncertainty and a vulnerability she had rarely seen in them. "But you are part of that world?"

"Yes," she said again, more softly.

"How is that possible?"

"I'm your path out of those nightmares, Dominique. I always have been."

"My 'beating heart and living soul,'" he quoted, searching her upturned face.

"As you are mine."

Their lips came together in a tender kiss that zinged through her body like a live current. He must have sensed it, too, because a moment later he had her hard against himself and deepened the kiss until the current turned to a smolder.

There was no rushing him this time as he explored her body, getting to know it anew, taking pleasure in igniting all her senses. The white-hot climax that seized her took her off-guard, and she struggled to gather her wits enough to prepare for what was next.

As before, when Dominique peaked, his true self erupted. He trembled, stared at her with the hyper-dilated eyes of the vampire in a timeless moment of understanding.

"*Mon amour*," he whispered, full of wonder.

Then he was gone.

This far north and this time of year, there was a stupid amount of daylight to get through. Cassidy spent the hours catching up on her sleep, checking in with the *V-zette*, answering email, getting caught up with news, and enjoying room service—several times—with an appetite that wouldn't quit.

It was well past eight o'clock before the bedspread burrito she had made of Dominique unraveled and promptly emptied his guts into the ice bucket she held at the ready.

"Why did you not stop me eating today?" Dominique groaned when he was done turning inside out and dropped his head into her lap.

"You're always hungry." She finger-combed his tousled hair. It slipped like satin through her hands. "Until your daytime self remembers what he's really hungry for, I won't stand in his way." Especially not for some of those appetites. The memory of their lovemaking still thrummed in her body.

Dominique untangled himself from the rest of the comforter and, noting his nakedness, slanted her a sultry look. "You wicked woman. Do you have him under your spell as completely as me?"

She gave him her most seductive leer as she leaned back on one hand and allowed her bathrobe to fall open a little more.

"*Femme méchante*," he told her in a husky whisper. "You drive me mad."

"And you love that about me."

"Beyond measure." He lowered his gaze, rueful. "I paid a high price to be here when no one expects me to be." He got up and placed a kiss on her forehead. "If I don't get out into the city and recover my strength—" Her hand, on his more sensitive anatomy, made him break off on a sharp inhale.

"It's been two weeks. You can recover some of your strength with me," she said, tilting her head to expose her best vein, all innocence. Her supposed safety be damned. She needed him to bite her, renew their bond, and then...

Dominique's eyes darkened with desire, but he took her hand from his cock and held it, rubbing her knuckles with his thumb.

Getting up, she untied her robe and pressed close to him, letting him feel her. Her lips found the pulse in his neck, his hair brushing her face. "Husband," she murmured. "Do thy duty."

"It is...not safe tonight." He sounded distracted, drawing in her scent. "I am too weak to...to..." He groaned at the renewed efforts of her hand.

"I'm willing to risk it for one short night."

"If anyone...gets into my thoughts and...learns about you—" Again, he inhaled, deeper this time, like he was feeding on air. Then he pushed back and held her at arm's length. He stared at her, his eyes flashing to full black, fire glowing in their depths.

With some reluctance, Cassidy banked her lust. "What?"

"Your scent. *Mon Dieu.* You have never smelled like this."

She lifted an arm and sniffed self-consciously. "Are you sure? I took a shower earlier."

An awed, tentative smile grew on his face as he studied her. "And your aura. It has...a new color."

"A new what?" Damn, she hated not being in his head. Hated not seeing what he saw, or knowing what he perceived through his supernatural senses. What little she heard of his thoughts through their touch felt scattered and insubstantial.

"There is a ribbon of emerald..." With his fingers, he traced a winding pattern over her shoulder and between her breasts. "It comes from...here."

Cassidy frowned down at his hand flattening over her belly. Her ravenous belly. As she thought about it, a weight seemed to settle there. Then her jaw dropped. "No."

"*Oui.*" He broke into a grin.

Oh God, oh my God. "This can't be right. I don't...I mean...I mean, I can't be...I...can't be—"

"*Enceinte? Oui, chérie,* you are pregnant." He held both her hands in his, squeezing them as a wave of dizziness washed over her. "I can see it in your aura. I can smell it in your scent."

"But...how is this possible?"

"We made love during the day today," he said, practically bubbling with excitement. "And the last time, too, *non?*"

Cassidy's head felt like an untethered balloon. She locked her knees. "Yes. Yes, we did. Could this really be happening?"

"You are carrying my child." On a downright giddy note, he added, "Unless there are other lovers you keep hidden from me?"

She stared at him, dazed. "As if I could, even if I wanted to." It was hard to breathe. Her vision swam with tears.

When he pulled her into his arms, she leaned against him and let the world come undone.

17

Puppy Dog Eyes

From the small deck behind her pool house home, Samantha watched night creep over the Intracoastal waterway, sipped from a cup of calming herbal tea, and waited.

Any moment now, the wine cellar in the house would crack open, releasing Serge and Natalia, who had gratefully accepted Dominique's invitation to remain at the house. Dominique trusted her, and that was good enough for Samantha. She had no concerns about the dainty Russian vampiress or her mortal lover who had slept most of the day in a guest room.

No, Natalia was not the vampire Samantha was worried about. It was Serge's over-the-top reaction to Étienne last night that had put her on guard—at least until Étienne distracted her again in the most delightful ways. In his human arms, the supernatural ceased to exist. She closed her eyes, remembering. God, she was falling hard.

"My golden treasure," a familiar supernatural voice purred into her ear. "Good evening to you."

Samantha cracked open one eye. "Hello Serge."

"How was your day?"

Now she opened both eyes and watched him curl up on a lounge chair. He was completely focused on her, clear-eyed and steady, but by no means calm. It was like he was looking to pounce on something. Like a cat.

"My day was wonderful." She smiled a little, remembering, and also maybe grateful that Serge hadn't fed from her in well over a week. His ability to read her thoughts would be severely diminished at this point.

Or maybe not.

"Will you show me?" he ventured hopefully.

Samantha's smile froze. That was his way of asking permission to feed. As far as she knew, she was the only one he ever asked, the only human he never compelled or coerced. She also knew how quickly that could change. "I'm not sure you'd like what you'd find."

Serge harrumphed. "Because of that man?"

"Your lord's cousin, Étienne, yes." No point denying it.

A dismissive gesture. "No matter. He is gone now. I'm pleased if you found some pleasure I can't provide."

Her heart squeezed. Those large, chocolate brown eyes reminded her of a puppy suddenly. A sad puppy. She put her hand on his arm. "Oh, Serge. You give me so much else. Your trust and friendship mean the world to me."

A shy smile and tiny lopsided shrug.

"And Étienne is not gone. He took Francesca to the airport late this afternoon, but he'll be back soon."

Serge's face sharpened. "Airport? Where is she going? She is under my protection."

"Calm down. She'll be fine. She talked to Dominique today—"

"Today? During the day, today?"

"—and thought he sounded strange." Samantha sighed. "So, she booked a flight to follow him."

Serge made one of those adorable little noises of bafflement. He looked away, probably thinking as she had, about the implications for Dominique. Well, not quite. "He is not going with her? He returns? Here?"

"Um. Yes." Étienne would have accompanied his aunt, had she asked, but Francesca had taken one look at Étienne and Samantha this morning and left her nephew where he was.

"I don't like it."

"Serge, why not? I haven't had an actual relationship in years. I don't know if this will go anywhere, but right now, it makes me happy. Don't you want me to be happy?"

He growled. Actually growled, God help her. The puppy eyes vanished, replaced by the hyper-dilated look of an agitated vampire.

"Um, Serge?"

"He is human."

"Yes, I noticed."

"Unreliable, human men. He will hurt you, break your heart."

"Well, good thing I'm a grown woman who knows what she's doing," she countered dryly. Though right at this moment, she wasn't so sure about that last bit. This was a side of Serge she had not seen before. One that didn't impress her. Maybe even frightened her a little.

Deep in the back of his eyes, the amber light of Dominique's influence shimmered. Love is what he craved, like all re-sired vampires. Apparently, sharing wasn't part of that impulse. "You are under my protection, golden one. Against all potential harm."

She squeezed his forearm. "I know, my friend. But I'm also human and not a child. I know the risks. I've taken them before, and I'll take them again. The rewards are worth it."

Puppy dog eyes again.

"You and I will always be close, Serge. I saved your life. You constantly protect mine. You have shown me things I never knew existed. You are the magic in my life. Nothing will ever change that." She rubbed her hand over his fuzzy forearm. "And if you want my blood tonight—with all the memories and scattered thoughts in my head—you can have it."

The tiniest of smiles flashed on his wide mouth, the tiniest air of capitulation. At least for now. He patted her hand where it lay on his arm. "I thank you for the offer, but I will decline. I need more than a sip this fine night."

"You're going out?" A strange mixture of disappointment and relief rose in her.

He picked up her hand and pressed a chivalrous kiss to her knuckles before getting up. "Indeed, I must." With a small, formal bow at the waist, he wished her a pleasant evening—and vanished.

"You too," she said to the empty air. "You too, my friend."

18

THE GLITTER OF ASHES

D espite the hunger gnawing at his entrails, it took more than an hour before he could bring himself to leave Cassidy. Kambyses once told him that before he was turned, Dominique's aura had been an emerald shade of green, the same as the new life now rooting in Cassidy's belly.

There was no doubt in Dominique's mind—he would be a father.

The joy bubbling through him was tangible and lightened his step as he set out to hunt, camouflaged in jeans, sneakers and a windbreaker. A pair of sunglasses hid the happy preternatural light in his eyes. Nothing obscured his smile.

Reconnoitering for blood-drinker activity was a challenge. Distractions abounded in this vibrant city that surrounded him like a colossal living machine of glass and steel. Lights glared, shimmered, and flashed everywhere. Scattered sirens and the rhythmic rush of traffic assailed his ears, along with voices, heartbeats, and distant thrums. The pervasive smells of damp pavement and exhaust fumes filled the air, but couldn't drown out the rich, tantalizing scent of the humanity milling all around him.

He headed south on Burrard Street for several blocks, deep into the downtown core, before realizing that he could never cover enough ground on foot. Not at the human speeds to which he would have to confine himself in such a highly surveilled environment. Blending in with the other pedestrians, he loitered at a busy intersection until the flow of traffic brought him what he sought.

The rider on the Ducati SuperSport waiting at the red light listened to his "request," but shook their head slowly. When Dominique raised the helmet's protective shield, the face of a young woman blinked back at him. He graced her with a disarming smile and his most compulsive voice. "You are thrilled to let me borrow your bike right now."

She was. More or less. "Okay."

Several passers-by regarded the exchange with some suspicion, but when the woman handed him the helmet with a smile and wished him "good luck," they turned away again, busy with their own concerns.

The light had changed and traffic was starting up again as he swung onto the seat. "What is your number?" he asked, and she told him. He committed it to memory with every intention of returning her ride when he was done with it. "*Merci, madame.*"

The machine rumbled between his legs. Though nowhere as fast as his tricked-out BMW at home, it served its purpose and carried him along the bustling city streets in anonymity. Carried him right past the glittering glass tower on Georgia Street he had seen in Natalia's mind as Adilla's base of operation in the human world. He combed the surrounding streets at length, seeking any sign of blood-drinkers, but no telltale cold white auras appeared anywhere. If there were two hundred of them in this city, they were not on the streets tonight. Nor did they loiter in the cafés, restaurants and bars he visited in search of easy blood, of which there was an embarrassment of riches. In dark and intimate corners, he tapped vein after vein, mind after mind, savoring the unique flavors and rich memories of humanity from every corner of the world. Hours passed as he happily lost himself in the euphoria of so much exotic variety.

Dominique didn't return to Adilla's headquarters until three in the morning, which was only a little over two hours before sunrise. How did vampires this far north cope in the summer? More night disappeared by the day, and it was only May. Maybe the long winter nights made up for this inconvenience?

There still were no blood-drinkers on Georgia Street. Dominique wasn't at a hundred percent, but felt far more confident in his abilities than earlier. At least confident enough to park the bike and try compelling himself past the guard stationed at the front door. If the human was already compelled to resist such a tactic, Dominique would retreat. To his surprise, the man didn't hesitate to let him into the marble and chrome lobby.

Dominique found the stairwell and sped up to the thirty-first floor. There, only the hum of traffic in the streets below disturbed the silence. No movement anywhere. Not even a heartbeat. Yet he proceeded with care, tucking his sunglasses away in his jacket, letting his senses expand. The smell of new carpeting and electronics rode the recycled air.

He had seen these dim corridors and common areas before, in Natalia's mind. Retracing her steps, he found his way to the upper floors and a corner conference room with seating for more than a dozen. Three of the walls were made of glass—one to the hallway, two to the night outside. The fourth wall contained what looked like a standard office door. He knew it was anything but. A core of steel lived under that benign wood façade, and anyone trapped inside had no hope of getting out. The door swung open to his touch, revealing a small, dark room. One side was another glass wall, a window facing east, looking out between glittering high rises, to the bay and mountains beyond. Two empty shackles hung high on the opposite wall. In between was nothing but the dry stench of ash.

Revolted, he lifted the back of his hand to his mouth. Vampire ash glittered everywhere, white and charcoal streaks smeared on the wall and the bare concrete floor. Dominique crouched beneath the shackles and traced a finger along the gritty seam where the floor met the wall. It was caked with ash. Aubrey hadn't been the first to meet the sun here.

The anger and grief that gripped him was strong enough to reach Cassidy despite their faded connection. He could feel her rising panic. She didn't want him being there.

He tried to calm them both with a sense of solitude. *No one else is here.*

Still, he sensed her silent demand that he get out of there. He almost heard her voice. And her heartbeat.

No, not almost. He *did* hear a heartbeat, but it wasn't hers.

Dominique stood and spun around in a single supernaturally fast movement.

The other vampire stood in the doorway as if he had been there for minutes instead of a second. A dark gray coat still swayed around him. His hands, covered in fine gloves, were clasped before him. The brim of a rakishly askew fedora shadowed his eyes.

Dominique tasted the air, looking for clues in this blood-drinker's scent as to his approximate age and strength. It reminded him of Serge. Dark and mossy, but not as wet. Older than three centuries then, but far from a millennium.

Esteban. The name came to him from Natalia's memories. Esteban de Santiago. Adilla's enforcer. Silent, brilliant, cunning—and dangerous enough to have surprised Dominique. In his present state anyway, which was far from optimal.

An impulse to flee beat at Dominique from Cassidy. He squashed it.

The man was petite, all but invisible in his neutral clothing, but when he looked up, a predatory gleam lit his dark eyes. "I don't suppose I need to ask who you are?" He sounded bored.

Dominique said nothing, intent on letting this creature reveal himself on his own terms.

"Dominique Marchant, is it?"

Still, he didn't react.

"I see. Well, I thought we might see you here before too long. But...you are not what I expected."

Dominique stifled an annoyed snort. Two years into his rule, and he still heard this on a regular basis. Although, in all fairness, in these casual street clothes and with his helmet hair plastered to his head, he wasn't his idea of a dominant blood-drinker either. To be even more honest, right at this moment, he was *not* the dominant blood-drinker. He had little more strength now than the average youngling.

"A common mistake, Esteban," he said flatly.

The brittle smile did not reach the Spaniard's eyes. "Some fool recently tried to convince us that you are the—what was it?—the root of our species? The 'lord' of us all?"

"Because it is so. Shall I show you?" Dominique held out his hand. His strength wouldn't hold up in a fight, but a re-siring he could manage. Not that he expected to be taken up on that offer.

Esteban scoffed. "So you take me for a fool as well? All I smell here"—he tipped his chin up and made a show of sniffing the air—"is youngling trouble."

The mush in Dominique's brain suddenly coalesced in a chilling realization. He was inside a room in which blood-drinkers were routinely executed—and the only way out was blocked by the individual who did the executing.

This must have shown in his face, for Esteban's smile widened into a grin.

"Adilla swore he would end you if you ever crossed his path."

"Then let him try. It is him I have come to see."

"Oh, well. I'm afraid you just missed him. In his absence, crossing my path is as good as crossing his. So..."

Dominique reached the door the instant the lock caught and latched. The sound of the heavy steel slab slamming home reverberated in the concrete walls and plate-glass window. He tamped down a spike of fear. He wasn't shackled. He'd been in worse traps. This was not a problem.

"You are a fool, Esteban," he called, both hands against the door and mustering all the nonchalance at his command. "If I die, we all die. Including you."

There was a long stretch of silence with a faint undercurrent of Esteban's heart, but then the other blood-drinker seemed to make up his mind, and the heartbeat, too, disappeared.

19

VAMPIRE SAMARITAN

Dominique stepped away from the door, staring at it as though it were a portal to another world. In a way it was—Adilla's world.

Summoning every shred of strength, he landed a massive kick against it. Every bone in his foot shattered on impact while the door itself didn't suffer so much as a dent. He swallowed an agonized scream in a vehement huff of "*Putain!*"

The phone in his pocket buzzed.

"What's going on?" Cassidy demanded the moment he swiped to accept the call.

"I found the place where Aubrey was executed."

"And?"

"And..." He turned around, scanning every square inch of the tiny prison. "I seem to be trapped in it."

"*What?*"

"I am not shackled, and dawn is almost two hours away. There is no cause for panic just yet." Though his gut disagreed. There, panic simmered like a vat of acid.

Frantic rustling sounded on her end. Sheets being tossed and drawers opened. Her voice muffled and garbled as she moved the phone. "...building that Natalia showed you? On Georgia Street?"

"What? Yes."

"Good. I'm coming to get you."

That vat of acid stepped up to a full boil. "No. No, do *not* leave there, and do *not* come here. Never come here. Do you understand? Not even during the day." Compelled humans operating on Adilla's behalf were bound to be in the area at all times, perhaps throughout the entire city. For all he knew, he was being monitored right now. He dared not mention her name or her location or reveal any clues as to her immense importance to him.

"Why? I thought there was no one else there?"

Dominique leaned one forearm against the concrete wall. "I did not exactly trap myself in here."

"Oh my God."

"Promise me you will stay where you are. Please. I will think of something."

"I don't like this." She sounded calmer. "I'll give you an hour. Then I will definitely think of something."

Dominique smiled to himself. His lioness had been well and truly roused. "Just stay there."

After the call disconnected, he paced the periphery of the room. It was little more than a storage closet, a heavily fortified one. He slammed several more kicks and punches at every wall with nothing but more broken bones to show for it. As his wrist knit back together yet again, he stood staring out the window at the traffic flowing far below. This glass he could break, but there were no ledges or handholds visible outside. A direct drop looked like the only option, but a fall from this height could well kill even an immortal, if his head hit the pavement hard enough to shatter. That wasn't a risk he wanted to take, at least not yet.

Half an hour later, Dominique had made small headway on a weak spot in one wall where a large chip of concrete had broken free under his assault. Several more, smaller ones followed, but progress was tediously slow. After every punch or kick, he had to wait for his bones to mend, and the healing interval was growing longer and longer as he exhausted what little strength he had left.

He was waiting to heal again when he heard another heart-beat. This one was slower than Esteban's, but also stronger as it approached in no particular hurry. Dominique didn't move or call out. His own racing heart would betray his presence to the newcomer well enough.

The lock unlatched, and the door swung into the room. A new blood-drinker surveyed him, but instead of Esteban's contempt, this man looked troubled. He was east asian, not tall, but built like a barrel, and possessed a quiet, imposing presence. He wore a long, tan overcoat that was unbuttoned, revealing a standard suit and tie. No hat or gloves. His hooded eyes flickered to the damaged wall before settling on the prisoner.

Dominique rose to his feet and moved toward the door. He was in far poorer shape now than he had been earlier, and this new vampire, judging by his dry scent, was easily twice Esteban's age. Dominique would take no chances about being trapped in here again, though he didn't relish a direct confrontation.

None was forthcoming. The other vampire stepped aside and let him pass. Dominique put the long conference table between them before he stopped. "Thank you."

His rescuer inclined his head and spoke in a distinctive baritone voice. "Just tell me this, young one. What did you do to piss him off?"

"I exist."

"Ah. The usual then."

Dominique shook out his hand to speed the healing process. "The usual?"

"This is the domain of the great Adilla," he said, waving both hands in the air, derision dripping from his tongue. "No vampire survives here without his favor. You wouldn't be the first new arrival to run afoul of him."

"He murdered my emissary." At the other vampire's questioning look, Dominique amended, "My friend."

"So you came running for revenge? Not wise."

"Since you are here, are you acting on his behalf as well, then?"

The broad, gentle face split into a savage grin that made Dominique's hackles rise. "He would love to kill me if he could, but I'm just a little too strong and too clever. I survive to be an eternal thorn in his side." The grin faded. "Fear not. Any foe of Adilla's is a friend of mine, and any victim of his is under my protection."

"Then I am in your debt. *Je vous remercie.*"

"You are lucky is what you are. Adilla and his sycophants left two nights ago for their summer quarters. So when I spotted his goon, Esteban, in the street earlier, I knew something ugly must be happening." He looked Dominique up and down. "Strange that he would stay behind for a mere youngling."

"I am a very big thorn," Dominique said, flashing an equally ferocious grin. In his present condition, he wouldn't even try to explain it. No blood-drinker in their right mind would believe a word of the truth from him right now. "My name is Dominique Marchant."

"Isao Kiyomori," the other vampire offered with a small bow before coming closer. "Put all fantasies of revenge aside and leave this city tonight. Esteban will come for your ashes tomorrow night. If he doesn't find them, he will find you. Am I making myself clear?"

Dominique considered his new ally. Isao smelled of deep woodland, confirming Dominique's estimate of his age. Maybe not an ancient one, but close, and not an entity to trifle with. "I do not have the luxury of seeking revenge, no matter how deserved. Nor do I have a choice about finding Adilla. Can you tell me where he is?"

"I could," Isao said after a moment's thought. "But I won't. I won't be responsible for your death. But understand this, young one. If you stay here, you are on your own. I save those I can, but I'm not carrying a battle to Adilla."

He brushed past Dominique and headed for the exit, but stopped when Dominique said, "Why is that, old man? If you oppose him, surely he has caused you grief?"

Isao didn't respond right away, and Dominique turned to see him paused in the doorway, one hand on the frame as if to steady himself. With quiet vehemence he said, "Adilla has caused me grief without end from the moment he turned me." Glancing over his shoulder, he added, "I cannot destroy him without destroying myself."

Dominique opened his mouth, but Isao was already gone. "I know," he said softly. "I know the feeling."

20

Necessary Evils

When Dominique emerged from his lair in the suite's closet, Cassidy embraced him. Her delicious, lush scent wafted around him as he held her close. Her delicious, lush, *pregnant* scent.

"Finally," she muttered against his shoulder. "The sun takes forever to set around here."

She was dressed to go out, and there were two other unexpected but familiar heartbeats thumping away in the suite's living room.

"How do you feel?" she asked, stepping back to appraise him with a critical eye.

"Restored," he assured her. After the previous night's trials, he had indulged in all the blood he could find until the sun was all but up. That, plus a full day spent at rest rather than pretending to be human, had restored him to the full and terrifying power of the Lord of Night.

"Maybe you can restore us tonight, too," she suggested, one arched brow saying all he could no longer see in her mind.

His teeth—and other parts of him—ached to oblige, but now was not the time. Their ritual was not something he wanted to share with their present company. "*Plus tard.*"

"Yes," she agreed with a sigh. "Definitely later."

Dominique swapped his wrinkled shirt for a fresh one, finger-combed his hair, and followed Cassidy into the living room.

Jackson and Garrett Striker rose from the sofa when they entered. Both their faces were lined with exhaustion, though Garrett's far more so than his nephew's. "Gentlemen. I did not expect you."

"Can't keep me down for long. You know that," Garrett said and smoothed his thinning hair against his skull. A strange discomfort edged his usually feral smile.

The bantering response gave Dominique pause. For all the time the hunters had worked for him, the moments they all occupied the same space could be counted on one hand. Unless he was moving in for a kill, Garrett kept his distance from all things vampire.

Dominique and Cassidy settled into the second sofa. She, too, watched Garrett with suspicion. As did Jackson.

The two hunters sat again. Jackson placed a small, flat case on the table. "You didn't ask for this, but the lab's been busy. I thought you might have a use for them, so I had them couriered today. There are three doses in here."

No need to ask three doses of what. Dominique was glad he survived the last of the suppressant. Now here were three more temptations. Three more opportunities to fight to be human again, fail again, weaken himself again—put himself and Cassidy at risk again.

"*Merci*," he said, but didn't touch the case. It sat like a coiled snake in his awareness as he summarized the events of the previous night for his visitors. Jackson looked grim when he heard about the trap, Garrett thoughtful.

"So they're not even in the city anymore?" Jackson asked.

"Most of them are gone, yes. But Isao tells me that Esteban will come looking for me if he doesn't find my ashes. Probably right about now."

"Does he have any idea where to start looking?" Garrett wondered.

"No. He has a name, nothing more. A name that is not associated with anything here, including this suite. The only way he can find me is if he, or someone he has compelled, sees me."

"Well, he won't know to look for us," Jackson offered. "If we can find him, we can do the usual tag, track, and trap for you."

Dominique searched Jackson's face and found the same sincerity that hummed in his voice. "No. It is not necessary for you to take such a risk." With a glance at Garrett, he added, "Neither of you appears to be at your best right now."

Garrett gave a grim nod. "I'm afraid that's true."

"Shouldn't you be in a hospital? In Germany?" Cassidy wondered, making no effort to veil her contempt.

"Yes, I guess I should be. But I felt I could do more good here."

"As what? Vampire bait?" she fired back.

"You would drag yourself through death's door for the promise of a prestigious kill?" Dominique asked.

Garrett touched his fingertips together. "If that's what you need from me, yes."

Dominique's eyes widened at the earnest declaration, and his jaw dropped a bit at his old foe's next words.

"Though I'll be better at it if I could get some magic juice from you."

Jackson looked at his uncle and sat back on the sofa, withdrawing from the conversation.

Dominique inclined his head. Very softly he said, "Are you asking for my blood?"

"I am." A glance at his nephew, who made a "you're on your own" gesture with one hand. "I already had the little we took from the guy who put me in the hospital. That got me this far, but I'm far from healed."

"*My* blood?" Dominique asked again, incredulous. "The blood of the vampire you tried to burn to death?"

"The irony isn't lost on me, if that's what you mean, but the circumstances have changed. I need to feel useful, and like it or not, the only way I can do that is through you. All I'm asking is that you help me be useful now."

Without taking his eyes off Garrett, Dominique reached over to the side table where glass tumblers rested upside down beside the ice bucket. He opened a gash in his wrist. By the time it sealed again, the glass was half filled with blood. He set it on the table before the hunter, a silent challenge.

Garrett was a sorry excuse for a human being, but he had also served Dominique well, despite his prejudices. He had earned himself a favor.

No one moved when Garrett reached for the glass. "Bottoms up." He stifled a gasp on the first swallow, but continued gulping until the blood was gone. Then he placed the empty tumbler down with exaggerated care, harrumphed several times, and shook his head. Color oozed back into his ashen face. The haze of pain left his eyes, and his heart beat with new vigor. "That has some serious kick to it."

"Are you feeling better now?" Jackson asked, sounding dubious.

Garrett prodded at his left side. "Still a little sore, but I'm good to go." Looking at Dominique, he added, "Thank you."

Dominique made no reply, still mystified by this extraordinary request.

Jackson broke the awkward silence. "So if you don't need us to bag this Esteban character for you, what's the plan for tonight?"

Dominique exchanged a glance with Cassidy, who looked as baffled as he felt. "I need to find Isao. He knows where his sire has gone."

"Hold on," Garrett said, lifting a hand. "His sire? Adilla is your Good Samaritan's *sire*?"

"So he claims."

"Then what, for the love of God, makes you think he'll help us put him down?"

"What makes you think I plan to destroy Adilla?"

"Well, it sure doesn't sound like he wants to play ball with you."

"He is not 'playing ball' because he does not know the rules of my game yet. Nor do I intend to condemn his descendants without very good reason."

"All right then. Isao it is. I say we hit the road, you and I, while we have plenty of night left." He got up and gestured at his nephew. "Jack will stay here and make sure Cassidy is safe."

Jackson blinked. "Wait. What?"

Dominique tilted his head at Garrett. While the man's enthusiasm was commendable, he couldn't imagine spending time alone in his company.

Cassidy's phone chose that moment to ring in the bedroom. She sprang up and rushed to get the call as though having expected it.

"As you can see, I'm in tip-top shape now," Garrett continued. "That's thanks to you, so let me repay you. I've got your back."

"You are no match against the blood-drinkers I have encountered here so far. Even *with* my blood," he added on a pointed note.

In the bedroom, Cassidy was speaking on her phone. He couldn't make out the words of the caller through all the surrounding mayhem, but the tiny voice itself sent a ripple of alarm up the back of his neck. "Stay here with Jackson," he said.

Garrett opened his mouth to argue, but Dominique shot up a hand. "*Assez.* Enough."

He got up and joined Cassidy, who had just disconnected the call. "Was that—?"

"Yes, it was. Your mother."

"Why is she calling you?"

"Because you don't answer your phone during the day. And because she wanted to know where you were." She hesitated. He waited. "So she could get a ride to the right hotel."

The tentative words slapped him in the face. "When?"

"This afternoon." Cassidy shrugged an apology. "She wants to know if you're available yet. She's down the hall."

21

The True Gentleman

Dominique never had a chance.

He knocked on his mother's hotel room door with every intention of sending her away. He didn't have time for her on this trip, nor was she safe here. Heaven help them if a hostile blood-drinker discovered her identity.

The moment she opened the door and planted kisses on his cheeks, a cloud of her beloved orange-spiced, lavender scent closed in and he was five years old again. She explained she had come because he sounded "strange" this morning on the phone, when he had called her from the plane. She was worried.

"I am well. Truly," he promised. "But my time is very limited here." To a little less than nine hours, to be exact, which was all the darkness he would get this night.

"*Ah, non.* I have come so far. And you were busy the entire day. Surely you can make some time for your mother tonight."

"I—"

"We will have a nice dinner at one of the finest restaurants in the city. You, me, and your lovely wife. I so want to get to know her better."

"*Maman,* this is not a good time."

"Words you will regret once I'm gone. Now go on. Get out of those rags and do something with that hair. We have reservations at Bishop's, and I am almost ready to go. I'll come to your room." Again, she kissed his cheeks and gripped his arm. "I have always wanted to see this city. We will have a fantastic time." With that, she closed the door in his face.

Dominique leaned his forehead against the door in silent capitulation. "*Merde.*" Had she always been this bossy? And why was being a blood-drinker—the Lord of Night, no less—no defense against her power over him?

Because she was his mother, of course. He cursed again and returned to his suite.

Garrett whistled softly when Dominique entered. "That's a new look for you."

Jackson looked at him in open-mouthed astonishment. The illusion of a vigorous mortal male he had spun for his mother was still in effect. He didn't dispel it, but he ordered them to dispel themselves—or tried to.

"What do you mean, we're not doing anything tonight?" Jackson asked.

"You two get caught up on your rest. I will search for Isao later on my own."

Cassidy looked at him with a small, knowing smile. "We're going out to dinner, aren't we."

"We are," he said darkly.

"I thought as much." She smoothed her blouse, the front of her skirt, brushed back a stray hair. Ready to go.

"Dinner?" Jackson wondered.

"You two. Out," Dominique snapped, and vanished into the bedroom to make himself presentable as ordered.

He heard his mother's voice again the moment the door opened to let out the hunters. "Oh, and who are you?"

They introduced themselves.

"No, no, no," Dominique chanted under his breath as he brushed his hair into submission.

"You are the same Jackson who is brother to Samantha? She is such a lovely young woman."

"That's me, yes."

"They were just leaving, *Maman*," he said, emerging from the bedroom.

Garrett's face lit up. "This beautiful lady is your *mother*?" Before Dominique could say anything, Garrett lifted her fingers to his lips. "It is such an honor to meet you, *madame*."

"Oh." Francesca looked surprised, but not displeased. "*Enchanté.*"

"My nephew and I work closely with your son and have for many years."

"In that case, you must join us for dinner. I want to hear all about your work."

Dominique shook his head. "*Non.*"

"It would be our pleasure. Wouldn't it, Jack?"

"What? Oh. Yes, of course."

Cassidy turned away to smother a grin. "Checkmate, my love," she said under her breath.

And so it was. Francesca ruled the evening. Or at least she did after he won his one and only argument with her, that being the question of where they would eat. He drew a firm line at parading his entire human entourage across a city where a hostile blood-drinker was looking for him.

Instead of ride-sharing it to Bishop's, they walked into Five Sails, one of the hotel's on-site restaurants. He allowed himself a moment's compulsion to get them seated right away despite having no reservations. As they were led to a table with a spectacular view of the night-black bay surrounded by a shimmering necklace of light, he scanned the area. He saw no blood-drinkers, nor humans who appeared to recognize him. Still, he kept his senses keyed for any signs of supernatural danger.

It was a human irritant, however, that continued to scratch at his nerves. Together with Cassidy and Jackson, he watched Garrett morph into an unlikely Prince Charming as he offered Francesca his arm, regaled her with compliments, and practiced his limited French on her.

"It is so refreshing to meet a true gentleman outside of France," Francesca told him.

"We're not complete heathens in the colonies," Garrett assured and took the seat beside her. "Especially not around a woman as stunning as yourself."

Dominique wrestled with the urge to drag Garrett away by the throat. The man was a monster in human guise who killed with abandon and had tortured him to within an inch of his immortal life. He was also a soldier, a warrior, and a hunter. And he had no business even *knowing* a woman like Francesca, much less speak to her like this.

The wine had been poured and the first course served by the time Dominique could see past the haze of fury far enough to glimpse what was really happening here. Though he didn't quite trust it until Francesca asked for the third time, "But what is it you do for my son's firm?"

The other times she inquired, Garrett delivered a vague answer with a bright smile and turned the conversation to France or Saint Barthélemy. "Whatever is necessary," he said now. "But as I was saying—"

"Jackson?" Francesca prompted. "What do you do?"

Jackson put his fork down and finished chewing a mouthful of salad. "Security, ma'am. We do security."

"Oh." Her lipsticked mouth became as round as her eyes. "Oh, I see. This is...secret work, *non*?"

"Very," Jackson confirmed.

"Basically, we have your son's back," Garrett added. He picked up his wine and gestured at Dominique with it. "No matter what sort of pickle he gets himself into, no matter what we need to do to get him out of it. Right, Nick?"

Dominique held the intense look that said he was in one of those pickles right now. "Apparently so."

Francesca placed her hand on Garrett's forearm, where it rested on the table. "Then you have my undying gratitude."

"What *is* going on with him?" Cassidy muttered into her water glass.

A mystery, Dominique decided. One he didn't know what to do with right now, except to be reluctantly grateful for.

"My daughter-in-law is under your protection, too?" Francesca inquired.

"Your—?" Jackson started.

Garrett's mind shifted more quickly. "Yes. Cassidy's safety is a top priority with us."

Cassidy groaned under her breath, no doubt recalling getting shot by this man. On purpose.

"I am so glad to know this." Francesca beamed at Cassidy, who seemed to drag a smile to her face by its scruff.

For two hours Dominique spun illusions of enjoying his nonexistent meal and watched Garrett steer Francesca around countless conversational land mines. She was stronger and more stubborn than Dominique remembered, and he wondered if the trauma of losing her husband and children had sparked this change. If so, she had, in a way, been forged by the same dark fire that had consumed him. She even appeared to find solace in the same against-all-odds hope and love that sustained her son. Dominique's heart pinched at the thought.

As the meal progressed, Cassidy touched less and less of her food, becoming increasingly quiet. By the time dessert was served, she swayed in her seat, a glassy sheen in her eyes. "Migraine," she whispered when she saw him studying her gray pallor.

Dominique requested the check and made their excuses the moment Garrett snatched it away and dropped his card on it. The hunters concurred. Francesca's disappointment at cutting the evening short was palpable, but she could not sway their united front.

Back in their suite, Cassidy beelined for the bathroom and lost what little she had eaten. Then she sprawled on the bed with a cold washcloth on her brow. "This whole thing is making my head explode," she groaned. "Literally."

Dominique didn't doubt it. There was also no doubt that there would be no romance tonight. In fact, when he sat beside her, she shooed him away. "Don't waste your night playing nursemaid. Go find this Isao guy."

He kissed her cheek and went to change into his leathers.

Where to begin the search? There had been no trace of Isao in Natalia's memories, much less his whereabouts. Nor had she been with the colony long enough to be familiar with their summer habits. Though Dominique had a good idea what he would do if he lived at this latitude and found his nights growing shorter and shorter—move south. Way south.

Garrett lay in wait for him in the hallway when Dominique emerged. "I'm coming with you."

"You are not." Dominique laced his voice with enough compulsion to convey the warning. Garrett was trained to resist it up to a point.

"You sound adamant," the old hunter observed, grim-faced, hands on his hips.

Dominique tilted his head in a gesture of astonishment.

"Okay, fine. But you have my number if you get into another pickle. Also, for what it's worth, I can see where you get your—well, everything. Your mother is quite a lady."

He stared. "Garrett Striker. That is not truly a compliment I hear, is it?"

The man worked his jaw as though trying to recall the words, but then capitulated with a shrug. "Take it any way you want, but know that it'll be my pleasure to keep an eye on her. For security," he added quickly.

Dominique arched a brow. "And *only* that." He leaned forward, lowering his voice. "Because she is a lady, but I know you are no gentleman."

He vanished before Garrett could even think about a reply.

22

LOST AND FOUND

D ominique cursed to himself. Hours of riding the borrowed Ducati through the downtown core and far into the city's outlying areas, and he had nothing to show for all his prowling. Not only was Vancouver a sprawling modern metropolis, it was also bereft of vampires. At least any that conveniently walked on the streets, which was the only realistic place he could search for them.

No bright vampire auras drifted in the sea of lights, nothing that stood out in the sensory cacophony. Nor was there any hint of blood-drinker in the air streaming past his nose, which was full of exhaust fumes and dumpster rot spiced with cannabis and brine. As for the dark web, only a handful of insubstantial entities drifted in his awareness, impossible to pin down without Cassidy's help.

He tensed in his seat while waiting for a light to go green at the bottom of a skyscraper canyon. With her condition being what it was—and a sense of wonder brought him up short every time he thought of it—he would have to learn to reach into that void without her human sensibilities to guide him. He was reasonably sure his bite wouldn't harm the baby, but giving her his blood for this deeper connection was something else again.

A misty rain had set in, coating his face through the open visor and trickling a chilly finger into the collar of his jacket, making him hunch his shoulders with more than just discouragement. All around, the city swelled with activity, bracing for the coming day. His window of opportunity was closing fast. Perhaps his time would be better spent discussing the situation with Cassidy?

Dominique looked around to find his bearings in relation to the hotel, when a black Ford Mustang cruised past with a blazing white aura at the wheel. He caught sight of her just as she saw him. Dark hair, warm makeup, lips parting in surprise. She didn't stop. Opening the throttle, he bolted after her, heedless of lights and honks and screeching breaks.

The Mustang wove through traffic, tires hissing on the wet asphalt, keeping just this side of the law. Dominique had no trouble staying with it while he considered the driver's identity. According to Isao, no vampires beside him survived in this city without Adilla's favor, but all of Adilla's colony, except perhaps for Esteban, had supposedly left the city. This made her either a friend of Isao's, a tool of Esteban's, or a clueless new arrival. Regardless, Dominique needed to know, and he needed to know it before the sun came up—even if that meant pursuing her straight into her lair.

He was torn between hoping she would lead him to Isao or lure him to Adilla. He would take either, but as she cruised along Highway 1, heading east and south for the better part of an hour, he hoped for the latter. If he could end this tonight and go home, he would.

By the time they reached Surrey, the ocean tang was a distant memory. The streets became narrower as they cut through commercial and residential neighborhoods and finally lost themselves in an industrial district dominated by mills, truck depots, and junkyards. With enough speed to send dirt and gravel flying, the Mustang turned into a deserted lot. What appeared to be a mid-sized warehouse waited there, windowless and shuttered, its loading docks empty.

Dominique caught her split-second glance in his direction as she got out of her car. Then the wet shadows swallowed an indistinct smear of motion as she disappeared. The sole visible door emitted a groaning squeal and fell shut behind her.

Through the veil of rain, Dominique couldn't see the sky brightening in the east, but he could feel the coming sun anyway. There was barely enough time to return to the hotel, but he had come too far to let this opportunity go now. He sensed no other blood-drinkers. Only the one he had pursued here, and who might or might not have the answers he needed.

He parked the bike, leaving it running, tossed the helmet aside and sped after her. If she hesitated so much as a second to volunteer those answers, he would rip them out of her head.

He got as far as the door.

The stale air that wafted out carried the stink of rancid blood and burned flesh. Every hair on his body lifted in silent alarm. Somewhere in the building's depths, another door clicked shut, taking her heartbeat with it. Hiding. But from what? The blood-drinker she had obviously led here? Why?

Dominique stepped back out into the rain and let the door close on a plaintive squeak. Answers or not, if he walked into another trap, there would be no hope for him this time.

Leaving the mystery of the warehouse where he found it, he made his way back to the hotel with ten minutes to spare—and a plan.

23

Less Than Your Best

Shortly after sunset, Jackson hobbled down the hall, dreading the moment he would have to knock on Dominique's door and report on this complete disaster of a day. This morning, it had been Dominique who had startled Jackson and Garrett out of bed with insistent pounding on their door. Before vanishing, he gave them an address in Surrey and terse instructions on what to do there.

Getting blown up had not been part of the plan.

By now, with the shock and adrenaline long gone, everything hurt. Between the bruises, cracked ribs, swollen and unreliable knee, and the angry red road rash that ran up the left side of his body and continued onto his face, Jackson's almost twenty-seven-year-old body had fast-forwarded to ninety-seven.

And explaining any of this to Dominique, of all people, was going to rankle.

The Lord of Night himself answered the door, rumpled and mussed from his rest. His hazel eyes widened as he looked Jackson up and down, taking in the bandages and stiff posture. "Come in, *chèr*. Sit."

When Jackson took a limping step toward the nearest chair, Dominique compounded his awkwardness by rushing to grab it and turn it so Jackson could drop into it with a minimum of effort.

Cassidy emerged from the bedroom and stopped short. "Oh my God. Jackson. That looks way worse than the few scratches and bruises you mentioned."

He gave a tight smile. The muscles in his face also hurt. He'd been popping ibuprofen like candy, the strongest thing he would take. His head needed to remain clear no matter how messed up the rest of him was. "I'll manage." He wiggled the finger stumps on his right hand. "I've been through worse. Remember?"

"*Mon Dieu*," Dominique murmured and pulled up another chair so he could sit facing Jackson. Cassidy settled into the sofa nearby, worry etched on her face.

The TV was on low, tuned to a local station and displaying an aerial view of a warehouse in flames. A banner along the bottom proclaimed: "Human Remains Found in Surrey Fire." Knowing their fuck-up would be widely reported, he had called Cassidy to let her know he and Garrett had walked away—more or less—but spared her every grim detail.

"Looks like you saw how our morning went down."

Dominique leaned his elbows on his thighs and clasped his hands. All calm business. "What happened?"

"You were right. It was a trap. One that was rigged to take out whoever might come to rescue anyone caught in it. And...I'm the one who tripped it," he finished. God, karma was a bitch.

The ghost of amused irony flickered across Dominique's face, but thankfully, he didn't mention the traps Jackson had set for him in the past. He still wasn't sure how it happened, but somehow the most powerful vampire on earth had become his closest friend. Dominique had been inside his head and knew him completely—scars, warts, demons, and all—and not only accepted him, but forgave him. His mind still boggled whenever he thought of it.

"Your uncle triggered the explosion?" Dominique prompted.

Jackson nodded. "Yes. He found one bomb and thought he disarmed it, but there was a backup firing mechanism. Thanks to that blood you gave him, he heard it trip a split second before all hell broke loose. Grabbed me and ran at pseudo-vamp speed to get us both out. The shock wave caught us and kicked our asses, though." Time had slowed to a crawl in that silence where the world had flipped and rushed past until the ground came up to wallop them, sending them bouncing and sliding like tossed rag dolls.

"He took the brunt of the impact, and, damn, he was a mess. Broken bones, split open his head, bled all over the place. But, again, with your blood, he healed up quick enough. Or so we thought. We got out of there before anyone showed up to ask questions, and we were almost back in the city when he came down with a massive headache and lost all sense of balance. I took him to the Vancouver General ER where we gave them a story about a random accident." He tried to shrug, and winced. "They're saying he has a concussion and want to keep him overnight for observation."

"*Merde.*"

"Right. He's becoming a regular at medical facilities the world over."

"Vampire blood doesn't heal concussions?" Cassidy wondered.

"He said he felt the 'magic juice' drain out of him in a hurry. Is that possible?"

"The healing power of the blood he consumed could well have been depleted by his injuries," Dominique said, thoughtful. "Who are the 'remains' the authorities claim to have found in the fire?"

"Ah, those. Well, they were remains already when we found them." He braced himself, then plunged in. "There was a furnace full of charred bones, and walk-in coolers that looked like people had been forced to stay in them. Some bloody tools, but nothing fresh. There was other stuff there, too. Hooks and chains, saws..." He broke off when he saw Cassidy put the back of her hand to her mouth. She looked almost as pale as

Dominique. "Well, it was a shop of horrors. Whatever the fire didn't destroy should have investigators speculating for years."

Cassidy tucked her legs underneath her, making herself smaller. "They have an entire city full of people to hunt and they don't need to kill. Why would they do something like this?"

"Convenience," Dominique said, grim-faced. "I suspect they bottled the blood. After it was suitably seasoned with fear."

Cassidy closed her eyes.

Jackson's stomach clenched. "You're putting a stop to that, right?"

"I intend to. I will find Isao tonight and track down this Adilla. He will change his ways or pay the price."

"What can I do?"

Dominique cocked one brow. "Not much, it appears."

"My body's banged up, but my head's in the game. I promise you."

"Hmm. You are useless like this." Getting up with the grace of a prowling panther, Dominique retrieved a glass from the tray, and, as he had the night before, sliced open his own vein to fill it.

"I—I really don't—" Jackson cleared his throat and tried again. "I'm not asking for blood." But his gaze was riveted to the crimson stream as he remembered the taste of the single drop that had turned his world upside down.

Dominique licked his wrist clean and presented the blood to Jackson. "You don't need to ask, *mon ami*." When Jackson hesitated, he added, "I am not asking you to take it. I am telling you. I depend on you with my life and the lives of my loved ones. I will not tolerate you being less than your best."

Jackson took the glass.

It was as he remembered—only worse. Like swallowing lightning. Heat hit his belly and exploded outward from there, melting away every ache and pain. He gasped and sputtered as his senses sharpened to an impossible degree. Fuck, he could even hear Dominique's heartbeat, all calm and distinct. Cassidy sounded like a sloshing mess in comparison. His own felt like it was attempting a prison break out of his ribcage.

"Oh God," he exclaimed. "How do you deal with this?"

A poignant smile was Dominique's only response. "Better?"

Jackson put the glass down and rolled his shoulders. Not a twinge or pinch or sting anywhere. He peeled off the bandage on the side of his face and felt the smooth new skin beneath. His whole body still tingled, still healed. His crazed senses dialed back several notches as the blood spent its power on fixing him. "Better." On a more grudging note, he added, "Thank you."

Dominique studied him, his eyes darkening. "Will you accept another gift?"

"Gift? What kind of gift?" Jackson tried to sound casual, though he was instantly wary.

"Truly a gift. For your birthday, if you will. It is soon, *non*?"

"Day after tomorrow." He straightened. "All right. Sure."

Instead of the wrapped package Jackson half-expected to appear out of thin air, Dominique extended his hand. "Do you trust me?"

A nervous snort escaped him. "Do you really still need to ask that?"

"Then give me your hand."

Not just his hand, he realized. More like the vein in the wrist attached to that hand. Dominique was asking for his blood again. Still more amazing was that Jackson wasn't about to bolt from the room—or say no. Not anymore. He held still as those uncanny teeth pricked his skin, tried not to imagine a supernatural awareness flowing through his brain, and definitely refused to think about any dreams he had after the last time Dominique had gotten his teeth into him.

It lasted only seconds before the vampire withdrew and sealed the punctures with a swipe of his tongue. His eyes glowed with golden light. Jackson fell into them without resistance, and he never even flinched when Dominique spoke, his voice seeming to resonate from another reality.

"From this moment on, Jackson Striker, no blood-drinker, no matter how strong, can wield power over you. No compulsion will ever touch you again without your permission. Your mind is now—and always will be—free."

<h1 style="text-align:center">24</h1>

<h1 style="text-align:center">Lock and Key</h1>

Dominique closed the door behind Jackson and turned back to Cassidy, tucked into the sofa's corner. She played with a strand of her loose hair as she watched him.

"That is quite the birthday gift," she mused.

"It is a weapon against his greatest fear." Jackson's spirit felt less battered now than the last time he had touched it. Stronger, too, but still unsettled. "Also, he might truly need it before we are done here."

She unfolded her legs and sighed. "Well, if that man wasn't half in love with you before, I suspect he is now."

"More than half," Dominique said, coming closer and making no effort to hide his pleased smile. Jackson's deepening trust and friendship was like a fine wine to his blood-drinker soul.

Cassidy raised a quizzical brow. "Oh? Should I be jealous?"

He held out his hand to her. "You know better." If Jackson's affection was the wine he enjoyed sipping, Cassidy's love was the emotional banquet that sustained him.

She let him pull her to her bare feet. "Prove it."

"*Avec plaisir*," he purred and drew her close, kissing her deep and slow until she melted against him with a languid moan, her question thoroughly answered.

Earlier tonight, she had come into his arms, exhausted, the moment he awoke in the back of the closet. "What is it, *mon coeur*?" he asked.

"I need you. I just need you." And with that, she had undone him in ways no one else ever could.

Now he continued to hold her, his fingers moving on her back, in her soft hair, asking a question without words or thought. She replied by taking his hand and leading him into the bedroom. She had enough of waiting and delays and excuses. As did he.

He didn't hesitate when she took him into her arms, his teeth finding their mark a second later. For a beat or two, reality was suspended as her intoxicating blood swept him away into mindless bliss. Then, her presence swelled in his awareness, warm as a tropical sunrise, calling him back from the brink and creating the unique entity that was forged of them both.

The lovemaking that followed was marked by a sharp new edge. Her roiling hormones saw to that, as did his growing desperation, and the danger that hung over them both. Together, it left them powerless with need—for each other, for release, for life.

In the aftermath, as they lay in a boneless sprawl, their memories flowed together like the confluence of two rivers, one light, the other dark. Bit by bit, they examined them. She experienced his pain and dread at becoming trapped in the execution chamber. He felt her acute anxiety at Jackson's news of the explosion.

Too close. All of it too close.

You need help, she thought, and studied his memories of Isao. *I like him. There's something steadfast about him. Like Aubrey.*

Another long moment drifted past. She waited. He hesitated.

As Serge had long ago prophesied, she was the key that unlocked his full power. But this required a taste of his blood to forge a bond beyond mere telepathy. Only then could she see the dark web and guide him to the minds of blood-drinkers not yet sired to him. It was how they had found Aubrey and so many others. It was how she now wanted to help him find Isao.

What about the child? Dominique wondered. Nothing would ever be more important than that.

She's part of you and will be fine. I know she will.

He propped himself up on one elbow and gazed down at her. "She?"

"I have a feeling," she said, smiling. The green tendril in her aura drifted around her neck, as though examining the place where his teeth had been. When he traced its path across her skin, it followed his fingertip, trailing a sparkling luminescent shimmer up the side of her face and down her freckled nose. Cassidy's smile grew into a grin. "See?"

"I like your feelings, *chérie.*"

She brushed the hair out of his face and stroked her thumb over his lower lip. "Let me help you."

For several more seconds, he watched the green wisp coil between them. Then he ran his tongue over one sharp canine. Blood pooled in his mouth when he kissed her again, letting her take it from him. She stifled a powerful gasp and gripped his shoulders hard, pulling him close. The hum of thousands of blood-drinker minds intensified as he saw the dark web through her heart. The ghosts came into focus, a few of them nearby. It was the brightest and oldest among these that he reached for.

Isao.

The other blood-drinker's shock reverberated through their joint mind. In a condo high up a building, only a few blocks away, Isao sprang up from his meditations with a fierce shout and snatched up two lethally sharp samurai swords not unlike Dominique's own. He crouched low, holding the blades pointed in two different directions, and growled.

Cassidy laughed out loud, and Dominique chuckled. He could not have found a more fitting ally.

Put those away, he told his new friend. *You won't need them to speak with me.*

25

ISAO KIYOMORI

For a meeting place, Isao selected Vancouver's Stanley Park, a vast, gently tamed temperate rain forest that formed the calm nucleus of the vibrant city. During the day, it bustled with tourists and locals alike. At this hour, before midnight and doused in a cold, soft rain, vagrants and vampires took their place.

Dominique covered the distance between the park and hotel on foot. As he reached the first interior trails, his phone sounded a polite beep from his back pocket. He paused long enough to see who it was, and on seeing Garrett Striker's name, paused some more. Garrett never contacted him if there wasn't a legitimate emergency brewing, but he was confined to a hospital and unlikely to need anything that his nephew couldn't provide. Dominique swiped to ignore.

Shielding himself from all eyes and ears, he continued to speed along, following the helpful signs to a large clearing near the far end of the park, a picnic area judging by the amenities. The field was empty except for a single figure in the corner farthest from the road. The blood-drinker aura was a beacon in the mist, inviting all comers—who would be greeted by the long, slender swords he held at the ready. Three others loitered in the surrounding woods. Their auras shimmered far enough away to act as a warning, but not a threat. The Lord of Night tried not to take offense. Isao didn't survive this long against powerful, vengeful vampires like Esteban and Adilla without constant vigilance.

Dominique stopped at the tree line and allowed himself to be seen—just when his phone chirped. Alerted by the sound, Isao spun in his direction only to see Dominique vanish once more when he recast the illusion and pulled out the offending device.

Need to see you. Urgent, read the text message. Garrett.

"*Merde.*" Now what? No matter. This would have to wait.

Dominique silenced the phone and approached Isao. With lightning swiftness, he relieved him of the two swords before allowing himself to become visible again. "I told you. You won't need these."

Isao staggered back several steps, but to his credit, did not protest or capitulate. He stared at Dominique, his hands empty.

Dominique tested the weapons, a long *katana* and shorter *wakizashi*. They were of exquisite workmanship, their balance in his hands flawless. Ivory art adorned the hilts, and the steel blades themselves were honed to edges so fine, those they struck down would never feel them. He took a few steps back, then worked the swords, letting them fly around his wrists, between his hands, and behind his back with millimeter precision. The cold steel hummed a song of violence and, he thought, honor.

Isao's expression was carefully blank, though his natural woody scent betrayed more than a hint of apprehension.

Dominique handed back the swords, hilt first. "*Magnifique.*"

Isao made a small, stiff bow and returned the weapons to the scabbards strapped to his waist beneath his trench coat. Dominique had made his point. Between his ability to vanish and his skill at wielding the swords, he could have cut Isao down with ease before he even knew what was happening.

"Are these from the age of your birth?"

"Thirteenth-century Japan," Isao replied brusquely. "A glorious age for the samurai."

"You are...a samurai?" Dominique couldn't hide his awe.

A curt nod.

"I am a fan."

"You know a little of the sword, I suppose," Isao allowed.

Dominique couldn't help himself. "Will you teach me more?"

Isao studied him, his face still inscrutable. "There is more to you than your youngling scent betrays."

"A little."

"And yet—" a small frown formed on his broad brow "—Esteban could trap you."

"I was not at my best that night."

"I see." Isao sidled deeper into the dark corners of the field. Dominique didn't move. "Does that happen often? You not being at your best?"

"It happens when I...do not get enough rest."

Isao cast him an uncertain look over his shoulder.

"Which is rare," Dominique assured and changed the subject. "Have you heard of the fire in Surrey today?"

Isao turned all the way back to Dominique, facing him from a good twenty feet away. "You know that place?"

"I have seen it. It belongs to Adilla?"

"Yes."

"What did he use it for?"

Another pause. "It's called the 'factory' and it was one of several. They process blood there." He moved back toward Dominique, his long coat swaying around him. "They find the lonely and destitute and compel them to tell whatever few people who may care that they are leaving the city for good. Then they report to one of these places where they are prepared, drained, and bottled."

"Fiendish," Dominique murmured, surprised by this clever, well-organized system of making large numbers disappear.

"What was your business there, young one?"

"I followed a blood-drinker, but I let her go when she disappeared inside."

"Wise decision. She likely was one of Esteban's soldiers. Her purpose was likely to lure you into another trap and finish you."

"Not just me. You, too. It was wired to explode if anyone tried to open the trap from the outside."

"That, regrettably, sounds like Esteban. He must have caught my scent in the office." A new suspicion sharpened his features. "How would you know this and survive?"

"I sent my human emissaries to investigate. They barely escaped." And one was being a literal pain in the ass. His phone vibrated against his buttocks, probably with another text from Garrett.

"Slaves," Isao said with a derisive snort.

Dominique made a small, ironic smile but didn't argue. There was no point explaining the Strikers right now, but he liked this man and his moral compass. So did Cassidy, whose presence lingered in his mind like a banked ember. He stuffed his hands into the front pockets of his jeans and did his best to look as non-threatening as possible, for he knew Isao was about to reach another conclusion.

"So much power in one so young. Who sired you?"

And there it was.

"The strongest of our kind." He took a step toward Isao. "A very ancient one who was weary of the dark. But instead of condemning his kingdom to end with him, he chose me as his heir. He no longer exists, but his essence and power do—in me."

Dominique could almost see the wheels turning behind Isao's narrowed eyes. It was a preposterous story, but it was also the only plausible explanation for the things Isao had seen Dominique do. "Then tell me his name," he whispered. "Tell me the name of the one who made you."

The smile turned brittle on Dominique's lips. "Kambyses."

No reaction from Isao. Or perhaps shock.

"You know the name?"

Isao nodded. "I have seen him in my sire's mind. The Lord of Night." The reverence in his voice bordered on fear.

Dominique said nothing as he let Isao absorb the implications.

"You're not here just to avenge a friend, are you?"

"No." His back pocket vibrated again. Damn that man. "Aubrey traveled the world on my behalf. He spread the word about me and the new way of things."

"Indeed. And what might this new way be?"

Dominique let his vampire rise and his pupils dilate. "No more feeding on terror. No more killing. We feed with compassion and in love."

Again, Isao seemed taken aback, this time by the glow in Dominique's eyes. Then he chuckled, a warm rumbling sound emanating from his barrel chest. "If that is what he told Adilla, I can see why he ended as he did. Adilla tolerates no authority but his own." He sobered before continuing, "He feeds on the worship of his followers. By the time they discover the deadly nature of his mercurial temper, it's too late. Any who leave, or even waver in their loyalties, are hunted down and destroyed."

"Except you?"

"I know him too well, I'm too old, and I have my swords. He can't harm me or those I protect. Though his pet, Esteban, continues to delude himself into believing he can. I have killed a dozen of his soldiers this past year alone." He paused. "Make no mistake. No one deserves my sword more than Adilla. But as my sire, he is safe from my wrath. He knows that when it comes to it, I will fight to protect his miserable hide." An unmistakable warning slid beneath the words.

Dominique's mouth twisted into a wry line as he thought of his own, far more volatile battles with Kambyses. "I have no intention of destroying one so old. I do not kill without good reason." Never mind that only days ago, Aubrey's horrific death qualified as such a reason. Things had become complicated since then and were getting more so by the moment.

"Oh, he will give you that. It's his way."

"Then I must seduce him first." He paused, lowering his voice. "I will find him, Isao, with or without your help. But I would prefer you as my ally."

Isao's shoulders squared. "Do you intend to seduce me as well, then?"

"I already have." As the words left his tongue, he cast an illusion over the proud samurai. The sky over their heads appeared to brighten. Within seconds, it turned from hazy black to velvet violet to resonant blue. The rain dissipated, replaced by a warm wind. Isao whirled around, face upturned, gaping. In the east, the molten edge of the sun crested the mountains in an explosion of light and warmth.

It was the sunrise Dominique imagined he would see here if he used one of the suppressant doses, assuming he could remember enough to cherish it. To Isao, however, the illusion was real—the first sunrise in centuries of darkness. Stunned, the samurai fell to his knees.

Dominique crouched before him and let the fantasy fade. As the night thickened again, the other blood-drinker looked at him, unguarded wonder in his face. "You would give me back the sun?"

"That I cannot do," Dominique said with genuine regret. "What I can do is free you from the lonely terror of our kind that was Kambyses's essence. I can give you peace. And I can give you love."

As he explained the re-siring process, Isao, still seated on his folded legs in the wet grass, listened intently and then thought with care when Dominique asked, "Will you allow this?"

The samurai was bright enough to understand that the question was one of courtesy only. His nod of agreement couldn't be described as enthusiastic, but at least it didn't feel resigned either.

Isao formally submitted by exposing his jugular. The Lord of Night accepted without hesitation.

Over eight hundred years of memories met him in the blood, rich with experience, tradition, and passion. Dominique dove into the centuries as though diving into an ocean, seeking Adilla. Adilla who had stolen Isao's life. Adilla who brooked no competition...

The flash of agony made Dominique jerk back. It came with the memory of a woman. Her smile was sweet, and her obsidian eyes glistened with gut-wrenching emotion in her blood-drinker pale face. Then her face tumbled away along with her head, disappearing in the tangled cloud of her long, black hair. Adilla stood over her body, her blood dripping from his sword. "You are mine, Isao," he said. "Mine alone."

"It was then that I left him," Isao whispered. *I made her. I loved her. She was everything to me, which was intolerable to him.*

Dominique's hand shook as he wiped his mouth. Would that have been his tale as well if he had turned Cassidy the way Kambyses almost forced him to do? How long would she have survived around the ancient madman? His heart broke for his new friend.

Isao's contempt for Adilla was boundless, and he held little hope for Dominique's plans to "seduce" Adilla into changing anything. Mostly he feared not for his own life should his sire perish, but for the lives of his younglings, his eternal companions. For their sake, he wasn't eager to show Dominique where to find Adilla. But given a choice between helping the new Lord of Night persuade Adilla to his cause and maybe dying, or refusing him right now and certainly dying, the former was the better bet. The more honorable way.

The doubt and anguish lay heavy on Dominique. He wanted to give Isao more than just his blood, more than just an abating of the lust for terror. He wanted to give him certainty.

Which is why, instead of cutting his palm to draw the blood that would complete Isao's re-siring, he embraced him and offered him his vein—and his mind.

26

The Fear of Death

An hour later, Dominique would have much preferred to spend the rest of the night ensconced in some dark corner of an atmospheric bar, enjoying deep conversation with his newest convert. Instead, he rode the Ducati through the biting wet chill and cursed under his breath every block of the way.

Isao had taken more blood than was necessary. Dominique didn't stop him. Neither did he stop him from riffling through his memories to learn what he needed to know of how Dominique came to be the Lord of Night. But he concealed those things he was not ready to share with another blood-drinker, regardless how dear: the suppressant, Cassidy's condition, his mortal family.

Garrett Striker, however, refused to be concealed.

The moment Dominique's phone buzzed in his pocket with an incoming call, he thought of the murderous old bastard and revealed his unorthodox relationship with the vampire hunters to Isao. The samurai's eyes widened, the new light in them as intense as red-hot steel.

"*Merde!* That man," Dominique fumed and yanked the phone from his pocket to catch the call before it dropped into voice mail. "*What* do you want?"

"I need to talk to you."

"Then talk to me."

"In person. Privately."

"I am busy."

"And I'm asking you to delay lording it over whoever for one lousy hour to come see the guy who almost died for you today. No, actually I'm not asking. I'm *begging* you. There. Happy now?"

The outburst was so out of character for the Garrett Striker Dominique knew—and loathed—that it gave him serious pause.

Perhaps he has a point, Isao offered through the temporary two-way link they had forged.

Dominique closed his eyes. True, the man had almost lost his life today while in service to him. Though one question took precedence. *Will I find Adilla this night?*

Not tonight. Isao showed him where Adilla could be found, and it was nowhere anyone would reach before sunrise.

"Fine," Dominique snapped. "I will be there within the hour."

He sensed Isao's mind already buzzing with questions from his younglings, who kept to the surrounding woods. His new friend would be busy for a while re-siring them and communicating all he had learned. "You will hear from me soon. Certainly before I seek Adilla. That, I promise you."

At Vancouver General, Dominique remained invisible as he parked the bike, slipped into the hospital's antiseptic miasma, and made his way to Garrett's room in no particular hurry. He was fairly sure he knew what the man would want from him, but how he asked for it left him baffled.

Even at this hour, the hospital was wide awake, with nurses making their rounds, dispensing medication, and providing assistance. One was leaving Garrett's room when Dominique arrived there. He slipped in before the door swung shut in her wake.

Strange how frail the fearsome hunter looked lying under the thin blankets, as though he had shrunk inside his skin and aged twenty years since the previous night. His slightly jowly face was gray with stubble, and his salt-and-pepper hair, usually so tidy, was in disarray. He lay staring at the window; though whatever he saw, the city gleaming beyond the rain-streaked pane probably wasn't it.

An empty plastic cup sat on the stand beside the bed. Without moving it, Dominique cut his wrist and deposited an inch of blood. It was the distinctive odor of this that the patient noticed before he ever saw Dominique, who had by then retreated to the visitor chair. "Is that what you want?"

"Dominique." Garrett ran a self-conscious hand over his hair and squared his shoulders. The melancholy of seconds ago evaporated. "I was hoping we had moved beyond these games."

"Habit, old man."

"You look drenched."

"Probably because it is raining."

"Yeah, it's wet here. And cold. They haven't been too generous with the blankets for this Florida boy." His fingers grabbed at the edge of said blanket.

Dominique waited.

"I guess that doesn't bother you, does it? Weather?"

"Surely you did not summon me away from my 'lording' business to discuss the weather."

"No. I didn't." Garrett struggled into a more upright position. When he glanced at the blood, his mouth worked as though already tasting it. He took the cup and held it in both hands. Some of the bravado ebbed out of his steely eyes. "Thank you for this, but...this won't fix what's really wrong with me."

"Which is a long list indeed," Dominique said dryly.

"Wiseass." He put the cup to his lips and knocked back the contents like a shot of crimson liquor. With eyes scrunched, he took several fortifying breaths. Dominique watched a silver sparkle build in the dark-gray aura.

"Well. That cleared a few things up," Garrett said and lay back into the pillows with a confident control over his limbs he didn't have only a minute ago. "For now."

Again, Dominique waited.

Garrett didn't look at him. "I'm dying, Nick," he began and swallowed hard. "I don't mean in the sense of 'we all die'—well, all of us mortals, anyway." He put the empty cup back on the table. "I'm sick. Really goddamned fucking sick. The doctors in Germany diagnosed me. I was hoping your blood would cure it, but..." He glanced at him. "These fine Canadian docs agree with their German colleagues. I've got a year. Probably less."

Dominique didn't quite know what to make of this revelation—or the maelstrom of mixed feelings running through him. He had hated this man and wished him dead. Yet he relied on him, too. Despite everything, a twisted honor dwelled in Garrett's blood-thirsty little soul. "What are they saying is wrong with you?"

"Chondrosarcoma. A fancy name for 'you're screwed.' Bone cancer. I've had pains for a while now, deep nagging stuff. I wrote it off as arthritis, popped some pills and hit the gym. Figured I was feeling my age." He shook his head, a grimace distorting his face. "Nope. A goddamn cancer is chewing on me. It's in my fucking arm. Can you believe that? And in my ribs. That's why one snapped when that prick we cornered in Germany rammed me. They're saying to try—*try*—and cure me, they'd have to start by taking off my right arm. At the shoulder." His eyes shimmered now. "After that, the chemo and radiation, and maybe, just *maybe*, they could stop the one in my chest."

Dominique had no words. He sat perfectly still, aware of nothing but the man in the bed, the heart racing beneath those fragile ribs, and the anger and fear oozing out of his pores.

Garrett briskly swiped a hand over one cheek. "You're the only one who knows. The only one I'm telling."

"Why?"

"Because...I can't live this way. And I don't want to die like that."

Dominique's brows gathered. "You...wish me to help you die?"

"What? No. I know how to use a gun. I don't need you for that."

"Then—"

"I want to live, Nick, and...I've decided that there's no price too high for that."

Dominique stared at him. He could not be hearing this, could he? Not from this man?

"What? You're going to make me say it?"

"Yes. I do not want to misunderstand."

"Fine. Dominique, I want you—no, I'm *asking* you to...consider—" He sucked at the air. His hands fisted in the blanket. "Goddamn it. I want you to turn me."

Yes, that was what Dominique thought he understood. Leaning forward in his seat, he rubbed the tips of his fingers together and spoke with care. "Not so long ago, you claimed you would rather die than consume even one drop of vampire blood. And when I threatened to turn you, you went into hiding on another continent."

"Death has a way of refocusing the mind."

"You do understand all the consequences, of course?"

"No sunlight. Need blood to survive. Great strength and immortality. Yes, I've known that for most of my sixty years on this earth."

"Also, complete submission to me as your lord and master. The world of night is not a democracy."

"Aren't you my boss already? You've got a good sense of integrity. I can work with that."

"You would lose your advantage of hunting during the day."

"I think I might do pretty well with the suppressant if I need to."

Unlike Dominique, who, despite all his powers and desperation to make it work, had yet to do so in any meaningful way. "Your mind would be forever linked to mine."

Garrett clenched his jaw. "I'd get used to it."

"I would not," Dominique said under his breath. He didn't even want to imagine such an intimate bond with a man who had so delighted in torturing him.

The patient shrugged by lifting both hands and putting them back down. "I can work on the other side of the world then. Whatever you need. Just say you'll think about it."

Dominique stood as though getting ready to leave.

"Please. If you tell me 'no' right now, I'll end it tonight."

He arched a questioning brow. "You don't have a gun here."

"There are cleaner ways in a place like this. Believe me, I know them all."

"I believe you." He eyed his former foe with care. Garrett, the blood-drinker, would be formidable. Still, having him in his head every time they were near each other was too high a price to grant this favor. Far too high.

Garrett extended his arm. "Here. Take some. Start the process maybe, or at least see for yourself how serious I am."

Dominique wanted to refuse, but the shimmering ribbons in the offered wrist held him spellbound. Blood, freely offered, was beguiling enough. Blood, freely offered by a foe? Irresistible.

He half-expected Garrett to snatch his arm back before he closed his hand around it. Instead, the patient lay back in mute surrender.

It didn't take much. A mere taste was enough. Fear was Dominique's first impression. Fear of death. Anxiety, too, over whether his request would be granted. Also, respect for the young vampire who had claimed a kingdom and knew how to keep his word. A fierce warrior spirit dwelled in this man, and a ruthless determination for anything he undertook—not unlike another mind he had touched tonight.

One thing that was not there was love. Garrett wanted to be turned to survive, and he justified this solution by acknowledging Dominique as worthy of being his master. But that was all.

This man would never love him any more than he loved anyone else.

"So, what will it be?" Garrett asked.

Dominique turned away from the window he had been staring out of as he processed all these impressions. "I will consider your request."

The body in the bed seemed to deflate a little. "Thanks. I'll take that for tonight."

Dominique was already at the door when Garrett added, "But don't consider too long. I haven't got forever."

27

A Simple Plan

At sundown, Cassidy was packed and ready to go. The plan was simple. Drive as far as they could get toward their destination in the Rocky Mountains—a solid nine hours away—during the not-quite-nine-hours-long night, pull Adilla out of his hole while the sun was high tomorrow, and have Dominique set him straight come night. Another day after that, two tops, and they'd be home again resuming their not-so-ordinary lives.

Simple. What could possibly go wrong?

She scoffed to herself as she zipped up her overnight bag. According to Jackson—not to mention history—plenty. He had unloaded the tools of his trade from the jet today—full-spectrum torches, canisters of silver, serrated daggers, body bags—all now tidied away in the back of a rented SUV. She guessed he shared this with her to make her feel better about how prepared he was.

He was also under the impression she would stay in Vancouver.

Fat chance.

Not after the day she had.

The days right after she and Dominique renewed their bond were never pleasant. But now, with her hormones agitating like popcorn in a microwave, she felt even more like she had been hollowed out with a rusty spoon while the sun was up. Part of her psyche collapsed once Dominique became unconscious, leaving her empty and incomplete. Like missing an arm or a leg—or both. And today, she didn't even have the luxury of having him physically near her. On learning that the vampire his life depended on slept in a hotel room closet, Isao had invited Dominique to spend his days in Vancouver safely tucked away in his own downtown lair. The samurai did not take no for an answer.

So Cassidy spent the soggy gray morning in Jackson's protective custody as he collected supplies for their trip. Along the way, Samantha called. "I thought you should know. Étienne is part of the club now."

"The club? What club?"

"Our club. The mortals-of-the world-of-night club."

"Oh, good God. What happened?"

"Serge happened."

Of course. What else? Samantha explained how the pirate vampire had been on a short fuse since Étienne's arrival, but it took her and Étienne getting amorous in the pool that finally triggered an explosion. "He went all fangs and eyes on him. Told him he didn't see a future for him with me and, I swear, was going to compel him to go away and forget me then and there. I stopped him just in time."

Cassidy lowered her head and pinched the bridge of her nose. Beside her, Jackson cursed. There was still enough of Dominique's blood in his system to allow him to hear both sides of the conversation just fine.

"Serge was crushed. He disappeared, and I haven't seen him since. I've never seen him so hurt."

"How did Étienne take it?"

"About how you'd expect. Shock, questioning reality, etcetera. Ryan and Natalia were a great help in convincing him he wasn't losing his mind. I think he'll be okay."

"So he knows about Dominique, then?" Cassidy asked, exchanging a look with Jackson.

"He put that together, yes. Once he did, I wasn't going to lie to him by denying it. The basics, anyway. Dominique can fill in the blanks for him. Assuming he'll let Étienne remember any of it," she added under her breath.

That was a big "if." Dominique's blood-drinker history was not for the fainthearted—or for his family. Which was why spending so much time with his mother presented such a problem for Cassidy. For all that she liked Francesca—French manners and no-nonsense sensibilities included—the longer they were together, the more Cassidy exhausted her ability to spin. There was so much she couldn't even allude to, much less talk about, to the mother of the man she loved, so much she knew that would cause Francesca anguish, or even destroy her.

She got plenty of practice holding her tongue that afternoon when Garrett, after making good his escape from Vancouver General, shepherded her and Francesca around Granville Island. To curtail conversation, as well as appease her appetite, Cassidy made a solid attempt at eating her way from one side of the food, art, and shopping mecca to the other. By the time she returned to her suite, she was ready to pass out in a carb and sugar-induced stupor.

The weather had not improved by the time she woke from her nap. Outside, the gray sky cloaked the gray high-rises and smothered the gray bay. Two more hours until sunset. Instead of giving in to the urge to curl up and bawl, Cassidy checked on the denizens of the *V-zette,* which turned out to be even more depressing. Waiting for her were several inquiries about Aubrey's whereabouts. With a heavy heart, she wrote a post announcing the gentleman vampire's death, though she kept the details vague, saying only that Dominique was handling the situation and everything was under control. Or would be. Soon.

She took a shower and packed, and watched the night creep in until at last she sensed Dominique waking in Isao's condo, several blocks away. As he made his way toward her, he absorbed her recollections of the day. And when he finally walked through the door, smelling of wet leather, city streets, and the incense Isao apparently favored, he embraced her without comment, needing her in his arms as much as she needed to be there. Night had come, and for a precious few moments, they basked in each other and the illusion that the world was safe again.

Then came the knock at the door. Dominique let in the visitors while Cassidy fetched her jacket.

Jackson's voice carried from the living room. "Everything is set. All we have to do is start driving."

"I spoke to Francesca and told her you'll be out for a few days to meet a new client in Alberta," Garrett added.

"*Merci*," Dominique said. Cassidy felt him ruminate as he watched the two hunters standing at the ready, both of them dressed in jeans and Gore-Tex jackets. He examined Garrett's thoughts in particular. Curious, Cassidy hung over his virtual shoulder. Nothing but an unfaltering commitment. Garrett still wanted what he had asked for the night before. He was also more than a little beguiled by Francesca, of whom he had been especially solicitous this afternoon—all in the name of "security." "Garrett, you will stay here and provide protection during the day. Isao will be downstairs at night."

Garrett's hesitation was slight. "If that's how you feel I can be most useful."

"I do."

"Okay. Then do you think I could get a little more magic juice before you go? Just in case?"

"Just in case," Dominique agreed. When he cut his wrist, Cassidy felt an echo of the slicing pain in her own flesh and smothered a gasp.

She waited until Garrett had downed his serving of "magic juice" before joining the group, travel bag in hand.

"That hit the spot. Thank you," he said as he set down the empty glass with an air of bravado Cassidy recognized for the show it was. Their afternoon outing had exhausted him, and even the powerful blood could only take him so far. Though she had been careful to conceal her knowledge of his condition all day, his expression told her she hadn't been able to keep the pity off her face now. She averted her gaze.

"Careful there, Garrett," Jackson said, eyeing his uncle askance. "You're turning into a junkie."

Garrett ignored him.

Dominique looked at her, his thoughts conflicted. "You will stay here, Cassie, *mon amour*," he said the moment that decision crystallized in his mind. The words and the thought created a disorienting echo effect.

"What? You can't mean that."

"This could become a very dangerous situation. As long as I do not have complete control over Adilla and his followers, I do not want you anywhere near them."

Indignant, she let her bag clunk to the floor and walked up to him. Jackson and Garrett squirmed where they stood, pretending not to hear, even though surely Dominique was using spoken words for their benefit.

"*Non, chérie.* It is for yours," he said. "I want there to be no misunderstanding. Much as I need you near me, you must remain here where you will be safe."

"Oh, come on. How complicated can this be? Jackson pulls this guy out of his hole tomorrow, and tomorrow night you show him who's boss. Then we go home. End of story."

"Not quite. This 'hole' is a repurposed mine, deep enough to lessen the sun's effect. Plus, there will be humans compelled to guard it. It is not a place I will let Jackson enter on his own, regardless of his impressive skills." *And you know why I cannot send Garrett.*

He's doped up on your blood. He could probably take the place down with his bare hands.

He is doped up on my blood to be the best guard for you and Francesca that he can be. But he is too fragile to face what we are likely to find.

The realization dawned on her with terrifying suddenness. "You're going to take the suppressant again, aren't you?" she said, all the air going out of her. "You're going to walk into that mine with Jackson. In the middle of the freaking day."

Dominique lowered his gaze. Behind him, Jackson looked aghast. Apparently, this was news to him, too.

"I keep my strength during the day."

"But you don't know you have it," she burst out, gesturing with both hands. "Plus, your daytime self hasn't seen Jackson since the day he tackled you in Mrs. Havashand's yard. I'm the only one he trusts. You can't let Jackson wake him up without me around. You just can't." She inhaled to say more, but then snapped her mouth shut and leveled a glare of pure challenge at him. *And you sure as hell can't be five-hundred-plus miles away from me. The link can't possibly stretch that far. I'd go out of my mind not knowing what was going on with you.*

Dominique pulled her into his arms. "I know," he said, answering both her words and her thoughts. "Jackson will have to make him remember, whether or not he wants to, and you cannot be anywhere near these blood-drinkers. Please understand."

She twisted her fingers into his shirt. An unsettling sensation stole over her, a feeling of being placed in a box and having a lid close over her head. A padded box for weak and precious things, locked up and guarded. What was she really, compared to Dominique or Jackson? Compared to all the forces at play here in the kingdom of night?

Nothing but an ordinary human woman. A *pregnant* human woman, God help her.

A liability.

His arms tightened around her. *Non,* he whispered in her mind. *You are my queen, the single most important person in all of this madness. Without you, there is no me—and no kingdom.*

28

THE ELEMENT OF SURPRISE

Jackson woke from the sort of deep, dreamless sleep he never experienced anymore. His demons, chained deep in the basement of his soul, wouldn't let him. On some level, he always heard them howl and whine, whether he thought of them or not.

Not tonight. Tonight, though he couldn't say how, they had been silenced by a vampire.

While driving east on the Trans-Canada Highway, they had discussed Dominique's birthday gift. Jackson didn't trust it. Dominique proved it by trying to compel him to sleep against his will. Sure enough, Jackson was awake for another two hours, thinking more than talking, aware all the time that Dominique could tune into his every thought and no longer caring. Sometimes Dominique even responded to questions Jackson dwelled on. After a while, he dozed off, feeling safer than he had in a long time.

An unfamiliar sense of peace lingered in him now as Jackson blinked at the traffic flowing around them in the predawn gray. Further out, hulking, jagged shadows loomed. The Rocky Mountains.

He stretched, his body stiff and uncooperative with sleep. Dominique didn't look at him. He stared straight ahead, maneuvering the car with one hand. No radio. Only the sound of the engine and the wind rushing past outside.

Jackson considered his profile, the sharp bone structure softened by the untamed dark hair. A study in contrasts and air-brushed perfection. So easy to see how his victims fell in love with him on the spot—the way Jackson had. In a strictly bromancy sort of way, of course.

A tiny smile tugged at the corner of Dominique's mouth, and Jackson busied himself adjusting his seat into an upright position. "How long do we have?"

"An hour before sunrise. Two until the lair." He glanced at Jackson. "You slept well?"

Only the best damn sleep of my life, he thought, but he didn't say so. He rolled his shoulders to limber them. "Get me some coffee, and I'll be ready to go."

"In the console."

A thermos sat in a receptacle between their seats. When he unsealed it, the heavenly aroma of fresh brewed enveloped his head. "Oh God. Thank you."

"There is some breakfast there for you as well. The best I could do with drive-through service."

The tidy paper bag was still warm. A biscuit stuffed with scrambled egg and a slab of sweetly salted Canadian bacon. The meal was a far cry from his usual protein shake, but under the circumstances, he wouldn't quibble. That Dominique thought about his mere mortal needs at all was amazing enough.

While he ate, Jackson checked his phone. A text message from Olivia—annotated with smiley faces, party hats, and happy hearts—had come in an hour ago and made him smile.

"*Bon anniversaire*," Dominique said, echoing the message's sentiment. "Happy birthday."

"Thanks." Jackson waved the phone. "Do you mind if I...?"

"Please do."

His call to Ollie was brief, but exactly the balm he craved right now. His sense of peace deepened at the sound of her voice. They made plans for a celebratory dinner when he returned, an event he thought might work well to share certain things with her. Assuming he could figure out how to talk to her about vampires without sounding like a lunatic.

"I will join you, if you like," Dominique said when Jackson was done with his call.

"What?"

"Your birthday dinner. You will need proof for what you plan to say to her, *non*?"

Jackson couldn't hide his astonishment. "You would do that? You would be okay with this?"

"You love this girl, so I am okay with you doing the right thing, *oui*. Very much okay."

"And let me guess. You'll compel her to be okay with it, too?"

"If you think I would need to do that, why do you want to tell her?"

"I don't think that at all."

"Then I will not." He waited a beat before adding, "But if she is not okay with the truth, it will be as if you never told her."

Jackson hadn't even thought beyond proving the supernatural to Ollie, but Dominique was right. The only thing worse than her not knowing would be her falling into an existential crisis over it.

"Fair enough," he agreed, and finished the breakfast sandwich. When he was done, he wiped his fingers on the paper napkin and reached for the coffee again.

"We will need help today," Dominique said.

"Yeah, I was wondering when you were going to figure that out."

"I knew this before we left, but my options were limited." He paused a beat before adding, "I believe we have lost the element of surprise. They know we are coming."

"How?"

He rubbed his chin and stared at the road disappearing beneath the hood of the SUV. "It doesn't matter. But we need to take more precautions. I don't know what going underground will mean in terms of how much the sun affects me, so we should go when it is strongest, straight overhead."

What aren't you telling me? Jackson thought. He remained quiet, giving the vampire every chance to answer that question, but Dominique ignored it, instead turning his head and raising an inquiring brow. "Agreed?"

Jackson toyed with the idea of asking out loud, realized that he probably still wouldn't get an answer, and looked away. "Agreed."

"Even so, we will be only one and a half men walking into the lair of hundreds, some of them exceedingly powerful."

"We have torches," he suggested.

Dominique shot him a cynical look. "Useless against human guards. Also, these humans will be compelled to protect their masters at all costs."

No arguing with that. "Okay. So what's your plan?"

Dominique flipped on the emergency flashers and moved the car into the outside lane. A devious smile played on his mouth. Jackson could have sworn he saw the tips of fangs in it.

"You should call 911," Dominique said as the car rolled to a stop on the shoulder.

"Why?"

"Obviously you are having an emergency, *non?*"

"Oh?" The vampire looked at him expectantly. "Oh. Right." They were out-manned and out-gunned and the targets knew they were coming. If that didn't qualify as an emergency, nothing did. He swiped open the phone, only half wondering if he really wanted to know what came next.

29

A Bit of Help

"The lovers are still busy out there," Étienne murmured. His lips moved against Samantha's neck, sending delicious shivers deep into her belly. "Maybe we should stay busy in here?"

In the hot-tub hideaway, Ryan was nearing climax, and he wasn't shy about vocalizing. They would have heard him even if Samantha's windows hadn't been open to catch the night breezes. The polite Canadian lost all semblance of restraint when he and Natalia were alone together. They might not even notice Samantha settling in for her pre-dawn meditation practice on the lawn, but the carrying on did nothing to inspire divine tranquility.

Étienne nuzzled behind her ear, the stubble on his jaw prickling against the tender skin there. "Mmmmm," she said, verging on letting him persuade her. Outside, Ryan went over the edge, Natalia right behind him with a cry just this side of human.

"Shall we try to outdo them, *chaton*?" Étienne whispered.

She giggled as she rolled toward him. "You are such a bad influence on my morning practice."

"But you don't really mind, do you?" The words were a heady, sultry purr of French seduction that melted her insides and drew her mouth to his.

His hand was making its way down her body when a strange voice broke the sensuous spell. She put a hand on Étienne's chest, stopping him, then pressed a finger to his lips. Together, they listened as an unfamiliar male voice greeted Natalia.

"How did you find me?" the vampiress demanded. "What do you want?"

"Didn't your time with us teach you anything? Esteban always knows where everyone is, sweetheart."

Samantha put a hand over her mouth. Étienne's eyes widened. "Vampire?" he whispered.

She nodded and slipped out of bed as quietly as she could to pull his discarded t-shirt over her head. Étienne followed suit, donning his shorts, stumbling in his haste. Samantha cringed at the noise they were making, then realized it didn't matter. Their heartbeats alone would give away their presence. To the intruder outside, they were mortals and, therefore, of no consequence.

"Of course, we had a bit of help. Didn't we, Ryan?" said another voice, also male but not so smarmy, almost bored.

Shock gripped her by the throat. Two. There were *two* strange vampires on the property. And she hadn't seen Serge since the blow up the night before. When she refused to capitulate to his adamant assertion that there was only misery in her and Étienne's future, he had disappeared in an offended huff.

She nudged aside the sheer curtain covering the sliding doors. Two figures stood between her pool house home and the hideaway grotto. Both were tall and dressed in black, one slim and graceful, the other bald and bulky.

Predators.

Serge, I need you! she called, praying he wasn't sulking a hundred miles away.

Étienne, standing behind her, closed a steadying hand on her shoulder.

Ryan appeared out of the shadowy recesses now in all his nude, bearded glory. "That's bullshit. Esteban doesn't even know I exist."

Slim, the laconic vampire who had made the accusation, ges-tured at a chair and shifted his voice into compulsion. "Have a seat, blood bag. And don't get up again."

Ryan sat.

"You see? You can be compelled just like anyone else."

A look of confusion crossed Ryan's face.

"How dare you speak such lies!" Wrapped in a towel, Natalia was the picture of indignation. "He is mine. I know his mind. Esteban never touched him."

"Guess Esteban knows how to hide a compulsion," gloat-ed the other vampire, a brutish mountain of a male. "Blood bag here's been reporting to Esteban every day without even knowing it." Pitching his voice into compulsion, he added, "But you'll know it now, won't you, blood bag?"

Ryan shook his head and began making low, choking noises, but he didn't get up. "No. No, please God, no."

No, please God, no, Samantha echoed silently. She had kept Natalia and Ryan apprised of events in Vancouver these past few days. If this was true—

"Say what you came to say, and go," Natalia demanded. "I am done with all of you." Her eyes had gone full vampire, glowing with Dominique's essence.

The duo studied her. The brute rubbed his gleaming bald head. Slim put his hands on his hips. "Well now, that's just it, princess. Once you're part of the colony, you're always part of the colony. No one leaves. I guess you weren't there long enough to figure that out."

Natalia took a tiny step back. Compared to them, she was pint-sized and could be a fraction of their age. Her voice changed, became hoarser, growling, the sound of a cornered vampire. "You should leave."

"Or what?" Brute glanced at Ryan, still seated, hands clamped around the armrests. "We know that impostor you swore yourself to is on his way to the summer lair. You know where that's going to end."

"He'll be dead soon enough," Slim clarified with little fanfare.

Samantha's surprised gasp drowned in a shriek of supernatural fury. Her human eyes couldn't comprehend what was happening until the glass door beside her blew in and something cannonballed into the room, taking the curtains with it. Étienne yanked her back and shoved her behind him just as the curtain rod came down, narrowly missing her head.

The cannonball turned out to be Slim. The skinny vampire hit the wall so hard, he shattered the artwork that hung there and bounced off. Like a cat, he landed in a crouch. His eyes flashed to full black, and the rest of him...the rest of him compacted into the skeletal form of a vampire at his most dangerous.

"*Mon Dieu*," Étienne whispered.

The vampire didn't even glance at them before he blurred back out the door, snarling like a thing straight out of hell. Apparently, Natalia had surprised them with her attack. She still had Dominique's blood in her system, lending her strength a vampire her age should not possess—and then some.

By the time Samantha and Étienne caught sight of her again, she had joined the ranks of things straight out of hell. A naked, snowy white figure carved of skin and bone, she had just swung around and driven a makeshift stake through Slim. The vampire doubled over around the business end of a palm frond protruding from his belly. That wasn't going to kill him, though—just slow him down long enough for Natalia to rip off his head with a loud, wet crack.

For a breathless moment, she stood over her kill, her platinum hair a damp mane around her head and shoulders. The head dangled by its jaw from her fingers, and her eyes burned bright in her blood-spattered skull face.

Ryan still sat tied to the chair with invisible tethers and stared at her in adoring wonder. "Natalia, my love."

She turned to him, to the love shining on his face, and never saw the brute coming. One moment she was whole, the next her head was gone. A fountain of blood exploded from her neck. Her body crumpled. Before she hit the ground, her killer shoved her over into the bubbling hot-tub with a vehement snarl. "Bitch!"

Samantha startled so badly she almost knocked over Étienne. Her heart flopped. Her breath hitched.

Her thoughts flat-lined.

Ryan screamed like an animal writhing on a spear.

Brute looked down at his cohort's sprawling carcass. "God damn bitch!"

With a series of grating thumps, Ryan hopped the patio chair across the pavers toward the vampire. He all but foamed with rage as he promised to rip the supernatural menace to pieces.

"Oh, no," Samantha murmured when she saw the menace turn to the human. "Oh, no, no, no." Before she knew what she was doing, she was out the door and running. Somewhere between the door and the bloody scene, her usual Zen self evaporated. In its place appeared an unrecognizable alien, a she-demon. "Get the fuck away from him!" she barked. "Harming those who are under the protection of the Lord of Night is a capital offense!"

Ryan stopped hopping the chair. Now he just sat and wailed.

Brute eyed her. Or rather, he leered at her. "Oh, is it now?" he cooed. "Then I guess I'll just have to go on offending."

Étienne suddenly jumped in front of her, hunched forward, arms wide, moving on the balls of his feet. "Do not compound your error beyond all hope of forgiveness," he warned. "We are your lord's family. Touch us and nothing can save you."

The vampire released his beast.

The terror that gripped Samantha's chest and turned her bowels to water was mercilessly swift.

Étienne grabbed a patio chair and brandished the legs toward the black-eyed, fanged, skeletal nightmare. "Samantha, run!"

She didn't. She knew there was no point. Plus, her legs had stopped working. In fact, they wobbled beneath her.

From out of nowhere, an arm flashed around the brute's massive trunk, pulling him back into a sharp arch even as a curly-haired head appeared and drove home a set of fearsome fangs. Within seconds, Brute became still and only stared, unseeing, into the sky.

When Serge had drunk his fill and pillaged the mind for all it could give, he severed the meaty head from the shoulders with a single blow of his hand. The head sailed off into the night in a pinwheel of blood. The body dropped into the carnage at his bare feet.

Samantha staggered. Her legs seemed to have disappeared. Étienne saved her from a crash to the ground by wrapping his arms around her. "It's over. They are gone," he said. "They're gone. You're safe."

She clung to him like a shipwrecked sailor to the only piece of flotsam in a heaving sea. Vomit seared the back of her throat. Her whole body shook from fear, adrenaline, and shock. She didn't look at Serge directly, but she saw him from the corner of her eye, heard him tell Ryan that he was free of every compulsion ever put on him.

The man fell forward out of his prison chair into the blood on the stones. On all fours, he scurried to the hot-tub and its grisly contents. There, he collapsed and howled with horror and grief.

Serge watched him for a long moment, tilting his head in that way he had when he saw futures dance in auras. When he turned away from Ryan, his face was empty, mask-like. Samantha could almost feel his unfocused gaze on her, searching her aura and perhaps Étienne's. Étienne who held her so tightly he seemed to be the only thing keeping her physically together.

From one moment to the next, Serge disappeared. But his parting words hung in the air. "All is as it must be."

30

FUNERALS

T hough the entire pool area was hidden from the prying eyes of neighbors, someone had heard enough to call the police. It was Étienne who opened the door and somehow persuaded the officers that the reported commotion had been nothing more sinister than a faulty TV volume control. Samantha stood by his side, trying not to look like the zombie she was. When the uniforms left, appeased, and the door closed again, she fell back into his arms. He held her, quietly caressing her back.

After a while, her brain started working again, and she stepped back with a sigh. "We should move them. While they're still manageable."

Étienne frowned. "*Quoi*?"

"C'mon."

It was shocking how swiftly and easily this relationship was progressing from first "*bonjour*" to "let's hide some bodies." He accepted her explanation about what would happen at sunrise without comment. Then, as though they had done it a dozen times before, Samantha and Étienne dragged two of the corpses deep into the foliage surrounding the pool where it would be simple to disperse the soon-to-be ashes.

With the third corpse, Natalia, Ryan adamantly refused their help. He lifted her body out of the hot-tub by himself and placed her on a satin bedsheet, arranging her head with the help of two pillows. Natalia Bogomolov looked almost whole and peaceful lying there, her small hands crossed over her sternum, another sheet draped to preserve her dignity. Ryan, attired only in his swim trunks, lay by her side and gently stroked her forehead with a thumb. In soft murmurs, he told her not to be afraid of the coming dawn, that he would stay with her, that they would be together again. Samantha's heart broke for him a little more with every word.

"Is this what Dominique has with Cassidy? This bond you told me about?" Étienne murmured. He sat on the grass with Samantha at a respectful distance from Ryan's tormented vigil.

"Yes," she whispered. "Just like that."

"Just like that," another voice echoed reverently.

Étienne startled, but Samantha smiled sadly as she turned to meet the puppy dog eyes. "Hello Serge."

"Golden one," he murmured. He was still damp from however he had rinsed off the night's gore, clothing included.

She reached out to touch him and was shocked to feel a moment of hesitation. "Thank you, Serge. For everything."

He looked at her hand on his forearm and reached for it, but stopped. Dark crescents of blood still marked his nail beds. "Are you feeling better?"

"I think so, yes. It's not my first blood bath, after all." Only the very worst. Is this what it had been like for Jackson, she wondered? To see his twin dismembered?

"Did you tell Dominique what happened here?" Serge asked.

She removed her hand and picked up the phone in her lap. "Yes. They know." She had only called Cassidy, who had been beside herself, and disconnected the call in her hurry to contact Dominique with the news.

Serge nodded. "Then all is as it must be."

There was a gut-wrenching sob from Ryan.

"Is he going to be all right?" she said so softly only Serge would have heard her.

The vampire watched the grieving man for a long moment. When he turned back, he didn't meet her eyes. "I must apologize, golden one. I have behaved...beastly these last few days."

"Very lucky for us this morning, *non?*" Étienne said, a nervous edge in his voice.

Serge shot him a look that said he wasn't talking to him, and the human man studied his coffee. Serge met Samantha's eyes. "I have found unimagined treasure in you, golden one. I knew you would not be mine forever, but I never wanted to believe that this...we could...could end so soon."

"Oh, Serge, please—"

He raised a hand to stop her. "Samantha Reynolds, you are free to do as you will with"—another glance at Étienne—"whoever you wish."

She blinked at him, mouth agape. Really? Was he saying she hadn't been free before?

Apparently still tapped into her mind, the vampire placed a hand on his breast and tried again. "What I am saying is...your destiny...it's no longer with me." He blinked, rubbed at his nose, squinted to the east where a bright ribbon of color grew over the barrier island. "Find your peace today, my friend."

With that, Serge blurred away into the shelter of the house and vault.

Samantha watched him go, trying to wrap her head around what had just happened.

"*Intéressant,*" Étienne said.

"Isn't it just?"

They sat in silence as the sun crested the horizon like a blob of lava creeping towards the dead vampires. The process wasn't instantaneous. For a minute or two, Natalia only looked more and more sunburned, her exposed skin turning from angry pink to blistering crimson to oozing burgundy. Then wisps of smoke drifted from her face and from beneath the sheet as her extremities charred. Dark tendrils shot from the blackened areas to take the rest of her, like cracks that widened into a final and all-consuming, glittering gray.

Ryan wept uncontrollably, his tears splashing across her delicate face as it disintegrated. The sheet that covered her collapsed. Some of the silvery ashes took flight in the morning breeze. Some of them clung to him.

While Étienne coaxed him away from the shifting pile on the sheet and into a lounge chair, Samantha made a strong cup of calming tea. Ryan sipped, but mostly just held it in his lap, untouched, adding tears to the contents. Étienne gathered up the sheet with the ashes and secured it into a tidy package. "I have a lovely bamboo box for her," Samantha offered.

There was no reaction.

Étienne shepherded Ryan into the house, convincing him to get some rest. By the time he returned, Samantha had poured the ashes into the box. Locking the lid, she placed her hands on the sun-moon, yin-yang design and offered a silent prayer to the universe for Natalia's soul.

"He is in shock," Étienne said quietly. "It will take a while for him to recover from this."

"A long while," Samantha agreed. Serge hadn't answered her question earlier, and it wasn't because he hadn't heard her. "We should spread out the rest before the lawn crew comes and wonders about them."

Moving on to actually disposing of bodies—not just hiding them—they worked side-by-side, spreading vampire remains with rakes and sweeping ashed blood from the pavers. Étienne followed her directions, absorbed in thought. Eventually he said, "Would this happen to Dominique, too?"

"Yes. It would." In fact, it almost had. Now that she had seen the complete process, she realized that she and Cassidy had saved him with only seconds to spare.

"But...he seems so different from these...beings. He looks...normal."

Samantha paused her sweeping and leaned on the broom with both hands. She had wondered when this question would come up. "You see what he wants you to see. But that isn't the Dominique I know. Not physically."

A thoughtful frown wrinkled his brow. "So he is completely like...what I saw here?"

A gusty breeze picked at Samantha's unraveling braid, and she pinned a long strand of blond hair behind one ear. The sun warmed her face, soothing and safe after the horrors of the morning. "Dominique can be anything he wants to be, but mostly...mostly he is breathtaking." *Like his cousin*, she amended to herself when she caught Étienne's impossibly blue eyes watching her. As though he had read her mind, his melancholy melted like butter in the curl of his sensual mouth.

"As are you," he said, leaning on his own broom, his words nearly lost in the palm fronds rattling in the breeze above them.

Heat bloomed in her cheeks. Feeling awkward as a teenager, she pushed the broom across the clean floor. "What I am is exhausted."

"You should be. You charged into a battle like a warrior."

She swept with more vigor. "Not my brightest move. We could have all died."

"Would they have spared us if we had tried to hide? Or run?"

She stopped sweeping. Her stomach clenched with the truth. "No. They would have killed everyone here."

"So you saved Ryan's life. And perhaps that is what brought Serge out of hiding to save us all."

"Maybe."

"You are *magnifique*, Samantha. A warrior's spirit with a pure heart." He put his broom aside, took hers, put that aside too, then gathered her hands in his and looked down at her upturned face. "I think your clairvoyant friend sees the truth." His voice dropped lower still. "You have captured my heart."

She felt herself falling into those sky-blue eyes with no hope of ever surfacing. That fight—if it had ever even been one—she had lost the moment he, armed with nothing but a chair, charged in to protect her against a raging vampire. Somewhere in her chest, something clicked into place, something she had never felt before.

Samantha squeezed his warm hands. "And you have captured mine, Étienne."

The kiss he bestowed on her was tender enough to steal whatever breath she had left—not from desire, but from the sense of absolute rightness, of connection. At that moment, it was as if they had known each other, not for days, but for decades.

With bashful smiles and long glances, they finished their sweeping before collaborating on a simple breakfast in her small kitchen. They talked as they ate—about immediate events at first, then venturing into their pasts, and suddenly...their future. They were busy plotting her visit to St. Barth when a meditative chime intruded on their growing bliss.

Samantha retrieved her phone from the kitchen counter. "Cassidy," she answered. "Please tell me there's good news."

"Not really. Is Étienne with you?"

She glanced at him. "Yes?"

"Francesca has been trying to reach him. She has news for him from France. Can you put him on?"

"Um. Sure."

With a puzzled look, Étienne took the phone when she handed it to him. The conversation was in French, and Samantha struggled to keep up, but his expression said this news wasn't good. Shock, surprise, strident denials. It was all there. As near as she could figure out, someone had died. Maybe.

Maybe?

"What's going on?" she asked when he disconnected.

"Supposedly Juliette has died."

Samantha's hand flew to her mouth. "Your sister? Oh, no. Étienne, I'm...wait. *Supposedly?*"

"Right." He chewed on his lower lip, mystified. "Something is wrong. She messaged me only last night. I need my phone." He paced into the bedroom.

Samantha followed. "That was hours ago." Even fewer hours ago, they had both seen just how quickly lives could end. "What happened?"

"*Tante* Francesca said it was an accident, but"—he grabbed his phone off the nightstand, swiped, searched and dialed—"but she said it happened last weekend. Ah, Juliette? *Bonjour. C'est Étienne. Comment vas-tu?*"

Not only was Juliette pleased to hear from her brother, she was perfectly fine. Not to mention alive.

"How bizarre," Samantha said after he disconnected. "What would make Francesca think Juliette had died?"

"Apparently Geneviève's husband told her so when she called to check on the restaurant."

"Geneviève? Francesca's daughter?"

"*Oui.* She and Juliette are fast friends, and she said she wanted to be at the funeral."

"Wait. Slow down." Samantha sat up in the chair she had dropped into. Alarms clanged in the back of her head. "Geneviève, Dominique's sister, said she was going to France for Juliette's funeral? When was this?"

"Saturday."

A chill of no name marched goosebumps up and down her arms. Today was Tuesday. "Did Juliette say Geneviève was with her in France?"

Étienne's eyes widened with dawning apprehension as he followed her reasoning. "*Non.* But she would have. She would have been very excited by a visit."

They looked at each other. Dominique often said his older sister was the most responsible person in the family. She had a loving husband, a toddler daughter, and a restaurant to manage. The last thing Geneviève was likely to do was disappear.

"We may have a problem," Samantha said. Though there really was no "may" about it. If Esteban's tentacles had reached into South Florida...they could also reach St. Barth.

31

Inconvenient Truths

Jackson packed away the empty syringe in its case, straightened Dominique's shirt, and waited. The sky brightened. The vampire's skin remained unmarred. For another minute, he looked peacefully asleep.

Then he woke.

His eyes widened in alarm as he sat upright, hands pushed flat against the door and center console.

"How do you feel?" Jackson ventured from the driver's seat.

"*Fils de pute!* Where am I, and what am I doing here with you?"

Jackson pointed to Dominique's phone propped on the dash. As it had for the last six or seven minutes, it still recorded their every word and action. "The answer to all your questions. Right there. Go on. We have time."

Dominique looked like he contemplated leaping out the door and making a run for the dense woods surrounding the rest area.

"Don't even think about it. *That* we definitely don't have time for."

Those eyes, so soft and troubled a minute ago, flashed hard, dark anger at him. A justified reaction, Jackson reminded himself. Their last encounter had been anything but cordial.

Dominique snatched up the phone, stopped the recording, and tapped to play. The video began with vampire Dominique speaking in French, his expression grim. This produced the expected scoff. "Another digital fabrication?" But he listened and soon grew quiet. Jackson heard his name, and Dominique cut him another kind of look. Uncertain but curious. The narrative continued to the administration of the shot, the silence that followed, the sudden, shocked awakening, and right on to the moment he had picked up the phone. When the video ended, Dominique dropped his hands into his lap and stared out the window at the misty forest in the wan morning light. His voice was just as vague. "What am I?"

"He didn't tell you that? On the video?"

"He said you would explain it only when I was ready to hear it." Dominique turned to face Jackson. "He said that you are...an intimate friend?"

"You could say that," he conceded with a touch of reluctance. Leave it to the bloodsucking bastard to call it an "intimate" friendship, whatever the hell that meant to him, but given the thoughtful calm that settled over Dominique, maybe that was the key to getting through to him. Intimacy was his language, after all, night or day. "So, are you ready? To hear it?"

Dominique gave the smallest of nods.

The truth fell off Jackson's tongue in all its dark, bloody, horrifying glory. "You, my friend, are a vampire."

For a full half minute, maybe more, there was no reaction. Dominique held his gaze, studied his face. "*Absurde.*"

"It's true. You are immortal, have incredible strength, along with some really terrifying powers, and, yes, you drink blood."

"You are mad." A vehement hiss of denial. But he wasn't running. Jackson considered that promising.

"Then explain what you just saw on your phone. You're the one who stopped the recording. It's unedited. So what was that?"

"I don't—"

"Your vampire self is as stubborn as you are. He wants to see the sun again, wants to be human again. I think he's nuts, but, yes, he—you—are my friend." Jackson took a deep breath. "We didn't start out that way, you and I, but you've earned my respect as a decent guy in a tough spot. I think I've earned yours as well or you wouldn't be trusting me with your life right now. Plus, I know you well enough to know that when you say you want something, I better not stand in your way."

He unzipped the black case and showed him the vials and syringes, one of them used. "I got this suppressant made for you, because that's what you wanted, but using it didn't go as you expected. You can't remember your other reality. Why? Because you don't want to. We've respected your wishes and kept you in the dark, so to speak, but we don't have time for that anymore. You need to be who and what you are when the sun's up, and you need to be that right now."

For long seconds, there was no reaction. "Why?" the vampire finally asked, sounding like he wasn't sure about wanting to know the answer.

Jackson sympathized, but took a breath and plunged in. "Because you're not just any vampire. You are the lord of them all. And there are about two hundred here who don't agree with your policies. We have to surprise them during the day. You got us some backup earlier." He glanced at the far end of the otherwise deserted lot. Two RCMP vehicles waited there—a huge 4x4 pickup and a slightly smaller SUV. The occupants had made the mistake of answering Jackson's request for help and now acted as their very compelled, very well-armed security detail. "But what we really need is your strength and speed."

A slow sneer spread over Dominique's face, the limits of his skepticism finally breached. "You must think I am soft in the head."

"No, actually, your head is unusually hard."

He leaned closer, pinning Jackson with his eyes. No hint of the supernatural in that look. Just a mind spinning the truth. "Vampires," he made air quotes with both hands, "are not awake during the day, *non*? So why do you need one to surprise them when they are asleep?"

"They're underground. It's possible they're deep enough where the sun won't have them as out of it as you would be up here. Also, you're much easier to travel with when you're not in a body bag," Jackson added, deadpan.

The derisive glower turned sour.

"Next question?"

Whatever Dominique was going to say was interrupted by his phone ringing in his hands. Cassidy's smiling face popped up on the screen. He answered with a hesitant "Hello?"

Her tiny voice stuttered. She must have hoped to catch the other version of him. A brief discussion in French ensued in which the word "vampire" featured prominently. Dominique's free hand alternated between wild gesticulation, shoving back his hair, and rubbing a spot over the bridge of his nose. Finally, he handed the phone to Jackson. "She wants to speak with you."

"Cass," he greeted, pressing the phone to his ear, hoping to keep her words from carrying. Dominique went back to staring out the window.

"You've got your hands full, I see," she said.

"It's been an interesting discussion."

"I did what I could, but I don't think he's fully ready yet. You'll need to push him, but be careful. There's a chance that when he remembers, he'll pass out. The sun can get to him then."

"Nice." Like he wasn't juggling enough shit storms already.

She promptly added another one. "Did he tell you about the attack at the house?"

"The what?"

"No, don't say anything. Just listen. I told him about this earlier, but his daylight self doesn't need to know."

He glanced at Dominique, who seemed lost in his own thoughts, then froze in his seat when Cassidy said, "Early this morning, two of Esteban's vampires tracked Natalia down at Dominique's house. It didn't end well."

"Sam?" was the first thing out of Jackson's mouth.

"She's shaken up, but unharmed. So is Étienne." Cassidy relayed the fractured and harrowing details Samantha had shared of the supernatural bloodbath that had taken place. Jackson was stunned speechless by the revelation that his gentle, peace-loving sister had been in the middle of that. "It gets worse." He couldn't imagine how until Cassidy told him about Ryan, Esteban's compelled spy. "Natalia wasn't the only one he reported on, Jack. Esteban knows you're coming."

Not sure if he could keep his face neutral, Jackson turned to stare out his side window. A gray chill settled on his shoulders. This explained vampire Dominique's cageyness earlier. They were both walking into a trap, their only advantage being knowledge of its existence and two RCMP patrols.

"Do they know where you are?"

"I don't know," she admitted with a trace of apprehension. "We told no one about the hotel we're in, but we're planning to be out all day today. And tonight, we'll have Isao and his crew. We should be okay. But listen. That's not why I called. There is something else he doesn't know about yet." Jackson heard her draw a shaky breath. "Dominique's sister is missing. Geneviève left Saint Barthélemy for France three days ago to attend a funeral for someone who turned out to be alive and well. She never got there."

32

WILDERNESS

"**I** am hungry," Dominique said the moment Jackson got off the phone. "And not for blood."

Nothing about his demeanor betrayed that he had heard a word of what Cassidy had shared with Jackson or her last request before terminating the call. "Take care of him for me, Jack."

With a small sigh, Jackson nodded and started the car. It was going to be a long day.

The first place they found serving at this hour was the Lost Moose Café, which was part of a two-hose gas station and had a distinct last-century, lost-in-the-woods feel. They pulled in, along with their armed escort, and parked near a muddy pickup truck and two camper trailers.

Compelled to accept every request from Jackson as if it were their own idea, the officers settled in another booth and ordered heaping plates of breakfast, fortifying themselves for the day's challenges. They were Jackson's secret weapon. No one knew about them, not even Cassidy, certainly not Esteban. Less certain was whether Esteban would know to expect Jackson and Dominique during the day or not.

The day-walking vampire laid into a plate of scrambled eggs with all the trimmings as though he hadn't eaten in a week. For once, he didn't complain about the taste and only glared at

Jackson when he explained what would happen to all that food come sundown.

Jackson knew denial when he saw it. Maybe a touch of fear, too. He wasn't about to add to it with Cassidy's suspicion that Geneviève might be in the clutches of Adilla's minions.

According to the map Dominique had marked up, the entrance to the mine Adilla had converted into a summer lair was only an hour ahead. An hour was too soon, the sun nowhere near high enough. They had to wait.

Jackson drove into the closest town, Banff, and took Dominique shopping. The picturesque resort town nestled at the base of a fog-shrouded Mount Rundle was cluttered with stores catering to outdoor enthusiasts and wealthy tourists. By the time he was done, they both cut dashing figures in sturdy trekking boots, convertible pants, hiking shirts, and utility vests. They were the personification of rugged outdoorsmen—even if one of them looked like he should strut the outfit down a Paris runway rather than a Canadian sidewalk.

"We need to look like we belong here," Jackson explained. "Their daytime security people will expect city-types or tourists. Dressed like this, we should be able to BS our way past them."

"You do this often? This BS thing?"

Jackson grimaced and scratched his chin, which was overdue for a shave. "It's my secret superpower."

They met their RCMP escorts in the agreed-upon location outside town and followed the 4x4 over the winding roads while the SUV brought up the rear. The passing landscape seemed to hold Dominique transfixed. A granite cliff towered to their right, while a glacier-fed river rushed to their left, and on the far bank, an unbroken blanket of evergreens sloped up to disappear into soggy gray mists. The smooth street snaking through it all and humming with traffic felt like an invader rather than a permanent fixture of infrastructure. But it beat tramping through the wilderness, Jackson thought, and hoped the road would take them all the way to their destination.

It didn't.

Just past noon, their escort slowed and turned by a plain brown sign marking the entrance to a campground. For several minutes they serpentined up the side of a mountain, engine gears grinding. Then, just as Jackson spied the first outposts of camp sites up ahead, the RCMP truck turned again, this time onto a muddy access road heading back down and barely wide enough for one vehicle. Gravel popped under their tires and the suspension swayed wildly over the uneven ruts.

"Are you sure this is where we want to go?" Dominique asked when the "Private Property: Trespassers Will Be Prosecuted" sign went by. It was bright red and impossible to miss.

"Very sure," Jackson said, setting his jaw. "Somewhere down there, a couple of hundred vampires are sleeping. The defenses are only going to get tighter from here on."

He felt Dominique's eyes on him, almost heard him thinking, too. "Don't doubt yourself, Nick. There is nothing here that can hurt you."

"Because I am immortal?" Only a slight scoff this time.

"Yes. And stronger than any of them."

The road ended, not at a mine entrance, but in a tiny village. Ten weather-beaten cabins clustered around a central square, which bordered a creek of gin-clear water. A newer-looking barn sat off to one side, surrounded by a vegetable garden and a lush pasture where several black-and-white cows grazed. Solar panels studded its sloped roof and topped the cabins as well. Chickens darted from the approaching cars and disappeared underneath a pickup truck and the rusting frame of a tractor.

A large-bellied man with bushy white hair and a thick mustache emerged from one cabin as they pulled up. He wore socks in his sandals and a pair of stained overalls over a faded blue-checked shirt. He looked a bit like an oversize duck as he waddled toward them on stocky legs.

"Terrifying security," Dominique murmured.

"Did you all get lost?" the duck called, jovial, as the officers, Jackson, and Dominique piled out of their cars.

"I don't know," Jackson said with an affable smile. "We're looking for a mine. Seen one around here?"

Officer Campbell answered in an official tone. "It's farther back in the woods, sir. There's a trail over there." He pointed to where another, still smaller road was blocked by a crossbar and a sign warning of rock fall ahead.

Both Campbell and his partner, Officer Rao, looked at them expectantly. Apparently, escorting them here and watching for trouble was as far as their compulsion had gone. Jackson coughed to buy time, composed himself, and stepped forward. "We're here with...the...Alberta Mines Inspection Commission," he improvised, hoping he sounded even remotely plausible and painfully aware that he probably was the only human here with a clear head.

The cops took it from there, parroting Jackson's words with grave authority.

"Inspection?" the duck man said, his hands disappearing behind the front panel of his overalls. "Oh, there's no need for that. We all know it's too dangerous to go in there, and not too many tourists lose their way down here."

"We know what we're doing," Jackson assured in his most confident tone.

"They know what they're doing," Campbell repeated. The more senior of the two officers, he propped his hands on his hips as he said this, drawing attention to his holstered pistol.

"They're experts," confirmed Rao. He was the fresher, younger one, but was tall and wide and all around intimidating.

"This is crazy," Dominique muttered from where he leaned against the rental's hood.

Jackson spoke out of the side of his mouth. "No, this is your magic at work."

The duck cast a doubtful look at Jackson and Dominique. While Jackson smiled and maintained an easy, open stance, Dominique stood with his arms crossed. He had tied his hair back and wore a new pair of aviator sunglasses against the day's gray light. Absolutely nothing about him screamed "mine inspector."

"Are you now," said the man, the welcome draining from his expression. Behind him, several more men and women emerged from two other cottages and the barn. They appeared to be in their late middle years, early retirees perhaps, living off the grid, with a few younger men sprinkled in.

"What's going on, Earl?" one of the latter, a tall, faded redhead, said. His fearsome scowl belied his almost delicate nasal voice.

"Mine inspectors," the duck, Earl, replied. The men raked Jackson and Dominique with hard, assessing looks that made Jackson miss his sidearm. "It's not any safer in there for you either, you know."

"We'll be fine," Jackson said. He popped the SUV's hatch and retrieved his backpack, which contained two folded body bags and his favorite Bowie knife. An assortment of climbing gear was clipped to the outside. He also grabbed three full-spectrum torches. With their hefty weight, these could double as clubs. He added one to the backpack and pushed another at Dominique. "Officers? Nick? Shall we?"

While Campbell and Rao headed for the access road, Dominique separated from the car with obvious reluctance, his expression unreadable, the skepticism ebbing. The sense of having walked into an alternate reality clearly wasn't lost on him.

"All right, all right, just a minute," Earl said. "Seems we can't convince you to keep your necks safe, so we might as well show you around. Terry?"

"Sure thing. Least we can do," Redhead agreed. "Tim, do you mind? Carl? Paul? Wanna go for a walk?"

Three others moved closer.

"No need," Jackson blurted. "Nick, tell them we'll be okay on our own."

Dominique gave him a peculiar look, but then did as told, repeating Jackson's words—with an edge of doubt and no hint of compulsion.

Jackson smothered a groan.

"From Quebec, eh?" Earl said, hearing Dominique's accent. His grin revealed stained teeth.

"Saint Barthélemy."

"Oh, *pardon-moi.*"

The sarcasm left Dominique unmoved. Or confused. Jackson couldn't tell which. Turning on a heel, he headed for the mine.

For a trail to a condemned mine, it was remarkably well-maintained as it curved through a narrow canyon of fragrant spruce. The rushing burble of the creek soon turned into a droning rumble. Then, around an abrupt turn, a sheer rock-face came into view, along with the black mouth of a cave. Two hundred yards away, a waterfall crashed to the ground, sending clouds of ghostly mist into the shadowy forest.

"There you go. The mine," the redhead, Terry, announced.

Jackson eyed the cavern, which seemed to stare back at him. It was big enough to swallow a locomotive—or two hundred vampires—with ease. "This doesn't look like any mine I've ever seen."

"It's not. It starts inside the cave."

"Nice." Ignoring the thud of his pulse in his temples, he flipped on the torch. "You should stay out here. Nick and I won't be long."

To his relief, the villagers didn't argue.

Dominique gave him another one of those looks that said he thought Jackson had lost his mind, but he took off his sunglasses and tucked them into a pocket on his vest, ready to follow him into the darkness.

Taking the flashlights from their utility belts, the officers tagged along.

The temperature dropped ten degrees when their group crossed into the cave, where they were met by a chilly breeze rushing from the depths. The beam of his torch cut through the gloom, revealing bits and pieces of civilization. Rusted winches and chains, an overturned bucket, and coils of frayed rope lay half buried in mud and gravel. The stacks of modern, camouflage-patterned crates gave him pause.

"Vampires," Dominique said in a dramatic whisper.

Shivers raced down Jackson's arms as he turned away from the crates. The actual vampire's light pointed straight up at the ceiling, where a cluster of bats shuffled and squeaked in the glare. "Wiseass."

Dominique chuckled.

"Over here," Rao called from farther in. "This looks man made."

So it was. The square tunnel was narrow, but tall enough to stand in, a path carved straight into the mountain. Several support struts were visible, but no end. Only black depths that swallowed their lights.

"Bingo," Jackson said, letting his beam follow a metal pipe as thick as his arm, which emerged near the tunnel's ceiling and snaked toward the cave's mouth. A power conduit, he reasoned, possibly data as well. Those solar panels, and the batteries they must be charging, clearly powered more than the cottages.

Dominique made a small worried noise. "Surely you don't expect us to—"

"That'll be far enough," Terry called.

A second later, Officer Campbell barked, "Drop your weapon!"

Weapon? Jackson spun around and straight into a blinding beam of light. Dominique turned away, shielding his eyes.

"Take cover," Rao commanded before echoing the order to drop weapons. He sounded like he was close to the ground now. Amidst the skittering beams, Jackson couldn't see a fucking thing.

The same was not true for the village men pointing those high beams at them. "I said that's far enough," Terry hollered and emphasized his words with a weapon's blast that reverberated in the cavern like a thunderclap. Campbell—or maybe it was Rao—returned fire, which was promptly met by more of the same. A deafening crescendo of gunfire followed.

Jackson grabbed Dominique's arm and hauled him toward a shadowy outcrop he prayed was substantial enough to stop bullets. Where the fuck had the villagers gotten those guns and lights? Had to be those crates by the entrance he hadn't checked. Fuck!

Just before he ducked behind the outcrop, Jackson cut off his torch. Dominique had dropped his and stumbled after him, blind and clumsy. Jackson yanked him down beside him, eliciting a pained cry from the vampire. "Keep your head down, you idiot. You're not so immortal that it can't get blown off."

Screams and shouts punctuated the gunfire, which raged for what felt like minutes but was probably only seconds. When the noise finally subsided, Jackson noticed Dominique curled beside him in the dirt, speaking in French as though reciting prayers or dispensing curses, maybe both.

"We told you it's not safe in here," Terry's nasal voice admonished. "Wouldn't listen, though, would you?"

"I got hit in the arm," one of his cohorts wailed.

"What a mess," another one spat.

"They had guns," Terry countered defensively. "Nobody said anything about them having guns."

Someone who sounded like Campbell cried out in obvious agony.

"Guess we save 'em," a fourth voice said from close by. "Let's be grateful nobody got killed this time."

From their hiding place, Jackson watched as one man walked up to Rao, who sat with hands raised and his face scrunching in the glare of a flashlight. The man picked up the discarded gun and ordered Rao to secure himself with his own cuffs.

Jackson pressed his lips to Dominique's ear. "This would be a *great* time for you to remember what you are. Because we are royally fucked if you don't."

Dominique said nothing. He was shaking.

"What the—"

Light burst over them. "Oh, man. Someone may have gotten killed after all," a disembodied voice said with genuine regret.

In the light, Jackson got his first good look at Dominique, who lay staring at him with unfocused eyes, his breathing shallow—his side covered in blood.

"Fuck, no." He unzipped Dominique's vest and pulled up the sopping-wet shirt. "You goddamn fucking bastards!"

Judging by the dark pool soaking into the grit beneath him, Jackson expected to find blood fountaining out of the vampire's innards. But there was only a thin trickle. He wiped at the wound. Not ragged. Just raw. And shrinking, slowly, right before his eyes.

"Well, I'll be damned," someone else said. Terry.

Four pairs of muddy shoes surrounded them now. The air reeked of clay, blood, and gunpowder.

Dominique moved his hand to the wound. Feeling it closing, he sucked in a gasp.

"It's about time," Jackson said, but there still was no sign of the vampire in those wide, glazed eyes.

Only shock.

33

EARLY RISER

*W*e're fucked. Screwed. Done for. Dead.

The words circled Jackson's thoughts like vultures as he circled his cell for the tenth or twentieth time, feeling his way, inch by inch, in the complete darkness, looking for a way out. Any way at all.

"Dispatch will send someone to check on us," Rao said. He had said it almost as many times as Jackson had orbited the cell and sounded a little less certain every time. Maybe they would. If so, they'd walk into the same trap.

And it wouldn't be soon enough.

The luminescent markers on Jackson's Tag Heuer watch glowed with the bad news. Two, maybe two-and-a-half hours until sunset, no more. He rubbed both hands over his face, heedless of the gritty grime stuck to his fingers. "Nick?"

"*Oui?*"

"How are you doing over there?"

Silence.

After witnessing Dominique's wounds closing, their captors knew he was different, and placed him in his own cell. Before the light was extinguished, Jackson counted four of these makeshift prisons—all empty—at the end of the long, skinny mineshaft boring into the mountain.

He had also spotted another shaft going straight down. There was no doubt about what would come crawling out of that hole before too long.

"Nick. Dominique. Listen to me, my friend. You are a vampire. You have the strength to break us out of this mess, but you need to do it soon. Like now. You hear me?"

A French curse floated his way, followed by, "I am chained to a wall, you imbecile. Don't you think if I could free myself I would? The more I move, the more my wrists burn."

"The shackles must be coated in silver then. I bet you're feeling it because the suppressant is wearing off, probably because you're starting to wake up. Well, wake up faster."

"You are *insane*!"

Jackson grabbed onto the bars he had just rediscovered and shook them as hard as he could. "For fuck's sake, Nick, you saw how you healed from a fucking gunshot wound. How much more proof do you need? You *are* a vampire."

Silence.

Furious, he slammed the heels of both hands against the cold, invisible iron. "*Goddamn it*, you stubborn bastard, you're a vampire. We've had our share of differences about that, believe me, but right now I really, *really* need you to be *all* vampire. We all do. Or—"

"Jackson, *ta gueule*."

"—we're going to die, you included, because there will be enough evil bloodsuckers coming for us at sundown to take you down, immortal or not."

The chains clinked again. "Be quiet, you fool."

Like hell he would. "You need to break the fucking chains, Dominique, and then break these bars. Your wrists will heal." He had no idea if Dominique would be strong enough to do either, even at night. Mind over matter, though. It's all they had left.

Silence as thick as the darkness.

"Well? What is it to be?" an unfamiliar voice queried, male, casual, and dispassionate. "Will you break your chains?"

An icy finger stirred Jackson's innards. No, this could not be happening. It was nowhere near sundown. He straightened, his wide-open eyes staring straight ahead, seeing nothing. This could *not* be a vampire. Not conscious. Not yet.

It was.

A light came on. After hours of complete darkness, the grimy fixture attached to the ceiling between the cells was blinding. The newcomer stood under the light, the pull chain still swaying. His features were cast in shadows, but Jackson made out a petite male dressed in simple black clothes with hands so pale they glowed.

Vampire.

Before sunset.

Holy shit, were they really that shielded from the sun's effects inside all this rock? But that made no sense. If that were the case, Dominique would have woken up by now and tossed his breakfast all over the place.

Then what the fuck?

The vampire ignored the humans, and Jackson lapsed into the mental exercises he used to keep his emotions under control, especially his fear. It wouldn't do for him to smell like a meal right now.

"All this effort I wasted trying to find you in the city, and here you are," the vampire told Dominique with a grand gesture of both hands. "God smiles on me this day."

His mouth hanging open, Dominique glanced at Jackson, who shook his head the tiniest bit. The less Dominique said, the better.

The other vampire—judging by the faint Spanish lilt, Jackson guessed it was none other than Esteban—retrieved a key from a shelf in the rock wall and used it to unlock Dominique's cell.

"And to find you like this, awake with me, is a splendid surprise, indeed." He stopped to study his prisoner, who stood with his arms spread high and wide by the chains, his shirt and vest caked in drying blood.

Dominique didn't move. His gaze was riveted to this creature that he didn't remember had tried to kill him twice before.

"You are not what you appear to be, Dominique Marchant, are you?"

"Apparently not," he replied faintly.

"Are you one of mine? Did one of my distant young ones make you? Is that how you come by the gift of cheating the sun?"

Dominique frowned. "Gift?"

"Did they not tell you? This is the gift I pass on to some of my young ones. And some of them to theirs. The gift of consciousness when the rest of us sleep."

A new worm of dread slithered into Jackson's mind. The vampire that had killed his brother had also been awake when he shouldn't have been. Lying in wait for them. Ambushing them.

Like this one was ambushing them.

His breath hitched. *No...*

Esteban still didn't acknowledge the humans. "But even that doesn't explain you, does it? You weren't here last night, and you would have had to face the sun itself to come here during the day." He tilted his head in thought. "So perhaps you compelled these mortals to bring you? That is an impressive feat for one so young. How do you have such power?"

Dominique tested the chains again. Hard. They held. "Do you truly expect me to answer your questions while you keep me shackled?" The sneer was tepid, uncertain. A gambit. Dominique, the vampire, was still MIA. The poor fool was running blind.

"I'm extending you a courtesy by asking. If you weren't so intriguing, I would have been rid of you by now." For another second, he remained calm. Then, his hand flashed out in a blur and grabbed a startled Dominique by the neck. "Tell me who sired you, or I will rip your baby brain to shreds."

Dominique wheezed. His eyes bugged.

"Tell me!"

"Kambyses," Jackson called, holding the bars in a death-defying grip. No matter what, he had to keep Esteban out of Dominique's muddled human head and learning just how vulnerable he was right now. "Kambyses sired him."

For the first time, Jackson found himself the target of Esteban's full attention. Eyes like wads of tar pressed into a ghost-pale face bore into him, and brutal fangs appeared in an otherwise refined, slack-jawed mouth. Dominique's current human self must be shitting himself right about now. Jackson wasn't far behind. *Keep it together, Striker. You don't spin this right, no one will ever find your body.*

"You have heard of Kambyses?" Jackson prompted. Esteban regarded him as if he were a dog using human speech. "The most powerful of you all? He had gifts nobody even imagined."

Leaving Dominique to gasp and wheeze, Esteban materialized before Jackson in a silent blur. Only the bars separated them. With the light behind him, Esteban's face was in shadows again, but the vampire's attention settled on Jackson like a physical weight. He took two small steps back.

"You," Esteban whispered. "I know you."

"I doubt that."

"Yes. I *know* you." The vampire closed his hands around the bars where Jackson's had just been. He was a full head shorter, but broad shouldered and powerful. "You were there the morning Santos died."

Jackson backed up farther. Every hair on his body stood on end. What the fuck was happening here?

"I know you...hunter," Esteban said. He keyed the lock to Jackson's cell and cornered him as a tiger cornered prey. A constant, inhuman growl vibrated in the surrounding air. Jackson fought to raise his anger, the fury that could mask his fear. He took another step back and bumped into solid rock.

"Santos was my oldest child. It was you and...your brother who came for him, wasn't it?" His cool breath brushed Jackson's face. "I was close, but still too far. I saw you come for him through his eyes. I felt the blow that took his life." He reached out to scrape a line across Jackson's larynx with a cold, hard fingernail. The growl dropped to a whisper. "But before that...before that, I shared his joy at tearing your brother's limbs and hearing the wet crack of his bones."

Jackson shuddered.

Esteban leaned closer, bracing one hand against the rough-hewn wall. "His skull smashed like a ripe melon." He illustrated by flicking apart his fingers in front of Jackson's face. "Pop."

Just like that, Jackson's burgeoning fear evaporated. The sire of his brother's killer, the reason this Santos was conscious enough to attack them, the ultimate catalyst for every nightmare that haunted Jackson since then—*that* monster stood right in front of him and prepared to destroy him too.

And there wasn't a single thing Jackson could do to stop it. He wouldn't even try.

Staring down into the black eyes, he gathered all the grief and rage that defined him into two words. "Fuck you."

Esteban grabbed Jackson by the scruff and yanked his face down to his own. "Is this why you're here? To finish me? Did you drag in that pitiful young one to bait me? Trick me? Coerce me? You are nothing, hunter. *Nothing!* Nothing but what I say you are." Compulsion resonated in the snarling voice. "And I say that you are mine to do with as I please. You are mine to grovel at my feet and to obey my every command for as long as I wish it. For. The. Rest. Of. Your. Miserable. Life."

Esteban released him with a shove that sent him smacking into the rock wall so hard he saw stars. The command vibrated in Jackson's bones—and dissipated. It was no match for the Lord of Night's earlier compulsion.

But his life depended on him making Esteban believe otherwise.

"As you wish," he said, doing everything in his power to sound calm and entranced despite his churning insides.

"I wish," Esteban reiterated with a dark growl. Then he surveyed the others in the cell with them. Rao and Campbell sat propped against a wall, both of them handcuffed, the latter looking dazed and clammy, his left leg soaked in blood. Jackson held his breath. His imagination served up several horrifying possible fates for them, including many Esteban might order him to execute.

To his unending relief, Esteban's interest in the officers appeared limited to being rid of them with the least amount of trouble. He hauled them to their feet and quickly drove his teeth into each neck. If he was surprised by what he didn't find in their heads—Dominique had erased himself from their memories as he compelled them—he didn't show it. Esteban poured his own blood into Campbell's wound, healing it. Shortly, the man regained his footing and moved with only a slight limp. Then, while breaking their cuffs with his fingers, Esteban put a new compulsion on them. "You are released from your duties here. Go home, clean up, burn your clothes. Nothing special happened today. You were never here. Let no one tell you otherwise. Go."

Without so much as a backward glance, they walked into the tunnel leading to the cavern and disappeared.

Only then did Jackson realize how much he was counting on Rao's assertions about someone coming to look for two missing officers. Now, no one would. Rao and Campbell wouldn't even remember him.

He was on his own.

Dominique had witnessed all this with a stillness that reeked of shock. He watched Esteban return as though watching a bear charging at him.

"Is the hunter your pawn, young one? Or are you his?" Esteban grabbed a hunk of Dominique's hair and pulled his head back. "I will have the truth from you."

Without further preamble, he latched onto Dominique's throat. The oblivious Lord of Night screamed and writhed, powerless as a fish in a net. Then twin pools of golden light flared in the shadows. For a breathless moment, Jackson watched comprehension dawn on Dominique's face.

Seconds later, the lights extinguished, and his face went as slack as his body.

34

QUEEN OF THE NIGHT

Fifteen minutes after the sun drowned in the Pacific, Cassidy felt like she was losing her mind. She paced through her suite, desperately groping for any sense of Dominique. There was nothing. Not even the flicker of a link she had still felt this morning, despite the enormous distance between them.

"When was the last time you called Jackson?" she asked Garrett, who stood, staring out the window, while she orbited the furniture. Ever the vigilant bodyguard, he had played tourist with Cassidy and Francesca again today, and, at Francesca's insistence, escorted them to dinner as well. Dominique's mother was now safely tucked into her room for the night, leaving Cassidy at last free to give full rein to her escalating anxieties.

"Every ten minutes for the last four hours. Texted, too. Nothing is getting through." The man who had carried on an animated conversation all day and all evening was gone. The hard-eyed hunter had re-emerged, looking even more intimidating than usual in his bespoke black suit and red silk tie. If they were in the States, she knew, he'd be packing a gun as well.

He turned to face her. "How about you? I take it you haven't sensed anything from Dominique yet?"

"Nothing. It's as if the earth swallowed him up."

"It did. They went into a mine."

"For an hour, not the rest of the freaking day. I don't like this. Not one bit."

"Operations sometimes have to change on a dime based on new information." Garrett didn't look convinced that this was the case here.

"Something is wrong. I'm sure of it."

"We don't really know anything yet."

"So? How long do you suggest we wait? Until they find Jackson's body and Dominique's ashes?" she snapped. No phone calls, she could understand. Technical issues happened. No trace of her brand new link with Dominique? There was no excuse for that except the very worst.

"Take it easy, Cassidy. Please." He held up a calming hand. "Panicking isn't going to help anybody."

She huffed out an aggravated breath and stopped to meet his gray eyes. They were the cool calm of a man absolutely sure of himself. "So, if not panicking, what do we do?"

"There's not much we can do. Not right now."

Cassidy heard the "not at night" he didn't say. "But there is someone who could do something."

Garrett nodded. "Isao, yes. I thought about that. But he doesn't know me."

Oh, he knows you, she thought, but was not about to divulge that Dominique's relationship with the Strikers was a source of great fascination for the samurai.

"Fine. Guess I need to do this myself." She adjusted her hair and straightened her brand new bolero jacket and silk blouse, which perfectly complimented the new flaring slacks and high heels. The clothes were courtesy of Francesca, who had declared herself Cassidy's personal shopper during their stay in the city.

"Do what by yourself?"

She snagged her Louis Vuitton purse, also new, from the sofa and stalked for the door. "Talk to Isao."

Garrett was suddenly beside her. "Wait. You can't just waltz up to a strange vampire by yourself."

"Of course not. Isao is not a strange vampire. He's sired to Dominique. Also, I am his queen," she said with somewhat more conviction than she felt. Dominique often referred to her as his queen, but she had yet to find reason to believe it, much less act on it, even with the Lord of Night himself by her side.

Garrett propped his hands on his hips, brow folding, but the expected argument did not materialize. "That you are," he said simply. "And I'm the queen's guard. Lead the way, my lady."

She nodded, unable to think of a single thing to say. Though nothing physical had changed with his words, something definitely had changed. Something subtle. Something that made things "real" for her as nothing else had. Queen—in spirit and in fact.

Queen of the night.

And it was as a queen, with her head held high and her expression confident, that she clicked across the hotel lobby in her stilettos with her personal guard trailing behind. She didn't miss the curious heads turning her way, wondering what celebrity she might be, and she noticed one in particular as she strode into the Coal Harbour Bar. A pale face with unnaturally intense eyes. A man in his thirties—at least when he had been turned—and definitely not Isao. Her heart jumped like a startled rabbit.

Garrett moved between Cassidy and this unexpected vampire. The stranger studied them before nodding toward the bar. She followed the look and spotted another man in a dark sweater, seated with his back to them. The neat black hair and perfect stillness were unmistakable.

Isao.

She nodded her acknowledgment to the strange vampire and moved in Isao's direction. So the samurai had brought reinforcements. Aside from being momentarily frightened out of her mind, she felt safer already.

As Cassidy approached, Isao turned from the untouched glass of brew on the bar and the hockey game on the large screen TV. His dark, almond-shaped eyes lingered on each of their faces in turn.

"Mr. Kiyomori?"

"Call me Isao," he said with an air of great formality and got to his feet to present a small bow. "How may I be of service, my lady?"

She took a relieved breath. This was going to be easier than she expected. Or far more complicated, she amended when she saw Isao's nostrils flare. His eyes widened slightly, and Cassidy realized the mistake she had made. Dominique wasn't the only vampire who could smell her condition, which Isao clearly just had.

"Have you heard from Dominique?" she said before he could say anything she preferred he didn't.

"No, my lady, I have not."

"Do you expect to?" Garrett asked.

Isao looked at Garrett with renewed interest.

"Mr. Striker is my daytime security detail," Cassidy introduced to cover the awkward moment.

"I know who he is," Isao murmured in a way that left no doubt about what all he knew. "I expect Dominique to contact me when he returns to the city sometime tonight." He held out his hand to Garrett, who hesitated only a second before taking it with the solid grip she imagined typical of professional hit men. "We should coordinate, you and I."

"We should," Garrett agreed.

"Perhaps you can coordinate on finding out where Dominique is," Cassidy suggested, struggling to keep the testiness out of her voice.

"Have you not heard from him, my lady?"

"Not even a whisper since early this morning."

"We can't reach him or Jackson on their phones either," Garrett added.

"They're in trouble. I know they are."

Isao thought for a moment. "Possibly."

"Excuse me?"

"If Adilla were to encounter Dominique, one of three things would happen. One is that Adilla would kill Dominique, another that Dominique would kill Adilla. In either scenario, I would be dead."

"Makes sense," Garrett agreed. "They're both alive, and Jackson hopefully, too."

"And the third thing?" Cassidy pushed, knowing already she wouldn't like the answer.

"The third potential outcome is that they're at a stalemate, with one holding control over the other," Isao said carefully.

"Shit," Garrett muttered.

Cassidy was the one to say it out loud. "So since we haven't heard anything, we're assuming that it's Adilla who holds the upper hand?"

"It would appear so."

Her chest tightened around her lungs. Suddenly she could hardly draw enough air to speak, and when she did, she sounded like she was wheezing instead of issuing commands. "Then what are you waiting for? Get on the road and help him."

"I cannot. My post is here, guarding you."

"I'm not the one whose death is going to take down half a million others," she hissed. Someone at the bar two seats away glanced in her direction. She looked away, blinking at the tears. Her hands clenched around the strap of her purse.

"I understand that," Isao said gently. "But I also know that my lord Dominique has the power and strength to prevail. He has many times before."

"Not after he's been awake all day," she ground out.

Isao stared at her, uncomprehending, and Cassidy knew she had revealed something else Dominique had chosen not to share with his latest convert. Oh well. He was in trouble and she was calling the shots now.

"It's a gift with a terrible price," she improvised. "As you well know, because you had to save his hide from Esteban the last time he did it."

The samurai looked dazed. "I see. And...he did this today?"

"Yes. He did."

"And he's a mess when he day-walks," Garrett confirmed.

"For how long?"

"Twenty-four hours."

"Then...if there is still no word from him tomorrow night...and I'm still alive...I will consider your request, my lady. Garrett, may I contact you later for an update?"

"Sure thing. Here." He reached inside his jacket and pulled out a card. "The business name is a fake, but the mobile is correct."

"Thank you." Isao handed him a card of his own.

Cassidy wanted to scream. "Really? We're just going to exchange cards tonight and hang out?"

"He has survived against impossible odds before," Isao said.

"This is diff—"

"He survives because of you, my lady." The samurai's quiet tone gained an edge as sharp as his weapons. He would suffer no more of her arguments. Not that she had any. She knew the truth. Dominique had told her so. *Without you, there is no me—and no kingdom.* She was his weakest link.

A tear broke free from her unblinking eye and slid down her cheek.

Isao softened. "Please understand. While I have great faith in his ability to triumph, I have no faith in my ability to survive him should anything happen to you—all of you," he cast a meaningful glance at her middle, "while you're under my protection."

When she said nothing, Isao turned to Garrett and asked about their plans and whereabouts for the rest of the night so he and his younglings could coordinate. With every word, Cassidy felt the lid on her box close tighter. The box for precious, guarded things—and pregnant mortal queens of immortal kingdoms.

God help her. If this is what it was like now, how would she ever survive this pregnancy?

35

Adilla Khan

There was vomit in Dominique's mouth, and his belly rippled as it tried to expel the last of the food he had eaten today. He was cold, his clothes damp. Behind his back, his wrists stung as though fettered in nettles. When he moved them, he realized they were shackled. There was also a hazy memory of being put in chains by humans.

During the day.

More memories came. Jackson exhorting him to break the chains, telling him what he was, a truth too impossible to believe, too terrifying to remember.

I will have the truth from you.

Dominique's thoughts snapped into focus. Esteban de Santiago had pushed into his mind. That was how he had woken up, remembered himself, and, like before, lost consciousness.

Esteban de Santiago was still there. In fact, he was cursing.

Dominique leaned his head against a hard surface that jiggled against his back and under his ass. Jackson stood behind Esteban, staring straight ahead, blind in this total darkness. All three of them were inside a cage, an elevator, dropping into nothingness. The weight of the sun lessened by the second. As it diminished, his mind cleared, and more murky memories rose. The ones from later in the day felt almost real. Those from earlier were specters that changed shape the harder he tried to focus on them.

Esteban shook his shoes and fine trousers. Whatever it was Dominique had foolishly eaten today had been disgorged all over the other vampire's shins and feet. "What is this nonsense? Food? Are you mad?"

The corner of Jackson's mouth betrayed laughter attempting to break free, but he otherwise appeared convincingly compelled, though of course he could not be.

The moment that thought crossed his mind, Dominique remembered Esteban's bite and erected his mental barriers. But Esteban was too distracted with the affront to his wardrobe to keep tabs on his prisoner's mind. "What do you think you are, you irrelevant child?"

Dominique pushed himself up the side of the elevator to stand and tower over the petite Spaniard. "I am your lord and master."

"Right." Esteban's will brushed against Dominique's defenses. "I can hardly wait to see you explain that to Adilla Khan."

"Neither can I," Dominique drawled. He adopted a careless air, though the blistering pain wrapping his wrists pushed his ability to concentrate to the brink. Any other night, he could have broken these shackles, but not after a day spent awake. He was as helpless as the last time Esteban had cornered him, except this time there would be no Isao to save him. This time—his single mortal ally notwithstanding—he was on his own.

The soupy gloom thinned as the lift slowed and clanked to a stop. Beyond the gate lay a small cavern, containing just enough light to allow sensitive eyes to adjust. A small archway opened onto another world entirely. There, a gilded hallway worthy of a palace stretched into the distance, ablaze with light from glittering chandeliers suspended from massive beams of burnished wood. Dozens of ponderous, iron-studded doors lined both sides of the hall. Massive tapestries depicting life-size scenes of historic battles and feasts covered the stone walls between them.

As they walked, the polished parquet floor creaked beneath the red silk runner covering the center of the hall. Murmuring voices drifted from up ahead, along with the softly haunting music of a drum-accompanied violin and piano. The voices and music sputtered to a halt when Esteban steered Dominique around a corner. They descended three broad stone steps into the midst of a gathering of blood-drinkers such as he had never seen. Hundreds of eyes—some of them darkening—found him and pinned him with intense curiosity. The vampires lounged on chairs, settees, or in piles of pillows on the floor in conversational clumps and were dressed in everything from business suits and cocktail gowns to blue jeans and saris. They were of different races, and judging by the miasma of scents mingling with the smell of blood, of vastly differing ages.

One thing they all had in common, though, was beauty. Every one of them could have compelled an army with a smile alone. Some probably had.

In contrast, the being seated on a dais at the other end of the hall would have been almost plain if not for the gold-embroidered purple regalia he wore. Or the gold-and-gemstone-encrusted throne he occupied.

Behind the throne and a little to the side, stood two others Dominique recognized from Isao's memories. Bhavanur, a young-looking man of uncommon loveliness, sparkled almost as much as his lord did. Markandeya, a regal, stone-faced man with thick gray hair and sharp eyes, had in life been Adilla's biological father. He now flanked his immortal son, wrapped in a drab gray cloak.

Adilla's voice was as hard and clear as the precious stones on his fingers. "Esteban. You have brought me a present."

Esteban shoved Dominique to his knees and dropped to the gleaming marble floor beside him. "My lord Adilla. The fool has brought himself. He desires an audience."

Every head swiveled to Adilla, who took his time finishing a crystal tumbler. When he held it out to the side, Bhavanur snatched up a decanter and scurried forward to refill his lord's glass with what could only have been blood. Blood no doubt drained from the innocents who had disappeared all over Vancouver. The same blood also filled countless other glasses in the room. This was how they survived here. And survived well, by the looks of them.

Adilla smiled as a snake might smile at approaching prey. "By all means, let him speak."

Esteban hauled Dominique up by an elbow and propelled him forward until they reached the dais, where he shoved him down again, smashing his knees hard into the floor.

Dominique caught Adilla's scent of a sun-warmed forest. A thousand years, probably more. But with his dark hair trimmed short and smoothed back from a wide forehead, he could have been anyone, anywhere, and in any age—except for the eyes. Mesmerizing even for a blood-drinker, their jade green depths glittered with ruthless power. They willed him to speak and give him an excuse to kill him. It wouldn't take much. And the only weapon in Dominique's arsenal right now was the truth.

It would have to be enough.

Not taking his eyes off Adilla, he rose to his feet. A shocked susurrus from the audience rose with him, but faltered into a horrified hush when he spoke. "Allow me to introduce myself. I am Dominique Marchant, the Lord of Night, and I kneel before no one."

The benevolence of seconds ago vaporized. Nostrils flaring, Adilla put down his drink. "You are either the most courageous creature I have ever seen...or the most foolish. But one thing you are most certainly not is the Lord of Night." He leaned forward a little, giving the impression of a snake again, this time preparing for a strike, and spoke in a hushed whisper. "I know the Lord of Night, you see. For he is my sire."

In the silence that followed, the tiny splats of blood dripping from Dominique's blistering wrists grew deafening.

"Then you should welcome me as a brother. I, too, am a child of Kambyses. And his heir," he finished on a growl. Whether or not he felt like it right now, he wasn't about to convince anyone if he didn't act like it.

"Outrageous," Bhavanur hissed with bared fangs.

Markandeya raised a single brow and crossed his arms.

Adilla chuckled, a humorless, patronizing sound, followed by a smattering of nervous laughter bubbling through the audience. "So you are a fool, then. You would have to be to believe this...if you know anything at all about Kambyses." He rose from his throne, a towering figure robed in purple and gold. "I am Adilla Khan, and I am the last the great Kambyses sired with his own blood. Not only was I strong enough to survive both his blood and his mind then, I am now the strongest he has ever made." His gaze swept over his followers as he made this pronouncement. They all lowered their eyes in deference, or perhaps just trying to escape his notice. "If he has any heir at all—as much as an immortal requires such a thing—that heir is I."

"Then come see the truth for yourself," Dominique said and bared his neck in invitation. If he could get Adilla to feed from him, he might be able to launch a re-siring by getting his own teeth into him and finish this madness. He fisted his shackled hands, forcing more blood from the expanding sores, seasoning the air with his vulnerable youngling tang.

In a flash, Adilla's eyes turned into obsidian glass—but it was Esteban who struck.

The Spaniard sprang up, forced Dominique to the ground with a vicious kick to the back of his knees. Then, he seized his head in both hands and battered into Dominique's mental defenses so hard his vision blurred. Since Esteban had already fed from him, Adilla wouldn't. Adilla would take what he wanted through his sire bond with Esteban.

So be it.

Before Esteban could overwhelm him and rampage through his mind, Dominique blasted him with his memories of Kambyses, his turning, their battles, and his ultimate victory over the five-thousand-year-old blood-drinker. He took care to abstract the actual transfer of the ancient essence, lest Adilla be tempted to try the same with him. Then he slammed the mental gates shut and jerked out of the startled Esteban's relaxing grip.

Esteban hissed. Several others, probably his younglings, shifted in their seats as they bore witness to what Dominique showed their sire.

"He knows the great one as he says," Esteban said aloud for those without telepathic links to him. "But he was not forged of his blood." He looked around. Their audience was wide-eyed and pale, even for vampires. "He claims to have slayed Kambyses and taken within himself the essence of our kind."

"As he wished," Dominique burst out. His head still rang from the assault, and the blistering burn in his wrists crawled up his forearms. The raw wounds didn't try to heal anymore. They just bled.

Adilla's eyes reverted to their shadowy moss green. "Brazen pup," he whispered.

Dominique's mouth twisted. "My most endearing trait, according to Kambyses." Taking Adilla's silence as a sign he might be getting somewhere, he pushed onward. "He gave me his kingdom to do with as I wished. And I wish there to be love and peace, not horror and fear. But it's not automatic. I need blood-drinkers like you, Adilla—old ones with great experience and wisdom—to help me make this happen." Adilla's chin rose slightly at the obsequious words. Dominique turned to the others. "Your lives are already bound to mine, but for you to hear me, too, you need to be re-sired by me." *Merde*, his arms were on fire. He had to convince someone to take the silver off him soon or he would go mad and act madder.

"Re-sire?" Adilla repeated. Calm. Glacially calm. "You wish to re-sire...me?"

Dominique got to his feet yet again. When Esteban reached for him, he snarled, but couldn't prevent being yanked back down. "I do, and I will," he promised through a pained grunt.

"I'm a prince who has known eleven hundred years of night, and you are what? A delusional youngling held by a mere pair of silver shackles?" His face distorted into a contemptuous sneer. "You are not worthy to gaze upon me, much less to receive my blood. For *any* purpose."

The speculative whispers in the hall died away into stillness.

Calm again, Adilla settled into his throne, wrapping himself in royal dignity, along with his robe. "You seem convinced that you did this thing. This taking of the essence from Kambyses."

"I did. Esteban saw it in my memories. You saw it through him."

Dominique bit his tongue until he tasted blood. Not to keep from saying more, but to distract himself from the agony in his arms and now shoulder blades. He fought not to tremble with it.

Adilla stroked a fingertip across his lower lip in thought. "Fortunately for you, young fool, I have spent centuries with Kambyses and know his ways like no other. I know the true extent of his power. If he wants you to believe that you killed him—"

"I did," Dominique hissed.

"—he can make it so. It is sadly obvious that you are his pawn, and your purpose is to test my loyalty to him." Adilla gestured with his bejeweled hands. "Will I believe and bow to you? Or will I doubt and kill you? These are the concerns he would want answered before he returns into my presence. And he is near," he concluded with an ominous air that drew several gasps. "I have felt his presence these past few nights."

For several seconds, Dominique even doubted himself and his own memories of what had happened. Then he realized Adilla was the first full child of Kambyses he had encountered since the transfer. It was possible that Adilla sensed Dominique—or no one at all.

The wild murmurings racing through the crowd seemed to please their lord, for his smile grew a little wider, a little less venomous, and a little more smug. Looking at the awe shining in their beautiful faces, it was easy to see that one of Adilla's charms for his followers was that he was sired by—and presumably had the favor of—the most powerful of them all. This was not an advantage Adilla would relinquish without a fight.

It was a privilege he would kill to preserve.

Aubrey had died for merely suggesting that another—a mere youngling, no less—had been more favored by the great one. "Of course, my loyalty is above reproach," Adilla said when the commotion faded to a low simmer. "So I will most certainly not yield to you. However, since we appear to be brothers of sorts"—he flapped one hand, dismissive—"I will grant you the opportunity to dispense with this charade and retract your claims. If you do, I will invite you to join my family." This with an expansive gesture to include the hall and everyone in it.

Cheers erupted, and somewhere in the haze of pain, Dominique understood why Adilla still suffered him to live. It was Adilla's greatest fear: the displeasure of Kambyses.

And what would displease the Lord of Night more than murdering his chosen emissary?

Too late, Dominique thought, displeased beyond measure.

Adilla continued speaking over the tumult. "I have made my colony the largest of its kind anywhere in the world. It is also, because of my wise guidance, by far the most prosperous." He paused, and adulation poured forth on cue. "My strategies and projects will bring us millennia of greatness. And you, dear young one, are welcome here. As is Kambyses himself, should he decide to grace us with his presence."

The cheering escalated. Only Markandeya did not appear to be a fan. No expression whatsoever registered on his face.

"So what do you say, brother?" The soft sneer on that last word wasn't lost on Dominique, who suddenly saw his true predicament. Adilla would not kill Kambyses's supposed messenger, not with hundreds of witnesses, and not without an excuse as solid as the rock walls. He was all but begging Dominique to give him that excuse by refusing his oh-so-benevolent offer. If Dominique accepted, Adilla would count it as a victory in the eyes of his devotees—and find another way to dispose of him in short order.

It was a game. A deadly and sadly typical game in the world of night as it used to be. Dominique had played a few of his own.

But no more.

Again, he leapt to his feet, and this time spun away from Esteban's lightning-fast grab. Between the pain and outrage, his control had reached its limits. "I say that I kneel before no one," he snarled. "Ever."

Silence again, thick as quicksand. In Dominique's expanding vision, a constellation of white blood-drinker auras glowed.

Adilla stared at him, expressionless. Stared at the golden light blazing in Dominique's eyes. "Perhaps I didn't make myself clear. I am giving you a rare opportunity to join more than a colony of blood-drinkers. We are a family." He held out his hand in what appeared to be a random direction. "*Your* family."

Something slammed down on his shoulders and pressed with the weight of a world. Esteban. Down he went. Add a cracked kneecap to his list of miseries. He couldn't even feel his arms anymore.

A new aura bobbed amidst the blaze of white. It wasn't Jackson. His aura was red, this one a vibrant blue. A stranger...

Realization punched his gut like a steam-powered fist. The blue bubble was a woman who should have been impossible in this place. She was a little more full-bodied than he remembered, but her scent shimmered with sage and herbs and the tropical sun. And her face, with their father's soft curves and mother's distinctive widow's peak, was unmistakable.

Four years of time vanished in an instant.

A garbled snarl emerged from his throat. "Geneviève."

His last surviving sibling didn't look at him, her attention for Adilla alone. Compelled. She might not even know there were others in the hall. Adilla held her under his spell as she took his hand and dropped to her knees. Her navy blue skirt flared out around her.

Dominique moaned. His entire body shook with pain.

With rage.

With helplessness.

"Geneviève, *ma petite chérie*. Look who has joined us," Adilla said in flawless French.

She looked as ordered, and when she spotted Dominique, her face brightened. "*Frère préféré!*" She saw only him, her "favorite brother," not his circumstances, bleeding and on his knees, nothing of the horrific reality. "Have you come to visit? Or to stay?"

"He will stay," Adilla assured. His smile didn't touch his eyes. "Now that he sees you so happy here, how can he not?"

Geneviève beamed at Adilla.

"No. No, you cannot," Dominique spluttered. This time, when he bolted to his feet, he leveled a solid kick at Esteban's ribs. At least one cracked audibly. The Spaniard, who had been trying to snatch at him, stepped back with a grunt. Dominique's not-yet-healed knee screamed and threatened to buckle.

Adilla pressed a kiss to Geneviève's knuckles before turning over her hand to expose the wrist. "We have gotten to know each other these past two nights, have we not, my dear?"

She continued to smile.

"No!"

Ink wells bloomed in Adilla's eyes as his fangs emerged.

"Do not touch her, you fucking piece of shit!" Dominique roared, but Adilla already had his teeth into her wrist—for perhaps the third time in as many nights. She was more than halfway turned.

Dominique's flesh rippled and compacted as his beast exploded to the surface. With a mighty jerk, his shackles snapped and his hands came free, darting out to either side of him. Silver-coated bracelets slipped over his bony, bloodied wrists and clattered to the floor. Adilla, under the influence of blood fresh from the vein, paid him no heed.

But others did.

Before Dominique could take more than a step in Adilla's direction, Esteban and two more closed in. He leapt into the air and kicked out with both feet. Esteban ducked out of the way, but the others fell back, howling, their noses smashed. His injured knee failed him on landing, pitching him sideways. Four more took advantage, grabbed him, and pinned him to the floor by his shoulders and legs.

Dominique screamed to the limits of his lungs, which was a hoarse croak compared to what it should have been. Frustration and anger burned through him. This is where his dream of seeing the sun again had brought him, here, to the brink of losing everything.

Everything.

Suddenly, that was precisely what he wanted. Lose everything, including his life. He would take them all with him, the world over. Geneviève would be free. Jackson would get her to the surface and take care of Cassidy and her child. They would all survive. As mortals.

All he had to do was die.

"I will never submit to you. I am your lord, not a test from an ancient one who could not tolerate your company," he screamed on an impulse he scarcely understood. Kambyses had never mentioned Adilla to him, but somewhere deep in Dominique's psyche rested the immense accumulation of Kambyses's memories that had come along with all his sire's blood. They were nothing Dominique could call up at will, but every now and then, like now, knowledge came to him out of nowhere. In this case, knowledge about an ambitious young prince in a long-vanished realm with no hope of ever gaining true power. He had manipulated Kambyses into bestowing the gift of immortality, and Kambyses, in turn, had abandoned him—after decades, not centuries.

"You disappointed him," Dominique continued in a guttural snarl. "He regretted making you as he regretted nothing else in all his eternal life. If you had not been the last who survived his blood, he would have put you down. *Like I will!*"

Appalled cries rose all around, and the vampires holding him hissed. Esteban appeared, and, in a flash, delivered a backhanded blow so violent Dominique's jaw fractured. Blood exploded in his mouth. Just as quickly, he spat it and a shattered tooth back into Esteban's sneering face. A claw hand shot toward him.

"Stop!" Adilla roared. The silence was instantaneous.

Sharp nails already pierced Dominique's skin and dug under his tendons, but hesitated. Then they withdrew, leaving him coughing and gagging. Instead of ripping out Dominique's gullet, Esteban wiped at the blood dripping from his face.

Adilla moved closer, towering above Dominique's prone form. "At my court, it is I who decides who lives and who dies."

The four holding him down murmured their obedient agreement.

"Brazen," Adilla said again, and shifted his weight. One of his feet moved as though preparing to crush his skull with a single stomp.

"You are a useless buffoon, drunk on your own imagined greatness," Dominique growled, using words that Kambyses had uttered verbatim. "You are not fit for immortality."

A thousand years ago, Adilla had responded by charging at Kambyses in a shrieking fury. Now he only stared down at Dominique as though seeing a ghost.

Dominique had said too much.

Adilla would know these words to be true memories. That Dominique knew them—regardless of how—was irrefutable evidence that his connection to Kambyses was profound.

"You will be mine," Dominique promised, hoping only to push the useless buffoon over the edge. "You will be mine or you will be dead."

Adilla shifted his weight back. The wheels spinning behind his unblinking jewel eyes settled into place. "I could not have said it more eloquently myself."

A tiny gesture to one side, then Dominique's feet were jammed together and bound tight enough to crush his ankles. A rope flew toward the ceiling and looped around a thick cross-beam, descended on the other side and grew taut. His bound feet shot in the air, following the rope, hauling him up to swing wildly toward the far end of the hall. Several blood-drinkers darted out of the way. Jackson, still by the grand main entrance, watched with an expression of helpless horror.

When Dominique swung back, Esteban caught him. He stripped off the vest and shirt, both tearing like tissues in his powerful hands, then pulled his arms straight down. Someone else wrapped another rope around his forearms, immobilizing him completely.

Adilla appeared in his upside down view of the world and smiled with cold malevolence. "If you have had so much of the great one's blood, by all means. I will gladly take you up on your offer. Bhavanur, bring a pitcher. A rare vintage must be shared with family."

Dominique's whole body went limp with shock. No, there would be no direct feeding. They would drain him. Drain him the way all those mortals back in the city had been drained.

The crowd's mood turned appreciative as celebratory music started up. Bhavanur appeared before him in a blur and grabbed his bound arms. A small silver blade flashed against his still raw wrists. Seconds later, Dominique heard his blood splatter into the belly of the requested pitcher.

Screaming with rage and more than a little fear, Dominique thrashed and flipped at the end of the rope. If he could reach his feet, maybe...

Hands grabbed for him, held him still and, once the blade re-opened his vein, directed the stream of blood into the receptacle.

Over Bhavanur's shoulder and past Adilla's purple robe, he saw Geneviève, his sister and once closest friend. She sat on the dais by the empty throne and stared at the spectacle with an empty face. She looked dead already, a corpse that forgot to lie down.

Tremors raced through Dominique's body. Tears blurred his vision.

He had failed.

Failed to assert himself. Failed to protect those he cared for. Failed as a wannabe human and as a blood-drinker lord. And failed to convince Adilla of anything that mattered. Whether Adilla believed there might be some truth to Dominique's story or only tried to avoid giving offense to Kambyses was irrelevant. The result was the same.

He would use Dominique, but he would not destroy him. Not now.

Not ever.

36

Morning Light

There was no doubt in Jackson's mind. It was his general uselessness as a mere mortal that saved him from the worst of the night. To vampires like Esteban, he was nothing but a docile food supply, a sheep, and he spent the interminable hours in the great hall of horrors doing all in his power to maintain the appearance of one.

He crouched in a back corner and focused on his breathing. The music played and the party rolled while his friend hung like a slab of meat, being bled until he became a skeletal, unrecognizable shadow of himself. Jackson couldn't afford even the slightest reaction. Any hint of fear spicing his scent or speeding up his heart was bound to attract the sort of attention that would get him killed.

But Esteban had not forgotten him. The slight figure of a male decked out in a shimmering lavender silk suit suddenly stood by Jackson's side to deliver a curt message. "Your lord requests you attend to him. Now." He shoved a pitcher into Jackson's hands and returned to Adilla's side in a blur.

The winter-fresh scent of Dominique's blood wafted from the pitcher. Jackson's stomach hitched. *Nothing. It's nothing*, he told himself, and began putting one foot in front of the other. He looked only at Esteban, seeing nothing and no one else, least of all Dominique. But he felt their curious eyes, hundreds of them.

Esteban had changed his vomit-soaked trousers for a fresh pair and occupied a small bench near Adilla's throne, which was apparently reserved for the favored few. He held out his glass. When Jackson filled it, he growled between grinning teeth, "Do *not* get sick, you filthy blood bag."

It was the one compulsion Jackson gladly accepted. He made good use of it and every other mental exercise in his bag of tricks as Esteban and Adilla reminisced about the bloodcurdling details of countless vampire atrocities—including Justin's death. This was followed by a vivid discussion about what to do with Jackson, complete with curious glances in his direction. He prayed he was too valuable as a toy to dispose of quickly, but made peace with the thought of dying at any moment. He had no control over anything except his own reaction. *Nothing, it's nothing,* he chanted in his mind over and over again. *Nothing at all.*

After a while, they tired of their game. Adilla moved on to enjoying members of his court heaping flattery upon him and groveling for favors while Esteban ordered Jackson to bring the pitcher with him to a quiet seat. There, he pulled out a smartphone and checked his email before contacting a long list of operatives and business partners via video. They might hail from long-gone centuries and sit under a mountain, but the colony maintained an admirable Wi-Fi connection to the world.

Jackson swayed on his feet, and half the crowd had already drifted away before Esteban decided what to do with his new sheep. "Go to the surface and attend to your needs," he said without looking at him. "Be in the cave two hours before nightfall."

All the way up the lift, Jackson continued his chant. *Nothing, it's nothing.* His knees wobbled with relief as he stumbled toward the early morning light in the cave's mouth. But not until fresh forest air filled his lungs and a glorious blue sky curved overhead did he allow himself to feel again. He sucked at the air, stuffing it into his tight chest until his ribs ached.

A dam broke and all the terror of the night hit him full force. *How the fuck am I still alive?* He clenched his hands into fists to stop them shaking. *Keep your shit together. You're a long way from getting out of this,* he admonished himself.

A very long way.

Dominique was still down there and in no shape to get out on his own, which meant Jackson would go back there. He had promised Cassidy. More than that, Jackson would not abandon his friend, even if he was the pain-in-the-ass lord of the vampires.

Fuck, what a mess.

As the sun broke over the peaks bordering the creek's far shore, Jackson staggered into the village, hoping against hope to find his car sitting where he had left it with keys in the ignition. Of course, it wasn't there. Hungry, thirsty and overdosed on adrenaline, he looked around in a daze when the front door of a nearby cottage opened.

"You came back from the cave," Earl called, sounding more than a little mystified. His bushy brows drew together. "Not many come back from there."

His wife, a ruddy-cheeked woman with a mop of faded brown curls, was less philosophical. "You must have had quite the night, young man. Come in, come in. We're just having breakfast."

As neither one of them wielded a shotgun, Jackson risked taking her up on the offer. He did his best not to gulp the fresh scrambled eggs and salty sausages heaped on his plate, but his appetite was such he wanted to unhinge his jaw and tip this and the next plate down his throat. Is this what it was like for a starving vampire? This gut-wrenching need for...something? He wondered if this was what Dominique would feel when he regained consciousness.

He wondered if he would want to be anywhere near him.

Taking the lead from his hosts, he kept the conversation to a minimum. Whatever they thought of him or where he came from, they didn't say. Somehow it was understood—he had returned from the cave; he was one of them and in service to the cave dwellers.

Earl's wife, June, had a mother-hen quality about her in both appearance and spirit as she doted on her guest. Jackson didn't even need to ask for a place to rest. When he stopped shoveling food in his mouth, she showed him to a small but tidy guest room upstairs and promised to keep down the noise in the house today.

Jackson used the last of his coherent thoughts to wedge a chair under the doorknob and locate and set an ancient analog travel alarm. Its insistent ticking on the nightstand dropped him into dreamless sleep within seconds.

Its shrieking ring pulled him back out only four hours later.

He stretched and shook out his limbs and considered his options. There really was only one. He had to wing it like never before and do it now, while the sun was at its highest. His phone had been taken from him when he was first put in the cell. God only knew where it was, but asking for it might well raise suspicions about his motives. Also, Garrett was too far away to help, and Cassidy was better off not knowing the details. In fact, he fervently hoped her link with Dominique couldn't reach this far.

Jackson was flying solo. No backup, no Garrett, no Grid. If he failed, he was dead.

I've lost my fucking mind, he thought as he made his way downstairs. He had a bride-to-be and a child on the way. The last thing he should do was risk his life for someone who couldn't die.

No, that wasn't it. There was more to do down there than to rescue His Badass Highness from this jam. There was Dominique's sister. She was a half-turned human in dire need of immediate rescuing.

And if he could relieve one Esteban de Santiago of his head along the way, so much the better.

A plan formed amidst his spinning thoughts as he moved down the creaking wooden stairway. Phase one required finding his car. Instead, he found Earl relaxing on the front porch after what—judging by his high color and mud-streaked overalls—appeared to be a long morning on the farm.

"Well, you're looking a bit better," his host greeted.

"I'm feeling much better, thanks," Jackson agreed with an amiable smile. He looked around the yard and bucolic scenery beyond. A handful of people moved in the garden plots, and someone was fishing in the creek, each of them intend on their own business. There was no conversation, no laughter, not even the sound of a radio. Somewhere a cow mooed. "Hey, you wouldn't happen to know where my car went, would you?"

"Oh? Going somewhere, son?" Earl wondered, sounding not quite casual.

"And leave all this? Are you kidding? But I have a bag in the back with a change of clothes I could use."

"Ah, all right. Come, I'll show you."

Jackson smiled and nodded as Earl got up and led the way.

The SUV had been moved behind the barn. With his back turned to Earl, he checked his bag and found the contents undisturbed: a change of clothes, toiletries, and—most important—the black leather case with the suppressant. The last, he tucked into his best pocket before zipping up the bag, grabbing it, and closing the hatch. Phase one was complete.

Phase two was related to phase one in ways he didn't care to contemplate. He launched into it on the way back to the house. "I'll need a couple of the guys to come back into the mine with me."

Earl stopped and looked at him, incredulous. "The mine? Why would you want to go back there?"

He made a show of looking uncertain. "I was asked to go back today." He dropped his voice a little. "By *them*."

For a moment, the large man with his hands tucked into the bib of his overalls didn't seem to have heard him. Jackson imagined he could see the compulsion churning in the pale eyes, trying to decide on a course of action. "And you need help?"

"Yeah. Some things need cleaning up." About two-hundred-odd things, in fact.

Earl scratched his beard. "Well, if you were told, I guess you can't say no."

Jackson remained straight-faced. "Why would I want to?"

"Right. Okay, c'mon. Let's get you your cleaning crew, then."

37

CLEANING CREW

T he crew was a little larger than Jackson had hoped. He was fairly certain he could handle two—so long as they didn't pull out their shotguns again—but three was pushing it. *Wing it*, he told himself, smiling and nodding.

They were three of the four men from the day before, but there was no animosity in them. No one mentioned the shootout, and all introduced themselves to Jackson as though they had only just met. He shook their hands. Terry, the lanky redhead with the wary scowl and nasal voice; Tim, his fresh-faced younger brother and steadfast shadow; and Carl, a large man whose jaw was in constant motion over a wad of tobacco.

Compulsion can be a beautiful thing, Jackson decided as he led the way to the cavern with his new companions. This time, they remained armed only with flashlights.

His backpack was still where it had been flung yesterday, all its contents intact. He pulled out the full-spectrum torch and lit up the small room bright as day.

The lift was still where he left it, thanks to the gate he had left open wide this morning, which blocked it from descending. If anyone noticed the glitch, they hadn't cared enough—or been unable—to pursue a fix that late in the morning.

My lucky day. Your loss.

When he stepped into the lift cage, all three men looked at him uncertainly. Terry scratched the back of his neck. "No one's ever been down there."

"I have. It's okay. Really."

The trio thought this over, their eyes drifting between Jackson and the lift. He tensed when Terry eyed the cell Jackson had languished in. "It's not safe," he concluded. The comment sounded automatic, like the compulsion it surely was.

"We'll be fine. *They* told me to come," Jackson said, hoping that "not safe" referred to *their* safety, not the safety of the vampires sleeping deep beneath their feet, who were definitely *not* so safe once he got down there.

The reminder of his supposed orders galvanized his helpers. Carl spat out a stream of tobacco juice. "Guess we better get going, then."

The lift sagged a little as they piled in. The motor ground to life above their heads and spewed oil-scented fumes that merged with the pong of warm male bodies in too-close quarters. Tension built like pressure with every foot they dropped, and the men held the overwhelming darkness at bay by keeping their flashlights trained on the coarse walls sliding up around them.

When the lift slowed and halted, they were surrounded by solid rock on three sides and nothing on the fourth. Jackson sucked in a breath. Without the electric lights in the hallway beyond this vestibule, the darkness was thick enough to cut. Thick enough to eat their lights. Thick enough to nurture things that could not abide the sun—maybe even at this time of day.

Shoving that grim possibility out of his mind, he opened the gate.

"I don't like this," Tim, the youngest of the trio, said.

"This won't take long. And it gets better just past there." Jackson walked through the arched passage to the underground compound's central hall. The wooden floors and silk rugs, the chandeliers and tapestries were all still there, silently waiting for the true night to return.

Terry made a low whistle as he swung his light around, the beam refracting in the chandeliers. "Will you look at that?"

"Epic," his brother concurred.

Carl spat his juice onto the polished wood beside the rug.

"Can't take you anywhere, can we?" Tim chastised.

"Shut up," Carl snorted.

For reconnaissance, Jackson tried several random doors lining the hallway. All of them were locked. If he wanted to find any specific vampires—or a human in need of rescuing—breaking them down would take a while. *Fuck.*

A half-acknowledged fear that Dominique might have been moved into one of these chambers evaporated the moment he made the final turn into the throne room. There he was, the Lord of Night, where Jackson had last seen him, hanging by his ankles, still as a corpse. His skeletal torso blazed like a lamp in the heavy darkness when his beam hit it. Then it turned bright pink. Jackson jerked the lethal torch light aside.

"What the fuck," Terry muttered. "Is this what we're cleaning up?"

"That's it," Jackson agreed.

"Sick," Tim said.

No argument there. Jackson swept his light around, confirming that the rest of the room contained only furnishings. A few shawls and other pieces of clothing lay scattered on seats, and many of the tables held glasses coated with blood. The hall was frozen in the damp, underground darkness, awaiting the return of its nightmarish inhabitants. One of the bloodstained pitchers sat on a table near him.

"Carl, can you find the end of the rope that's keeping him up there and get him down?" Jackson said, shrugging out of his backpack and dumping it on the nearest seat.

With his flashlight, the man traced the rope to the rafters and back down, then ambled off toward the far end without comment. The beams of the brothers sliced through the crushing darkness, glinting off dead chandeliers and crystal tumblers.

Jackson grabbed the pitcher. It came off the table with a sickeningly sticky noise. The smell of blood wafted out, making his jaw tighten. He was about to fling the pitcher away when he realized it wasn't empty. A thin layer of half-congealed blood sloshed at the bottom. He froze for a moment before lowering it. "Terry, see if you can find some cleaning supplies somewhere. We need to get this blood off the floor." Turning to Tim, he added, "And bins to collect all these filthy glasses."

"And do what with 'em?"

"I told you. We're here to clean."

"Oh. Right."

The brothers moved off toward the gilded throne and the archways lining the wall behind it.

Dominique swayed and bounced as Carl loosened the line and lowered him into a cadaverous heap on the ground.

Jackson propped his powerful light on his backpack so it wouldn't touch Dominique, but also glare in Carl's direction, blinding the man. He ignored the resulting holler of protest, grabbed the pitcher, raised it to his lips, and tipped it up.

The blood tasted of ice-encrusted iron and was about as cold against his tongue, triggering his gag reflex. As the slimy mass slid down his craw, he tried not to think of bloated corpses. Then a muted jolt hit, nowhere near what it was fresh from the vein but enough. Warmth suffused him, and some new strength. The footsteps of the men grew louder in his ears, and his eyes no longer saw nothingness in the far reaches of the hall, but a fuzzy collection of shapes and passageways.

Jackson wiped at his mouth with his shirtsleeve, set the vile pitcher down, and turned his attention to Dominique. He grabbed one bony shoulder and rolled the would-be carcass to his back. The sight before him made his gorge rise. The bastards had bled Dominique as close to death as it was possible for a vampire to get. His body had struggled to compensate, creating the blood he needed to survive at the expense of almost every bit of soft tissue he possessed. By now, his skin stretched over bones and little else. In human terms, he was a famine victim. In vampire terms, he was incapacitated and one blow away from permanent death.

"This is fucking insane," he muttered under his breath. Pulling the leather case from his vest pocket, he quickly loaded one of the remaining two syringes. He should just stick Dominique in a body bag and hope to God that he could convince the trio that hauling him out of here and driving away with him was following his orders. And if the suppressant didn't work, he might yet resort to that.

Though much more horrifying was the thought of what would happen if the suppressant actually *did* work under these circumstances. Jackson didn't see how it could, but the odds of getting Dominique out of here—to say nothing of rescuing or killing anyone or anything else—were much improved if he could function autonomously.

With his fingertips, Jackson located the weak flutter just beneath Dominique's sternum where the belly had caved in. Aiming the needle, he jabbed it deep and pressed the plunger.

He filled the wait that followed by pulling the Bowie knife from his pack and cutting the bindings from Dominique's forearms. There was still no sign of life when the tread of heavy boots approached behind him. "So what's the plan for"—Carl's flashlight fell over the vampire's inert form—"that."

"I'm hoping he'll just walk out of here."

The other man snorted. "Right. He looks to be done walking."

Jackson stared at Dominique's blood-smeared skull face, willing him to wake. *C'mon, c'mon, c'mon.*

More footsteps, Terry's this time, accompanied by a hollow rattling. The son of a bitch had actually found a mop and bucket. Who knew bloodsuckers could be so domestic?

Dominique's chest rose and fell with a tiny breath. Jackson swallowed his relief—and his horror. "Rise and shine, sleeping beauty," he whispered.

The eyelids struggled against the dried blood gluing them shut before opening into narrow slits.

Carl scuttled backward with a gasp. "Holy shit!"

"It's okay," Jackson assured, raising a calming hand.

"Holy fuck, how is that thing alive?"

The clattering bucket sped up. Tim's flashlight swung in their direction from the room's far corner. Soon all three would converge on him—or race for the lift. Since neither outcome fit into Jackson's ad-hoc plans, he got up, took two giant steps, and leveled a massive right hook at Carl's jaw—all in a single fluid motion that felt more like a dance move than the contorted attack that it was. The large man keeled over onto one of the ornate tables, which collapsed in a mass of splinters.

The bucket clanged to the ground. Not so the mop. The moment Jackson turned around, he spotted the handle coming for his head in a wide arc. Jackson grabbed it and yanked hard. Terry jerked forward. His feet tripped against Dominique's side as Jackson's fist rammed home into Terry's gut. With a loud *oomph*, the redhead doubled over and came down on top of Dominique, who jerked up, his wasted arms flailing, mouth gaping, and blood-caked hair standing on end.

"Welcome back," Jackson said as he shook out his hand. Pointing to the man squirming by his side, he added, "Lunch is served."

Dominique stared. At him. At Carl spread-eagled in the debris. At Terry groaning beside him. Then he saw his blood-covered hands. He held up the bony claws in front of his emaciated face. A dry hiss rattled in his throat.

Jackson was grateful there wasn't a mirror handy, and he congratulated himself for remaining so calm. He kept his gaze locked on Dominique's eyes, which remained human and very much confused. "You've been bled out all night. You need to—"

A small sound made him spin around in time to see the shadowy figure of Tim wielding a large tray in two hands. "You touch my brother, you die, you asshole!"

As Jackson snapped up his arm to block the blow, he spotted Terry staggering to his feet and reach for the discarded Bowie knife. Jackson spun to kick it away past the bewildered Dominique just as the tray crashed down on the finger stumps on Jackson's right hand. Pain shot all the way up to his shoulder, but he ripped the tray out of Tim's hands and whapped it against the side of the boy's head hard enough to make him reel and trip. Terry charged him with an outraged yell, but a hard kick to his solar plexus pitched him into a group of chairs which scattered on impact. Both brothers groaned but stayed where they landed. Jackson flung the tray away.

Dominique crept backwards on the trembling spindles of his arms and legs. The pants flapping around his bony hips threatened to slide off and hobble him. He continued to hiss, his vocal cords sounding like they had withered away to the consistency of dental floss. Raw panic lit his enormous eyes.

"Easy," Jackson cooed and made quieting motions with his hands. "Easy. You're going to be okay. Relax."

Dominique halted his retreat, but it was hard to tell if that was because of Jackson's words or his strength giving out.

"You'll feel better in a moment, I promise." Jackson retrieved the knife from under the sofa. Dominique hissed again, but this time the sound shifted, darkened, and morphed into a deep, wet growl.

The small hairs all over Jackson's body rose in primal alarm. "Easy," he whispered, backing away. "Easy." Without letting Dominique out of his sight, he crouched beside the still-unconscious bulk of Carl and brought the knife edge to the man's wrist. He made a shallow scratch, barely enough to draw a line of blood.

Dominique's eyes riveted to the injury. The growling stopped.

Jackson eased out of the way. "This is what you're hungry for," he murmured, his voice just this side of unsteady. A part of him recoiled at what he was doing. Only a small part, though, and growing fainter by the moment. "You know you want it. Go and get it."

The vampire's gaze flickered to him, and his mouth opened a little wider. Then the fresh wound captured his attention again. He crawled forward as though fighting the pull of an invisible string.

Jackson wiped the back of his hand over his mouth, ignoring the soft tremor in his fingers. If this didn't work...

Dominique was still undecided when Carl came to with a groan. He blinked at the surrounding shapes in the reflected half-light. When he realized what hovered over him, he yelped and tried to roll away.

The starving vampire pounced with a speed that belied his withered body. Pinned to the ground, Carl thrashed and screamed with unmitigated fear. The whites in Dominique's eyes disappeared. For another small eternity, he hesitated, and Jackson rode a razor's edge between raw terror and roaring anticipation.

Then indecision poured out of Dominique the way his blood had poured out of him all night. He shoved the terrified face aside, drove his teeth into the fleshy neck, and fed.

38

THE SPACE BETWEEN

"Are you back yet?"

The words slithered between his thoughts like eels. He understood them, but their meaning eluded him. As did the identity of the man who spoke them. He thought he knew him, this bronzed, muscled creature with the cutting bright eyes. He thought he could trust him. Which is why he tried so hard to understand.

"Guess not," said the man and glanced at his watch again. "Just relax. It'll come." But the worry in the pinched face told Dominique that maybe it—whatever it was—might not come.

Dominique looked around for "it." Evergreens towered like fragrant walls, holding back a flood of shadows. They were alone here. The man sat on top of a picnic table. Dominique stood before him. Every few seconds, the sound of a car passing somewhere out of sight overpowered the wind soughing in the branches.

His companion muttered below his breath, and Dominique turned back to him.

"The sun's been down five minutes. Talk to me. Do you know who I am?"

"A friend." The words rolled like pebbles in his mouth.

"Right." The friend rubbed his face with one hand, pulling at his chin, frustrated. "And you are?"

"Dominique."

"What are you?"

The pebbles turned to concrete. His mind emptied.

"Fuck." He slid off the table. "Fine. Let me remind you." Before Dominique could fathom what he was about, the friend produced a pocket knife, unfolded it, and ran the edge over the pad of his thumb. The welling blood sparkled with luminous beauty, and the meaty metallic smell of it hit Dominique with tangible force.

"Anything?"

He swallowed hard and hunched his shoulders against a sudden chill. He didn't move as the friend pressed the injured thumb to Dominique's mouth. Blood seeped between his lips. The concrete in his mind crumbled. The blockage disappeared.

Darkness spewed forth.

Dominique reared back and gasped. Reality crystallized around him in all its terror and fury.

The blood-drinkers he had been too weak to fight.

His sister among them.

The half-asleep fog he had awakened to.

The darkness he escaped—and was still trying to escape.

The darkness that defined him.

"*Je m'souviens*," he said. "I'm back."

Jackson retreated several steps and sucked the blood off his thumb. "About fucking time."

Dominique doubled over, but his stomach only rolled for a second or two before settling down. He had consumed no solid food this day. His hands looked thin as they clasped his knees, and his whole body felt fragile as glass.

Hunger gnawed at him...even though he had fed.

He looked up. "Did I take their lives? The men you brought?"

"You remember what happened?"

"Maybe." He straightened. His leather jacket flapped open over his bare chest, and a pair of cargo pants rode far too low on his skinny hips. His heart pushed sand through his veins. He would need more. Much, much more. "Like fading dreams. Nightmares," he amended. "You came for me."

"I wanted to get Geneviève. I kinda needed you."

Renewed despair hit him. He tried to sift through Jackson's memories of the day, but couldn't quite muster the necessary focus. Still, on some level, he already knew. "We did not find her."

Jackson shook his head. "No. You were a useless zombie to-day. I tried to get you to break down those doors, but you didn't have the strength. It was better for us to get as far away from there as possible before we got anywhere close to sunset."

"Did you try to stop me from taking lives, too?"

"Yes."

Dominique remembered the blood's scalding heat in his belly. So much blood. "You failed."

Jackson's jaw tightened. "With the first one, yes. The other two ran when they figured out what was going on." He paused. "I don't know if you heard me or not when you tracked them down, but you stopped before they were too far gone."

"I heard you," Dominique said softly. Jackson's cursed demands had been desperate enough to reach him, even as the blood filled him. He had taken too many lives before becoming Lord of Night, but none since. Any life sacrificed to sustain him was a life too many. "*Merci.*"

"You listened to me when I told you to compel them to think their friend died of an accident. They carried him to the surface with us and then let us drive away. And here we are." He waved a hand at the wilderness and picnic tables.

"Which is where?"

"We're about halfway back to Vancouver. Far enough from them for the moment, I think."

Halfway. In the middle. Like him. Balancing on an invisible edge. Not just between geographic locations, but between his sister to the east and Cassidy to the west, and more than that even—he balanced between his past and his future. Between day and night.

Between humanity and…not.

"You have to recover," Jackson said as though reading his mind. "Don't even think about going back for your sister while you're like this. She has a couple more days."

"Do you know how she got here?"

Jackson filled him in on Cassidy's unthinkable news that morning about a compelled spy right there in his lair. Natalia's and Ryan's "escape" from the colony hadn't been good fortune so much as it had been Esteban's plot. The fragile little Russian blood-drinker was nothing but a tool used and disposed on a whim. Given what she and Ryan saw during their brief stay at Dominique's house, it would have been simple to find vulnerable mortals with whom to coerce and torment him.

He scrubbed both hands over his face and let the frustration wash over him and away. His need to charge to his sister's rescue bordered on overwhelming, but in his current condition, he would end up right back where he had been, hung up and drained. And this time Jackson would not be suffered to live.

There were other consequences as well. Through Natalia, Esteban had been a step ahead of Dominique almost from the moment she crossed Aubrey's path. He must feel very sure of his victory to order his unwitting spies destroyed now. Also, he had been in Dominique's muddled head. There was no telling what else he had learned, including Cassidy's importance and location.

Reaching out to her, Dominique sensed she was safe—at least for now.

"Does Cassidy know what happened to us?" he wondered.

"Yes. You compelled Earl to give our phones back before we left. I called her as soon as I could get mine charged enough to turn on and find a signal. All is quiet in the city, but she's beside herself with worry. Garrett said she even tried to badger Isao into coming after us."

Dominique smiled wistfully. He almost felt sorry for the proud samurai, but was grateful for his steadfast vigilance.

Jackson pulled the keys from his vest pocket. "We need to keep moving. And I need to get some food."

"As do I," Dominique murmured.

"Yes," Jackson said with a long exhale. "I imagine you do. I'll find us a fast-food joint with lots of customers, but..." He drifted off and Dominique met his eyes. "If you need something right now, well..."

"Are you offering me—"

"My blood, yes." He shrugged awkwardly. "If you need it. Like a snack, I guess."

Before he knew he was doing it, Dominique embraced Jackson, his once-enemy who had risked his life to save him and risked it again now by offering himself to a starving vampire. For long seconds, Jackson's pulse thundered in his ears, and the heat of his skin burned against his lips. But what Dominique savored most of all was the genuine affection behind this unexpected offer. Which is why, even though his belly cramped with hunger, he kept his lethal teeth firmly sheathed.

"*Merci, mon ami.*" He stepped back to meet Jackson's eyes. "You have given me enough for one day. And...I will need far more than a snack."

39

THE END OF LIES

After Dominique had tapped enough veins to pass for a merely ailing human rather than one a step past death's door, he drove the rental fast and sure along the winding highway back to Vancouver and Cassidy. Jackson succumbed to his exhaustion in the passenger seat, but Dominique's mind spun faster than the wheels on the pavement.

The Lord of Night was not invincible. What a fool he had been to think otherwise and toy with the suppressant, a fire more dangerous than the sun. He had risked not only his life and Jackson's, but the lives of every blood-drinker in existence. Even his human family was now in peril. All because he had been too bewitched by the promise of daylight to pay attention. He had underestimated Adilla and Esteban, and given them all the time they needed to uncover his weaknesses, even handed himself over to them at his most vulnerable.

His fault, all of it.

He cursed under his breath. Indecision. He wallowed in it. Ambivalence kept him suspended between worlds. It was a luxury he could ill afford.

And yet he wallowed.

The sun still called to him, perhaps more than ever.

A little after one in the morning, he pulled into the Pan Pacific's parkade and woke Jackson. Then he tuned into the dark web to locate Isao. There were three others who now appeared to him as bright beacons instead of ghosts. They moved in various parts of the hotel complex, patrolling for threats.

My lord.

Isao's silent greeting felt tense, putting Dominique instantly on guard. *What happened?*

Nothing here. Pause. *A great many things with you, as I understand it.*

I survived, Dominique countered as he paced toward the parkade's hotel entrance. *What is it you think you understand?*

Garrett has told me what you tried to do. As well as the result.

Taken aback, Dominique's long stride faltered. An alliance had been forged, Isao informed him, between himself and the wily old vampire hunter. Information sharing was part of this agreement. All in the name of security, of course.

"*Merde*," he said faintly.

"What?" Jackson said.

Another bright presence approached, causing Dominique to curse again. He raked the fingers of both hands through his sticky hair and plowed through the door into the hotel's staid and air-conditioned inner sanctum.

"What the—oh," Jackson said when he spotted the female blood-drinker at the far end of the hall. She was petite, Japanese, and looked runway-model-fragile in her stylish coat and thigh-high boots, but her eyes gleamed as hard as black steel, and the spikes of her hair looked sharp enough to draw blood. Surprise made her delicate features go slack.

"Friend or foe?" Jackson queried out of the side of his mouth.

"Spy of a friend," Dominique growled. The starved prisoner look he currently sported wasn't lost on Makoto, nor was the stench of blood still clinging to his skin. Both she and her sire, Isao, were now very much aware of just how close to death he had come. How close they had all come.

I have failed you, my lord, Isao said on a wave of profound shock.

On the contrary, Dominique countered, choosing to misunderstand. *You have kept my family safe. For that, you will forever have my gratitude.*

But I failed to prepare you adequately for Adilla. You underestimated him and put us all at risk.

"Not a mistake I will make again. Of that, you can be very sure," Dominique muttered as he swept past Makoto. She was little more than a century old, but at the moment she was easily his better. He was vulnerable, which made them all vulnerable, a state of affairs that did not sit well with Isao and his spawn.

Not a mistake I will make again, either, Isao promised solemnly and proceeded to lay out the situation in more detail than Dominique cared to contemplate right now. *With your sister, Adilla has gained a grave advantage over you. He will use her to provoke you until he breaks you to his will. Or until one or both of you—and many or all of us—have turned to ash. Nor can you turn your back on him now. He will not let your challenge go unanswered. Not in a thousand years of night.*

An excellent argument for Adilla's destruction, Dominique thought, but swallowed the impulse before it could reach anyone who would object to that course of action. *Adilla will submit. Even if I have to keep him in chains for the rest of time.*

This appeared to mollify the blood-drinkers in the hotel, for no further chastising was forthcoming. He counted himself fortunate that they needed him to live as much as Adilla.

"What just happened?" Jackson wondered once they had stepped into the lift and the doors sealed.

Dominique leaned his head against the wall behind him. "Politics."

"Oh, nice." Picking up on the weary tone, he let that answer lie. Jackson gestured with his phone and continued. "Garrett texted. They're all waiting in your suite."

Dominique already knew. Cassidy's presence in his mind had grown steadily stronger for hours, instilling him with new determination. But while she knew of his turmoil, she was also preoccupied with keeping Francesca from despairing over her missing daughter and absent son, or worse, calling the authorities.

Looking down at himself, he realized he was far more the picture of a battlefield survivor than the confident man of business his mother would expect. The wounds had healed and most of the blood was wiped away, but it still caked his hair and edged his fingernails. "May I borrow your bathroom? And your closet?"

"Um. Sure."

Dominique made quick but thorough use of the shower in Jackson's suite before donning the same boots and black leather jacket, along with a pair of Jackson's jeans and a fresh T-shirt. Damp and reeking of the hotel's floral soap, he headed for his own suite, Jackson trailing behind.

At the end of the hall near a fire exit, he spotted another of Isao's younglings, his oldest. With his wild, russet hair and broad face, Kostya looked a little like a taller, brawnier, better-dressed version of Serge and not much older, too.

He barely had time to acknowledge Kostya's small bow of greeting before Cassidy opened the door and rushed into his arms. Purple smudges of exhaustion shadowed her eyes. "Cassie *amour*," he whispered as he tucked her close against his chest and inside his soul. *Mon coeur, mon tout.* A sense of peace brushed his mind as he buried his face in the loose knot of hair at the back of her head. A sense of comfort and completion. A sense of home.

"Dominique?" His mother stood just inside the suite, holding open the door, her features drawn with anxiety and a touch of displeasure. She believed he was returning from a business trip, one that had taken far too long given the current family crisis. Only when she didn't come forward to greet him did he realize he had forgotten to alter his appearance. She was staring at him, seeing him the way he truly was: gaunt, pale, and not quite human.

"*Maman*," he said, releasing Cassidy.

Garrett, standing back, nodded a grim-faced greeting.

As Dominique stepped into the suite, Francesca reached for his face, her eyes searching his. He caught her hands in his own. "*Maman*. Are you well?"

"What...what happened to you?"

For a long, long moment, Dominique didn't know how to answer that question. Then he reeled from the shock that he considered answering it at all.

Cassidy gave him a mental nudge. *Do something. Just a small compulsion. Set her mind at ease and tell her you know where Geneviève is. Then let her get some rest.*

He didn't.

He couldn't.

He couldn't utter one more lie or spin one more deception. Not to her. Not to himself. "*Je suis mort*," he whispered. "The son you knew is dead."

Cassidy inhaled sharply. Garrett crossed his arms and looked at the floor while Jackson shook his head in mute disapproval.

Francesca's blue eyes, always so strong and confident, slowly narrowed with doubt and the shadow of something Dominique had never seen there before—fear. "What are you talking about?"

Dominique brought her hands to his mouth and kissed her knuckles. She grasped his fingers as though reaching for a lifeline, unaware that this lifeline was about to pull her to the bottom of an ocean she never knew existed.

"Don't do this," Garrett said under his breath. "She's suffered enough."

"*Oui*. She has," Dominique agreed. He guided her to the sofa and sat, pulling her down beside him. "She has suffered lies and questions without answers, and she will suffer them no more."

Dominique laid out his story before her. It was the tale of how he, her beloved son, aspiring chef and celebrated playboy living a carefree life, drew the attention of the ancient Kambyses. He told her how he was transformed, his human life stolen. He told her of the subsequent torture he endured and his eventual escape. He told her of the solace he found with Cassidy. He even told her of how he came to take Kambyses's place in the world of night. And he told her about Adilla and Esteban and how they challenged him and had almost killed him. The only thing he did not tell her was his part in the deaths of his father and younger sister, which, together with his disappearance, had destroyed her world.

Then he told her about Geneviève. "She is safe for a little while longer, but she has become a bargaining chip in a power struggle that I will not lose, no matter the price. She *will* survive. As a mortal. That I swear to you."

Francesca had listened to every word with a face that had gone blank of all expression. No shock. No surprise. No reaction beyond the occasional glance at the others in the room. Now that he was done, she dragged her hands from his grasp, brushed a knuckle over her lips, and cleared her throat. Her face might be carefully schooled, but her heartbeat was not. Dominique heard it racing out of control. When she finally collected herself, she looked up at him. "Why would you tell me such things, Dominique?"

His eyes stung. "Because you deserve to know the truth. And because...I am so very tired."

"So you believe this, then? You truly believe you are a...vampire?"

"I truly wish I were not."

"I see." She glanced around. "And you, Cassidy? Garrett? You believe this as well?" They let their silence speak for them. She didn't listen. "Why would you encourage him like this? He is obviously unwell. You are taking advantage of a damaged mind."

"*Maman*," Dominique tried, reaching for her hand.

She grabbed his wrist hard before he could say anything more, her fierce tone dropping low. "Listen to me, *mon fils*. I don't know how I missed this until now, but you are not well.

Maybe it is drugs, or maybe a virus really did get to you and made you think such things, but you need help, and I will help you. Do you understand? You are safe now."

Dominique's mouth pulled into a bitter smile. There she was, his mother. Never one to suffer defeat, always charging into the situation, taking control. "You cannot fix this, *Maman*."

"Don't be absurd. You are delusional, and these people are letting you believe it because they want to get their hands on your money." She leaned forward, voice going soft, earnest. "You are not a vampire, *mon chéri*. There is no such thing. You are just ill, and you can be helped." She grasped his hand harder. "You *can* be helped."

Please compel her to forget this conversation and let her go, Cassidy begged.

Instead, Dominique slowly let the vampire rise, darkening his eyes until the whites disappeared. The sharp points of his canines emerged. His mother blinked, then straightened.

"There is no help for me," he said, his voice inhumanly resonant. "My only salvation lies in acceptance of this truth. By me and by those I love."

"You selfish bastard," Garrett grumbled.

Dominique looked at the man who had begged him to turn him because he didn't want to die. "You would know, of course."

Color suffused Garrett's wan face. Even with the blood, he was not holding up well. His disease would get the better of him before much longer.

He held out his hand to Garrett in silent invitation to begin the process that would, eventually, transform him. The old hunter's mouth flattened. He stared at Dominique, stared at what he would become, and walked forward. Sitting on the coffee table in front of Dominique, he pushed up the sleeve of his jacket and placed his bare wrist into the waiting hand.

"Garrett? What is this?" Francesca asked.

"The selfish fucking truth," he snapped hoarsely. To Dominique, he added, "Get on with it, then."

Dominique did.

In full view of all that remained of his past life, he sank his teeth into Garrett's wrist. With a deep sigh, he closed his eyes and let the blood come to drown out the silent horror on his mother's face.

40

CROSSING LINES

S trange how you didn't see them coming, these moments, these lines, that divided life into what was and what is. Lines that once crossed, can never be uncrossed. Cassidy could only stand and watch, breathless and numb, as Dominique crossed such a line—and dragged everyone else in the room along with him.

If Garrett, legendary destroyer of vampires, had any doubts about transforming into one of the beings he had spent a lifetime hunting, by surrendering his vein a second time so soon after the first, he was leaving them behind. His nephew, who had spent his life keeping terrifying secrets, stood uncharacteristically slack-jawed as he witnessed Dominique not just share such a secret with someone he loved, but practically beat the woman over the head with it. And Cassidy...Cassidy sensed Dominique's very essence shift. A new edge surfaced in his being, sharp as a samurai sword, slashing the doubts that defined him for as long as she had known him. More than that, Cassidy could feel that razor edge slice up against his humanity, and...and suddenly she couldn't breathe.

He was with her an instant later, his impossibly thin, yet impossibly strong arms around her, holding her upright, suspending her above the panic attack opening beneath her feet. *No, Cassie* amour. *I survive because of you. I grow because of you. I am because of you. Nothing can ever change that.*

She held on to him until the moment passed and her world stabilized. She had not lost him, and would not lose him, not to doubts, benevolent intentions, or to fate. They lived in a storm right now, both their lives changing, but through it all, they remained each others' haven.

They would always be each others' haven.

"*Je vois*," Francesca said into the silence and Cassidy met her wide, still gaze. The woman had paled with shock, but color was already beginning to seep back into her face, her no-nonsense, practical nature fighting to reassert itself in this new reality. "I see."

Garrett rubbed his wrist, straightened his sleeve, and moved to the credenza, where he opened the ice bucket and doled cubes into glasses before filling them with bottled water. Jackson joined him and took two of the tumblers, sipping from one and taking the other to Cassidy.

"Thanks," she said, wishing it were wine, but also grateful it wasn't. Her head was swimming quite enough already.

Garrett took the other two glasses, setting one next to Francesca, who watched him with an expression of horrified wonder. He gave her a small, tense smile and retreated. "*Merci*," she murmured and picked up the glass with both hands. After drinking half, she cradled it in her lap.

Another full minute passed in suffocating silence. Cassidy watched the woman's face harden even as her eyes brimmed. Finally, Francesca nodded to herself, drank the rest of the water, produced a handkerchief, and wiped her face. Then, she began asking pointed questions. How strong was he, really? How immortal? What were his limitations? Who was this vampire who dared to kidnap Geneviève? And what would Dominique do about getting her back?

"Everything I can, *Maman*." He reached out to reassure her, but she flinched before she caught herself, and Dominique stayed his hand. Cassidy felt his stinging disappointment. His mother may appear to accept the situation, but she was far from comfortable with it. She still sat on the sofa, stick-straight and wary, Cassidy by her side, Dominique seated on the table, facing her.

"Staying in the area and waiting to try that stunt again at sunset was out of the question," Jackson protested when his uncle questioned him on his tactics. "Dominique was barely awake. I wasn't about to risk—"

Garrett raised a placating hand. "Easy, Jack. I wasn't there. What counts is that you secured both of you. But that doesn't change the fact that we need to get back there with some element of surprise."

"Why are we not calling the police?" Francesca insisted. "Geneviève is being held captive. The authorities need to be informed."

For a moment, everyone was silent. Then Cassidy, whom Francesca seemed to gravitate to now, said, "You'd be condemning them to death."

"We would have to tell them they need to leave before sunset, of course."

"Do you think they would believe you?" Cassidy asked gently and watched the woman's composure waver.

"Cassidy is right," Garrett said. "We can't risk getting ignorant humans involved."

She fidgeted with the handkerchief in her lap. "Then what will you do, Dominique?"

Her son leaned forward, elbows on his knees. He had taken off his jacket, and the navy blue T-shirt he wore did little to hide his wasted physique. Some lines were the usual hard muscle, but mostly they were bone. "I cannot risk traveling by day again. I need to be there and at full strength right at sunset, without alerting the human guards that anything is amiss."

What he didn't say, but what Cassidy felt slither in his thoughts, was that there would be no hope for Geneviève otherwise. Assuming Adilla hadn't changed his mind about her and she wasn't already dead.

"We can transport you," Jackson suggested. "Fly you out while you're sleeping."

Both Dominique and Cassidy gave Jackson a long look.

"Fuck. You know you can trust me."

"I do, *chèr*. But I don't trust all the others along the way who would see you transporting me. Anyone could be under Esteban's command."

"Even if we fly at night, we would have to take the jet to Calgary," Garrett reasoned. "That's an hour and a half. Add another two hours on the road after that, and the night is half over."

"What if he wakes up on the plane?" Jackson suggested.

Dominique raked the fingers of both hands through his damp hair. "Still too long. I must be there at sunset."

Silence descended as everyone fell into their own thoughts.

Francesca was the first to speak. "If you are there right at sunset...can you defy all these...vampires by yourself? Are you that strong?"

Dominique gave his mother a weary sideways smile. "It is only two of them I need to worry about, and as long as I get a day's rest, I will be strong enough." To emphasize this point, he conjured the illusion he had been showing her before, the version of him she remembered: sun-bronzed, strong, and human. The moment she inhaled sharply, he let it go, the effort to maintain it too great and no longer necessary. "They will submit or die. The rest will fall into line."

You hope, Cassidy said. He didn't argue. He knew it was a gamble. The others could turn on him as easily as submit, especially Bhavanur and Markandeya, who were just as old and strong as Adilla. And two hundred vampires were two hundred vampires. Regardless of how powerful Dominique was, there would be only one of him.

"What we need is to get you there during the day," Jackson said. He stood with his arms crossed, staring out the window at

North Vancouver glowing on the bay's far shore. "And we need to do it as inconspicuously as possible."

"You could bag me and drive me back there." He said it with a straight face, but Cassidy felt the reluctance behind the words.

I would come with you and watch over you, she let him know quickly.

"That's what I was thinking, but not in the SUV." Jackson turned away from the window to face them. "We need to be completely under the radar. Totally unexpected."

"I'm listening," Garrett prompted.

Jackson raised his hands and lowered them, palms up, as though presenting his proposal on a platter. "RV."

Cassidy's brows lifted.

Dominique smiled.

Garrett nodded.

Francesca looked between them. "I do not understand. What are you saying, Jackson?"

"RV. Recreational vehicle," Garrett explained.

"I saw them all over the road when we drove out there," Jackson elaborated. "There's a campsite on the access road to the village. We'd have every legitimate reason to be there. Plus, there would be bunks in the back. Dominique could be bagged in one, and I could grab a nap, too. Not to mention not having to stop to get food."

"*Savant*," Dominique murmured. "This could work."

"It'll work a lot better if you have someone you can trade off driving with," Garrett said. "Count me in."

"And me," Cassidy added. "You're not driving his unconscious self around during the day without me."

Dominique gave her a sharp look that felt like a slap to her brain. *You stay here.*

"What do you mean, I stay here?" she retorted, stunned.

Francesca's head swiveled to her. "What?"

"I'm definitely *not* staying here while you go running off into danger again."

"You will be safer here," Dominique countered. His words and his thoughts echoed each other. His hollowed eyes grew adamant.

"You will be safer with me near you." She was reaching, and she knew it. There wasn't much she could do for him beyond being close enough to touch his mind. "I won't spend another day not knowing what's happening to you or if you're even still alive."

"If you go there, you become a target, Cassidy." Dominique all but growled the words. Francesca stilled, suspended in the growing tension between them. "That *salaud*, Esteban, had his teeth in me. He could have pulled anything out of my addled head before I passed out. You may not be safe even here."

Cassidy got to her feet. "So much more reason for me to come with you then."

"So much more reason for you to get on a plane and go back to Florida," Dominique snapped, getting up as well. His wild hair fell into his drawn face, giving him the look of homicidal madness.

"Not happening." She tipped her chin up in defiance. "I belong with you. I'm coming with you."

"*Fille naïve!* Why can you not see that I cannot focus on what I need to do if I have to worry about you?"

"Foolish vampire. Why can't you see that if anything happens to you, I would sooner be dead?"

"Because this is not about just you anymore, Cassie. Your responsibility needs to be to the child you carry."

She sucked at the air with shock as her hands flew to her belly. *How dare you!* Every eye in the room raked over her. This was definitely not how she had planned to cross this particular line and announce this bit of news.

Neither had Dominique. He dropped his face in both hands. *Désolé, mon coeur.*

Cassidy closed her eyes. He could be sorry all he wanted, but not only was the news out now, his comment also confirmed what she already suspected. In the eyes of those around her, including the man she loved, she had been reduced to the status of a vessel for a being no bigger than a grain of sand.

Francesca was the first to speak. "Is this...is this true? Cassidy, you are expecting a child?"

Cassidy swallowed hard and opened her eyes. There was no point denying what two different vampires, a conspicuous absence of her usually timely period, and this morning's pregnancy test confirmed. "Yes. I am."

A tiny frown marred the skin between Francesca's shaped brows as she no doubt sifted through a flood of new information. "Then Dominique is correct. Of course, you must take care of yourself and not rush into danger."

Cassidy's hands curled into fists by her sides, and a small cry of sheer frustration burst out of her. "I didn't sign up for this."

Garrett exchanged a look with his nephew, and then considered Dominique as he scratched at his chin. "Would I be totally out of line if I asked how this—" an open-handed gesture at Cassidy "—happened?"

"The suppressant?" Jackson wondered with quiet awe.

Dominique nodded. "The child is mine."

Francesca's head snapped up. "What? This is possible? Even though you are—" She stopped, uncertain.

"Not human, *Maman*. No, it should not be possible, but the suppressant that lets me...function during the day seems to have made it so." His dimpled smile broadened, becoming adorably sheepish. "I am to be a father."

"Congratulations," Jackson said.

"*Merci, mon ami.*"

"I'll be damned," Garrett muttered.

Francesca reached for Cassidy and pulled her down to the sofa beside her. Then she clasped her hand in both of hers so firmly Cassidy thought she might need to fight to get it back. "This is a miracle then, *non*? A miracle child of my lost son."

She opened her mouth, but couldn't find the words in light of what she saw on Francesca's face. All the hard edges softened, and her smile was as watery as her eyes. "A miracle from God."

A grain-sized ball and chain with the weight of a world, Cassidy corrected.

Dominique's mind brushed against hers in warm apology. With a deep sigh, she capitulated. She would have gladly battled the vampire for the right to join him in danger. But against the mother determined to latch onto a "miracle" grandchild, Cassidy knew she had no chance. The light in Francesca's eyes told her that the woman would sooner lock her into a room before she let her out of her sight, much less risk her life.

And Dominique would cheerfully help her lock the door and hide the key.

41

Don't Move

Cassidy stared out at Vancouver Harbour sparkling in the morning sun and clutched her phone to her ear. On the call's other end, Samantha sniffled.

"Serge never answered me when I asked him if Ryan would be okay. I should have known what that meant. I should have spoken to him, gotten him help. At the very least, not let him out of my sight."

"I'm so sorry I'm not there for you right now," Cassidy whispered, wiping at her eyes. Francesca was out in the sitting room, waiting for her to get ready for breakfast, and this was the sort of news the woman didn't need to hear so soon after the night's revelations.

"Étienne is here," Samantha said. "He's an enormous help."

Something about the way Samantha said his name made Cassidy smile despite the grim conversation.

"He was with me when we found Ryan in the hot tub this morning." A shaky inhalation full of emotional struggle. "He slit his wrists. The note he left said he wanted to die where Natalia had died."

Oh God, Cassidy thought, closing her eyes. The despair the man must have felt circled her like a black hole.

"When she died, he died, too. These last couple of days, he was just an empty shell. Just sat and stared into space."

Empty the way I will be empty if anything happens to Dominique. No, nothing and no one would keep her from going back to that cavern of horrors with him, least of all Dominique. She'd hitch a ride in that RV, even if she had to zip herself into that body bag with him. He could hardly argue during the daytime. And by sundown it would be too late.

Voices in the sitting room brought her out of her dark plotting. Jackson, their security detail, had arrived to escort them to breakfast. "I have to go, Sam. Please call me if there's any more news."

Cassidy splashed enough cold water onto her face to wash away the redness, finished dressing, and tied her hair into a ponytail. But when she stepped out of the bedroom, Jackson wasn't fooled.

"What's wrong?"

She glanced at Francesca. The pinched eyes and thin mouth betrayed a quiet storm of anxiety. "It's been a long night for all of us," Cassidy said, silently begging Jackson to leave it at that.

He did. "You'll both feel better after you eat."

"Will Garrett join us?" Francesca asked.

"He's out getting the RV he found us last night. We'll need to take off as soon as we can if we're going to make it there by nightfall. Are you all packed?"

"*Oui*, I am."

"Cassidy?"

"Sure." Several cases and bags were lined up in the bedroom, ready for transport to a new, undisclosed location. Among the planned precautions was that she and Francesca should book themselves into another hotel during the day, using cash and fake ID's, then call in two of Isao's younglings tonight to stand guard.

Dominique was with Isao and Kostya in Isao's downtown lair, awaiting pickup when the RV was ready to go. She smiled to herself as she considered her own plans. As the only one who knew where the vampires were hiding—not to mention the holder of the key and security codes required to access them—there was no chance that RV was leaving town without her.

"I was thinking we should try to get an appointment at a clinic for you today, my dear," Francesca said.

"What? Why?"

"You are pregnant," she said as if Cassidy had gone daft.

"For two weeks," Cassidy protested. Hell, her only symptom so far was an increased appetite—for everything.

"The sooner you receive prenatal care, the better for you and the baby."

"Good point," Jackson seconded. "Given the circumstances, you need to stay on top of this." Seeing Cassidy's irate glare, he quickly amended, "But I'm sure you can wait until we get home. Ollie can set you up with her doctor."

"Ollie?" Francesca asked.

"Olivia, my fiancée. She's pregnant, too."

"*Merveilleux!*" She clapped her hands in delight. "Cassidy, *chèrie*, you will have a friend to share this journey with you."

Cassidy refrained from mentioning that she had yet to meet this Olivia. "I'm sure we'll be besties," she murmured.

Francesca carried on for a while longer, completely enchanted with the idea that both her son and his friend should become fathers at the same time. Within seconds, she had moved on to the children growing up together, attending school together, and everyone visiting on St. Barth, the parties she would host, and the meals she would serve. Even who she would invite.

Cassidy and Jackson exchanged a look, both of them recognizing the babbling for the desperate hope for happier times to come that it was.

I should have known.

Samantha's words, which had at first stirred only a whisper of unease in the back of Cassidy's mind, suddenly clanged louder than a firehouse alarm bell. Serge hadn't told Samantha about Ryan's future because Ryan didn't have one.

Serge had also never seen a child as a consequence of Dominique's day-walking.

I should have known.

A chill raced up her arms. Her hand moved to cover her belly in a protective gesture. Should she know not to force the issue about traveling into danger with Dominique? Would she lose the child if she did? But how could she not go?

A knock at the door made her jump.

"Maintenance," someone called from the hall.

"Time to go," Jackson said, apparently eager for the excuse to stop the torrent of words from Francesca.

"Maintenance?" Cassidy wondered. It must be a code word Jackson and Garrett were using. Though that didn't sound like Garrett.

Before she could question it, Jackson had opened the door.

The guy on the other side was two heads taller than Jackson and three times as wide. He wore what could well have been the official uniform of the hotel's maintenance staff, but instead of stating his business in an apologetic, Canadian manner, he simply walked in—along with two other, only slightly smaller men.

Jackson put up a hand. "Just a second."

The maintenance crew shoved Jackson aside and swarmed through the suite, tearing open doors and prodding under furniture.

"What the hell are you doing? What are you looking for?" Cassidy cried. A small part of her still clung to the idea that this was all an innocent misunderstanding.

No one bothered to reply.

Jackson grabbed the arm of the first giant through the door. "You need to leave right now, buddy."

A meaty fist arched around toward his face. Jackson ducked just in time and landed a solid punch in the guy's gut. The mountain of a man swayed, but remained upright.

Francesca screamed.

Cassidy went mute with shock.

An attack. This was an attack. The empty eyes and single-minded pursuit of these men reeked of compulsion. They were looking for a sleeping vampire who had had the good sense not to be here today.

But that wasn't all they were after.

The giant scooped Jackson up in a crushing hold that took his feet clear off the ground. Cassidy was about to rush to his aid when a hand came down hard on her shoulder. All the martial arts training Dominique had insisted she do kicked into autopilot. She reached for the wrist and whirled around, twisting, holding nothing back. Tendons popped beneath her fingers. With a strangled cry, her would-be assailant crashed to the floor and smashed his face into the rug.

Francesca improvised a weapon from her sizable designer bag. With ear-piercing shrieks and a flurry of French outrage, she swung it at the head of the man trying to gain control over her.

"Fucking son of a bitch," Jackson snarled. Somehow he had gotten out of the hold he was in and turned on the bear of a man who still staggered, off balance.

The guy Cassidy had leveled crawled on the floor, only to get clocked again when Francesca's bag-cudgel sailed past and toppled a table lamp on him. Francesca's screams became agonized. Her attacker had her hands trapped behind her back and jerked them up high between her shoulder blades.

With a wild shriek, Cassidy vaulted onto the man's back. Her arms snaked around his muscular neck, her legs around his middle. She squeezed, intending murder.

Francesca, released, fell forward. Her assailant, now top-heavy with Cassidy on his back, spun around, gasped, and teetered. His arms waved wildly, grappling for balance.

Something thin and long glinted in his hand.

Shit.

"Drop the knife," she shouted over a calamitous crash behind her. If that was Jackson who had just hurtled into that desk, and if there were more weapons about to appear, this battle was all but over. "I said drop the fucking knife!"

He didn't. He swung it down and back at her hips and legs. Cassidy felt several sharp punches, but no cuts or stabs. She extended the thumb on her free hand and went for the face, determined to relieve him of an eyeball to get him to drop the knife.

"Cassidy, let go," Jackson ordered. "I've got this."

Her thumb had already disappeared into a slippery socket. The man howled and thrashed, but still didn't relinquish the weapon. Not a knife, she saw, but a screwdriver, covered in blood and arcing straight at her face.

She jerked back, out of reach. The maneuver threw them both off balance. Together they flailed, bounced off the edge of a sofa, and hit the floor with a hard thump. All his weight landed on top of her.

Cassidy's spine shoved up to meet her sternum, exploding every molecule of air out of her body.

Jackson dragged her assailant off her. The guy clutched at his bleeding left eye, a snarl distorting his unshaven face. "Bitch!"

Jackson's fist found his jaw with a meaty smack that keeled him over and away from her.

Her chest was pancake-flat and on fire. She tried to roll over while her mouth worked like a landed fish. No air would come, not even a trickle.

"No no no no. Stay put," Jackson said, keeping her on her back. Blood dribbled down his face. Cassidy had a good mind to add to his injuries if he didn't let go of her.

Francesca leaned over her, wild-eyed, a sleeve torn from her blouse, hair sticking out all around her head. "*Mon Dieu. Mon Dieu, non.*"

"Cassidy, can you hear me?" Jackson said, still trying to hold her down. "Do you understand?"

She nodded as she batted at his hands, opened her mouth wider, and writhed her body, fighting to get air back into her lungs somehow. Her heart pounded in her head like a steel-spiked hammer. *Let go of me! I can't breathe!*

"The air will come back. Just relax. Don't move." His gaze flickered down her body and back up. "Whatever you do, don't move."

42

ÇA SUFFIT

Dominique knew a moment of panic when he couldn't hear the familiar thump of Cassidy's heart. Instead, there was a muffled chorus of voices and traffic, and the distant rumble of thunder.

Then he remembered that Cassidy's absence was according to plan.

What was not according to plan was that when he unzipped himself from the body bag he had slipped into this morning together with his dragon swords, he was still on the bed in Isao's private sanctuary with two other body bags tucked in beside him. No one had come during the day to collect them for the journey back to Adilla's underground palace.

As he stood and slung the swords across his back, he reached out for Cassidy. Did she change her mind about letting Jackson and Garrett transport them all out of here? If so, she must have also left the area, perhaps even the city, because he detected no trace of her anywhere.

Another bag stirred to life, and he sensed another mind wondering the same thing.

"Something is wrong," Dominique said. "Gather your family."

By the time Isao was awake enough to respond silently in the affirmative, he had already rushed out of the immaculate, antique-stuffed condo and was halfway down the stairwell. Less than two minutes later, he burst out of another stairwell and found Jackson waiting for him in the empty hallway by the door to Dominique's suite—which was barred with yellow crime scene tape. Worse, the smell of blood drenched the air.

His heart squeezed into a small, quivering ball. "Where is she?"

"Cassidy is in the hospital, but she's expected to make a full recovery," Jackson said quickly. A bandage marred his forehead near his hairline, and an antiseptic odor clung to his clothes as though he only just came from there. "If you can't sense her, it's because she's doped up on pain meds, but she'll be fine. Your mom is shaken up, but physically okay. She's with Cassidy and is waiting for you."

Dominique's heart unclenched just a little. "What happened? Who hurt her?"

The elevator dinged down the hall and a family of tourists spilled out, complete with hyperactive preschoolers.

"Let's take this inside," Jackson suggested, gesturing toward his suite. Dominique followed, bristling with impatience, worry, and anger. The thoughts and memories he could make out from Jackson were disjointed and chaotic and full of screams that scraped his nerves.

Jackson closed the door behind them. "You should sit down."

"Tell me—"

"Please. Sit." The soft tone brought Dominique up short. Turmoil roiled in his friend's tired eyes.

Dominique's stomach turned over in slow-motion. He found a chair that allowed the scabbards to hang to either side of him.

Jackson sat, facing him. Behind him, Vancouver glittered with a sinister new energy. Lightning flickered beyond the high-rises.

"Three men came this morning, posing as hotel maintenance workers. They were obviously looking for you. When they couldn't find you, they tried to take Cassidy and your mother instead. The men were compelled and not all that clever, just brutes, but they had tools. One of them used a screwdriver as a weapon when Cassidy tackled him."

Tackled him? Dominique almost didn't hear the rest of Jackson's words, too caught up in the disjointed memories shooting out of him like strobe lights. Francesca screaming, hysterical. Pain throbbing in Jackson's head. Anger that the blood Dominique had given him had spent itself, giving him no advantage. Rage that he had been caught off-guard. Fear that he would fail to keep them safe.

And Cassidy...Cassidy clinging to the back of a dead-eyed man, shrieking with fear-fueled anger.

"What?" Dominique said.

"I said she was so hopped up on adrenaline, she didn't even know she got stabbed."

An image of Cassidy on the ground, fighting for air, terror in her eyes, going flour-pale while protruding from her abdomen...

All of Dominique's blood seemed to leave his extremities at once. Jackson remained silent, rubbing his fingertips together, waiting.

"What else?"

"She'll be fine, but she—" he swallowed. Dominique heard the words in Jackson's thoughts as he fought to voice them. He wanted to clamp his hand across his friend's mouth so they would never emerge. "She lost the baby."

The gruff whisper crackled in Dominique's bones.

"She hemorrhaged. They tried everything to save her womb, but in the end, it was all they could do to save her."

Dominique closed his eyes.

"She doesn't know yet. She's still too drugged to know what's going on. I'm sorry, Dominique. I really am."

If he weren't sitting already, he was sure he'd crumple to the ground. Instead, he dropped his head into his hands and let the grief surge through him in devastating waves. "*Elle est en vie*," he whispered over and over. She is alive. She is alive.

But the child was dead. The child that was to be his future, the proof of his humanity, reborn. The child that would...*could* never be.

Tears dripped from his eyes. The child was as impossible and short-lived as his own abortive attempts to reclaim his humanity. That, too, was forever dead, for he would never again take the suppressant. And Cassidy would never again conceive. Not by him or anyone.

Elle est en vie.

Cassidy lived. She was all he had left. She was all he ever truly had in this cursed life, always walking by his side without hesitation and always hounded by danger. Danger for which he was responsible. Just as he was responsible for the deaths of members of his mortal family and endangering those who survived.

All those deaths, all those threats, every one of them because of his one unrelenting need to be human again.

Ça suffit, he thought. Enough. He was done with dreaming and hoping and ambivalence. Done endangering the lives of those he loved. Most of all, he was done being something he could never be again.

When Dominique lifted his head, his eyes were still wet, but his grief had hardened into something cold and new and dark.

Jackson didn't move, but the sight of Dominique's face made his cherry red aura flinch. He knew that what he was in the room with now was infinitely more dangerous than what it had been two minutes ago. "Nick?" he said carefully. "You okay?"

Dominique said nothing. Instead, he sat and listened to the wet heartbeats and murmuring voices in the building all around, a river of humanity flowing past and over and under him, but no longer touching him. Two were closer than the others. Jackson's and...

He turned his head to the closed bedroom door as he reached into Jackson's mind for the information he sought.

"That's not Garrett," Jackson said and jumped up when Dominique got to his feet. "But it's *not* the guy who stabbed her, either."

43

TRUTH AND TREACHERY

Dominique was in the bedroom and followed the intruder's heartbeat into the adjacent bathroom before the warning had fully left Jackson's lips. In the Jacuzzi tub, trussed up and gagged with duct tape, was a large human male dressed in stained blue coveralls. His longish, dull blond hair tangled around his head, and a dried crust of blood covered part of his face. His eyes were open but flat, showing no interest in his situation.

Jackson came up behind Dominique. "The other two were conscious enough to run, but this one was still out cold. So I dragged him over here and secured him before the police got here. I thought you might want to talk to him."

"That I do." Dominique let his fangs emerge. "*Merci beaucoup.*"

There was no time for tenderness. This man had been ruthlessly compelled. Only an equally ruthless counter-compulsion would break through. Shoving the head aside, he went for the blood. Within seconds, Dominique found what he needed, the vampire who had cast the compulsion. It was a female he had seen before—behind the wheel of a Ford Mustang that had led him to a booby-trapped warehouse. Her victim knew her as Annabel, and he had done her bidding for months as her daytime eyes, ears, and hands.

He even knew her lair.

Dominique absorbed it all. Then he blasted it out of the human's mind. By the time he was done, the man knew only that he needed to clean himself up, go home and sleep off a hangover, then look for a new job in the morning.

"When he wakes up, let him go," Dominique said as he splashed water on his chin to remove a smear of blood. "He will be no more trouble."

Jackson, who stood with arms crossed just outside the bathroom door, watched him dry his face. "What about the vampire who compelled him?"

"Will be no more trouble by dawn." He reached for Isao, sending him an image of where he was going and who he was after. "I will contact you when I get back."

He didn't wait for Jackson's response. The moment Dominique was out the door, he disappeared down the nearest stairwell and into the parkade where he had left the borrowed Ducati SuperSport. He sensed Isao and two others just outside, but was still surprised when he found them astride motorcycles as well. There even was an extra bike, carrying two "ghosts," something of which he took only fleeting notice. As Dominique gunned the Ducati down the street and heard the roar of four other bikes giving chase, the web trembled with his rage.

We felt your need to act and made ready to join you, Isao said, responding to his half-formed questions.

Did others around the world experience this as well? Did Serge? And what of the two behind him who were not sired to him?

They are under my protection and will submit tonight, Isao promised.

Dominique refocused on reaching Annabel as fast as possible. That she was Esteban's operative was a given. Where she had struck once, she could strike again. And where there was one like her, there could be more.

In Surrey, they roared past the burned-out warehouse and continued for several more blocks before turning into the parking lot for a row of townhouses. Dominique led the way, retracing the path Annabel's slave had taken countless times. He broke down the front door with a single kick, sending it flying across the room. Then he stood and listened.

Cool wind gusted past him, ruffled a discarded magazine, and swirled back, redolent with a young blood-drinker's fresh scent. Upstairs, a TV was on, and a faucet ran. But that was all. No sounds of movement. No beating hearts.

She was gone.

Douglas pushed past him and swept through the sparsely furnished rooms, long coat flapping in his wake. As a mortal, the kind-faced, unassuming man had been a police detective and the only human ever to unravel the mystery of Isao Kiyomori. Impressed with his skills, the samurai had befriended him and eventually offered him immortality.

The detective now wielded his skills at hyper-speed, scanning every inch, absorbing details Dominique would not have known to notice—such as the corner of a curtain caught in an upstairs balcony door. Douglas snapped the curtain aside, and Dominique looked through the glass just in time to watch the telltale glow of a blood-drinker aura disappear into a stand of trees at the edge of the development. He threw the door open with a crash and flowed over the rail.

The soft rain turned into a million stinging needles against his face as he moved too fast for even most supernatural eyes to track. His entourage followed, but soon fell behind, none of them capable of keeping up with a well-rested and well-fed Lord of Night. Annabel was moving at a relative jog when he stopped in front of her. With a surprised yelp, she leapt straight into the air. Her bare feet slipped in the leafy mud when she landed, sending her sprawling, but she was up again in an instant.

"Stop," Dominique commanded with compulsion in his voice. She remained rooted to the spot and stared at him with undisguised hostility. She wore only undergarments, dirt splattered her legs, and wet hair clung to her shoulders. "You have one and only one opportunity to explain yourself. Speak."

Her eyes turned black and huge, consuming her face, and her mouth opened in a fanged grimace of defiance.

"So be it." He grabbed a fistful of hair and went for her blood without ceremony, finding a mind boiling with fury. Esteban had sired her, rescuing her from a destitute existence only a decade ago, and her devotion to him was complete. If there were others in the city like her, she neither knew nor cared. Getting leverage over Dominique was her sole mission at the moment, and to that end, nothing was off limits. Not even...

A strangled cry brought Dominique back to the moment. He stepped back and watched Annabel sway before falling to her knees. Five others surrounded him now, the eyes of three of them glowing in the misty darkness. It was one of the two ghosts—a young female with heavy makeup, black hair and yellow roots—who had cried out. An equally young male held her close. They had been teenagers when they were made not that long ago, a pair of pale street urchins sheltering from a brutal world.

Dominique watched them as he filtered through all the information he had just learned. *Merde.* Just when he thought he had found the bottom of this miserable treachery.

Turning back to the more immediate issue cowering at his feet, he let his anger vibrate in his voice. "Annabel Carmen Almiron Rivas. Do you submit to me?"

Pointless to ask. He knew what her answer would be, could feel it scream in her blood, and saw it in her beast-black eyes when she lifted her face into the rain. "Never!"

He watched her gather herself to leap at him, and the impulse to end her shot through him, but his hand didn't move toward his sword. In fact, he didn't move at all.

He didn't have to.

His wish had already become Isao's command.

The samurai's *katana* flashed in a silent arc.

Annabel's body dropped in a sprawling heap long before her head stopped bouncing over the uneven ground.

"We need to move up our departure," Dominique said without preamble as he walked into the Strikers' hotel suite just past eleven o'clock.

Garrett, who had opened the door in a paisley silk robe, didn't hesitate. "Okay. When?"

"Tonight. I want us to be underway and clear of this city as soon as possible."

"What happened?" Jackson asked, rubbing his eyes as he staggered out of the suite's bedroom in boxer briefs and a T-shirt.

"The blood-drinker who sent the attackers is dead, but she had a spy in Isao's camp. Adilla and Esteban know I plan to return during the day with reinforcements."

"Fuck," Jackson muttered. "I thought Isao was such a pro?"

"He is," Garrett argued. "He was tricked, I take it?"

"He was. He took in youngling twins who could no longer stomach the colony's rules. One of them had a history with the woman we killed tonight, and that woman took full advantage of this to manipulate the girl into revealing everything she learned about Isao's family and, by extension, us."

"And took it straight to Esteban," Jackson concluded, shaking his head. "Fuck."

"We now must move before they realize we know this and send other operatives. We also need to take added precautions." Dominique laid these out as he saw them, and the hunters added a few of their own until a workable plan had solidified.

"So they're all coming now?" Garrett asked at one point.

"They all want to come. Since none of us will remain, there is no need to maintain security here."

Garrett and Jackson exchanged a dubious look.

"They are sired to me now. I know their minds." Though Isao had been willing to execute Carly on the spot for her hapless treachery, Dominique offered the girl a re-siring with the understanding that if he found deceit in her heart, she would still die. She submitted, sobbing, at her brother's urging—and lived. Her brother, Lyle, submitted eagerly, his heart pure and possessed of a great deal more common sense than his twin.

"I can trust them all," Dominique confirmed. Isao and his younglings were formidable, but how useful a pair of teenage blood-drinkers could be in this situation was debatable. Lyle was eager enough, but Carly had given herself over to boundless despair over Annabel's deception.

Their discussions completed, Dominique reinforced his human army of two by pouring a measure of blood for each, and then left them to their preparations.

His next stop was Vancouver General. But before meeting the emotional cataclysm awaiting him there, he made a call. Samantha picked up on the second ring, and as he had hoped, Serge was nearby. The old pirate had yet to embrace the magic of his own mobile phone.

"All is quiet here, blood-child," Serge reported. "Morbid quiet," he added, and filled Dominique in on the suicide of Natalia's companion. "There was no future cast in his light," he concluded. "Without her, his life didn't exist."

Dominique half sagged against a wall under a dripping awning. The rain and wind had followed him into the city. "What do you see for Cassidy?"

This brought a snort. "You know I need to see someone's light with my own eyes to know what shadows it casts in time."

"*Bien.* What *did* you see for her the last time you saw her?"

"What I always see. She is the key to you, blood-child. She sets you free."

"Did you ever see a child for us?"

"A child? No. No child." No hedging or hesitation in that gruff voice, nothing to hide or obscure. "Not possible, that."

"It was possible, Serge," he said softly. "But she lost the child today." Dominique braced for the inevitable declaration of all things being as they must be, but for once, the oracle stayed his tongue. "What did you see for me in what is coming?"

The reply was swift and sure. "You will face Adilla alone."

"*Non.* I am bringing others."

"Are you?" A rising note of worry in that tone. Serge caught himself a moment later. "No matter. You must deal with him alone, and you must consider all the lives tied to his."

"All the lives tied to his are close at hand. He destroys his companions rather than allowing them to leave him. Including his younglings."

"Not all," Serge blurted. "Not all are with him."

"I know. One of his most powerful has joined forces with me. I know he will keep Adilla from serious harm as surely as he will keep me." Or try to. For all his strength and skill, Isao was no match for either Adilla or Dominique.

The relief in Serge's voice was obvious. "This is most fortunate."

"Oh? Why is that?"

"All those blood-drinker lives that will be saved when Adilla lives."

Dominique rubbed at his forehead, trying to massage bits and pieces of information together in his brain. "Including...yours?"

Another weighty silence. He could almost see his friend pick at one of the Hawaiian shirts he favored.

"Adilla is your sire, is he not?"

The answer was long in coming. "Yes."

"I can see why you would try to kill him."

"Tried, yes. And failed. Good thing, that. I didn't know what it would mean for me if he died. But he left me alone after that. Tiresome idiot, that one. Mad with greed and a glutton for power. Always was. Easy for him to make bodies over nothing."

"He almost made a body of me. Still, I will do all I can to not make a body of him. I will not bring harm to you or Isao. Did you not see this in my light?"

"I saw only that you will confront him." Serge's voice dropped to an anxious whisper. "Beyond that...I saw nothing."

44

CHOICES

A shower of sparks in the darkness. She watched them, mesmerized, a million tiny suns, falling into an infinite void. More came. More fell.

Drink, mon amour. Drink.

Was she drinking? Drinking the light? It tasted of rain falling on snow. Of nights frozen in time. Of love, and of tears.

She tuned into her body in stages. Her mouth was dry, her tongue sticky. A manic, thumping energy vibrated in her chest. Arms and legs lay still, heavy and glued in place. Her belly...

With a gasp, Cassidy came awake.

It took a moment for her eyes to focus, several more to recognize her dim surroundings as a hospital room. She had no trouble recognizing the man in black leathers sitting on the side of her bed, the hilts of his swords protruding over his shoulders. It was his light-shower blood that coated her mouth.

"What—"

Dominique placed a finger against her lips. *Shhh. Let her sleep.* He glanced at the recliner in the room's corner. Stretched out in it, covered in a blanket, was Francesca.

Cassidy lifted her arm to reach for him, only to find tubes and wires running from her body into a wilderness of bags and carted equipment. So familiar, all this. She'd been here before, been near death before.

Her right thigh and hip buzzed with strange electricity, and her mid-section twinged and churned. *What's happening to me?*

I gave you my blood. It is healing you and burning all the drugs out of your system.

Healing me? From what?

Dominique wove his fingers with hers, squeezing gently. Colossal emotions moved in the shadows of his eyes. *What do you remember?*

She dredged through her reluctant memory banks. When Francesca stirred in her sleep, she recalled being with her at the hotel. It was morning. Jackson came. And then...and then...

It all came rushing in at once. The attack. The fight. The blood. So much blood. Jackson told her not to move. She'd rolled her eyes down. Saw something protrude from her gut. Then nothing.

Until now.

Beneath the covers, her free hand crept toward her middle. Bumps and lumps under the hospital gown. Bandages.

Dominique lowered his forehead to hers, enveloping her in the smells of leather, rain, and night. *During the fight, you were stabbed several times. You lost a great deal of blood.*

She let that sink in, remembered the moments she'd been hit, the moments she, in her frenzy, had registered them as punches, not stabs. More. There was more. More loomed just beyond the grasp of her understanding. *That's not all I lost. Is it?*

Non. Not all.

Her fingers went limp in his hand. Heat stung her eyes. *I lost the child.*

Dominique cradled her face the way he cradled her quaking mind. She made not a sound as her tears flowed and she held on to him, but her heart wailed into the emptiness that radiated out from her belly. So much more than a new life had been destroyed there. Hope had been murdered in its cradle. Hope for even a sliver of light in Dominique's eternal darkness.

You are my light, Cassie, he thought at her fervently. *I need no more. I never did.*

But you wanted this. You wanted this so badly, and I wanted to give it to you so much more than I even realized.

But I cannot have it, chérie. Fathering mortal children is not to be for me. Not anymore. Just like the light of day can never be mine again, and every other human thing is lost to me.

The fatalistic tone rallied her. "No," she whispered. "No." *Not true. We did this once. We can do it again.*

No. We will not. We cannot, he said with unnerving quiet.

When this is over, you'll take another shot. We'll...

We cannot. At her mounting confusion, he added, *Your body was damaged in ways my blood can never repair.*

Only then did it occur to her to consider the details of her injury and the implications. She had been stabbed in the abdomen hard enough to lose a pregnancy. Her uterus would have been punctured. Likely hemorrhaged. Probably removed.

No, not *probably.*

Definitely removed. To save her life. She saw the truth of that now in Dominique's mind. Jackson had told him. The doctors had told Jackson.

Strange, the dazed calm that settled over her. It had about it the flavor of the irrefutable and inescapable. She had never wanted children, but there had always been the option to change her mind. She *had* changed her mind for Dominique, but now, at the ripe old age of twenty-five, that choice was gone for good. For her, anyway. For Dominique—

He stirred in her mind, expanding her awareness far beyond mortal limits. Sometimes, like now, when they were this close, she thought she could touch the edge of eternity.

My eternity includes nothing but the night, and no one but you. I am done with the day. I have all I will ever need. Everything is...as it must be.

Serge had uttered these words countless times over the years, and Dominique had always scorned them. No more. Everything is as it must be. It always had been. And the single-most important of these things was that she and Dominique were together.

She brought her hand to his neck, her thumb brushing the hard muscle and thick veins there, throbbing with supernatural power. Power he never wanted, along with responsibilities he wanted even less. Power without direction—until now.

Done with the day, she repeated, feeling the enormity of that statement.

He sat back and gazed at her with a seductive tilt of his lip. The tiny dragons in his sword hilts gleamed in the low light to either side of him. *I am the Lord of Night, am I not?*

Cassidy swallowed the lump in her throat. The Dominique she had once known—the youngling vampire tormented by doubt and longing and regret—was gone. Before her sat a being, a man, who had at last embraced his destiny: a blood-drinker of beguiling beauty and staggering power.

"That you are, my love," she whispered. "That you are."

The woman in the recliner stirred, and Cassidy held her breath, afraid she had awakened her. He glanced over his shoulder at his mother, who blinked at them.

"Dominique," she cried, tossing the blanket aside and struggling out of the awkward chair. This morning's bright, stylish outfit had been replaced by a simple pair of black slacks, non-descript cardigan, and an efficient pair of shoes.

Dominique rose but didn't move toward her, letting her decide how much she wanted to be in contact with him, or even if at all. She lifted her hands as if to embrace her son, but then clasped them tight together as though in prayer.

He spared her further awkwardness with a smile. "I hear you are quite the combatant, *Maman*. You walked away without a scratch."

"Not quite." She rubbed her lower back with a small wince before turning to the bed. "But nothing compared to poor Cassidy."

"She is fine."

Francesca's mouth dropped open. "*Quoi?*"

"It's true," Cassidy confirmed, sitting up. Their conversation had left her a little dazed, and she was still digesting the news of her altered physical circumstances, but her injuries had stopped fizzing. Dominique's blood had completed its work. She pushed her tangled hair off her face and flicked at the tubes and wires attached to her body. "Just need to get myself unhooked, and I'm ready to go."

"How is this possible?" Francesca asked.

Dominique gave his mother a coy look. "I am magic, *non?*" She studied him with fearsome wonder.

A small vibration in Dominique's pocket made him pull his phone out and read the new text. "We should go."

"Go? Go where?" Even as Cassidy asked, she tapped into the answers welling up from Dominique's mind. A game of subterfuge was afoot. Two jets would leave Vancouver, one going to Calgary, the other to Florida. The former would carry seven vampires and two reformed vampire hunters. As for the latter—

She took a deep breath to launch into vehement protests when Dominique placed a finger on his lips. *I know. Not here.*

Cassidy snapped her mouth shut, her teeth clacking together with temper, and ripped at the monitor pads attached to her chest. *No way in hell am I going back to Florida while you stay up here with your posse. That's just not happening.*

With a knowing smile, Dominique helped her pull the IV needles out of her arms and healed the punctures. *Far be it for me to tell you otherwise.*

Well, I'm glad we got that straight, your highness.

A pale, slender vampiress stepped into the room without a sound. She wore a short, belted raincoat and short, spiky hair. "The car is downstairs, my lord." With a nod to Cassidy, she added, "My lady."

"Makoto," Cassidy acknowledged, recognizing her from Dominique's memories. The vampiress was Isao's devoted companion for over a century. She was also an avid student of the sword, and chances were good she carried a blade beneath that coat and could use it in less time than it took to blink. She had been their supernatural security detail here since right after sundown.

Not that Francesca had known this, judging by how she regarded Makoto now as though seeing a venomous spider slither out of her shoe. She blanched, half-crossed her arms, and plucked at the collar of her blouse. "You are one, too? A...vampire?"

"I am," Makoto confirmed with a solemn nod.

While Francesca turned away, murmuring a prayer under her breath, Cassidy realized she had no clothes beyond the hospital gown and a pair of non-skid socks. Dominique's grin widened at her dark scowl. "You wear it well." *Your luggage will be at the airport. You can change on the plane.* He pulled a blanket off the bed and was about to wrap it around her shoulders when Makoto took off her coat and held it for Cassidy to slip into. Sure enough, there was a small sword slung across her back.

"Thank you. But are you sure?" Cassidy asked, eyeing the now-visible weapon.

"I am honored to assist."

And, of course, Dominique made them all invisible as they walked out, Makoto in the lead. Dominique brought up the rear, herding his reticent mother.

At the entrance, Douglas, attired in his usual trench coat, waited with a spacious Cadillac. They climbed in, Cassidy in the rear seat between Makoto to one side and Francesca—wedged against the door and clutching her bag like a shield—to the other. Once they were on their way, Dominique—in the front seat, holding his swords—filled his mother in on the plan. "Your luggage is waiting for you at the airport, *Maman*. Which plane you get on is up to you."

Her wide eyes flickered between the two vampires in the front. "I will go nowhere without my daughter."

"This will mean spending time on a small plane with seven like me."

Francesca looked like she was skirting a panic attack with only three in the car. "But you are their *patron*, their boss, *non*?"

"They are bound to me. They will protect, not hurt you." Still more softly, he added, "But if you wish it, you do not even have to see them."

It's what he wanted, Cassidy sensed. More than just Francesca's acceptance of what he had become by locking herself into a plane with seven vampires, this was a matter of security. Their foes had found both the house in Florida and the hotel in Vancouver. Calgary wasn't on their radar yet, and hopefully wouldn't be before Dominique had settled his differences with Adilla. It was the safest place to be.

Francesca's reasoning was far simpler. Her shoulders squared with resolve. "I will not go home," she said. "Not without my only living child."

45

BAGGED CONTENTS

Jackson kept a low profile in Calgary. Like Dominique, he would be recognizable to any member of the colony. Unlike the Lord of Night, he didn't have the luxury of cloaking himself in obscurity. So while Dominique shadowed Cassidy and Francesca as they checked in at Le Germain Hotel under assumed identities, Jackson kept Dominique's swords company in the back of their hired ride.

For being so short—not even ninety minutes—the flight from Vancouver in the middle of the night ranked as one of the longest in Jackson's life. The posh cabin of Garrett's G450 had been crammed with seven vampires and four humans, and between Carly's catatonic vamp state and Francesca's mounting anxiety, every one of them had been on edge.

But the worst part for Jackson was seeing Cassidy so drawn and exhausted as she curled against Dominique's shoulder. Some security he had turned out to be. The loss she and Dominique incurred because of Jackson's carelessness sat on him like an elephant. Especially considering the other news he received today.

Being on this plane with Dominique didn't help either. It wasn't the same plane Jackson had trapped him in three years ago, but it was the same model with similar decor. Back then, he had been beside himself with rage over failing to kill Dominique. Now he was beside himself with guilt over having tried so hard.

The car's passenger door opened and Dominique dropped into the seat. "They are settled," he reported. "And there is no trace of blood-drinkers in the area."

The driver, as thoroughly compelled as the pilots had been to hear and see nothing out of the ordinary, pulled the car out of the lot and merged into the early morning traffic.

"I called Sam," Jackson said, toying with his phone and trying to purge the dark thoughts from his head before they hit Dominique's radar. "She and Étienne will leave the house for a while. In case there are any more unwelcome guests."

Dominique didn't look at him. "I know."

"Shit. Are you really in my head all the time right now?"

"Only when I want to be. Or when your thinking becomes exceptionally noisy."

"Nice."

Dominique turned in his seat. "Jackson. I do not blame you for what happened to Cassidy. She lives. Truly, that is all that matters. And I am eternally grateful for your help in keeping her that way. Again. You are making a habit of saving her when I cannot."

"But—"

"But the plane, *oui*," he said with a pained little noise and a mischievous glint in his eyes. "True. That I may never forgive."

Jackson leaned back and plastered his hands over his face. *Stop. Just stop.* "I know what you're trying to do, and it so happens that I don't *want* to feel better, okay?"

"I would be a poor friend if I allowed that," Dominique said, serious again. "Not with this waiting for you."

"What? Is that...? Give me my phone." He snatched the device out of Dominique's unresisting hand. It was open to Ollie's text message which had reached him while Cassidy was fighting for her life in the OR. "Look what we did!" his bride wrote along with a long string of excited emojis—and a black-and-white image of her first ultrasound. Jackson felt hit over the head all over again. Twins. They were going to have twin girls.

"Congratulations," Dominique whispered.

Jackson wrestled with his emotions for the better part of a mile. He chewed his lower lip, rubbed his chin, the back of his head, but he didn't trust his voice to utter his greatest fear. *What if I fail them, too?*

"You will not. I will not permit it."

"You?" he croaked.

"*Oui. Moi.* They will need *un oncle, non?*" The mischief was back.

God help them, he thought, and put the phone away. "Maybe we should get out of this mess in one piece before we redraw my family tree."

"We will," Dominique said, sobering again. "The only way we can fail is if I end up at Adilla's mercy. And that will never happen again."

Could not happen again. Not if any of them were going to walk away from this. Jackson wondered if Dominique would try to sacrifice himself again to take them all down, if it came to that.

"I could try," Dominique mused, turning back to the city lights sweeping past. "But Isao and his young ones would sacrifice themselves to stop me first."

I would stop you, too, Jackson thought before he could stop himself and was grateful that this merited no comment beyond a twitch of Dominique's lip.

As per plan, the car deposited them at a mall parking lot just off the Trans-Canada. One by one, Isao's group melted out of the shadows surrounding a Canadian Tire store and formed a loose protective ring around their lord and Jackson.

Everyone was now armed, not just Isao and Makoto, the professional sword-slingers who had brought their weapons on the plane with them. Somewhere, the other four had found similar weapons in the past hour and now carried them with varying degrees of confidence. As they waited, Lyle tried to teach his sister how to handle her knife. Supernatural speed did not help the girl hold on to it as it continued to slip from her fingers. Should she end up in a confrontation with anything more than an ordinary mortal, Jackson pegged her chances of survival somewhere south of none. Dominique shifted beside him, and Jackson thought he heard the Lord of Night sigh.

The Sunseeker RV that lumbered into the lot was the size of a small, boxy bus and wore the dull patina of generous use. Garrett put it in park and opened the door. "Pool's open."

"Nice ride," Jackson said as he climbed in. The vehicle belonged to a local relative of a contact who owed Garrett a favor. For organizing the impossible in no time flat, Garrett was one resourceful son of a bitch.

"That he is," Dominique agreed as he looked around.

The interior was spotless, if dated, and reeked of old dampness and fried onions. There was a bedroom sectioned off in the back, along with a small lavatory. The rest of the space contained two fold-out bunk beds, a common area with a sofa and a dinette booth, and a tiny kitchen of sorts. Several large duffels piled in the middle of it all.

The vampires staked out their spots as Garrett got them moving. Jackson settled in the copilot seat and fired up the GPS on his phone. "Looks like we could be there in a couple of hours."

"Sun will be up in an hour," Garrett said. "We'll wait out the day somewhere off the beaten path and then head in just before dark. The fewer people see us there, the better."

Things quieted down behind them by the time they left city limits. Jackson peered over his shoulder. Dominique sat in the booth, one leg drawn up, watching him and Garrett, and no doubt riffling through their heads at will. Isao and Makoto sat opposite him, hands joined on the table, absorbed in their own silent communication. Douglas and Kostya occupied opposite ends of the sofa, Douglas dealing a deck of cards between them.

The twins huddled on one of the fold-down bunks in the back. Lyle still murmured to his sister as her arms and legs twisted together in constant motion as though warding off an army of invisible ants. Her wide eyes stared from beneath her unkempt multi-colored hair and shimmered with barely contained panic. Jackson had never seen anyone look more terrified and lost.

They would all feel the sun coming by now. But instead of following their instinct to hide away in a dark, secure place, they would put their unconscious, vulnerable bodies into the hands of not just mortals, but accomplished vampire hunters. And they would do this at the request of their lord and master.

No wonder they were all busy distracting themselves. In their own way, every one of them must be as close to freaking out as the poor, unfiltered Carly.

He caught Dominique's eye. *We'll keep you safe today. I won't fail you.*

The Lord of Night smiled. "I know," he mouthed.

There are bags in the duffels. Maybe they'll feel better if you hand them out.

The "bags" were body bags, which only upset Carly more until Douglas showed her that the material was light-tight and could not be torn by mere mortal strength. Just the same, she jammed her bagged self into the tiny shower stall. Lyle dutifully zipped himself up on the toilet beside her.

Fuck, Jackson thought. So much for enjoying the conveniences of home on the road.

Dominique, his own body bag tucked under his arm, shot him a look. "You can move them later," he whispered.

You know I will.

The murmuring in the bathroom continued for several more minutes as the others settled into their chosen berths. Garrett pulled off the highway and followed the signs to a campground. They rolled through the quiet, predawn forest all the way to the back where it appeared nothing but bears and deer had set paw and hoof since fall.

The engine cut off, and a whimper issued from the bathroom. A few more rustles, a small gasp from a bag on the bunks, and finally silence.

Jackson and Garrett sat until the sun fell in brilliant shafts all around them. A breeze full of moss and wood rot swirled through the open windows. From an unseen nearby campsite, pots clanged and voices rose in greeting over the warbling birdsong.

So peaceful, this bucolic scene. So deadly to the oblivious souls behind them.

"What amazes me is that they let us do this," Jackson said. "Knowing what they probably do about us."

When his uncle said nothing, Jackson turned to see him looking out his side window, then raise a hand to rub at his eyes. Jackson frowned. This was the first he knew of Garrett being allergic to anything.

Garrett cleared his throat. "Yeah, well. What really amazes me is that I won't kill them all. A year ago, I would have."

"Even Dominique?"

"Even him."

Jackson thought for a moment. "What changed?"

"I'm tired, kid. Old and tired." He shrugged one shoulder and leveled an askance look at his nephew. "And I'm hungry. C'mon. The fridge is stocked. Let's have something to eat and get some shut-eye while it's quiet."

"Yeah," Jackson said thoughtfully as he watched his uncle go to pull a pan and utensils out of the cubbies. This couldn't be the Striker Foundation's most ruthless hunter in history going soft on vampires, could it? That would be unthinkable. Yet, the trust Dominique suddenly placed in Garrett was nothing short of unprecedented. Why?

"You just gonna sit there and let me do all the work around here?" Garrett groused, pulling Jackson out of his speculations.

The fragrant smells of bacon and coffee began to overpower the whiff of old onion. "There's a bathroom that needs clearing out before one of us needs to take a crap."

Jackson got up and shook the questions out of his head. "Right. Where do you think we should put them?"

Garrett looked around and gestured with the spatula. "Let's keep the sofa and the bunk over the cockpit for us later. Stick them in the booth. We'll eat at the picnic table outside."

46

SUNLIGHT

He was back.

Dominique knew it even before he opened his eyes. That strange world was about to claim him again. The one that had nothing to do with reality. The dream state populated by people he never met, claiming to be his closest friends or lovers. People claiming to be monsters.

People claiming *he* was a monster.

One of these individuals hovered over him now in a twilight fog, blurred and indistinct. He turned his face away from the bees that drove their stingers into his eyeballs.

"Dominique, wake up. We need you. The real you."

The real him? Something shifted around in his head, like two transparent pictures aligning in space, struggling to line up and come into focus, both as real as they were alien. The enormity of what was taking shape made him pant for air, and the memories that seeped in from everywhere made him shake. Darkness beckoned. Blessed nothingness.

"Don't you dare," Jackson snarled and grabbed him by the lapels of his jacket. "Stay with me. I used the last shot on you, and if you don't get with the program right now, you're never waking up again. You hear me?"

That didn't sound like a bad thing, not at all—the things he had done deserved a death sentence—but the desperation in his friend's voice seized him. Something was very wrong, and it was more than that he was a vampire. Or even a vampire conscious during the day. Much more.

"Would you miss me, Jackson?" The words rolled around his reluctant tongue and fell out of his mouth like random marbles.

"Not as much as Cassidy would. Now, please get the fuck up," Jackson hissed under his breath.

Keeping his eyes to narrow slits, Dominique twisted away from the thin shade covering the rear wall of the tiny bedroom and bumped up against another body, this one still as death and secured in a body bag. A third bag lay against his other side. Wedged between them were the scabbards of several swords, including his own.

"You brought friends," Jackson whispered as he hurried to unzip Dominique's bag all the way to his feet. "We're almost back to the cavern, but we got intercepted. I was taking a piss, so they don't know I'm back here. They're armed and trigger-happy, and there are more of them than I want to risk taking on."

Dominique's heart slammed against his ribs, and he couldn't stop sucking at the air as though he needed it again. His legs felt like they belonged to someone else as he found the floor with his feet. "There are too many for you, even with my blood?"

"That won't save me from a bullet to the head, and—" Jackson froze. "You remember."

"*Oui.* I remember everything. From both of me." He tried to look at Jackson, but the bees were back in his eyes again and he covered them with one hand. "But I am blind and useless." And would stay useless well into the night if experience was anything to go by. He'd be at a disadvantage again. Geneviève was all but lost. "What made you do this?" The angry growl he aimed for emerged as a whine. Trying to read the situation from Jackson's mind was like flipping pages in a mud-covered book.

Jackson shoved something at him. Dominique grasped it, felt sunglasses, and pushed them onto his face as Jackson spoke in hushed tones. "The moment we turned off the main road, we got pulled over by one cop that turned into four before I could zip up my fly, all of them armed to the teeth. They got one look at the bags in the booth and—"

"Goddamn it! I said leave that where it is," Garrett bellowed from the other side of the door.

A male voice calmly told him to step aside. Sounds of a scuffle ensued. A hard thump and a low grunt of pain finished it. "Son of a *bitch!*"

Jackson leaned over the bed and moved the shade up just enough to see the scene outside. Dominique winced and put up a hand against the light blazing in. It felt like the blast from an oven. Tears burst from his burning eyes, but with the sunglasses he could just make out two uniformed figures standing over a long, dark smudge lying on the side of the road. Two others joined them, another smudge swinging between them. A body bag.

"Ah, *non.*"

The door burst open and filled with a disheveled Garrett cradling his arm. "Are you just going to hide back here while they drag out our entire cargo at gunpoint?" Spotting Dominique hunched on the bed, he added, "And what the *hell* did you do?"

"I got us help," Jackson said.

"Oh, this ought to be good. What fraction of his head do we get this time?"

"All of it," Dominique said.

Garrett stepped into the space between the bathroom and bunk beds, clearing the doorway. "Then get your all-of-it out there before they kill another one of your flock."

Another one? Dominique maneuvered his string-puppet body to the front of the RV, stubbing his toes twice, once half-falling on top of a still, bagged body, and holding on to various bulkheads as he went. Never had his arms and legs been less cooperative, and when he got to the open door, they declared an all-out strike. It was as if something inside him with a mind of its own refused to step out there into all that sunlight. That something, his true vampire self, found itself half-awake and trapped in a nightmare. The edges of his vision darkened. Oblivion reached for him. Just pass out like he did before, like every fiber of his being screamed to do when the sun was up. Run, hide, seek the darkness.

"*Ça va*," he reassured himself and forced his gaze to the scene outside, to the officer bending over, reaching for the zipper on the second bag. Two others turned back to the RV for the next bag. "*C'est d'accord.*" This was okay. This worked. He knew it did. He had walked in this inferno without so much as a blister before, without even thinking about it. He could do it again.

That realization rushed at him like a gust of wind. Within moments, the fog cleared from his mind, his vision sharpened, and his limbs grew strong. Leaping out into the pool of fire, he grabbed the wrist of the man unzipping the second bag. "*Arrêtez.* Stop."

The officer looked up in open-mouthed surprise. "Step back immediately," he said and tried to jerk his hand free, only to drop to his knees with a strangled shriek when his bones cracked in Dominique's grip.

His partner drew his sidearm. "Hands up and get on your knees," he barked. The two officers who had been on their way to retrieve another bag turned back, hands going to their weapons as well.

Dominique zipped the bag back up and forced compulsion into his voice. "Put your guns away and listen carefully." The weapons lowered slowly. "You have found nothing here. You stopped no one. You are having an uneventful day and will continue on your way." They exchanged puzzled glances. Another compulsion had a hold of them, a powerful one, and Dominique was nowhere near strong enough right now to counter it. He had seconds before they forgot he ever spoke and would hear nothing else he had to say.

At which point, he would have to kill them.

Dominique closed his burning eyes and lowered his head. Sunlight beat against him in white-hot waves. But he wasn't burning. The pain wasn't real. It was merely what he imagined he should feel, what his vampire self dreaded the most. Grinding his teeth in concentration, he crushed the panic in his chest and pulled his most powerful self out of the very marrow of his bones.

Then he cast a psychic cloak around himself.

Around the body bags.

Around the RV.

"What the—" one officer said.

"Where did he go?"

Several seconds later, "Where did who go, Josh?"

"What? I—nobody. What are you talking about?"

"Shit. My wrist is killing me."

"That's what you get for punching random trees," chided the only woman in the group. "If you boys are done with your pissing contest, I have a patrol to finish."

Within a minute, all four of them had retreated to their various vehicles and pulled out. Only when they were out of sight did Dominique release the cloak.

A blanket settled over him. "Here. Looks like you could use this."

Dominique gathered the fabric around his shoulders, hiding his hands and cowling his head in shadow. The illusion of pain faded and his thoughts cleared. He touched the body bag before him, relieved to feel the round lump of a solid head. The occupant would survive.

The same could not be said for the blood-drinker in the first bag, which had been unzipped and spread open from top to bottom. Tendrils of dark gray skittered across Carly's blistered and smoking skin. They widened into tracks of ash that spidered all over her bare arms, shoulders, neck and sweetly childish face. Even her bi-colored hair wilted away to sooty dust. There was no trace of this morning's terror. She was dead.

"Jesus," Garrett muttered as he joined Dominique and Jackson. "Poor kid."

Dominique held out his hand to cast a shadow over the disintegrating body. His skin prickled but stayed pristine, blazing white at the end of his black sleeve. He was immune, at least for this day, and could walk in the sun to bear witness to the fate he cheated.

"Sorry," Jackson said. "I know this was the last thing you wanted today."

"*Au contraire.* This is the one thing I have always wanted." Even when he decided he would never have this again, he had still craved it. Even when he tried to drown his hunger for the sun in the same abyss into which he had plunged his hunger for terror, he knew it would never leave him.

Not until now.

He could see the heat shimmer in the late afternoon sunlight that slanted through the woods and across the road. He could hear the sun thunder in the sky. It beat against his body with tangible force.

No, this wasn't the world he remembered, or the sun he once loved. He no longer belonged here. In body, mind and spirit, he truly was a creature of the night.

"How do you feel?" Garrett asked.

Dominique pulled his hand back beneath the blanket. "Like an impostor."

"We should pack these up and keep going before we run out of daylight," Jackson said. He leaned down to zip up Carly's remains.

"Are you certain this is what you want, Garrett?" Dominique said quietly. "To be this vulnerable?"

Jackson stopped the zipper halfway up. The breeze caught a wisp of ash escaping by his hand.

Garrett didn't respond until Dominique turned to him. "I'm being eaten alive by something even your blood can't fix. I'm so fragile, the bastards broke my arm just shoving me aside. How much more vulnerable can I possibly get?"

"Look at her."

He did, but avoided his nephew's questioning stare. The muscles in his jaw bunched.

"The same sunlight that warms you now will do that to you if you proceed."

Garrett's mouth pinched to the size of a pea. "Well. If that's how I go, it's a damn sight better than what's waiting for me now."

"Wait," Jackson said. He closed the bag and stood. "Are you saying what I think you're saying? You...want to be turned?"

"Nothing gets by you, does it?" Garrett groused.

"What the fuck. Why?"

"Why not?"

"But—"

"We don't have time for this. Pack these kids up and let's get back on the road. I'll tell you all about it while you drive."

47

Not As Expected

W ith a good deal less emotion than when he first made his case, Garrett, his arm now secured in a makeshift sling, told his nephew about his diagnosis and the treatment path he could not abide. "It is what it is," he concluded matter-of-factly. "We all die some time. I'm just not ready to die now. Or any time soon." He glanced at Dominique, who sat curled in the booth behind them. "If the night will have me, I'll welcome it."

Jackson looked as stunned as Dominique had ever seen him. He drove the RV with one hand, a can of caffeine in the other, staring straight ahead. The rattle of the engine was the only sound.

"Well. I see you've got this," Garrett said after a length of awkward silence. "Think I'll go see about getting this sling to fit better." He gave Dominique a long look as he passed. A look that said, "Now the decision feels real."

Once Garrett rummaged in the back, Jackson pitched his voice so only Dominique could hear him. "Are you really going to do this?"

"His request is genuine," Dominique murmured. "If not for the blood I gave him this week, he would be bed-bound and hooked to machines already."

"So you're going to do a compassion turning?"

"Would you prefer he dies a miserable death in the clutches of your so-called health-care system?"

"Shit, no. The bastard is more of a father to me than my father is."

"But you cannot imagine him as a blood-drinker."

"Be honest. Neither can you. Not after your history with him."

Dominique sighed and was momentarily distracted by the sensation of his lungs expanding with a need for air he hadn't felt in years.

"You haven't answered my question," Jackson muttered. His knuckles went white around the wheel. "Are you going to do this?"

"I don't know, Jackson. I truly don't."

They had almost an hour to sunset and were on target to reach their destination a comfortable twenty-five minutes before that. Dominique used the time to make a phone call. Service was spotty, but after several attempts, he heard Cassidy's voice wobble through the connection.

"Dominique?" Surprise and concern in that one word.

"*Mon amour*," he greeted.

"What happened? Why did Jackson wake you up?" The words came tense and full of restraint.

"Cassie, it is I. All of me. Awake."

The connection went silent. He looked at the phone to confirm the call was still active. It was. "Cassie? *Amour?*"

"Oh my God. You're awake. Fully awake?" Hard to say if that tremble in her voice was emotional or technical.

"*Oui.* At last." He had shed the blanket, though not the sunglasses, as he watched the walls of green pass the window beside him. The light still prickled over his skin and made his eyes water, but his vampire's panic had subsided.

"It's not what you hoped it would be, is it?" she asked, sensitive to his every mood even now, when she couldn't possibly be aware of his muddled thoughts.

Dominique closed his eyes. "*Non.*" That was true of so many things right now.

"Well. At least now you know for sure."

That he did. But at what price? This madness could yet cost countless lives tonight when he faced Adilla once more at a disadvantage. Including the lives of those who slept around him now and had placed their fate in him.

"So if you weren't awake right now, they would all be dead already," Cassidy reasoned after he summarized events for her.

"But if I had never dabbled with this folly in the first place, none of us would have to be here now. Geneviève would not be here now," he clarified. So strange to have these discussions with her aloud and trying to convey the depths of his feelings in words and tone.

"Are you going to wait another day, then?" she asked, tentative hope in her voice.

He considered this. Dismissed it. "The risk of being discovered again is too great. Garrett is too fragile. Jackson is only one. There are no more shots to wake me up, and…Geneviève will not last that long. It doesn't matter how weak I will be, I cannot afford not to end this. Somehow."

A short time later, Jackson eased their giant box on wheels into the campground and slipped into a vacant spot next to a party in high gear. Several families had gathered around a set of grills that smoked and sizzled with their dinner. Children darted underfoot. Pop music streamed from a wireless speaker.

Garrett eyed them suspiciously. "Could be sentries. Probably compelled."

Dominique snorted. "What they are is fresh blood, you fool. Why else do you think Adilla encourages a campground this close to his lair?"

"Jeez," Jackson said.

Garrett gave Dominique a look that hovered somewhere between horrified and resigned.

Several greetings floated their way when they emerged from the RV. "You look like you had a long day on the road," one woman called, all smiles. "Want to join us for dinner? We've brought way too much."

While Jackson and Garrett looked at each other as though trying to decide if they should bring weapons, Dominique turned his most beguiling dimpled smile on the woman. "We would love to, *chère. Merci*."

She chuckled throatily, her cheeks coloring. "Well, c'mon over. You're in for a treat. Bryce here makes the best burgers in the neighborhood." At the grill, a man in a cheerful "Kiss the Cook" apron waved a spatula in acknowledgment.

"Wait. What are you doing?" Jackson's tone said he suspected him of being up to the very worst.

Dominique laughed, feeling freer than he had in years. "I am going to have my last solid food ever. And I intend to enjoy every bite."

48

CERTAINTY

Jackson finished his "best burger in the neighborhood" at a brisk pace and chased it with another energy drink. Well rested, and loaded with carbs, protein, and caffeine, he was ready for whatever the night would throw at him. While he ate, he made minimum conversation with their hosts and kept his eyes glued to where the Lord of Night was enjoying his last supper on a rock outcrop overlooking a rushing stream.

Beside him, Garrett polished off the helping Jackson had cut up for him so he could eat it one-handed with a plastic fork. "I think I need more magic juice. This arm is taking too damn long to heal."

"Won't that interfere with your plans?"

"I'm just trying not to fall apart while we're all still in this hot mess. The rest is for later."

Jackson shook his head. "I don't suppose you've talked with Dad about this?"

"Hell no."

He played with his drink can and considered the question that had weighed on him since he first heard about his uncle's intentions. "What are you going to do if he asks me to put you down?"

Garrett gave him a narrow look. "That's not the question, now, is it?"

"What do you mean?"

"The question really is: what are *you* going to do *when* Warren asks you to put me down?"

Son of a bitch. Leave it to Garrett to get right to the point. His actual father or the man who had acted as his father? Which would he choose? His hand clenched around the can until it crinkled.

"Doesn't matter, kid," Garrett declared and wiped his mouth with a paper napkin. "You couldn't, even if you tried. I taught you everything you know about hunting, and I intend to be any hunter's worst nightmare."

"I'm sure you—" Jackson looked around. The quiet figure in the black leathers was gone. "Where did he go?"

"Probably puking his guts out in the woods." Garrett put his napkin down and checked his watch. "Sunset."

"Shit. I wish I didn't have to give him that shot today."

"They'd all be dead if you hadn't, and my plans would have changed to picking out a plot at the cemetery. They have a chance now. As do I, I might add."

An agonized and decidedly inhuman scream issued from the motor home, bringing all activity to an abrupt halt. Someone turned off the music. "What was that?"

"Oh God," Jackson said. "Lyle."

He tore open the door and burst into the RV. Carly's bag gaped open on teenage-girl-clothing awash in gray ash. Kneeling over it, face distorted in a mask of agony and ash-covered hands raised in fists, was the forever-teenage boy.

Seeing Jackson, Lyle's eyes snapped to deep, black pits glowing with hellfire in a face gone skull thin. His guttural snarl was not even close to human. "What did she ever do to you?"

The entire forest seemed to fall silent, every mortal thing alert for the predator that had its sights set on Jackson. Not a muscle in his body responded. He stood nailed to the spot, catapulted back in time to his brother facing just such a creature. He could already see the blood-spattered aftermath, the torn limbs, the smashed skull...

Death flew at him. And he couldn't move.

Then death was snatched out of the air and hurtled into the shadowy interior. Kostya's enormous arms circled the enraged vampire from behind. Isao grabbed the pointy jaw. "This is not his doing."

"They were supposed to watch over us, and Carly is dead," Lyle howled. "My sister—my family—is *dead!*"

"I'm sorry," Jackson said, clutching at both sides of the door because he didn't quite trust his knocking knees. "I'm so sorry."

"Move," Dominique whispered behind him and Jackson, startled, jerked aside, letting him pass.

The Lord of Night grabbed Lyle's head in both hands and spoke low and fast in words as soothing as they were commanding. It took a minute, maybe two, but slowly Lyle's face filled out again, and his eyes lost their dark fire.

"Adilla and Esteban will pay for what they have done to you and your sister, to all of us," Dominique promised. "Tonight, they will pay."

Lyle gave a tiny nod and Dominique patted his cheek before releasing him. "Time to go."

The vampires stepped out of the camper. When he passed Jackson, Lyle ducked his tear-stained face, the mop of yellow hair falling over his eyes. "Sorry."

"I understand," was all Jackson could manage. When everyone but Dominique was out, he slipped up the steps and found the Lord of Night slinging his swords across his back. "What's the plan?"

"Stay out of our way," Dominique said as he tied his hair back with swift movements.

"I know that cave now. I know the setup. I have your blood." Not to mention enough caffeine to fuel a small jet. "I'm an asset."

"You are mortal."

"What?"

Dominique grabbed him by the shoulders. "Tonight, I cannot protect you. Stay here with Garrett and be ready to leave quickly."

"I want Esteban," Jackson ground out. There. He'd said it. Admitted it to himself at last. This was as close as he would ever get to his brother's killer, and he was not about to let this chance at retribution slip past.

Dominique searched his face. "I know, *chèr*. I know. But not tonight. Tonight you would not survive." His lips twitched. "I would miss you."

Before Jackson could respond, Dominique had exited the RV.

The humans in the neighboring camp had all stopped to gawk at the vampires. When the woman who had first invited them spotted Dominique, she called, "How was that burger, Nick?"

Every other vampire eye swerved to Dominique, who smiled graciously and placed a splayed hand on his chest. "The best I shall ever have, *madame. Merci de tout cœur.*"

She pushed a cloud of frizzy hair behind an ear and blushed. "Well, there's more if you and your friends—" Her brow folded into a frown. Around her, the others resumed eating, talking, playing games. The speaker throbbed back to life. Looking at Jackson and Garrett, she said, "Would you like another burger?"

Garrett waved his good arm. "Thanks, but no."

Jackson looked between the humans and Dominique whose amiable air had evaporated into something far darker. They couldn't see him anymore, or any of the vampires. *How the fuck are you doing this after being awake today?*

Dominique glanced at him but made no reply. An instant later he had blurred away, the others zipping after him.

"Son of a bitch." Jackson shook his head.

"So he's at full power tonight," Garrett said. "We may have a chance of getting out of this yet."

Their neighbors paid no attention to them anymore. They had already forgotten Dominique and the inhuman spectacle of a grieving vampire. Over twenty humans. Not just random passersby, but fully aware of—and intently focused on—him. Compelled without a word in a matter of seconds. Jackson had never seen Dominique do anything on this scale, even at his best. "Full power," he repeated. "And then some."

49

WAIT

They did not approach the cavern as Dominique and Jackson had before, by the route amenable to humans. They came through the woods from the campground, along the stream, and then down a jagged cliff face beside a roaring waterfall. The holds were so small and random and slippery, nothing but a supernatural entity would consider descending that way at night with neither light nor climbing gear. This was the path the colony used to reach the campground and its easy fresh blood.

It was not a path Dominique would have dared travel if he were not in full possession of his faculties. Or perhaps not even then. Not before now.

Unlike his previous attempts at day-walking, this day had not exhausted him. Far from it. The battle was done, his triumph over his fractured mind complete, and the two sides of him had more than made their peace—they had meshed into a surprising synergy. More power coursed through him than he could ever have imagined possible.

When the day had drained from the sky, darkness crept over the forest and back into his soul. He no longer dreaded the hunger for blood and the lust for life sharpening his senses. Instead, he welcomed them, even as he vomited his hamburger dinner into the creek, and the dark forces that defined him ignited into an inferno. Only the night before, this level of power rushing through him would have terrified him, made him believe he would burn up or explode or lose his mind. No more. This is what he truly was. Master of the dark.

Lord of Night.

As the one most familiar with the cliff path, Isao took the lead. Dominique shadowed him, copying his movements. Douglas came behind him, followed by Lyle, Kostya, and Makoto. Massive sheets of water swept past them within an arm's length.

"Don't you dare fall on me," Lyle hissed when Kostya's bulk crested the edge above him.

"Shut up and pay attention," the big blood-drinker grumbled.

But it wasn't Kostya who lost his grip in the slick mists. A tumbling rock hit Dominique in the shoulder an instant before Douglas flailed into space on his way to the boulders fifty feet below.

Dominique reached out his hand, grabbing for the man's arm, but only caught a fistful of leather trench coat. It was enough. His own tentative hold slid under the jerk of extra weight, and he found himself grateful that it wasn't Kostya he had to catch. For a moment, the former detective dangled like a half-drowned cat in his coat, staring up at Dominique with a look of mute surprise. Far below, the rock hit the boulders, its clattering not quite masked by the pounding water. He sent a wave of calm at Douglas and waited for him to find a grip on the wall again before releasing his hold.

Isao's silent gratitude washed over Dominique. Even for an immortal, an uncontrolled drop to the rocks from this height could have been fatal.

Unfortunately, the rock that had fallen could be fatal for them all. Whatever element of surprise they had left after their delay at the campground approached non-existent.

Or perhaps it never existed at all.

Esteban waited for them.

Edged in the soft silver of a half-moon and with his arms crossed, he leaned on a small boulder at the cave's entrance and looked almost bored when Dominique's group materialized out of the woods. Esteban's black slacks and shirt were pressed and spotless, and the fine leather loafers on his feet were placed with care on a clean rock. There was not a weapon in sight.

Dominique let his vision expand, let his eyes glow with his power, and saw Esteban's aura flare to life around him—and the five others standing at some distance in the darkness behind him. Their scent rode the chilly wind belching out of the cavern and betrayed something more than the youngling soldiers he expected.

Elite guards, Isao provided helpfully. *Not to be taken lightly.*

Despite his impatience, Dominique stopped himself from reaching for his weapons and issued a silent command for the others to do likewise. He knew a trap when he smelled it. The shape of this one he couldn't guess just yet, but he dared not underestimate the Spaniard. He would have to wait and stay vigilant and hope he would be fast enough to counter the ambush when it sprang.

And spring it would, and soon. Esteban's self-satisfied expression said as much. As did the subtle shifting of the others. Unlike their master, they were well armed and appeared to know what to do with their assortment of swords, pipes, and chains.

It was tempting to cast himself and his group in invisibility and walk past this crude welcome committee, but that would have left a dangerous foe in his back and no knowledge of what lay ahead.

"I was beginning to think you had lost your way," Esteban greeted. "It's not that far from Calgary, after all."

The implication behind those words made Dominique go supernaturally still.

"Oh yes. I know all about that little shell game you tried to pull with your planes. I have eyes and ears everywhere." He dropped his voice and leaned forward. "All the time."

Dominique reached for Cassidy not even a hundred miles away. She and Francesca lived. But that was all he could determine at this distance. He swerved to Garrett and Jackson. *Get away from here*, he commanded. *And confirm everyone's safety. Now.*

He sensed Garrett's instant acknowledgment up in the campground as he grabbed his phone. Jackson...Jackson he sensed somewhere else entirely. *Merde. You stubborn bastard!*

Jackson fought him like a charging bull rhino, revenge blazing in his heart. The hunter took ruthless advantage of the gift of freedom Dominique had given him. *Putain d'idiot! You will get yourself killed*, he argued. It didn't matter. Jackson would never hear his words, only feel his commands.

His response, however, was very clear. *Too fucking bad. I'm not going back.*

"This can't be that much of a surprise to you, can it?" Esteban wondered when Dominique remained silent in his unwelcome distraction.

Not yet ten minutes into this night and already surprises battered him from every direction. Before he could begin to fear what else might conspire against him, he shoved Jackson out of his mind and poured calm into his voice. "Not at all. But you should know that you have one less spy tonight."

"Really. Well, that explains her silence then." Esteban licked his lips thoughtfully as he regarded Lyle. The turmoil and recent memories raging in the youngster's head would be a virtual news bulletin to his sire.

Dominique kept his own mind as shuttered as his face, taking no chances that any of the serum Esteban had gotten into him still lingered.

"I am here for Adilla." He took several steps toward Esteban. The guards drifted closer. He ignored them. "I made him a promise that I intend to keep."

"And he's expecting you. He will be so pleased that you have accepted his invitation to join us. As his equal." Not even a trace of a sneer in that statement.

Dominique arched a brow. "I promised he would submit to me or die." Very succinctly, he spoke the words reflecting what Adilla had screamed at Aubrey, and which he would hear now through Esteban. A sentiment that, true as it was, Dominique had never fully embraced—until now. "I am the one true heir to Kambyses. I have...no equal."

Unease fell on the shuffling guards and permeated the damp evening air, together with the high-pitched squeaks and frantic flutters of bats, and...the clink of chains.

Esteban stared at him as though transfixed by the unearthly amber glow in Dominique's eyes.

"Adilla knows I am what I claim to be," Dominique said. "But you do not, do you, Esteban? You would have had your slaves finish me today, and, with me, all of us."

The Spaniard's thin lips stretched into a humorless smile as he pushed away from the boulder. The others closed ranks behind him. "Foolish young one. Adilla's wishes are my commands. He is my sire. Nothing I do ever happens without his consent." He leveled a contemptuous look at Isao's group. "Those who shun his favor are not welcome here."

Isao scoffed. "We are fit only to be discarded in the sun? Yes, that is how those who have Adilla's *favor* usually end up as well. You best take care, Esteban. Your time is coming."

"Ah, my dear brother, Isao. Still the cynic after all these centuries. How I have missed you not."

"You're my fucking sire, you motherfucker." Lyle's hoarse shout almost made Dominique wince in sympathy. The boy bristled with pain and rage.

"Not now, young one," Kostya warned and reached for the boy's arm.

Lyle tried to twist away, shaking his head. "You are Carly's sire! Do you even care that she's dead?"

Esteban unfolded his arms and pocketed his hands as he moved forward just enough to force Dominique to turn his back to the guards, who remained where they were. Isao and Makoto watched them, their hands moving to the hilts of their weapons.

"Oh, I think everyone here will agree that she and you are a waste of perfectly good blood. You were weak as mortals, and now you are a useless immortal."

"Just because we didn't inherit your goddamn special fucking 'gift,' you ca—"

Dominique threw up his hand in a "Stop!" gesture. *Enough.*

Lyle snapped his mouth shut.

That rattle of chains from the cave grew louder.

"Well. There may be hope for him yet," Esteban mocked. "You can make his case to Adilla. He might reconsider. As I'm sure you will reconsider his offer once you understand my lord's generous terms."

"His terms are of no concern to me beyond his willingness to submit." Wary impatience nipped at the back of Dominique's brain. Why were they tarrying here?

"Just the same, he has made you a gift."

Merde! He could even smell Jackson now. Peeling off a tiny part of his attention, Dominique spun a small illusion. "A gift?"

The feral expression on Esteban's face made the hairs on the back of Dominique's neck rise in alarm. Moving like a rattlesnake coiling to strike, he turned back to the cavern. "A token of his esteem for you."

The wall of guards stepped aside. Two more blood-drinker auras glowed behind them. One of these kept a firm hold on the other, who shuffled along in shackles and chains that clattered over the stone floor.

The smell of purest snow wafted off...her.

A sense of unreality crawled over Dominique's body. "*Non.*"

It was too soon. It could not be. He had to force himself to look at her, this newly made youngling, to see the long blue skirt she wore, and the stained pinstripe blouse. The sensible shoes were gone, her white feet filthy and bony. Her black hair hung in a tangled mass, the widow's peak a small dagger in the skeletal mask of her face. And the eyes...windows into a void that saw nothing, recognized nothing, craved nothing.

Nothing but blood.

The wind rose in a mighty gust and moaned through the cavern. Moaned as Dominique's soul moaned. He was too late.

Geneviève.

"My lord Adilla has generously accepted your beloved sister into our ranks and granted her immortal life."

There it was, the shape of the trap. Blackmail. Coercion. Adilla would not submit. But killing him would now also kill Geneviève.

Though he remained motionless, a tremor ran through Dominique's bones. There was more. He sensed it in Esteban's smug demeanor and heard it in the jangling weapons behind him. Something was closing in as surely as Jackson was skulking in the woods.

Wait, he told himself. *Wait*, he told all the minds he could touch. *Wait.*

"Have you nothing to say to this poor child?" Esteban asked with a casual gesture at Geneviève. She shook so hard her shackles rattled, seized by a need for something she did not yet comprehend.

"Adilla's...esteem for me does not extend to feeding her?" The words felt flat on his tongue. *Wait.*

"Nonsense. Who better than her brother to introduce her to the sweet pleasures of the hunt?"

Hunt? Geneviève wouldn't be doing any hunting for many nights yet. She would fall on and drain every mortal thing to cross her path. Left on her own, she would lay waste to the village within the hour and the campground soon thereafter.

Wait.

"You might as well," Esteban said with a low, impatient growl when Dominique continued to stand in silence. "We have a little time before our guests arrive."

Wait.

Guests? Dominique turned to the Spaniard, saw his mouth widen with a fanged grin, and both knew and feared what he would say.

"Your mother is on her way here to join us." He chuckled. "And, of course, darling Cassidy."

Dominique waited no more.

50

MONSTERS CANNOT LOVE

Cassidy tried to ignore Francesca practicing with the light gun. Every time the awkward device whined to life, painting a neat circle of brilliance on the rug, the wall, the bed, the table, she shuddered a little. She could almost smell Dominique's roasting skin again.

"You probably shouldn't run down the battery on that thing."

Francesca turned off the gun and placed it in her lap, covering it with her elegant hands, which looked like they had never held a weapon more dangerous than a paring knife. "So you do believe we might need this...this gun?"

"I don't see how. But since we have it, we might as well keep it operational." The monstrosity—a clunky early version of the full-spectrum torches the Strikers used now—had shown up in Francesca's luggage along with several small canisters of silver dust spray. A gift from Garrett, Cassidy suspected, one she had been all for abandoning with their luggage back at Le Germain Hotel. As per the plan she and Dominique had hatched, no one, not even she, would know where she and Francesca would end up. Therefore, no weapons would be required.

Francesca disagreed. She had stuffed the lot into a satchel and slung this over her shoulder like a coat of armor. Cassidy sighed and nodded. There was no point in telling her that if a vampire came close enough for them to have to use these weapons, it would be too late.

Cassidy returned the remains of the turkey sandwich to its bag. She had picked it up this afternoon during their random travels on Calgary's public transit systems, which had landed them here at a Best Western on the outskirts of the city. The hotel was far from the downtown Le Germain in both distance and luxury. With a little luck, this translated into being well off the radar of any vampires in the area.

When she turned to the side to take a peek past the drawn curtains, her belly twinged. Dominique's blood had done all it could to put her guts back together in record time, but her middle still felt like a ragged hollow, especially during the day. Last night, with Dominique at her side, his sober acceptance of what they lost permeated her. But at daybreak, everything changed. The child, that tiny part of him that had been with her twenty-four seven, was no more and would never be again. If she weren't running for her life, she would have curled up in a ball and howled.

Outside, the day had long melted into night. Dominique wasn't close enough for her to hear his thoughts, but she sensed his continued presence in the world. For now, that would have to do. One more night on her own. Then she could afford to fall apart.

She dropped the curtain and handed Francesca one of the silver spray containers. "Here. Hold on to this." Another one went into the back pocket of her jeans beneath the hem of a bulky sweatshirt.

Francesca studied the innocuous weapon before slipping it into the pocket of her designer slacks. "It is hard to believe that they should be so fragile, given what they are."

"Sensitive," Cassidy corrected. "What they are is sensitive. A little light and silver will cause them grief, but it won't kill a vampire." At least not one that wasn't confined to a cage. What she knew of Garrett's interrogation practices still screamed in the back of her mind. The urge to pull the silver from her pocket and hurl it across the room was almost overwhelming.

"Do you know how many he has killed?"

Cassidy gave a derisive snort. "I'm not sure even Garrett knows how many he's turned to ash. Hundreds for sure. Maybe thousands." Reading Francesca's expression as shock at the revelation about her suitor, she added, "The hunt is his life's purpose. He's good at it."

Francesca's hands closed on the light gun. "I meant...Dominique. How many...people has he killed?"

Ice slid down Cassidy's spine.

"He says he no longer kills when he...drinks." Delicate fingers described a circle near her throat before returning to the weapon. "But that means he did kill at some point, *non?*"

"At some point," Cassidy conceded faintly.

"Do you know? How many?"

Quite a few. Dominique's early, out-of-control hunts had produced a great deal of carnage, details of which she often wished she didn't know as well as she did. She pressed her hands together between her knees and tried to sound casual. "Why would you want to know such a thing?"

"Because he...he is my son." She tucked her lock of silver hair behind one ear and moistened her lips. "I want to know what his life has been like. And I do not believe he has told me everything about what happened to him. Has he?"

No point denying that. Cassidy didn't even try. Neither was she about to volunteer anything. She managed a tiny smile. "He has told you everything he can live with, Francesca. The rest—" She shook her head. "The rest are private demons that will haunt him for the rest of...well, time, I guess."

"He feels remorse?"

Francesca's doubtful tone grated on Cassidy's nerves. "Yes. He does. To a degree incomprehensible by human minds. The same as he feels everything else. Your son bears the scars of what happened to him, but he is the same man. Only his body has changed."

The older woman's eyes crinkled with tension. "He was always such a loving and happy young man. Now...so much darkness."

"He is reshaping the world of night to suit him. It's why he's out there right now teaching a thousand-year-old monster to love."

She looked away, thoughtfully stroking the gun in her lap. Her words, when they came, were barely more than a breath. "Monsters cannot love."

Cassidy stared at her, speechless. During the flight, when Francesca had skirted a full-blown panic attack, Dominique had pounded the last nail into the coffin containing his human life by compelling his mother. Around vampires she was to never know fear, he told her. Nor would any other compulsion ever influence her. But how she felt about the supernatural—about him—he had left untouched.

And here it was.

Monsters cannot love.

"Dominique is not a monster," Cassidy whispered. Before she could say any more, a knock sounded at the door. "Yes?"

"Room service," a young male voice replied.

Both women glanced at the remnants of their earlier meals, then at each other. Cassidy took the light gun from Francesca's lap, stood, and forced an airy tone. "Wrong door. We didn't order any."

Seconds ticked by. Her pulse pounded in her ears. Any vampire outside that door would hear it, along with Francesca's. When he spoke again, the bored tone was gone, replaced by the unmistakable timber of compulsion. "You placed an order. You want what I bring."

Cassidy took a shaky breath and exchanged another look with Francesca, who blinked in surprise, then glanced at the window.

She shook her head. They were on the fourth floor. The window was not an escape option.

"Open the door," demanded a second, deeper voice. More ineffective compulsion.

Cassidy powered up the light gun and pointed it at the door with both hands. "We're busy."

The low, furious growl sounded like it came from a large animal. A monster.

Francesca got up, her movements still stiff from her battle the day before, and edged closer to Cassidy.

With a thunderous boom, the heavy hotel room door tore out of the wall, frame and all, and crashed into the room.

Cassidy pulled the trigger before she could see the invader. An ear-splitting shriek pierced her ears, followed by silence.

The gun whined in her hands, grew warm. The battery indicator registered more than half full, but for how long would that last? All night? She didn't dare turn it off.

Francesca went for her phone. "911?"

Cassidy knew better, but nodded anyway. Too little, too late. Too crazy to report.

Voices in the hallway. Asking questions. Protesting. Compulsion. The voices went away. Through the open door, the square of hallway lit up midday bright remained empty. The gun whined louder. The handle grew slippery in her sweaty palms. She held it tighter.

Francesca cursed at her phone. Her call wasn't going through.

A small thud from the window made Cassidy swallow her heart. Before she could utter a meaningless warning, Francesca grabbed the curtain and pulled it aside—and screamed.

Cassidy turned just in time to see the full-fledged beast clinging to the wall outside slam his skeletal fist through the glass. After that, everything happened very fast and precisely as she knew it would.

They had, after all, only one light gun.

She swung the beam around and lit him up just as he climbed through the shards of glass. There was only a glimpse of the skull face turning bright red. Then the gun tore out of her hand and hurtled at the window with such force the glass that remained shattered and blew out.

Picked up and tossed, Cassidy hurtled toward the bed like a stringless puppet. She flailed wildly to keep from bouncing clear off the mattress. As she flipped around, she saw Francesca face-to-face with the beast that had come through the window, her arm raised high, wielding a...plastic fork?

In a flash, a claw hand captured her wrist, eliciting a sharp cry. The beast roared into her face in all its horrifying glory, angled its head, and...

The other vampire flew at his partner and nailed him to the nearest wall by his skinny neck. "Stop," he snarled. It was the deep-voiced one. The one obviously in charge. "Lose it now, and you know what Esteban will do to you."

The beast subsided, but it remained close to the surface, just behind the hyper-dilated eyes in a coarse, tattooed face. His cohort let him go. Also dressed in a hoodie and jeans, he had a calmer but far more dangerous look about him.

Cassidy scrambled into a sitting position and marshaled every ounce of outrage she could muster. "How *dare* you? Do you have any idea who we are?"

"Shut up," boss vamp snapped, using compulsion again.

"Clearly you don't, or you wouldn't be trying that foolish trick on us." She got to her feet and locked her knees to keep them from buckling. Her head swam on top of her shoulders. Emotions she didn't recognize boiled inside her. "I am your queen, you fool. Explain yourself. What is the meaning of this?"

This declaration gave the two blood-drinkers a moment's pause.

Boss vamp mocked a bow in her direction. "No, I'd say it's you who doesn't know who *we* are, or you wouldn't have bothered trying to hide from us. The only thing you surprised us with is that you are here at all. You have no idea how many eyes and ears we control in this city. Or how many of us there really are. Do you?"

This was true. Bad as the situation was, knowing it was set in motion the moment she stepped off the plane somehow made it worse—made her deflate and feel more helpless.

The venomous little smile on the vampire's face vanished. "We're going on a road trip, your highness. And you really need to shut up."

<h1 style="text-align:center">51</h1>

<h1 style="text-align:center">MAKING BODIES</h1>

No one would tell Jackson to stay behind and wait while justice came for his brother's killer—not even the Lord of Night. With vampire blood still cruising in his system, he made it to the cavern in record time, ready to follow Dominique and his minions down into the mine. They should have been through here minutes ago and the place deserted. Instead, he heard voices from around the last bend, barely audible over the waterfall's rumble. Clearly, something was not going according to plan.

Shit. What else is new?

Keeping low to the ground and his feet soft, he entered the woods and moved forward, only too aware how visible he would be to vampire eyes. A massive log, musty with rot, provided some cover for his advance. At its splintered end, he peered over the top, between several clusters of fan-shaped mushrooms, and studied the situation.

A dozen vampires faced off in the rocky clearing before the cavern's maw. Their hands and faces glowed in the thin moonlight, and the wind toyed with their shadowy clothes and glistening hair. Esteban's soldiers shifted like a restless pack of wolves, eager for a kill. Dominique's group watched with their hands on the hilts of their weapons while Dominique himself stood between the two factions, as warily rigid as Esteban was casually relaxed.

Fuck. This has got ambush written all over it.

Something was moving in the cavern, but Jackson lost track of it when he felt Dominique shoving at him again, willing him to leave with a bloodcurdling sense of danger. Jaws clenched so hard his teeth ached, Jackson pushed back against the wordless command. *I'm staying!*

A mental slap upside the head made his brain ring. He could almost hear the colorful French that no doubt accompanied it. Then the connection broke so fast, vertigo seized him. Shifting his feet to stay upright, he stepped on a muddy rock and lost his balance entirely.

Crack!

The branch breaking under his ass sounded like a gunshot in his ears. Every vampire for a mile around must have heard it. Breath caught, blood pounding, he reached for the mini torch in his pocket. He waited, listening.

Nothing happened.

In the clearing, Esteban was holding forth, but no one came for the clumsy mortal in the woods. Jackson poked his head up among the mushrooms again. Another figure hunched before Dominique now, female and in chains, and...

"Oh, God." The words were out of his mouth before he could stop them. Still, nobody looked in his direction. It was like he wasn't there.

Then it hit him: for these vampires, he *really* wasn't there. Unable to budge him, Dominique must be using his psychic voodoo to erase him from the awareness of everyone here.

Emboldened, Jackson rose to his full height to get a better view. His gut dropped. The woman in chains was Geneviève, and...she was no longer human.

The total lack of heat in Dominique's reaction to finding his sister turned into a vampire sent a chill down Jackson's spine. He knew his friend, the lord of the vampires. That wasn't simple anger beneath that glacial tone. Not even grief.

It was wrath.

Esteban taunted him while his wolf pack watched. They were all sleek and powerful, and they were all on guard. But they weren't prepared for Esteban uttering the one name—the one threat—that unleashed the Lord of Night's wrath.

"...and, of course, darling Cassidy."

Dominique had his jaws clamped to Esteban's jugular so fast the wolves startled, uncomprehending. By the time they moved in to help, Isao and the others were there, all their weapons drawn. Together, they created a defensive ring, surrounding Dominique and Esteban, who twisted in Dominique's arms like a pinned worm. The wolves snarled their fury.

Jackson slipped around the log and rushed forward. Justice was being served, and invisible or not, he needed to be front and center. But before he could take three steps, the handful of Esteban's guards morphed into ten. Then twenty...thirty...more. Too many.

Vampires swarmed out of the cavern's depths, moonlight glinting off a wild assortment of weaponry, ranging from swords and chains to axes and pipes. Figures blurred and flickered everywhere, gray smears frozen in flashes of stillness, as though caught in a strobe light. The whoosh and clash of steel meeting steel at extreme velocity cut through the forest night. So did shrieks of outrage and howls of pain.

Five vampires suddenly appeared near Jackson. Two were the trench-coated figure of Douglas, Geneviève clutched in his arms. Three more surrounded them, armed with a knife, sword, chain whip, and fangs. Douglas hunched over Geneviève, shielding her, but the attack never came.

Instead, the sweet metal stench of vampire blood exploded in the damp air, and the three would-be assailants collapsed to the ground with surprised yelps. Dominique towered over them, both his swords dripping blood. Enraged as he was, he still maintained his no-kill policy; he only cut their legs out from under them. As they writhed and cursed, Douglas gathered up Geneviève and vanished into the forest. Dominique spun around to dispatch two more combatants coming after him—taking their arms this time—before disappearing back into the battle.

The temporarily slain fighters located their severed limbs and shoved them back onto bleeding stumps, the ones with arms helping those without. Whole again, they, too, bolted back into the fray.

The entire exchange took mere seconds, and Jackson was sure the only reason he could follow it at all was because of his enhanced senses. Or maybe because it was so much slower than the rest of the fighting, which looked like a featureless whirl of activity in comparison—except for one small group. Standing well clear of the chaos was Esteban, flanked by four others. Blood splatters covered his face, and there now was a sword in his hand, though he appeared more interested in directing the supernatural warriors than joining their ranks.

The clearing reverberated with dark growls, punctuated by bright shrieks. Bodies or—more often—pieces of bodies came sailing out of the combat zone. Mostly, the dismembered limbs were caught and re-attached before they hit the ground. Some, however, went flying into the forest. Jackson didn't even have time to duck when a leg crashed into the tree behind him, bounced off, and narrowly missed kicking him in the head with its muddy boot.

Fuck. He slipped halfway behind another tree and tried to find an opening for himself to be useful, when he spotted Lyle. Brandishing his two knives like machine guns pointing out to either side of him, the boy stormed into battle. Jackson's heart squeezed in sympathy; he knew a suicide mission when he saw one. So did Kostya. The hulking vampire tried to block his charge from the worst of the fighting, but Lyle wanted none of that. When he made to dart around his protector again, Kostya hooked Lyle's skinny frame in one massive arm and dragged him away in a blur. They stopped right in front of Jackson's tree.

"Let go of me, you fucking moron!"

"I won't let you—"

"Watch out!" Jackson yelled. But the streak of movement he saw heading their way had already arrived and struck with savage speed.

Kostya's head lifted from his broad shoulders and dropped with the weighty thump of a bowling ball. His body collapsed, releasing Lyle, who whirled around just in time to raise one of his knives and block another lethal strike. In almost the same motion, he thrust his second knife deep between the assailant's ribs.

For a moment, the kid only gawked at the vampire swaying at the end of his hilt, both of them clearly surprised by this turn of events. Then he twisted the blade hard, causing a massive gush of blood to erupt from the chest. He must have snatched his attacker's weapon as it fell and swung it hard, because the next thing Jackson saw was another headless body drop.

"Are you all drunk? You outnumber them ten to one, you incompetent fools," Esteban shouted over the battlefield. "Let's get on with this! Capture the pretender and kill the rest!"

Lyle wasted no time. Hefting his new weapon, a machete, he skulked toward Esteban.

Jackson wasted no time, either. Snatching up Kostya's sword, he hurried after the young vampire, who promptly found himself challenged.

"Going somewhere, pup?"

Lyle held the machete up in front of him. "Don't even think about it, Gregory. I'm older than you, and stronger."

"You're a boy and always will be."

And those were the last words out of Gregory's mouth. Running up behind him, Jackson swung the sword in a well-practiced move, separating vampire head from vampire body.

Lyle gaped, but not at Jackson. Jackson was still invisible, and as far as Lyle was concerned, Gregory had just spontaneously lost his head.

"You're welcome," Jackson said. No reaction. They couldn't hear him either. That poor fool, Kostya, had never heard his warning.

Catching a blur from the corner of his eye, Jackson spun around and flailed when he almost slipped again on the gore-slick rocks. Another one of the rabid wolf pack ran straight into his swerving blade and effectively decapitated herself. Blood fanned out in every direction, slapping Jackson in the face.

Startled out of his astonishment, Lyle leapt backward, shook his head, then turned and headed for Esteban again. This time, he moved faster than his ghostly guardian had any hope of keeping up with.

"You're going to get yourself killed, you little shit!" Jackson yelled, even as a sword whistled behind him. He dove forward, stumbling over a dismembered arm, and lurched away from the vampire who tripped over the body Jackson had just made. He hadn't hit the ground yet before Makoto's *katana* slashed through both of the stumbling vampire's legs and one remaining arm. The tip of her blade caught Jackson's shoulder and missed his head by a fraction of an inch. "Fuck!" Never mind Lyle getting killed. Jackson was going to get himself killed even faster if he didn't get his invisible mortal ass out of the war zone.

He scrambled forward, only to get hit by Lyle's hurtling body. The boy righted himself and crouched low, growling.

It took Jackson a moment to realize that the racket of conflict had died down. Only scattered snarls and curses remained. Bodies and limbs lay scattered, the macabre contents of hell spilled from the mouth of the cavern. Many still tried to crawl, but most lay motionless and cadaver-thin, neutralized at last by the repeated amputations and hemorrhaging. The chill wind reeked of gore, and blood dripped from Dominique's, Isao's, and Makato's lethally elegant swords. The three of them stood in the middle of the carnage, facing Esteban, who held his still-clean blade and clearly struggled to find words.

"Do you still think I am underestimating my situation?" Dominique said with the icy calm of a glacier.

The response was a guttural growl. Esteban hadn't gone full-on out-of-control vampire beast, but he wasn't far from it. "You crude, pitiful *joke* of a baby vampire," he roared. "You will pay for this insult!"

"No insult, Esteban. An opportunity." Dominique gestured at the carnage. "Most of them still live. If you submit, they will continue to live. Very generous terms, *non*?"

"Hell, no!" Lyle shrieked, getting to his feet. "He has to die for what—"

A dagger flew from Esteban's hand and buried itself in Lyle's chest. An instant later, Esteban—now brandishing two swords—charged at Dominique, who appeared to have expected the move and blocked him with ease. They froze, face-to-face through their crossed blades, laser focused, taking each others' measure. Then Esteban slowly stepped back. But the moment Dominique lowered his weapons, the Spaniard moved so fast, he practically vanished. If Dominique was surprised, it was hard to tell. They both dissolved into spectral blurs of motion. Even the staccato clash of their swords took on an eerie echo.

Lyle dropped to his knees, blood pouring out of his nose and mouth, and Jackson hurried to his side. Maybe there was no point pulling a dagger out of someone so hell-bent on dying, but Jackson did it anyway. The kid's glowing eyes widened with astonishment. Jackson grabbed his hand, letting him feel what he couldn't see. With a gasp, understanding dawned on Lyle's face. Then his eyes finally focused on him.

"I've got this, brother," Jackson said.

"Kill him," Lyle mouthed.

"And you? You're going to die, too, then. You know that, right?"

Lyle only nodded.

Jackson sucked in his lips the way he sucked in his emotions. He knew that look. He had seen it in the mirror often enough. Without his twin, Lyle was half. He was done.

The boy closed his eyes and went as pale and still as a corpse, waiting to become one, which, given the way Dominique and Esteban were going at it, could happen at any second. But with over four centuries of practice and strength to call on, the Spaniard proved to be a real challenge. The combatants' ghostly shapes bent and twisted, their whirling blades missing each other by nanoseconds and millimeters.

Or...so it seemed.

Isao and Makoto stood by, but made no move to intervene. Jackson was pretty sure those two weren't suicidal. Just as he reasoned that something else was happening here, it happened.

Esteban cried out when Dominique's *katana* slid through his shoulder. The tip of Dominique's shorter blade first sent Esteban's second sword flying and then jabbed under his jaw, forcing up his head, pinioning him in place, preventing him from snatching up his severed arm. Immobilized, Esteban stood, blood pouring from his shoulder and flowing along Dominique's sword...a mere five feet away from Jackson.

Dominique's eyes were living flames in the darkness. "If you care anything at all for yourself or your spawn, you *will* submit to me." He sounded calm, not like someone who had just been fighting for his life. Because he hadn't, Jackson realized. This is precisely where Dominique wanted Esteban. He wanted him to know that even his very best effort wouldn't be enough.

And so close to Jackson, too. That couldn't be an accident. With a tight hold on Kostya's sword, he stood up.

Esteban's lips drew back in a vicious sneer. "Just because you have tapped a powerful vein, you are not the master of me. You are nothing but a pretentious youngling fool."

"Who is holding a sword to your throat," Makoto pointed out.

"You are condemning all your spawn to death, Esteban," Isao's rumbling baritone added. "When you could give them true peace."

"You're the last one I had thought would buy into this drivel, Isao. You, all of you, have earned yourself Adilla's eternal wrath!"

"Which means nothing to me," Dominique murmured. There was a strange reverberation in his voice. As he continued, it morphed further, becoming an otherworldly presence that took wing on the night, carried by the wind out of the cave, the forest, even the sky. "Because it *is* nothing. Just like the tantrum of a spoiled child is nothing compared to a father's grief...or a brother's broken soul."

The surreal soundscape thrummed in the air for several more seconds as Dominique stepped back and withdrew the sword point from Esteban's jawline. No one moved, least of all Esteban, who stood slack-jawed, his obsidian eyes locked on the true Lord of Night as if he had never seen him before.

Jackson certainly hadn't seen this side of Dominique before, and he was more than a little rattled himself, but the nudge pressing into his mind was unmistakable. As was the slight nod Dominique gave him, a gesture of permission or encouragement, likely both.

Touching the twin St. Christopher medallions around his neck, Jackson took a deep breath and looked up into the lake of stars glittering between the treetops. *Brother, are you seeing this? Are you with me, Justin?*

The answer came not in words or thoughts, but in a familiar sense of calm settling over him. The hunt was on, the prey cornered, a kill imminent. Sword in hand, he stepped in front of the vampire ultimately responsible for his brother's death. With sweet satisfaction, he saw realization dawn on the Spaniard's face. "You..."

"Me," he said and raised the sword. "Feel the wrath, Esteban. Feel *my* wrath."

If Esteban had any thought of defending himself or taking flight, those impulses never translated to his feet. "You," he said again.

Then Jackson's sword found its mark, and he said no more.

52

THE SILVER GAMBIT

"**I** need to use a toilet."

Cassidy glanced at her fellow captive beside her in the backseat. They had just merged into highway traffic and were picking up speed. Francesca stared straight ahead, eyes unfocused, her face the color of milk in the strobes of passing headlights. The bruise spreading on her cheek stood out in ugly relief. These were the first words she had uttered since regaining consciousness in Cassidy's lap almost ten minutes ago.

Their captors skipped restraints and gags, relying on their supernatural speed and strength instead. Cassidy knew better than to run, much less try to solicit help from anyone they encountered. That she and Francesca still lived was a good sign. It meant someone valued them as hostages, and the only reason for that would be to gain Dominique's cooperation. For which purpose didn't matter. The important thing was that she would be with him before the night was over, and as long as she stayed alive and conscious, they would find a way out of this together.

Francesca was of a different opinion. She flat-out begged for help from the couple who shared the elevator with them on the way down. When the woman looked at the vampires with alarm, the thug vamp yanked her close and delivered a swift bite. Boss vamp told the man that his companion was fainting and the two of them were alone in the elevator. By the time the doors opened, the man was oblivious to all but the unconscious woman in his arms with the blood soaking the collar of her blouse.

In the lobby, Francesca screamed as if possessed—shrill and desperate—for all of two seconds. That's how long it took before she was backhanded so hard she passed out herself. Cassidy scrambled to catch her and soften the fall.

"Fucking bitch," boss vamp cursed. Then he turned to face the handful of shocked mortals who witnessed the scene. "You see nothing out of the ordinary." His voice rolled with compulsion. Most people resumed their business with only a small shake of the head. A few needed a more personal follow-up compulsion.

Francesca was dumped into the backseat of their current ride, Cassidy shoved in right behind her. "You're going to regret this," Cassidy promised as the car squealed out of the lot. They ignored her.

Downtown traffic mired them at one stop light after another. She watched the pedestrians who might have given them cover, if not for Francesca, who was in no condition to bolt. Not that they would have gotten far. These two clowns could be tapped into the minds of anyone who would see them. A neural network of surveillance spanning a city. Two human women didn't have a chance.

"I need to use a toilet," Francesca said again now, calm and polite, and Cassidy wondered if her mind had cracked at last. Francesca's hands lay flat on her thighs. Only the pinkie finger of her left hand moved—along a cylindrical shape in her trouser pocket.

Cassidy's breath caught.

Thug vamp didn't bother turning in the passenger seat to deliver a shot of compulsion. "No, you don't."

"Not too bright, are you?" Cassidy ventured. She didn't shift in her seat but became aware of the small, hard object in her back pocket.

Thug swiveled his head around. "Shut the fuck up already." More compulsion.

Cassidy forced a derisive smile. "We may be mere mortals, but we are under the protection of someone far more powerful than you. We can't be compelled." This earned her a fanged snarl.

Boss vamp at the wheel clapped a warning hand to the thug's arm. "Knock it off. She's just trying to bait you. Ignore it."

"I'm just trying to tell both of you the facts, gentlemen," Cassidy continued. Provocation was the last thing on her mind, but maybe she could convince them to see the error of their ways before Francesca provoked them to a point where they would lose control and forget about their orders to deliver them alive. "Wouldn't you rather live your own lives than be forever—literally forever—under Esteban's boot heel? Or Adilla's? I mean, that guy is just unhinged. No telling what—"

"I. Need. A. Toilet."

Francesca still stared straight ahead. The car was moving fast now. Far too fast to distract a driver, even one with supernatural reflexes. Cassidy hoped to God that wasn't her plan, prayed that Francesca wouldn't pull out that canister before they had stopped.

"For fuck's sake. Cross your legs," boss vamp said. He was past trying compulsion on them.

"I am an old woman who has had three children. My control is limited."

"Try harder."

Breathless, Cassidy watched Francesca's mouth twitch and her eyes narrow. "Too late."

Boss vamp smacked a fist at the steering wheel and took his foot off the gas. "You can go piss in the bushes then."

"What the fuck are you doing?" the thug spluttered as the car decelerated with several hard jerks and veered into the outside lane.

"Do you know how hard it is to get piss out of upholstery?"

Under the cover of being jostled about, Francesca pulled the silver canister out of her pocket. Cassidy followed suit, thinking she was just getting prepared. Not so. Next thing she knew, Francesca had stuck her hand out between the window and the passenger seat and jammed down the trigger.

The oily stream struck thug vamp full in the face and splattered away in glittering filaments. His deafening shriek had a tangible force in the car's sealed confines. He pawed at his eyes, but only got more silver-laced oil all over his face and hands.

It took boss vamp precious seconds to figure out what the hell was going on, but when he did, he turned in his seat and reached for Francesca.

Which was when Cassidy unloaded her canister into his face.

Their combined screams rattled her brain. Francesca pressed her hands to both ears and doubled over in her seat. Cassidy didn't have that luxury because now the car was out of control and drifting back into traffic. Squealing tires shadowed them. The furious blast of a truck horn sounded practically on top of them.

Heart galloping in her mouth, Cassidy lunged forward and grabbed for the abandoned wheel. The center console slammed into her tender gut. Headlights glared out the front window. She twisted the wheel away. More honking. Taillights, brake lights, swerving, spinning...

The vampires still screamed and thrashed in their seats. Silver glitter everywhere. The smell of blood in the air now, too. From the corner of her eye, she saw hands covered in oozing sores, frantically wiping against already glittering jeans.

Suddenly, the screams became gasps. The hands spread into claws, jerked and fluttered, and went limp.

Silence.

Cassidy had the car moving in a straight line now, which she hoped was an actual lane of traffic. They were slowing down by the second. Keeping one hand ready to grab the wheel, she contorted herself all the way to the front where she straddled the console. The driver did not protest. She spared just enough of a glance to realize that he would never protest again. His face was a grotesque mask of sparkle, his mouth gaping and eye sockets caved in.

Jamming her left leg down beside his, she found the gas and then the brake after maneuvering the vehicle onto the shoulder. She pushed the shift into park.

Her hands trembled on the controls. Vomit tickled the back of her throat. Too close. Much, much too close.

Traffic whooshed past as though nothing had happened. That wouldn't last. Guaranteed someone had called in their drunken careening, probably reported their plates. Emergency responders were minutes, if not seconds, away. And there would be no vampires around to convince them of anything.

"Francesca," Cassidy said, voice unsteady. "Help me get this guy out of the driver's seat. Hurry." When there was no response, she turned around. Blood trickled from a new gash in Francesca's forehead. She looked every inch the shell-shock victim. "Francesca. Now. We need to keep moving."

Dazed, she took hold of the vampire carcass with both hands. Together, they tugged and shoved him into the back. Thug vamp slouched in the passenger seat. Cassidy pulled the hoodie over his head to hide the hideous effects of the silver oil from casual glances.

Putting the car into gear and remembering to politely use the directional signals like anyone else who hadn't just zig-zagged across a highway with two dead vampires, Cassidy slotted them back into traffic. Belatedly, she realized she wasn't seat-belted and reached to remedy that. All very normal. Just out for an evening ride. Nothing to see here. A sign going by announced the next exit in five kilometers. With a little luck, they might slip off the highway and disappear before anyone came looking for them.

"What happened?" Francesca asked.

Cassidy swallowed the immediate "You almost killed us," and offered a more restrained, "They weren't going to kill us, you know. Once we got to Dominique, we would have been okay."

"I did not think we were...okay."

Cassidy bit back another retort.

"You said silver could only hurt them. Not kill them."

The words pulled a chill up her spine when she grasped what had really happened here. The vampires had died—permanently died—from...silver?

"It doesn't," she said, trying to think past the chaos in her head. "Something else killed them." And then it hit her. Hard. "Their sire is dead. Esteban is dead."

She reached out to Dominique. He was still there, alive and humming with frenzied activity. A wave of relief echoed across the distance. Almost missing the exit, she had to swerve abruptly to make it onto the ramp. Luckily, no one was there to protest or get hit, but in the rearview mirror, far behind them, a patrol car activated its flashers.

Cassidy was about to go straight at the first light when a siren blared nearby. Mouth dry and hands gripping the wheel, she followed the car in front of her to a stop on the side of the road. Moments later, a fire truck howled past. The police escort in its wake gave her a fresh start, but took no note of them.

Not until they had traveled several more miles and made a number of casual turns without flashing lights or sirens erupting, did Cassidy allow herself a shaky breath of relief. She checked on Francesca in the rearview mirror. The woman studied the corpse propped up beside her as she dabbed at her forehead with the sleeve of her cardigan. The shock was fading from her eyes. "I think you saved our lives, Francesca. If they had died like that while we were in traffic, we would have crashed."

She remained silent, and Cassidy could only imagine what was going on in her head. In the last hour, she had been taken hostage and physically assaulted, witnessed terrifying transformations and callous disregard for human life, and seen vampires drop dead of what must seem like magical processes. In other words, everything Dominique had tried to protect her from had happened to her. This was the world of night at its worst, the world of loveless monsters.

The world ruled by her son.

"See if you can find a phone on him," Cassidy suggested, and not just to give Francesca something to do and stop thinking. "We need to talk to someone who knows how to hide bodies."

53

Abyss

Dead. Every one of Esteban's immortal elites was dead—from the single stroke of a sword.

Dominique stared down at the gray husks of blood-drinkers scattered across the clearing. Their empty eye sockets stared back. More than these had died tonight. All of Esteban's younglings and all of theirs and so on, all littered the dark places of the world.

How many? How many had he spawned over four and a half centuries? Or did it matter? His ability and that of his younglings to remain conscious long into the day was an aberration that threatened all vampires everywhere and could well have undermined the peace Dominique envisioned. In a way, he was glad the scheming blood-drinker who had so prided himself on being the true power behind Adilla's throne had refused to submit. It made it possible to live with the decision to allow Jackson his revenge.

"Why the fuck am I still alive?" Lyle sat up among the corpses. He was splattered in blood and his limbs spasmed a little. Wailing, he staggered to his feet. "Why am I still alive?"

Dominique, too, was mystified, but seeing the light in Lyle's eyes, he realized there was only one reason that made any sense. "Because you belong to me now."

"But...but I *felt* him die. I felt his mind disappear. The blood bond...it's gone." He sounded borderline frantic.

"The blood bond is not what tied your life to his. It never was," Dominique explained, thinking out loud. He looked to where Isao crouched over Kostya's body, his head hanging low. Makoto knelt by his side, one comforting arm around his shoulders. "Your lives are linked through the serum that infected you and altered your genetic code," Dominique continued, speaking to Isao and Makoto as much as to Lyle. "That code altered again when you were re-sired."

Makoto met his eyes. Isao raised his head. Dominique saw the moment the samurai understood that his existence no longer depended on Adilla's. Thoughts of murder followed hard and fast.

We cannot, Dominique cautioned. His own thoughts swung from wondering how much longer they had before Adilla came charging out of that cavern to... "Geneviève."

At Dominique's command, Douglas had carried her away when the fighting began. Now it took him somewhat longer to return. When he stepped into the clearing, Geneviève hung in his arms—still and gray.

"Oh, no," Jackson moaned before Dominique even allowed himself to comprehend the truth.

The sister who had been like a second mother and closest friend, whom he had cherished and cared for and laughed with—that sister had been reduced to an empty, lifeless husk.

"I'm so sorry, my lord," Douglas murmured.

Dominique brushed the back of one finger over her sunken cheek and waited for despair to rise. None came. There was only a pinch of sadness for the life cut too short, for the husband who would mourn her, for the daughter who would grow up without her.

"I don't understand," Jackson said. "I saw Adilla feed on her. How can Esteban have been her serum sire?"

"Adilla rarely bestows the honor of being sired by him," Isao said. His face was hard with grief and anger. "When he fed on her in public, it must only have been that once and only to exercise his power over you, my lord. Nothing more."

"Esteban was her true sire," Dominique said.

"And I killed Esteban." The sword in Jackson's hand trembled. The stunned euphoria of moments ago drained away as quickly as his blood left his face. "I...I killed your sister."

"*Non*, you did not. She was dead the moment they found her." Geneviève's body felt light as nothing when he lifted it from Douglas's arms and placed it on the ground. "If you had not killed Esteban, I would have. And if Geneviève had not died this night, she would have died a thousand deaths every night hereafter. Her spirit would have broken in this life." He kept his gaze on her beautiful black hair, the only part of her that still looked alive, and stroked his hand over it in farewell. "It is better for her this way."

He turned away from the corpse of his former life and reached out for Garrett. The old hunter was unmolested and had been busy with his phone. "Everyone else is safe," Dominique told Jackson. After processing his own relief, he added, "Your sword saved Cassidy and my mother."

Jackson gave a grim nod.

The group gathered around Dominique, another body short now, with the loss of the gentle giant, Kostya. They were spattered with blood, their weapons soaked in it, but all looked ready for more.

"We finish this tonight," Dominique said. "But we kill only if necessary. Too much blood has been spilled already."

Douglas nodded and Makoto said, "As you command." Lyle still looked disappointed at having survived, but he, too, gave a grudging nod.

Isao met Dominique's gaze but committed to nothing. Beneath that quiet façade, barely contained emotion boiled. There was an emptiness in his soul where Kostya had dwelled for over two and a half centuries, and only one entity he blamed for that. "We should go, my lord."

"What about him?" Lyle asked, pointing at Jackson with his machete.

"He'll be useless," Makoto said.

"Gee, thanks." Jackson checked his shoulder, which was soaked in blood. "Thanks for this, too, while we're at it."

She raised one of her fine brows.

"I can find my way back to the campground."

"We cannot protect you if we separate," Dominique said. Though no vampires lurked nearby now, that could change if there were others farther out returning to the colony. Leaving Jackson to wander the woods, smelling of blood and gore, could be condemning him to death. "You have to remain with us."

"I'll only slow you down."

"No, you won't. I'll take you," Lyle said and handed his machete to Douglas. In the next instant, he had slung the much larger Jackson across his shoulders as though he were no more than a sack of feathers. "I owe you."

The sack of feathers grunted and flailed, his sword swinging erratically.

Makoto grabbed the blade out of Jackson's hand. "I'll take that. Before you disembowel someone."

No more needed to be said. Isao vanished into the cavern. The rest followed.

They got as far as the room with the prison cells, where Douglas pulled the thin chain hanging from the ceiling fixture. The light confirmed what their night vision had already revealed. Where the lift cage should have been waiting, only a hole in the floor remained.

Isao pushed the call button. Nothing happened. "It's locked at the bottom."

"Their way of keeping us out?" Douglas wondered. "They have to know what happened up here."

"There is another way into the lair," Isao said. "But it's treacherous."

"Treacherous" was a colossal understatement if Isao's random memories were any indication, but the alternative was to wait for Adilla at the surface and lose the element of surprise. "Lead the way."

After the briefest of hesitations, Isao streaked away. They followed him out of the mine shaft, through the cavern, and into a labyrinth of caves full of perilous dips and narrows, loose rubble and crumbling cliffs. The darkness was complete, and it was cold, rendering their infrared vision dim and unreliable until suddenly that, too, was gone.

They stopped to consider the abyss that lay before them. Freezing cold air gushed out of the fissure, appearing to them like an impenetrable black wall. A challenge even for blood-drinkers, the drop-off would have been impossible for mortals. It was a security system more effective than any gates or locked lifts or an army of human guards. Those who had tried and failed to breach it in the past were still here. The faint, musty odor of their deaths rode on the icy currents.

Adilla also disposes of his bodies here, Isao provided as he studied the situation.

"Are we there?" Jackson whispered into the quiet. His mortal heart hammered at their sensitive ears. Far behind them, a loose rock rattled down another invisible cliff.

"Oh, we're somewhere all right," Lyle grumbled. "Just can't fucking see it."

"You never traveled this way when you were here, Lyle?" Douglas asked.

"Nope. Carly never wanted to come this way."

"There's a light in my back pocket, if that would help?" Jackson said. Under his breath, he added, "It sure would help me."

Everyone turned to the bright red aura among them, and Dominique realized what light he was talking about. "It would," he said and went to dig the small blowtorch out of Jackson's pocket. Pointing it across the chasm, he clicked it on.

The beam barely reached the other side. The ledge that was supposed to be there was hidden behind a sheet metal wall. Only one small opening was visible by the entrance to another cave.

"Fuck," Jackson gasped. "I did *not* need to see that."

"I did. Thank you," Isao said faintly. "The barrier is new." No need to add that anyone leaping blindly for any place other than the opening was as good as dead.

Jackson's weapon had saved them all.

Isao retreated far enough to get a running start and leapt along the shaft of illumination. Once he landed safely, Dominique turned off the light. Isao's brilliant aura was now the beacon the rest of them would aim for.

"Watch the wind," Isao called. "It's not stable."

"Holy fuck," Jackson muttered.

"I don't think I can do this," Lyle said. "Not with..."

Dominique held out his arms. "Give him to me."

Lyle handed over the sack of feathers, which felt not all so light as it attached itself to Dominique's back like an overgrown barnacle. The crossed sword scabbards squeezed between them.

A miasma of anxiety enveloped Jackson. "Can *you* do this?"

"I do not intend to die tonight."

Makoto and Douglas sailed over the abyss next, the former with the grace of an eagle in flight, the latter like a cannonball. Lyle threw himself across with a terrified scream. Only the young blood-drinker's toes caught the brink, and if not for Douglas's swift grab, he would have been lost.

"What's this? You no longer want to die?" Makoto wondered.

"Shit. Not like this, no."

Dominique retreated as far as he could to gather momentum, but Jackson's bulk threw him off balance. The moment his feet left the edge and they hit the turbulence, he knew they were in trouble. "Hold tight," he ordered his passenger, who already held tight enough to crack ribs. *We will not die tonight.*

Fighting to change their trajectory, Dominique twisted in the pummeling wind like a rudderless weather vane. It was no use. They were flying fast enough to reach the other side, but they wouldn't land anywhere near the cluster of horrified onlookers.

A sudden memory of a playful Serge leaping off Dominique's bike and onto the sides of moving semi-trucks made him extend his hands like talons—or grappling hooks. A second later, he hit the invisible sheet metal with a resounding boom. As Serge's fingers had with the trucks, Dominique's fingers, too, pierced straight through. Grabbing the sharp edges, he stuck.

The sudden stop caused his passenger to jerk and gasp. "Hold on," Dominique repeated. "We are not there yet." He kept his voice soft and sure, not only for Jackson's benefit. Off to the side, two body lengths away, four glowing faces peered around the edge of the barrier. Their eyes and mouths were round with shock.

While sending Serge silent prayers of thanks, Dominique began slamming his fingers into the metal, hand over hand, and clawed his way toward the edge. There, the others grabbed him and Jackson the moment they were within reach and pulled them around to safety.

Jackson's hold on him never wavered, but a violent tremor raced through his body. Dominique took a reassuring hold of his friend's forearm clamped around his neck. "It is over."

No one said a word. They all had felt the brush of death's wings and were far too glad to be alive to be angry about the close call or cast blame for it. Dominique let his own relief radiate out to them. "Where to next, Isao?"

Their journey continued ever-deeper into the mountain, along steep, serpentine inclines. They leapt numerous smaller crevasses with ease and navigated countless caves that had been enhanced and connected over the ages by the blood-drinkers who called these depths home. But they found no more drop-offs hidden in streams of cold air reeking of death.

The commotion in the underground palace reached them long before they rounded the last turn, and none of it involved music or merriment. Light seeped beneath a heavy fabric which covered a narrow exit. Isao drew his sword and sliced a massive gash into the obstruction, which turned out to be one of the heavy decorative tapestries lining the central hallway. One by one, they squeezed out, eyes watering in the chandelier lights. Several more gray corpses sprawled in the hall.

As he found his own feet again, Jackson looked like a man who wasn't sure he had won his argument with death. His fierce emotional control had finally shattered. The smell of terror still clung to him and even intensified now that he was back where he had spent an entire night fighting for his life. It wasn't a battle he would win again. One whiff and the denizens of the underground palace would tear him to pieces.

Dominique grabbed him by the arm. "Allow me a suggestion before you lose the rest of your mind?"

A dazed nod.

He pitched his voice toward compulsion. "You are safe with us. Whatever you see or hear or feel, you will be safe. Do you understand?"

With closed eyes, Jackson accepted the "suggestion" and let it work on him. He relaxed, nodded again, and scrubbed his blood-smeared face with both hands. "Thanks."

When Dominique released him, Jackson held out a hand to Makoto. She obliged by returning his sword. It still reeked of Esteban's blood, and Dominique thought Jackson might be safer soaked in fear after all.

54

No Equal

Moving in complete silence, Dominique took the lead toward the bedlam echoing from the audience chamber. Together, he and his mostly blood-drinker entourage marched through the entrance arches and stopped to take in the spectacle.

Gray bodies lay scattered where they had dropped, several dozen of them, men and women in court finery with surprise frozen on their ghoulish faces. The remaining blood-drinkers—well over a hundred—milled among the corpses, their eyes filled with disbelief, questions falling from their lips. How could this be? What did it mean? Who would dare?

Some were silent as they hunched over their fallen friends and lovers, their heads hanging in shock and despair.

Dominique cast a sidelong glance at Jackson, who maintained a white-knuckled grip on the weapon that had wrought this carnage. His jaw muscles twitched, but his mind remained free of fear, if not doubt.

Adilla had his back turned to them as he walked toward the gilded throne. His two shadows trailed behind him like extensions of his deep-purple robes. One of these, Bhavanur, was beside himself. "This is an *outrage*. An affront to you and your glory that cannot go unanswered," he hissed. Markandeya stayed farther back, keeping his own council.

Rage vibrated in Adilla's low voice. "It will not go unanswered. Be assured of that."

"I can take a group to the surface and hunt them down. They won't get far."

Adilla settled onto his throne and glared at the young-looking man, who appeared about as capable of combat as a butterfly.

Bhavanur shrank back with a demure, "If you wish it, my lord."

Dominique inhaled deeply, drinking in the blood and ash and death that perfumed the air, and let it out on a long, quiet exhale. A few of the blood-drinkers closest to the entrance, who weren't completely focused on a fallen comrade or their lord, finally took notice of him.

Awareness rippled through the court on a wave of gasps and hisses. A few, uncertain, retreated to their lord's side, clustering around the dais. Most, however, gathered themselves, preparing to spring at the intruders and destroy them at Adilla's most subtle command.

The air throbbed with animosity.

While the others held their weapons at the ready, Dominique kept his blades in their scabbards. All the fighters, security guards, and spies had fallen with their sire. Those who survived carried no weapons beyond their formidable supernatural abilities. Yet, their sheer numbers gave them reckless courage. Most hovered on the brink of releasing their beasts.

Isao's silent warning prickled in Dominique's mind, but he brushed it off. These blood-drinkers were angry and afraid, and they needed to see that the Lord of Night had no quarrel with them—not unless they defied him directly.

Far more dangerous was their master.

Adilla pinned Dominique with obsidian eyes, which consumed his increasingly skeletal, stark white face. Immortal rage incarnate. He rose from his throne to tower over them all, his voice a hoarse rustle. "You *dare* to show yourself in my presence?"

Dominique took several slow steps into the room and spoke with velvet menace. "You dare to defy me? You dare to threaten my family?"

Intense hissing filled the hall.

"Your *family*? The mortals you cannot live without, like some depraved newborn moping after his past life?" Spittle flew from Adilla's lips. "They are *nothing*. *Nothing* beside my immortal glory. *Nothing* compared to a single immortal life. *Let alone seventy-three!*" he finished with a roar that reverberated from the walls. His rage caught in the crowd like fire in kindling. Several shrieked as they darted closer.

Dominique maintained his cavalier quiet and waited for the uproar to settle a bit. Then he graced Adilla with a condescending smile. "As I told you, you will be mine."

"You pretentious babe," Adilla snarled. "You and this band of vermin you dragged into your lunacy have no hope against my superior strength."

"Then what are you waiting for?" Isao called. "Or are you so afraid of getting your hands dirty that you would have us slaughter these helpless panderers first?"

Adilla's nostrils flared. Isao knew how to push his sire's buttons. But his sire also had access to his mind, something Dominique sensed Isao was not only not fighting, but inviting. Isao showed Adilla his memories of the battle. He showed him the ease with which they had subdued the elite guard.

And he showed him Esteban's death in vivid detail.

Adilla's gaze flew to Jackson. "A *human*," he sneered. "My most loyal aide, a true warrior of the ages...slain by a *human*?"

Every eye turned to the sole mortal in the room. The hissing shifted back into growling. Instead of wisely remaining quiet, Jackson brandished his bloodied sword in challenge. "Want to be next?"

Dominique stifled a wince. That compulsion might have worked a little too well. Before the anger simmering in the hall could morph into a bloodbath, Dominique moved to the center of the chamber and raised his voice. "Esteban did not have to die. He had a choice. As do you, Adilla Khan, and all of you." He swept his arms wide toward the mob. "Submit to me and find peace. Or refuse...and meet Esteban's fate."

In their agitated state, the threat was apparently stronger than the offer, for the outrage that erupted was instantaneous. They brandished their fangs, flashed their black eyes, released their beasts. An army of monsters tethered by the thinnest of leashes.

Their master considered for a long while before quieting them with a gesture of his bejeweled hand. His beast retreated, replaced by an expression of cool amusement as he descended from the dais. "This is where you fail, young pretender. Perhaps you could surprise Esteban with your cleverness, but me? Me, you will have to defeat on your own merit, because I will not submit to you or anyone. And Isao—" His smile widened into smug malevolence. "Isao and his babes are not foolish enough to let you try."

"On the contrary. We intend to help," Isao said, bloodlust in his voice.

Dominique pulled his lips into a semblance of a smile as his vision expanded and eyes darkened to reveal their unearthly golden fire. "Do you recognize the boy with us?" he asked without turning away from Adilla. "Lyle is one of Esteban's young ones. But now he is also mine. Unlike my sister, he survives. And he will continue to do so as long as I live. The same is true for Isao and his younglings. Your demise will not matter to them."

The low warning growls faltered, became a hum of uncertain murmurs. As a former member of the colony, they would know Lyle and his parentage. Now that facts had been laid before them, they drew new and more accurate conclusions about Dominique and his claim.

Adilla stared at Lyle as though wanting to grind his bones into the ground.

"So what will it be, Adilla? Will you submit and join me? Or shall I end you? Are there any of your spawn here who would like to pledge themselves to me first? I will welcome them into my heart." Dominique held out his arms wide in invitation.

Back by the throne, Bhavanur and Markandeya exchanged a worried look that spoke volumes. They would know their lord well enough to understand how this would end.

"Enough!" Adilla roared. "Enough of these games and deceptions. Remove them from my sight!" No one moved. "*Now!*"

The colony cowered.

Adilla Khan lost his last measure of self-control.

In a blur, he charged at Dominique, who needed only a thought to vanish. To the eyes of the stunned onlookers, he dematerialized into a cloud of black smoke that slithered away in a dozen writhing snakes, while he himself stepped aside, unseen, from the spot Isao rushed to fill. Adilla stopped a microsecond before the tip of Isao's *katana* found his throat.

"Give me an excuse, you insufferable waste of blood," the samurai snarled. "Any excuse will do."

Douglas and Lyle moved in to flank their human charge, while Makoto took up position behind Isao and surveyed the crowd for threats.

Invisible, Dominique settled onto the throne. He leaned back, propping one ankle over the opposite knee, and conjured the snakes of smoke again. They rushed from every corner of the chamber, arced toward the throne and re-formed there as his solid, once-more-visible self. Part of him wished Cassidy was here to see this. It was her innocent question to him early in their relationship that had given him this idea. *Can you turn into smoke?* Yes. Now he could. Because of her. The memory made him smile over his steepled fingers.

A smothering silence descended. One and all, the blood-drinkers gaped at Dominique. Markandeya and Bhavanur realized just how close he was and darted away like startled fish.

Adilla turned away from Isao and his blade. The wrath in his jade eyes was only slightly tempered by shock. He was the only one here who would have ever witnessed such power in Kambyses—a power that was now Dominique's.

The Lord of Night spoke into the hush. "You will find me a most generous lord, Adilla. You may keep your...kingdom." A dismissive wave at the glittering opulence. "All those who wish to continue their servitude to you are free to do so. But those who wish otherwise will also be free to pursue their own existence in whatever way they see fit."

Adilla was beyond words. With a primal scream, he released his beast.

Isao swung his sword, but it slashed through empty air as Adilla was already gone, catapulting toward the throne in a single mighty leap.

Dominique didn't wait for him to land. He shot up and forward to meet him in mid-flight. Even before they crashed to the polished stone floor, he ripped open Adilla's jugular. Ancient blood spurted into his face and mouth, thick with time and power. Claw-like hands tore at his jacket and shoulders, but to no avail. He took the blood as fast as it would come, all but inhaling it along with a thousand years of memories. All that time, and still Adilla hungered with the same voracity as the mortal he had been: privileged but with no hope of greatness until a mysterious traveler showed him what could be. Adilla had begged Kambyses for the power to rule without question, answerable to none.

You answer now, Adilla. You answer to me. Come. Dominique opened himself to the beast that fought him, showed him the peace he would know if he surrendered, tried to soothe the blazing, all-consuming fury in this magnificent, timeless being.

It did not cease.

It did not falter.

If anything, it burned hotter. Brighter. Fiercer.

Incredibly, faced with a world rushing to obliterate him, Adilla raced to meet it. He would not, could not—not ever—be questioned, be conquered, be less than everything. Every fiber in his being raged: *I have no equal!*

Then so be it. Dominique knew a moment's regret as he continued to drink. What a waste of so much experience. What a waste of such a life. Or...maybe not. The more he saw of Adilla's centuries of existence, the more these years felt the same, shallow and bland as puddles in any street. From the moment he had been old enough to reason—and reasoned himself the center of a world that would not have him—Adilla had festered with resentment, and nothing Dominique could say or do or force on him would change that. Not now. Not in a thousand years more.

He drank.

There had been a chance, a slim one, that his bite would react with the blood Adilla consumed two nights earlier and trigger a re-siring. It didn't. Too much time had passed, and Dominique found himself relieved.

All of Adilla's surviving younglings were here, except one: Serge. Dominique saw his friend as a mortal frightened by his own gifts, turned into a blood-drinker by an Adilla who craved only to hear about his own glorious future. Death by fire is what that future would hold, according to Serge. Adilla tossed him aside in disgust and left him defenseless against those who would not tolerate a newborn without a sire to control him.

But Serge had kept to himself. Serge had thrived. And three hundred years later, Serge had sent Dominique to his door. *You will face Adilla. Alone.*

Adilla shuddered.

Dominique continued to drink.

Except for Isao and Serge, no other spawn of Adilla's had ever left his side. If they tried, they died. Those he created were his and his alone, and they were all here along with those he had seduced into his sphere along the way.

Dominique drank until his belly ached. He drank until he was plump with blood. He drank until the beast clutched in his arms ceased to struggle, his movements becoming feeble and uncoordinated and, at last, still.

But Adilla's mind seethed.

There was no ultimate essence to pull from this body to end him like there had been with Kambyses. Even with his veins dry, Adilla continued, physically helpless but conscious, blasting rage like a sun blasted fire.

"You belong to me, Adilla Khan," Dominique said when he finally stopped drinking. The lavishly robed, emaciated body was a gangly puppet draped in his arms.

When he stood, he realize that Isao, Makoto, Douglas, Lyle and Jackson surrounded him, their weapons held ready to fend off anyone who might have wanted to rush to Adilla's aid. No one did. No one except for his two oldest younglings. They stood just out of reach of the swords. Tears streamed down Bhavanur's cheeks, but Markandeya only stared, blank-faced.

Dominique walked between them and placed Adilla on the marble slabs before the throne with all the respect worthy of a fallen ancient one. Then he ascended the dais to stand beside the empty throne.

Every eye was on him. Except for a few muffled sobs, the hall was silent.

"I am the Lord of Night," Dominique began, a small part of him marveling at the new conviction in his voice. "And I will have peace in my kingdom for all its citizens. The world of night is a world of refuge. Of love, compassion, and respect for all living things, immortal and other." He let that sink in before laying out the re-siring process and how it would change them. He also informed them of the two primary rules of his kingdom: no killing and no turning anyone against their will. "Beyond this, you are free to live your eternal lives how ever you wish and anywhere you choose."

Several individuals exchanged hesitant looks. The soft wailing in the back quieted.

"This is the same offer I made Adilla," Dominique continued with a long look at the motionless form on the floor. "He refused. To preserve the peace for all, I will not allow him to continue. Those of you who claim him in your sire line will survive—as long as you accept my offer first."

Uncertain glances darted between Lyle, the corpses scattered on the ground, and Adilla's quiet figure before settling back on Dominique.

Dominique let them take his measure. They had no reason to trust his word, and every reason to suspect ulterior motives. It's what they knew from Adilla, after all. But the facts remained. Adilla lay defeated. He would manipulate them no more. And the blood-drinker who had bested him stood before them, not studded in jewels and trailing a cape, but wrapped in leather and covered in blood.

Markandeya, who had stared at his helpless son with what appeared to be no particular emotion, was the first to sink to one knee. "He brought me into this life for no reason other than to declare himself my master for eternity. All these centuries later, I can honestly say that I am done, and gladly so."

"As am I," another man said, dropping to a knee. He was a tall, elegant figure with long waves of chestnut hair. Recalling what he knew of this one from Adilla's mind, Dominique glanced at Jackson and already looked forward to introducing them.

All around the room, others now knelt as well, singly and in groups of twos and threes and fours, some eager, others sullen, until all but Bhavanur were on their knees. He looked around, eyes narrow, shoulders riding up to his ears. "Traitors," he whispered. A moment later he shrieked, "*Traitors!*"

When no one even lifted their eyes in his direction, Bhavanur whirled around to Dominique, his boyish, tear-stained face distorted by outrage. "You are an animal, a monster! I will *never* be yours! I will—" Whatever he had been about to threaten, nobody would ever know. His head separated from the rest of him and tumbled away in the wake of Isao's sword.

Dominique nodded to the samurai in silent gratitude.

"Submission is not optional," Isao intoned into the hush, clarifying what Dominique could not say without being branded the same sort of tyrant he had just deposed. On a thunderous bellow, he added, "Approach your lord!"

The male who had been the second to submit was now the first to move. He shuffled forward—on his knees.

"No," Dominique said, stopping him. "On your feet. Upright like the proud creature of the night that you are."

He hesitated, but complied, though his gaze remained downcast until he stood directly before Dominique and bared his neck.

The Lord of Night embraced him, pierced the vein, and marveled at the tale he found unfolding in the five-hundred-year-old mind. When he cut his palm and offered his own blood, Dominique smiled. "Welcome, Leonidas."

55

GHOSTS

Standing in the predawn quiet, Dominique turned his face to the fading stars and listened. Cool wind soughed in the surrounding forest, drenched with pungent resins, damp earth, and sweet dew. Nearby, a drowsy songbird warbled tentatively. In the distance, the waterfall rumbled.

And unfurling quietly, powerfully from his core, infusing the very fabric of the night, was the dark web. Never had there been so many aligned with it, so many minds bound to him, so near to him. He felt rooted at the web's center as its source and its master, protected and protector, inevitable and right.

Only one small flicker of discord remained, and only Dominique still heard it.

"It is not too late for you," he said without looking at the gaunt form by his feet. Of the dozens laid out in neat rows across the clearing, Adilla was the only one still living. "You can still have the peace you sense in your young ones now."

By now, Adilla's body had regenerated a little of the blood it had lost. While he couldn't do more than twitch his cadaverous fingers, his mind was stronger, aware of everything—and burning with undiluted resentment.

For long minutes, Dominique listened to Adilla's mute rage, listened for any shadow of doubt or fear or even a question, any opening at all. There was none. Not even the coming of the sun's inferno deterred him, which would be no small thing; old as he was, he would likely remain conscious through much of it. Dominique's skin prickled with the memory of his own close encounter with the sun. It was not an agony he would wish on anyone, not even an enemy determined to destroy him.

"You have existed over a thousand years, Adilla. In all that time, have you truly found nothing to live for?"

The torrent of rage hesitated, surprised by a question rarely considered, if ever.

Wind gusted through the trees with a sorrowful moan. *Ghosts,* Dominique thought. The night was full of them. How many of all these dead had mattered to Adilla? Esteban maybe? Bhavanur at least?

"Kambysessssss," Adilla rasped.

Dominique gazed at the withered face.

His mouth uncooperative, Adilla continued silently. *Kambyses was the only one ever worthy of me. You took that from me, but you can never take his place. Never!*

"But I have," Dominique murmured. "As was his will. Does that mean nothing to you?"

You tricked him!

Had he? Dominique sifted through his memories of the games Kambyses played with him and all his younglings, manipulating them into doing exactly what he wanted—including his own death. The one instant in which Dominique had the upper hand changed nothing. It had merely brought on the inevitable sooner.

Adilla, watching these unguarded thoughts, growled quietly, and, by the end, mentally thrummed with fury. *You understand nothing. I can never forgive you for what you did. Get away from me, you stupid child. Get away from me, and leave me to the sun.*

There was no point, Dominique realized, in trying to sway him. His first impression of Adilla had been correct: power was all. Power to drown the insecurities that plagued him. Power to appease the anger that ruled him. Power that, in life, Adilla never had. And as a blood-drinker, all his power was derived from his association with Kambyses and the imagined promise of taking his place. Without that, only the fear and anger remained. If a millennium of night couldn't change that, a ten-minute conversation wasn't about to either. Still...

Dominique waited as the shadows melted. Night creatures rustled away. Exuberant bird song announced the coming day. And against his back, the dragon swords grew heavy. He had brought them to the surface as he often brought them anywhere—without really knowing why. He trusted that the reason would reveal itself, and so it did again now.

The sun roared ever louder in his ears and daylight thickened into a tangible force, making his flesh crawl around his bones. But there was no panic. For him, the cave's refuge waited only steps away. Not so for the immobilized Adilla. The ancient one's hollowed eyes were wide and quiet, the sky's purple light reflecting in their fathomless depths. In his mind, the first tendrils of fear stirred.

"Is it still what you want?" Dominique asked, though how genuine a conversion at this point would be was debatable.

Shut up and burn with me or leave me the fuck alone.

He sighed. "That...I cannot do." As he unsheathed one of his swords, the embedded dragon settled in his hand, radiating calm certainty. "From the moment Kambyses first drank from me, it has been my destiny to rule the world of night, to do with it as I choose. My choice has always been to bring peace to those who inhabit it. One way or another. Even to you."

Adilla's obsidian eyes locked on Dominique's, ignoring the sword glinting against the morning sky. *You are not worthy of me!*

A single slash is all it took to silence the outrage for good. A moment later, there was one last flicker of something that might have been gratitude...or contempt. Maybe both, or neither. Then...nothing.

"Rest in peace, Adilla Khan."

The wind sighed as the clearing brightened, and Dominique's skin prickled. Glancing up, he saw the treetops catch fire in the sun's first blood-orange rays. He watched the spectacle until his eyes watered, until the lethargy dragged at his limbs, and apprehension overpowered wonder.

Then he turned toward the cave, the darkness, and the future.

***

While Jackson and Garrett monitored the makeshift graveyard and scattered the ashes after the sun processed the remains, Dominique spent the day in the underground palace. There, sheltered from the sun's direct influence, most of the blood-drinkers stayed conscious for several hours past sunrise and spent that time swarming around him.

A few remained subdued, grieving for friends lost during the battle, but most were openly curious. Many practically buzzed with excitement. When he settled on an ordinary sofa rather than on the throne, they pulled other seats close until they surrounded him. They shared their tales of woe and spoke of their plans now that their lives were their own—in some cases, for the first time ever. They crawled out of the shells in which they had cowered. They showered their new lord with gratitude and love.

Dominique basked in every moment, feeding on their emotions and letting them vibrate back out into the web. Any second now, he was sure, he would pass out with the sheer, drunken euphoria of it all.

Eventually, he did pass out, because eventually, the sun's power reached even here. But he was the last to lose consciousness, long after the others had fallen one by one into their oblivion, leaving him with the silence, his thoughts, and the unnerving sense of unimaginable quantities of rock suspended above him. Adilla had found this comforting and thought of the mountain as a shield against the larger world he could never subdue. Dominique found the sensation claustrophobic.

He distracted himself with thoughts of Cassidy. Earlier, he had connected his phone to the colony's Wi-Fi and started a video chat with her. He only wanted to see her and make sure she was safe, but soon he had a steady stream of blood-drinkers hanging over his shoulder, introducing themselves to their queen. She welcomed them with a confident grace and humor that made his chest swell with pride and his heart overflow with love. Before another night passed, he would be one with her again, hold her in his arms again, love her again. The anticipation brought on a whole different kind of euphoria.

Night had barely settled when Dominique and his hundred-plus new followers emerged from the depths into the cool damp left by a rainy afternoon. They all carried bags of personal belongings, and most soon vanished into the darkness with varying degrees of excitement and anxiety. None intended to return here. The villagers had already been compelled to consider the cavern and its mine devoid of all interest. He made sure that in the days and weeks to come, they would seal the place up, erasing it from existence.

Six of the new converts, four men and two women, joined Dominique's original group in the RV and made themselves as comfortable as was reasonable, given the cramped conditions. As the miles passed, the vehicle filled with lively discussions about centuries of art and politics and history, both personal and global. Mostly they spoke in English, but references from several other languages peppered the conversations. New experiences were shared, old ones recalled. Connections were made, friendships formed and renewed.

While Jackson manned the wheel, Garrett joined in the discussions, adding the "modern human" perspective whenever he thought appropriate, which was often. His broken bones had mended thanks to more blood, and his spirits soared. A pseudo-mania shone in his eyes, the defiant, burning life of one racing toward death.

Of their six guests, one man had joined them solely because of Lyle, whom he said reminded him of his own long-dead brother. Looking close to the same age, but separated by many decades of time, the two huddled in the back of the RV, quietly plotting their new life.

Four of the others were two couples who asked to travel with Dominique to Florida. From there, they planned to continue to their native South America, where they would operate as official emissaries of the Lord of Night.

Then there was Leonidas.

The quiet blood-drinker had attached himself to Jackson the moment he learned of his prominent role in the Striker family history. He sat in the copilot seat and shared what he knew of his long-ago friend Lars, the Striker ancestor whose murder had created the Striker's sworn mission to annihilate the vampire species.

"We almost succeeded, too," Jackson said. "If it hadn't been for Dominique taking over and convincing us to give his way a try."

Leonidas exchanged a long look with Dominique before speaking again. "In all that time, how many did you kill, Jackson?"

The human man shrugged. "We're good at what we do." His hands tightened around the wheel. "Very good."

"I see." Leonidas became a little paler. "Will you believe me when I say that I was not responsible for Lars's death?"

Jackson continued to stare at the road. "It was Adilla, wasn't it?"

"Yes," Leonidas said, the raucous background chatter almost drowning him out. "It was when I learned that, in Adilla's world, there is...was only room for Adilla."

Jackson's mouth twisted with irony. "And all these centuries later, that one kill came back to end him. Karma's a bitch, isn't she?"

A slow smile spread across Leonidas's handsome face as he regarded his friend's descendant. "Yes. She certainly is."

Oui, c'est vrais, Dominique agreed as he sifted through what he recalled of Adilla's memories. It had taken half a millennium, but the raging jealousy and ego that destroyed so many had ultimately come full circle and destroyed Adilla himself.

The equivalent of a polite knock on his mental door made Dominique look up and meet Isao's solemn gaze. *Have you decided about Garrett Striker, my lord?*

Dominique glanced at the human, who was engrossed in a rousing exchange about medieval weapons technology with one of their immortal guests. Only last month, this scene would have been unthinkable. Garrett would not have set foot among this company without a solid plan to kill them all. No such thoughts crossed his mind now. In fact, he looked as close to enjoying himself as Dominique had ever seen him.

And yet...their history...

Would make an intimate bond uncomfortable? Isao ventured.

Dominique looked back at Isao. *There is only one I ever hope to make. Garrett is not that one.*

Then, with your permission, I would like to be the one to sire him. When Dominique just stared at him, the samurai slowly drummed the fingers of one hand on the table and continued. *Normally, I wouldn't consider such a step for a mortal I have known so briefly, but Garrett is running out of time.*

Dominique wondered if Garrett was begging every blood-drinker he met to turn him, but he saw in his thoughts—and in Isao's—that this was not the case. Garrett didn't know what Isao contemplated. *In my memories of him, you have seen what he is capable of. Why do you want to turn someone like that?*

Because I have also seen what drives him, my lord, and I have worked with him these past few nights. He is a soul shaped of true suffering, and possessed of a will to live that has caused him to transcend even himself. With a glance at Makoto, seated beside him, he added, *We have discussed this—Makoto, Douglas, and I—and we all agree on admitting him to our family.*

Dominique rubbed his chin, feeling the barest trace of a beard there. *Will you all serve me then, as he does now? As my personal guard?*

On my honor, my lord. Eternally.

Then, if he will have you, you are welcome to him.

Isao inclined his head in acknowledgment. Not much chance of Garrett rejecting such a powerful and sympathetic warrior soul mate for his sire. Amazing how he hadn't seen their similarities earlier.

At a fuel stop, after the RV had lumbered its way out of the mountains, Dominique relieved Jackson at the wheel. He needed to separate himself from the hubbub brewing in the camper. Also, he needed time to think about what awaited him in the glittering city rising out of the flat Alberta prairie ahead. He would have another conversation there tonight, a conversation he hoped wouldn't end the way he already knew it would. He knew his mother too well.

The closer they came to Calgary, the stronger his connection to Cassidy grew. His vague awareness of her blossomed into a warm hum that became distinct thoughts. *Geneviève isn't with you, is she?*

He glanced at the canvas shopping bag on the floorboard by Leonidas's feet. Wrapped inside was a large, beat-up tin Jackson had found in the village. Inside that was all that remained of Geneviève Guérin.

Oh, no.

There was nothing I knew to do at the time to save her, and that...is as it should be. He briefly marveled at how Serge's infuriatingly frequent words to that effect had lost their power to irritate. *She would have hated living in this world.*

Francesca...

I will tell her, chérie. We are almost there.

After their harrowing escape of the night before, Cassidy and Francesca had changed hotels yet again, just in case a rogue element still operated in the city. Dominique pulled the RV into the most remote corner of the Comfort Inn lot and shut off the engine. While the blood-drinkers spread out, exploring the pleasures of hunting for love instead of terror, Jackson busied himself with cleaning and prepping the vehicle for return to its owner.

It was Garrett who accompanied Dominique and the canvas bag to the second floor room where Cassidy and Francesca waited.

Cassidy felt him coming and was out the door and in his arms before he could knock. Dominique crushed her against his body, his one free hand moving up her back and around her shoulders. He buried his face in her hair, closed his eyes, and inhaled her sweet, beloved warmth.

The moment of peace only lasted until Francesca spoke. "Geneviève? *Où est-elle?*"

No greeting to her son. No relief that he survived what she knew was a dangerous struggle. Only "Where is she?" Where is the daughter he promised to return to her?

"Let's sit down," Garrett suggested, ushering her deeper into the room.

The worry on Francesca's face became wariness as Cassidy sat next to her on one of the two queen beds and took Francesca's hand in hers.

Dominique placed the canvas bag on the desk before them and watched his mother's face for a long moment. A mottled bruise bloomed on her left cheek, and a small bandage was partially hidden under the lock of silver sweeping from her widow's peak. Slowly, understanding dawned. Then her expression hardened with defiance worthy of a warrior. *So be it*, he thought and said, "I miscalculated, *Maman*. I did not realize how powerful and determined my enemies truly were."

Francesca swallowed. Her eyes glistened.

Pulling up a chair, Dominique sat and leaned forward, doing everything he could to look as "normal" as possible without using his supernatural gifts. He had even changed out of his leathers into a pair of Jackson's jeans, a sweatshirt, and a pair of running shoes. His hair was loose and mostly free of dried blood. "They had claimed Geneviève as one of their own before I found her." He looked at the bag. "She did not survive the battle. I brought back what remains."

Francesca's throat bobbed again, her attention locking onto the now-sinister bag. "You...you...murdered her?"

"*Non*. Of course not. I retrieved her and tried to keep her safe. But when her sire was killed, all his spawn died with him, including her."

"You murdered my daughter," she whispered.

"No, he didn't," Cassidy said and put an arm around Francesca. "Of course, he didn't. He was tricked into believing someone else was her sire."

"He tried to help her," Garrett, standing beside Francesca, added, his tone consoling. "He was the only one who could have helped her."

"Yet you allowed her to die." The tears broke free. She looked down at her clasped hands, where the knuckles turned white. "You allowed her to die."

"*Maman*, I—"

Her shoulders stiffened, which was all the warning he got. Then her eyes pinned him. They glittered with far more than grief, and her voice shook. "You are their so-called leader. You knew what would happen, and yet you allowed it to happen anyway. You allowed my last living child to be murdered."

A dozen defenses rushed to his tongue. He uttered none of them. Nothing he could say would sound like anything other than a meaningless excuse.

Francesca's face distorted into something beyond misery. Something that made his heart hitch. This wasn't just a grief-stricken mother lashing out. No, this was an impenetrable wall rising against him. A wall she had built since the moment she learned the truth about him. Though he had watched her construct it, he had refused to see it. Not until now, when the last brick slid into place. He was her son, and she would forever love the memory of him...but she could never love what he had become.

As of this moment, there was nothing more that would ever bind them.

Sadness filled Cassidy as she witnessed this revelation in his thoughts. Her unacknowledged embrace of Francesca loosened, preparing to be shrugged off the way Francesca was shrugging off her son.

It was contempt he saw in his mother's face, hateful and raw. "You...you *abomination*."

Dominique didn't flinch. The words felt like the ghosts of a sad, half-forgotten reality.

Cassidy recoiled. "Francesca, you don't know—"

"I know all I need to know," she snapped. With small, angry movements, she swiped at her eyes. "I have seen all I need to see. And I have reasoned out everything you did not tell me."

Garrett reached for her shoulder. "Francesca, don't."

She slapped his hand away and stood. "How was it exactly that my husband died, Dominique? Your father? The love of my life?"

He closed his eyes. Hung his head.

"And Anastasie? My sweet, innocent baby?"

Dominique said not a word. He let it happen and pass around him and over him and through him like so many more ghosts.

They joined the other shades still haunting the murky corners of his being—the sun, a human life, a family of his own.

"They were both found decapitated and not a drop of blood in them. It was not just your *kind* that did this, was it?" Her voice dropped to a hoarse whisper. "*It was you.*"

The ghosts shrieked in his skull, but no one spoke. Or moved.

Francesca threw a shuddering breath. "So you know this, Cassidy? Garrett?"

Silence.

"I see. You all know this, and still...you are with him. What kind of monsters are you?"

"Well, I almost killed him once," Garrett offered.

"Almost? Only almost?"

"Dominique didn't know what he was doing," Cassidy tried. "He has been plagued with guilt ever since. I had to stop him from killing himself over it several times."

This seemed to give her pause. Her tone softened, but not her venom. "I was happier believing my son was dead. I was happier not knowing all of this. He might as well kill me, too, and finish destroying our family."

Dominique finally raised his head. "You are right, *Maman.*" She flinched a little, apparently not as eager to die as she claimed. "It is all my fault," he clarified with a derisive smile. "I was a fool to rescue Ana from her attackers the way I did, drawing the attention of the immortal who stole my life from me and, for a while, even my sanity. Everything I have done since, and will ever do again, springs from that one moment in which I made—what?—the wrong decision?" he finished on a soft, mocking note.

She stared at him. Her lower lip trembled.

"I did not think so." He stood and stepped closer. She shrank back. "Do not for a moment think that I have suffered no regrets over what I have done. The guilt you try to heap on me is inconsequential compared to the guilt I have already lived with and already resolved. I will take the blame, if you will, but I will not apologize for what I cannot control. I will not apologize for cruel and random fate."

Her silent tears flowed freely now.

"Everything is as it must be," he said as if intoning a prayer. "Including this moment in which we must part for good." Sorrow welled up, but faded when he began to see Francesca Marchant, his mother, for what she truly was to him now—another ghost.

He forced a smile to soften the words. "I love you, *Maman.* But there is no place for me in your life anymore. And no place for you in mine. We remind each other too much of everything we have lost, do we not?"

She gave the smallest of nods.

"With your permission, I can make it so that I am dead to you again. You will remember nothing of what happened here."

Francesca glanced at the bag. "She will still be gone."

"*Oui.* She will. But you will remember a different reason." Though what he could concoct that would explain a woman who said she was going to France for a funeral turning up in ashes in Canada escaped him at the moment.

"*Non.* I do not permit it." The contempt was back, harsher than ever. "Do not touch me with your evil magic. I want to remember the truth. Either way, my son is as dead to me as the rest of my family."

"You can't mean that, Francesca," Cassidy said, heartbreak in her face.

Garrett shook his head, but remained silent.

"She means it," Dominique confirmed. His mother was not one for thoughtless decisions. And she never changed her mind.

Francesca glared at him. "Get out. I can't stand the sight of you."

Dominique pursed his lips and verged on turning himself, Cassidy and Garrett invisible on the spot. But he decided against it. He wasn't about to be that accommodating in providing further proof of his "evil magic." Let her last memory of her son, the Lord of Night, be as human as possible.

Cassidy came to his side. He put an arm around her shoulder, felt her shake with suppressed emotion, and pressed a kiss to her temple. White-hot heat radiated off her. More than her body, it was her spirit that enveloped him in life and love and light, banishing all the ghosts from his awareness.

Including his mother.

Do we have a place to go? he wondered.

Yes. I took another room for us. She expected to share this one with Geneviève tonight.

And so, she will, Dominique thought with a last look at the bag. He bid his sister a silent farewell and left the ghosts to wail in the past.

56

FOREVER

Six months later...

"**Y**ou look delicious," whispered the Lord of Night in a husky voice that sent delightful goosebumps racing over Cassidy's skin.

She graced him with her most seductive smile. "You like the new dress, do you?" The style was her favorite off-one-shoulder design. It also hugged her torso and waist, and caressed her legs in graceful drapes of blue and green.

Dominique's hazel eyes danced with mischief. "What dress?"

Amazing how he could still make her blush, still stir her like this, even with their minds so intimately joined. They had renewed their bond only last night and were as close to being one soul in two bodies as ever.

When he held out his hands, she took them and tipped up her face for a deep, achingly tender kiss. The love behind it wrapped around her as his arms would have, if he wasn't mindful of where such an embrace would lead—and just how much time she had spent on getting her hair into that up-do confection.

They separated with a sigh, their lips clinging for a little longer before Cassidy stepped back and gave him an appraising look. He struck a pose, modeling the suit and dress shirt like the sultry *GQ* cover model he resembled. No tie, collar rakishly undone, eyes burning beneath the dark slashes of his brows. He had cut his hair on the sides and back, adding an air of sophistication, but that thick, rebellious thatch of ebony still fell over his forehead, unless—like now—it was tamed into submission.

"Well, if the maid of honor looks delicious, the best man is downright scrumptious," she purred and took hold of his offered arm. Dominique winked at her. Together they emerged onto the second-floor landing, overlooking the foyer and living room.

The place was an unrecognizable hive of activity. Early guests milled below, sipping drinks. The catering staff circulated among them, carrying platters heaped with hors d'oeuvres. Heady aromas of roasting meats, strong alcohol, and sweet perfumes drifted in the air.

Most amazing of all, not all the guests were human.

A handful of vampires were in attendance—some by invitation, others current visitors in residence—and they were not skulking the shadows for unsuspecting prey. Isao and his brood saw to that. Cassidy spotted Garrett having a stern word with one of the immortal houseguests who acted a little too interested in a plunging neckline. The vampires carried untouched beverages or sipped goblets of sparkling water as they chatted with the human guests, who seemed to find them fascinating conversationalists.

Cassidy heaved a deep, contented sigh as she soaked up the laughter and life that bounced off the walls, filled the house, and nearly overpowered the upbeat Celtic music streaming in the background. So many people under their roof, enjoying themselves, humming with happy anticipation, celebrating love...Dominique would be punch drunk on it all before the night was through, and she right along with him.

Only a tiny frisson of regret scratched at her heart as they descended the stairs. "Aubrey would have loved this."

"*Oui*. He would. Francesca, too," he added after a pause. His mother had sent her regrets from her new home in Provence. On her way from Canada, she had stopped in St. Barth just long enough to pack up her life and ship it to France. She signed the restaurant over to Étienne the morning she boarded a flight to Paris. Never, she swore, would she set foot back in the Caribbean or the Americas. Her life there was over, all the people in it dead. Her only grandchild, Geneviève's daughter, would be welcome to visit when she was old enough, but that was all.

No one pointed out that plenty of vampires lived in Europe.

At the front door, Jackson greeted a newly arrived couple who were some of the over two dozen people Dominique had flown in from France for the event. They spoke no English and Jackson no French, but the warm welcome and invitation to eat and drink required no translation.

Dominique and Cassidy extended their own warm welcomes. They had never met most of their guests and knew only that they were friends and relatives of the groom. The guests, in turn, knew only that Dominique was their generous host and footed the entire bill for his cousin's wedding—including all the first-class travel expenses for the overseas attendees. The faces of the new arrivals were polite, but it was clear that they were taken aback by Dominique's youth and dazzled by his stark beauty, which he made no attempt to conceal with a more human appearance.

Au contraire, mon amour, Dominique said. *They wonder at the most beautiful woman in the room at my side.*

She chuckled. *That'll only last until the bride appears. Trust me.*

The brother of said bride cut a dashing figure with his golden tan and tailored suit. Jackson didn't even miss a beat when Dominique greeted him with a kiss on each cheek. It was the traditional French manner of greeting friends and family, and after their harrowing trials six months ago, they definitely qualified as friends. Soon they would be family, too.

Jackson's bride-to-be was less nonchalant. Olivia looked flustered when the vampire kissed her cheeks. Though Jackson, Dominique, and Cassidy had explained—not to mention proved—the supernatural facts to her months ago, her world apparently still hadn't quite righted itself.

Dominique murmured a compliment about how radiant she looked, which caused her cheeks to bloom with color. With her twins due in less than a month, Olivia was indeed radiant, but also huge. She looked about as comfortable in her sapphire dress as a beach ball trapped in a potato sack.

With an encouraging smile, Cassidy took the young woman's hand in hers. "How are you feeling, Olivia?"

"Oh, good, thanks. Just, you know, adjusting." The sidelong glance she darted at Dominique made it clear she wasn't referring to the fishbowl in her belly.

Dominique understood. With a parting kiss for Cassidy, he excused himself to attend to his duties as both Lord of Night and the best man.

Jackson put a supporting arm around Olivia's back. "You okay, babe?"

"I will be." She smoothed her bright pixie-cut hair with one nervous hand. "But, shit. I forgot how imposing he is." This was the first time Olivia had encountered Dominique since meeting him.

"You never get used to it," Jackson told her, his eyes scanning the room for the other vampires. "You just relax and go with it."

Olivia looked up at her future husband, love in her blue eyes and stubbornness in her firm chin. "Thank you, Jackson. For volunteering to trust me with this knowledge."

"Oh? You think you would have figured this out on your own, do you?"

"Well, I did minor in psychology, so..."

Cassidy snorted. "I didn't even need that."

Both women laughed as Jackson's expression soured.

Cassidy couldn't help but wonder how different her own life would have been if Jackson *had* told her about his vampire hunting before she met Dominique and formed a very different opinion of the supernatural. Whatever that life might have been, one thing was certain—she would not be standing here, big as a tent, glowing with devotion to Jackson.

No, this moment and everything that conspired to create it over the years would never have happened. She wouldn't have known Dominique, he certainly wouldn't be the Lord of Night, and his subjects would still live in shadows, still feed on terror. They would also still be pursued by a lone hunter, nursing bitter rage.

And Cassidy? She would have found herself married to that man of rage whose ultimate priority would forever be the next kill. Maybe she would have filled the emptiness with work or children, or both, assuming she had stayed at all. Jackson and Olivia had the kind of relationship Cassidy could have never had with him, and she was truly happy for them.

She was even more pleased with the way her own life was turning out. At least at night.

"Shall we go see how the bride is doing?" Cassidy suggested.

"Yes. Let's." Olivia set herself in motion, her waddling steps hidden by the long, blue gown draping off her belly. As she followed Cassidy down the path to the pool house, she said, "I still can't believe Sam wanted me in her wedding party in this condition."

Cassidy smiled over her shoulder. "You look wonderful, Ollie. Really."

"I'll try not to go into labor before the I-do's."

"I don't think Samantha would mind," Cassidy confirmed with a giggle, certain that as long as the groom was there, the bride would object to nothing.

Samantha had followed Étienne to St. Barth a week after he left to help Francesca wind down her life there. Her two-week visit had turned into two months. When he came to see her again in Florida shortly after that, he brought a ring. He proposed to her out by the pool at sunrise, on the very spot where they had lost their hearts to each other after charging into battle with a furious vampire. "It was inevitable," Samantha often said. "We both knew it then and there. We are a team."

She looked somewhat less thrilled now when Cassidy and Olivia entered the pool house. The bride stood in front of a bathroom mirror while her mother fussed over her hair, and a photographer snapped pictures non-stop.

"If I had known you didn't hire a stylist, I would have brought mine," Lillian said. "This hair is much too long to do anything with."

"It works fine in a braid, Mom. It always has."

"No daughter of mine is getting married with her hair in such a mess."

The "mess" hung down to Samantha's waist in a gorgeous wheat-colored mass. The photographer swooped in for close-ups. *Snap-snap-snap...*

Samantha made a small, impatient sound. "Mother, please. Just let me work with it."

"Perhaps you will permit me to try?"

All eyes turned to Estelle. Of the four bridesmaids, she was the only one who wasn't a member of Samantha's yoga community. Also, she was the only vampire. Her hands wrung before her, uncertain. Interacting with humans she wasn't hunting—even having several know her true nature—was still a novelty for her, to say nothing of a photographer recording her every move. She had well and truly moved out of the shadows. "I used to style my mother's hair, which was very similar."

"Please do," Samantha said with an encouraging smile.

Lillian grudgingly stepped aside and prepared to pay close attention. No matter how much attention she paid, though, she wouldn't see the truth about Estelle, and it wasn't because of a communal effort to keep her in the dark. Her son and his bride had offered to enlighten her about their family's clandestine operations. She refused. "I know there are things going on in my life I don't fully understand," she had told Jackson. "But I understand enough to know that I don't want to know more."

Olivia, who had not yet met Estelle, leaned close to Cassidy and whispered, "Is she…?"

"Mhm."

A grin spread over her face. "I love it."

When Lillian glanced in their direction, Olivia amended, "I love what Estelle is doing." The half-up do taking shape on the bride's head promised to be as relaxed as it was elegant. The photographer focused on Estelle's hands, never pointing the camera at her face. Cassidy suspected a bit of compulsion had come his way.

"I do, too," another bridesmaid announced from the bathroom door. "Estelle, can you redo mine when you're done?"

"But of course, Evelyn." The vampire beamed, and Cassidy caught a happy golden flicker in her eyes.

She decided to use the cheerful atmosphere to sneak in a loaded question. "Lillian, I haven't seen your husband yet. Is he with you?"

The mother of the bride looked pained. "He was held up with business when I left."

I just bet he was, Cassidy thought. When Warren Striker learned about the venue and the guest list, he had put it to his stepdaughter in no uncertain terms: the wedding and reception would be during the day at the Striker mansion or he wouldn't pay a cent for it. To her mother's consternation, Samantha had shrugged and walked away.

"He said he might come later," Lillian added.

Cassidy dragged a cheery expression onto her face. *Packing a full-spectrum torch, no doubt.* "Oh, good."

Estelle finished her work and released Samantha, photographer in tow, to Cassidy and Lillian, who helped her with the dress. In true Samantha fashion, the gown was a thing of simple beauty that, together with her graceful new hair style, lent her an almost ethereal air.

Cassidy stepped back to admire. "You are a true vision, my friend. Étienne may forget how to speak when he sees you."

Lillian sighed. "Not the gown I would have wished for you, but very lovely, I agree."

A knock at the door sent an attendant scurrying to open it. Garrett eased into the room. "Security check," he announced solemnly.

At the sound of his unfamiliar voice, Brinkley, watching the bustle from a pillow nest on the sofa, began growling quietly. The cat had finally made his peace with the permanent vampire residents of the house, but new ones were still suspect.

Garrett's eyes narrowed at Brinkley before they found Estelle. "Is everything okay in here?"

"Security check?" Lillian exclaimed. "Seriously, Garrett. Don't spoil the evening by being so grim." She swept up to her brother-in-law and planted a kiss on his cheek, a gesture that made the new vampire squirm. It hadn't been an easy transition for him. His disease had caused the process to spin out of control several times and would have killed him if his sire had been anyone less powerful and experienced than Isao.

"Just doing my job, Lillian," he said with a dazzling smile which betrayed not a hint of fang. "It's great to see you. You're looking good."

"As do you," she said, sounding not completely sure. She had to notice the paleness of his skin, the sharper edges of his features, the clarity of his eyes, harder and colder than they had ever been. What was she thinking as she stared at a brand new vampire fighting to maintain his self-control? "It's been an age. Where have you been hiding? In a crypt?"

Olivia covered a sputter with a cough as she went to sit beside the agitated Brinkley.

"Feels like it sometimes," Garrett agreed. "We've been busy expanding our operation. I'm sure Warren told you."

Cassidy's brows jumped up her forehead. Was that compulsion in those last words?

Lillian nodded. "Yes, I know. But promise you'll be by the house soon? The place feels so empty these days."

"Sure." His cheer faltered a little. "Soon." Or as soon as Warren would make an exception to his no-vampires-under-my-roof-ever rule. He shot another look at Estelle, both a question and a warning. "Is everything okay here?"

The vampiress was the picture of serenity as she made final adjustments to Evelyn's hair. "Everything is beautiful, good sir."

"Okay then. Fifteen minutes till show time."

"The bride is ready," Cassidy confirmed. She did a quick check-in with Dominique. "As is the groom." At Lillian's odd look, she added, "Well, I would hope."

Fifteen minutes later, the groom was waiting at the arbor that had been set up in the backyard. That was as much as Cassidy saw before she started her walk down the grassy aisle. Two walls of people smiled at her and the other jewel-toned dresses floating past, even as they craned their necks for a first glimpse of the bride. The only one Cassidy had eyes for, however, was the best man. It was him she was moving toward, step by step, heartbeat by heartbeat. Everything and everyone else vanished. Only she and Dominique remained under the balmy night sky, coming together again as they had from the beginning, but also as they never had before. Here, now, amidst a sacred celebration of love, something shifted beneath her feet. Something...inevitable.

Je t'aime, Cassidy. Toujours et pour toujours.

And I love you, Dominique. Forever and ever, she repeated, feeling the words thrum in her blood like a vow.

She took her assigned place at the front, aware of nothing but the man standing at the groom's side. Though both looked straight ahead, their minds twined together until they verged on fusing and leaving the immediate reality of the moment. *There is time,* Dominique said as he released his invisible embrace on her a little. *Endless time.*

Yes. Endless.

Appreciative murmurs rose when the bride appeared. Samantha was like a comet in the night, and Étienne indeed looked gobsmacked. Almost as startling was the virtual stranger escorting her down the aisle. It was the shoes that threw Cassidy most of all. She had never seen Serge wear them. But not only was he shod, he wore a tailored suit, sported not a smudge of grub on his clean-shaven face, and had styled his mop of wild curls into a semblance of civility. It was Serge 2.0.

His smitten gaze flickered toward the woman responsible for this miraculous transformation. Since arriving a month ago to pledge herself to the new Lord of Night, Estelle and the pirate had fallen hopelessly under each other's spell. Over five decades his senior, she was worldly and sophisticated, and all the motivation Serge needed to at last embrace the twenty-first century.

The ceremony—conducted in both English and French by the minister flown in from St. Barth—held the assembled crowd of four-hundred-plus in rapt attention. More than a few eyes glistened with happy tears by the time the couple enjoyed their first kiss as husband and wife. Love swirled in the air like an intoxicating mist, and every vampire there wore an expression of bright-eyed euphoria. Hyper-aware of it all through Dominique, Cassidy's head swam with it too, the effect resembling fine champagne fizzing in her blood.

Nothing, she decided, nothing at all could ruin her mood this night. Though she had to remind herself of this when she came face to face with her father, his new wife Iris by his side. The cynic in Cassidy noted again that, as his business partner's widow, the woman had brought substantial assets into the relationship, allowing Gil Chandler to recover from the financial ruin of his last divorce. But tonight she saw what looked like genuine affection in the looks and small touches they exchanged. Though reluctant to admit it, she had to concede that her philandering coward of a father might have learned his lesson.

"Baby girl," he greeted with an exuberant smack of a kiss to her cheek. "You look incredible." After greeting Dominique as well, in an only slightly more restrained fashion, he continued with, "So? You two have been engaged for—what?—more than two years now? When are you making it official?"

Cassidy glanced at the platinum and sapphire band encircling her finger. Dominique had given it to her as a promise of his undying devotion and marriage if she wanted it. She hadn't wanted it, not then and not now. At least not by any human standards. Different, deeper, and far more permanent bonds existed in the world they inhabited.

When she looked up at Dominique, a knowing smile lit his eyes. "Soon," she said.

"Very soon," he confirmed softly.

"Well, I'll be," Gil hooted. "I'm standing by to walk you down the aisle. You just say the word." Lowering his voice a little, he continued, "But I hope you'll forgive me if I can't afford quite this kind of shindig." His finger circled to encompass the inside of the reception tent. Chandeliers hung over the sea of chattering people, a four-piece band provided live entertainment, and dozens of servers bustled between the flower-festooned tables.

Cassidy laughed, surprisingly moved by the sincerity in his voice. As if it hadn't been a decade since she had done it last, she leaned forward and pecked a kiss on his cheek. "No worries, Dad. We've got this covered."

Gil beamed and clasped her hand in both of his. "But anything you need that I can give. Even the shirt off my back. I'm only a phone call away."

"I know."

"Love you, baby girl." He turned away to shepherd Iris toward the next knot of people he wanted to mingle with—but not fast enough to hide the shimmer in his eyes.

Cassidy stared after the man she had sworn to hate for the rest of her life. Dominique cast a shield of invisibility about them, giving her time to collect herself. After a while, he said, "It truly is a night for miracles."

And another one was on approach. Not only had Warren Striker arrived at the first notes of the bridal march, he now followed Jackson to a far corner of the tent—the same corner where Garrett had stationed himself to keep watch for misbehaving vampires. Isao moved to his new youngling's side, clearly sensing the potential for emotional havoc about to unfold. And there was Leonidas trailing in his wake, watching the Striker patriarch with great interest. Jackson had volunteered as an official intermediary. Judging by his father's stern face, a peace deal was by no means certain.

Dominique nuzzled at her ear. "Would you like to dance, my lady?"

She turned to place her hand in his. "Any time." *For all time.*

On the dance floor, he took her into his arms and put her new ballroom dance skills to the test. To prepare for the wedding, Cassidy had taken classes. This was something she wouldn't be able to do just by tuning into his head. For this, she had to be independent of him and literally think on her feet.

They began slowly, feeling their way around each other and the music with all the excitement of new discovery. Unlike her, he had learned these steps years ago in his human life, and they came back to him with ease. Her initial uncertainty soon gave way to her feet flying along, following his lead. She trusted in his timing and strength as he swung her through breathtaking dips and dizzying twirls. By the second dance, they were the couple everyone else watched and cheered.

"I think we're stealing the bride and groom's thunder," she said, laughing and breathless at the end of a racy tango.

"I don't think they mind," he replied with a glance at the newlyweds, who clapped in enthusiastic support. He raised her hand high and together they took a deep bow to raucous applause, the gracious hosts, the Lord of Night and his queen.

The band shifted into the slower gear of "Unchained Melody," and she moved into his arms, her entire body vibrating with happiness. Rocking gently now in a sea of couples, their souls merged once more.

Samantha and Étienne danced nearby. Cassidy's heart pinched. *I'm going to miss her so much.* Dominique's private jet would whisk them away to Paris later tonight. The couple planned to spend the better part of a month traveling the French countryside, visiting family, even Francesca, before settling on St. Barth. While Étienne would manage the restaurant, Samantha had big plans for setting up a yoga studio and hosting workshops with renowned instructors. Their days would be full of life and their nights full of passion. Samantha had found her fairytale, and Cassidy was thrilled for her friend, even if her own days looked positively dull in comparison.

Dominique stroked the back of her neck with his thumb. *The day is no longer your domain.*

It was true, she had to admit. When there wasn't some business that required her to be up and about, Cassidy's days were mostly spent in bed. Rare was the moment that she stepped into direct sunlight anymore to relish its warmth on her skin. Rarer still were the moments that he looked for these memories in her mind. It was the magical light of the moon she craved now, the quiet power of darkness, and the cool, earthy aroma of her lover. The lover who no longer grieved his mortal life, nor needed her to be his tether to humanity, but needed her just the same.

The lover who patiently waited for her to join him in the eternal world of night.

"Tell me, Cassie, *mon amour*," he murmured, his breath against her damp skin making her shiver. "Tell me what you want. Tell me in words."

In words. Because only as words would her decision become...official.

Cassidy swayed to the music that spoke of hunger and touch, need and love. Swayed in time and in the arms of the man who was the only true anchor she had ever known—and would always know.

She tipped her head back just a little and felt her body melt when his lips found the delicate skin beneath the corner of her left jaw. Only hours before, his teeth had pierced the pulse beating there.

"I'm ready, my love," she whispered and felt those teeth again. "I'm ready for forever."

Thank You For Reading

If you enjoyed this book and have a moment, please consider leaving a brief review wherever you purchased this book or on Goodreads to help others discover this series. Thank you!

If you would like a free eBook, sign up for my mailing list and also be the first to find out about new releases and special offers.

Mailing list signup: https://skryder.com/mailinglist

Acknowledgements

As always, a big, big thank you to my family for their continued support and encouragement. Without you, there would be no me.

Heaps of thanks also go to:

Second edition editor, Aleksina Teto, who never fails to go above and beyond.

First reader Máirín Fisher-Fleming, who was honest enough to say "No!" after reading the first draft.

Queens among fans, Lorraine and Toni, who have provided insights into these characters even I didn't see coming.

Rosie and Bill M. for bringing Eli/Brinkley into my life, however briefly, and being some of the best neighbors anyone could ask for.

And all the writers who have encouraged and inspired me over the years, and all the readers who have entered my world. You are the reason this book exists.

About the Author

S.K. Ryder writes paranormal and science fiction fantasy featuring fish-out-of-water characters forced to deal with reality gone wrong. Her stories reflect her deep love of nature and are filled with adventure, suspense, humor, and romance. Though she currently calls South Florida home, she has lived in Germany and Canada and has traveled widely, usually in the hot pursuit of wild and scenic spaces. When not writing or working as a freelance programmer, she enjoys plotting her next scuba diving or river rafting trip, beach combing, or just getting lost in a book. Should push comes to shove, she can also bake a halfway decent cake and stand on her head, though not (usually) at the same time.

Find her online at https://skryder.com

BOOKS BY S.K. RYDER

DARK DESTINIES SERIES

Dark Awakening (Prequel)
Dark Heart of the Sun (Book 1)
Dark Lord of the Night (Book 2)
Dark Reign of Forever (Book 3)

For a complete list, visit:
https://books2read.com/SK-Ryder